IN THE COMPANY OF DECENT MEN

Andy Horne

In the Company of Decent Men

Published by Clovercroft Publishing, Franklin, Tennessee

Published in association with Larry Carpenter of Christian Book Services, LLC

www.christianbookservices.com

Cover Design by Debbie Manning Sheppard

Interior Design and Copy Edit by Adept Content Solutions

Printed in the United States of America

978-1-945507-16-8

DEDICATION

Rear Admiral Roy F. Hoffmann, USN (Ret.)
1894–

Captain Charles Moulton Plumly, USN (Ret.)
1931–2015

Captain Bill Warren Fugit, USA (Ret.)
1943–2015

Lieutenant Michael R. Bernique, USN (Ret.)
1943–2016

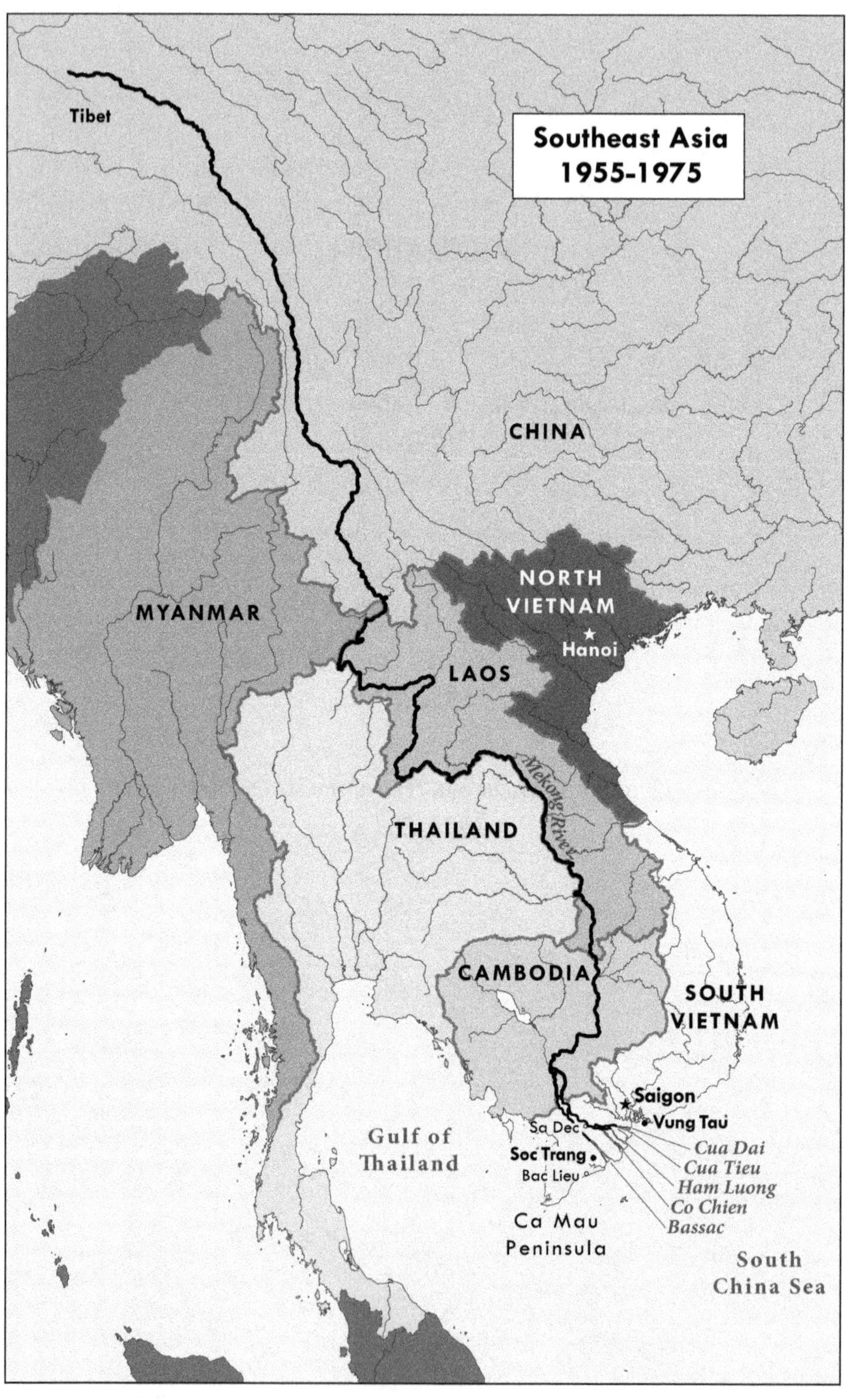
Southeast Asia
1955-1975
Tibet
CHINA
MYANMAR
NORTH
VIETNAM
Hanoi
LAOS
Mekong River
THAILAND
CAMBODIA
SOUTH
VIETNAM
Saigon
Vung Tau
Sa Dec
Soc Trang
Bac Lieu
Cua Dai
Cua Tieu
Ham Luong
Co Chien
Bassac
Gulf of
Thailand
Ca Mau
Peninsula
South
China Sea

INTRODUCTION

The Mekong River's virgin sources flow from the steep mountain gorges of western China and the Tibetan plateau. The river meanders twenty-six hundred miles through Burma, Thailand, Laos, and Cambodia, into southern Vietnam. Gathering more water, silt, and debris each year, this slurry of material moves toward the South China Sea. For eons, the prehistory boundary of that sea receded from the advancing delta created by the deposited silt and waste of Southeast Asia. With successive floods and deposits, the elevation of the land increased, and the reach of the delta grew.

Leaving Cambodia, the Mekong divides into nine tributaries known to the Vietnamese as the Nine Dragons River. The five major tributaries, large in their own right, are known by many names, but for the purposes of this story, they are the Bassac, Co Chien, Ham Long, Cua Tieu, and Cua Dai Rivers. The Bassac is well southwest of Saigon, and the other four rivers are successively closer to that city.

Saigon, no longer a politically correct map reference on the eastern side of the Delta, today is officially and publicly called Ho Chi Minh City. Its ordinary citizens stubbornly and privately use its historic name.

Like the strands of a cobweb, the Mekong Delta is also overlain with lesser-known rivers of varying width, depth, and length, such as the Saigon, Soirap, and Can Tho Rivers. These rivers are unknown except to locals and the combatants who fought there. The Bo De, Dam Doi, and Cua Lon Rivers could have been on the moon as far as Americans back home were concerned.

Many canals, often nameless, are the etchings of nature, caused by the inability of the Mekong branches and other rivers to fully drain the land. Others are the consequence of centuries of backbreaking, relentless labor of the civilizations that flourished there.

Delta waterways, dotted with floating water hyacinth and debris, move as though at flood level. Strong, rising tides force their way up these rivers and canals many miles, periodically causing the seaward flow to first stop and then reverse for a time. Mud-sided river and canal banks become overrun with water for a few hours until the tide ebbs and resumes its course to the sea. Mangroves and jungle-bordered cultivated and fallow rice fields lay over decay, silt, and sand.

A Western traveler to the Delta senses that Noah's flood has yet to fully recede. Only with time does a visitor understand the relationship of the land, the river, and its people. Here the people live at the sufferance of the water that surrounds them. They live, grow crops, raise children, and die, all on terms demanded by these waters.

There are three further natural conditions that significantly affect life and death in Vietnam: two distinctly different monsoon seasons and typhoons. The northeast monsoon runs from October through March and is wet and chilly in the northern half of the country. In that same period, the seas are rough along the southern coast of Vietnam, but the weather there is generally dry and somewhat cooler.

The southwest monsoon begins in about April and continues until October. The air temperatures rise. The seas are calmer, but along with the calm comes the rainy season in the Mekong Delta. Rainfall often obscures any distinction between the coastal lands and the rivers.

The lower Micronesian islands, north of the equator and Australia, is the spawning area for typhoons in the Pacific region. Spun into life as tropical depressions, they move west and northwest into the Philippine and South China Seas. In combination with other influences, the tracks of these storms may wander, picking up strength and mass and deciding which part of the Pacific Rim to assault with their high winds, rain, and surges of sea. While the broadly stated season for typhoons is from July through November, these monsters of the western Pacific read no calendars.

Humans have inhabited the Delta since the Stone Age. Ethnic Chams were among the first societies to live there and in the region of present-day Cambodia. The Viets, a rice-growing and fishing culture, migrated from the north along the coastal lowlands of the South China Sea and displaced the Chams, forcing them back into Cambodia. The region's abundant water and rich soil has always invited outsiders.

For two thousand years, the people of the Delta suffered invasion: the Siamese, Chinese, Khmers, French, Japanese, and the Americans invaded. Even their brothers from the north were invaders. Only the Americans never came to possess the land.

As World War II drew to a close in 1945, American political administrations, joined by Congress, became increasingly concerned with the violent worldwide expansion of communism. Militant communism, posing as an internal or domestic conflict, through violence threatened peaceful political processes throughout entire regions. Characterized by assassinations of community leaders and terrorist attacks on public institutions and innocent civilians, the communist movement spread in Europe, Asia, and Central America.

Repressive and totalitarian communist governments took over countries in Europe and Asia formerly subjugated by the defeated Axis powers. By 1950, communist governments dominated by the Soviet Union controlled all of Eastern Europe.

On June 25, 1950, North Korean communist forces invaded the Republic of South Korea in an effort to crush their fledgling democratic government. The United Nations, in what was interestingly called a "police action," fought a bloody, three-year war on the Korean peninsula, repelling the North Koreans and later their Chinese communist allies. While America provided the majority of logistical and military forces, this was an international effort of twenty-two nations to restore peace and freedom in South Korea. By war's end, 54,000 Americans had died.

In 1955, France withdrew from Southeast Asia, and the United States government progressively deepened its military involvement in South Vietnam, following its policy of containment. That policy called for resistance, not always at every opportunity and sometimes incrementally, of militant communism, even if that meant stepping into what others argued to be a civil war. Containment became a costly euphemism for avoiding victory.

American presence and casualties rose in 1965. While not a United Nations effort, at least forty nations provided assistance to the South Vietnamese government in its struggle with the north. Eight of those countries provided direct military assistance: the United States, Republic of Korea, Thailand, Australia, New Zealand, the Philippines, the Republic of China, and Spain. Casualties for the insurgent Vietnamese National Liberation Front, otherwise known as the Viet Cong, and the North Vietnamese Army forces operating in the south increased dramatically.

The American public increasingly rejected the human and monetary price of containment, and as American casualties climbed, support for the war fell. By war's end in 1975, 58,000 Americans had perished. It would be another fifteen years before containment's virtues and values, if any to the world, were realized by the collapse of the Soviet Union and bankruptcy of communism as an abstract social and economic philosophy.

In 1968, America began its long, painful process of going home. While training and equipping the South Vietnamese government to fight on its own, Americans continued to fight and die for another five years. The vain hope was that the Republic could endure alone this bloody war of attrition and that somehow the death and destruction would be worthy of the effort.

For those Americans fighting in Vietnam, the hope was more personal: to do what they were trained to do, to survive, and then to return home and get on with their lives. At the fighting man's level, preoccupation with policy or management issues of the war was counterproductive to these hopes, especially for physical survival. That, too, proved vain for many, but all survivors were changed.

Only the Delta remained constant in its timeless muddy courses to the sea. Whether any of the inhabitants, invaders, or visitors lived, died, or endured was irrelevant to the Delta. This is a story of then and now.

The Present

CHAPTER 1
Morning in Iowa

Bill Boston was a survivor. His dark blue Chevrolet Suburban moved slowly along the asphalt country road, eased onto a smaller, gravel road overgrown with weeds, and stopped at a chained, aging gate to a farm property. He unlocked the chain and stepped carefully across the cattle guard to open the gate. Driving an eighth of a mile into what might have been a parking area near a boarded-up farmhouse and deteriorating barn, he got out of the truck and paused.

Tall weeds and sparse brush commanded the ground outside a chain-link fence surrounding the house. The yard within the fence was also overgrown with high grass. Paint on the farmhouse, like the barn, had mostly peeled away. The yard gate was unlocked. Bill walked from one side of the house back around to the other and then to the front, inspecting for any exterior damage. At the front door, he worked the lock and went in.

Beams of early morning light filtered in through the open door and cracks between the boards over the windows, revealing a parlor apparently undisturbed for years. Blowing on an entryway side table, Boston watched the dust cloud rise. Moving to the back door behind the kitchen, he opened that door, creating a flow of air through the house. Returning briefly to the front porch, he pulled off two of the boards covering the large window in the living room.

What had been a pleasant parlor now contained a cheap, black-and-white checkered sofa centered on the room's one long wall. Wooden Teac-brand stereo speakers doubling as end tables flanked the sofa. A thick, dark-stained wooden cargo hatch cover resting on cinder blocks functioned as a coffee table. Cigarette burns and rings of stains marred all of these pieces. A light film of dust was everywhere.

Tacked above the sofa were old curling photographs, plaques, and Navy memorabilia arranged in some attempt at order. Another decorative feature of the room probably set it apart from all of the other old, unattended farmhouses in the area. There were empty bottles along virtually every inch of baseboard in the room. There were no beer cans or beer bottles, just carefully placed half-gallon whiskey and jug wine bottles of all brands and tastes. The wine bottles had one common feature—screw caps. All labels faced the center of the room.

Following a short inspection of the other rooms of the house, Bill returned to the living room and pulled the sofa away for access to the wall behind it. He removed only the photographs, pausing momentarily to study some, and stacking them neatly on one of the Teac speakers. The plaques and other souvenirs remained in place.

Centered on the wall was a wood-framed, eight-by-ten-inch photograph, showing a group of smiling unkempt young Vietnamese and American men in various versions of military garb. The framing obscured a portion of the right edge of the group. Smiles contrasted with the hollow-eyed fatigue of the group.

These young warriors brandished an array of American-made weapons, primarily M-16 automatic rifles. One American held high an M-79 grenade launcher, another a twelve-gauge stubby pump shotgun, and a third casually fondled a Thompson .45-caliber submachine gun. One young, grinning Vietnamese hefted a rag mop. Each person also held a can of beer. In the background could be seen a cluster of moored patrol boats, among them a light breeze moved sufficiently to show the Stars and Stripes and small yellow-and-red flags of the Republic of South Vietnam.

On the concrete dock in front of the group, in very neat rows segregated according to type of device, were six AK-47 automatic rifles with curved magazines, ten B-40 rocket-propelled grenades (RPGs), a launch tube, four Chinese CKC Mauser-type rifles, and a wooden box angled toward the camera to reveal an array of documents. In front of the weapons and documents was the blue-and-red flag of the Vietcong, the Vietnamese Communist insurgents.

More than twenty years had passed since Bill Boston had seen the inside of the farmhouse. Following separation from the Navy, he spent almost two years of civilian life holed up in the old family farm. Early in his residency, Bill grubbed out a vegetable garden at a back corner of the yard, now reclaimed by prairie grasses. Occasionally, he made supply runs into town in a 1956 half-ton Chevrolet pickup his dad bought the year before his death. The old truck now rested in the barn. The family business paid Bill a small biweekly salary for a meaningless title without specific duties. When money ran low, Bill dipped into his Navy savings.

When female companionship was desired, he mounted his 1951 Indian eighty-cubic-inch motorcycle. Bill's father had bought the Blackhawk Chief as an investment in what his dad hoped would be a revitalized competition between Harleys and Indians. Bill's father did not live to see the competition go in favor of Harley Davidson or the sweet emergence of the Indian as a collector's item. The bike was good for trolling up a woman from some of the low-rent bars in town or the other communities in East Central Iowa. These women would not have favorably impressed Bill's family nor would his life of pointless solitude, routinely soaked in alcohol.

One day more than two decades ago, Bill got up off the couch, stuffed a few clothes in a backpack, took a brief moment's look around the house, and walked out. He took up residence in a small, furnished apartment in town and appeared the next morning at the family's business. Over the next few months he returned to the farm only to retrieve a piece or two of furniture or kitchenware and to prepare the pickup truck for long-term storage.

For a time, Bill's older brother, Tommy, kept the yard and surrounding grounds mowed, but he eventually stopped that maintenance and boarded up the house. After all, the old house was just that—old and part of a dark time for Bill and the family and best forgotten. The last time Bill even went on the property was ten years ago to check on the cover he had placed over the old truck. The Indian motorcycle already had a new home in Bill's three-car garage back in town.

Bill became an incidental drinker and was never again given to wild carousing. He discussed the war only on the few occasions that he saw friends who had served in the military during that period and never with others. Even now, there were flashes of scenes he told himself to forget. In recent years, he accepted these flashes as normal. He ignored these mind's-eye images like a television program without sound. They were a part of him, maybe a better part, and always would be.

Sometimes he allowed those memories their rein. Sitting on the porch steps of this old Midwestern house, he remembered a particularly bad time in November 1969.

November 1969

CHAPTER 2
Coastal Mekong Delta

Leaden skies concealed the setting sun. Transition to blackness was almost immediate. The jungle-fringed canal in the Tan Phu Special Zone, by night controlled by the enemy, was a little over twenty yards wide. A light, salty breeze moved down the canal to its meeting with the Co Chien River. The tide was rising against this utter darkness and silence.

A low, distinct, gargling sound moved with the tide and into the breeze. Two large dark shapes almost as long as the width of the canal glided through the water. The second vessel slowed as its engine became silent and eased into the side of the vegetation and stopped. The vines, tree limbs, and leaves cushioned its arrival against the bank, distorting the distinct profile of mast, antennae, and radar.

The lead vessel continued beyond a slight bend in the canal and stopped the single engine that had been running. The boat lost its forward movement just as its bow nosed under a small overhanging tree. Hands, bow and stern, moored the vessel to the jungle vegetation with no more than the equivalent of kite string. Silence reigned.

In the darkened pilothouse of each boat, a small field radio had its dial light masked and its volume at the lowest setting. Keying the handset produced an almost inaudible "tick" at a receiving radio. Moments after the lead boat settled in, the boat officer keyed his handset one time to which two ticks came in response. It was fifteen minutes past the hour. Such reassuring ticking signals would be repeated every fifteen minutes until the mission concluded or intruders were confronted.

Over the main cabin near the port-side opening into the pilothouse, each boat officer earlier had placed, in fixed order of preference, devices to be used in the event this night's ambush became more than just an exercise in stealth.

The second boat's officer, Lt. (jg) Sam Taylor, arranged from his left to right, six hand-held flares, caps reversed and ready for ignition, four concussion grenades, and six forty-millimeter buckshot rounds for the already-loaded M-79 grenade launcher laying further to his right.

Ens. Bill Boston, the lead boat officer, preferred three concussion grenades followed by seven hand-held flares, one .38-caliber six-shot revolver, and a Thompson .45-caliber submachine gun. His men were armed with M-16 assault rifles or manned .50-caliber machine guns, one on the afterdeck and two above the pilothouse.

Men on each vessel wore jungle fatigues, shirts buttoned at the neck and wrists. Each wore a round, soft-cloth fatigue cap and flak vests. Some wore helmets. The boat officer wore no boots or shoes of any kind, only olive-drab socks. Dark green or gray woolen blankets were spread on the deck of each boat to muffle the sound of even socked feet.

Only boat officers moved about. Very slowly and carefully placing each step, the officer passed from man to man, wordlessly checking their continued readiness. A pat on the shoulder might be responded to by an upturned thumb or a whispered, "I'm OK." At half past the hour came the expected one tick responded with two ticks.

Thirty-eight minutes into the second hour of silent waiting, Boston ticked three times. Taylor ticked once and began moving aft.

"Stand by," Taylor whispered. He could hear the slight purring sound of small engines. "On my command, fire only at targets back-lit by Mr. Boston's flares."

Twenty-three seconds later, a flare climbed into the sky above the lead boat and shooting erupted. Heavy three-shot bursts from a Tommy gun and booming .50-caliber explosions underscored the sharp, whacking staccato of M-16s and coughing sounds of an M-79 grenade launcher. The shooting stopped as another flare arched up. Dull booms announced the use of concussion grenades to bring up anyone trying to escape under water. Two short bursts of M-16 fire followed.

As a third flare went up, two sampans came around the bend, their occupants leaning forward as if to help their small, long shaft engines which were straining for distance between themselves and death behind them.

"Wait, wait" was not heard by all on the second patrol boat but was instinctively understood. When Taylor began to shout, "Now," the rest of the word was drowned in the eruption of gunfire. Two flares were sent aloft together. Four men in the two sampans at once knew they were about to die.

One .50-caliber slug hit the forward occupant of the first sampan, throwing him back against his companion. The companion sprawled backwards because the same slug shattered his skull. As he was struck, the AK-47 he was trying to raise was sent spiraling into the canal. The two corpses were hit by other shooting but remained in the sampan.

The men in the second sampan went to the water without fighting. Two more flares went up, followed by two concussion grenades splashing near where the men had disappeared. Muffled explosions roiled the water. First one and then another head emerged only to be torn apart by concentrated M-16 fire.

The commands now were neither whispered nor shouted. "Cease fire. Engines up. Grab those two sampans. Check for weapons and documents." A single flare was ignited.

The second patrol boat's twin diesel engines coughed to life and pushed its bow toward the canal bank as a pivot point to swing its stern for a turnaround. As the stern swung across the canal, it blocked the drift of the two sampans. Sailors lay outstretched across the deck, holding the sides of the first sampan as others rifled the pockets of the corpses, handing things up to other men. The corpses were then rolled into the water. As this was accomplished, the sampan was tipped to one side and partially filled with water. The same searching procedure occurred with the now-unoccupied second sampan. As this activity ended, the patrol boat continued pivoting into the middle of the canal with each sampan held alongside.

A final flare went up. On command, each sampan was released and allowed to drift. Just as each passed down the side of the patrol boat, a concussion grenade was lobbed into the partially water-filled hull. The weight of the water pressed the force of the subsequent explosion down through the hull, effectively breaking the back of each sampan. Broken bows and sterns now pointed to the sky.

Passing through the debris, the lead patrol boat joined its partner for the short trip to the Co Chien River. Before reaching the relative safety of the open waters of the river, the breeze died, and a heavy rain began.

CHAPTER 3

Cat and Mouse

Deadly serious waiting games of cat and mouse were played every night of the war. Contests on the water determining winners and losers were normally resolved within the space of a few seconds up to two minutes. Such fighting was rarely a draw. The purpose of these violent confrontations was to starve the war's furnace of its fuel by interrupting the flow and concentration of men, weapons, and supplies into and within South Vietnam.

This interdiction was a major component of the American military's mission in Vietnam. As a barrier of ships and aircraft successfully closed sea routes, enemy forces and supplies entered South Vietnam from the lands adjacent to it. The Ho Chi Minh Trail, in reality a band of routes running from Laos into Cambodia along the western border of South Vietnam, used entry points at various places along that line.

Once men and material crossed into South Vietnam, further distribution was made often at night on trails and waterways all over the countryside. The work was labor intensive, tedious, and dangerous.

To interrupt this movement, a variety of assets were used; surveillance and attack aircraft, patrol boats, and men on the ground cast a ragged net over the land. By day the work of the Navy patrol forces was direct and to the point. Coastal vessels and river traffic was stopped and searched for contraband of military significance.

Inspecting patrol boat officers, however, exercised considerable discretion with some bias favoring other kinds of offenders. Tax or duty avoidance shipments, common smuggling in other parts of the world, were not treated as contraband by American Swift Boat crews.

Daytime raids of at least two and sometimes more boats entered areas known to be enemy infested. Frequently, these raids had air cover available; often it was not. Sometimes these boats carried troops, Vietnamese and American, to sweep the land for a few hours. Occasionally Swifts entered canals just to shell bunkers or draw fire for retaliation by air. Day work, often dull, was periodically dangerous, sometimes noisy, and always obvious. Night work was careful and quiet, at least until something happened.

CHAPTER 4
Co Chien River

An unusual flash of lightning and rumbling thunder, masked the ignition of a star shell fired from somewhere in the rain-soaked jungle. The swaying, unnatural illumination revealed sheets of torrential rainfall dominating the flat landscape and the river beyond.

In the middle of the Co Chien River, Swift Boat PCF-59, carefully approached the side of another Swift, PCF-37. Just as the two craft were about to touch, a shirtless person darted from the pilothouse of the approaching boat and leapt to the 37 Boat. As the figure found shelter, the 59 Boat veered off, taking station behind and to the side of its companion. The two craft moved slowly upriver.

A Swift Boat is a twenty-two-ton, heavily armed, fifty-foot, shallow draft aluminum patrol craft made in Berwick, Louisiana by the Steward Seacraft Company. Its silhouette is similar to utility boats servicing oil platforms and other offshore facilities in the Gulf of Mexico. These boats are known also by the US Navy designation as PCF or Patrol Craft-Fast, Mark 1. First introduced into the war in Vietnam in 1966, they are driven by two powerful diesel engines emitting a throaty, even growl.

The boat is armed with paired .50-caliber, aircraft-type, ring-mounted machine guns forward over the pilothouse, another .50-caliber machine gun mounted in piggyback fashion over an eighty-one millimeter mortar fixed to the afterdeck, and an M-60 light machine gun most often mounted on the Sampson post at the bow in front of the pilothouse. The post has a mounting plate that can accommodate a Mark Nineteen forty-millimeter, rapid-fire grenade launcher.

These boats also carried an assortment of other weapons issued, captured or, in some cases, informally acquired by barter or theft. Some of these weapons were unauthorized at the command level of the American Navy. Fragmentation hand grenades were not permitted on the boats since water-borne combat would not call for them and posed, at close quarters, more danger for its users. Concussion grenades were a most effective deterrent to swimmers trying to attack a boat. Light anti-tank weapons (LAWS) and shoulder-fired rockets also were not permitted on the correct belief that its back blast could damage the boat or injure the crew. Not all boats complied with command prohibitions.

The authorized crew consisted of five enlisted personnel led by one officer in charge (O-in-C). In the early years full lieutenants and lieutenants, junior grade nearing promotion, commanded these boats. Many were then regular Navy officers. As time passed, full lieutenants became less common and reserve officers were in the majority. These officers normally were a lieutenant, junior grade or an ensign, twenty-three to twenty-seven years old. Occasionally, an older officer, maybe with fleet experience, as old as thirty years, would volunteer for this duty. Rank was less significant in the operation of these boats than "snap" and patrol experience. The crew's ages ranged from eighteen to their early thirties, but most were quite young. All were volunteers, and almost all of the officers and men developed a fierce love for their boats.

Beginning in 1969, some boats began carrying from one to four Vietnamese Navy trainees, including a junior officer. Language skills and interest of teachers and students varied. Not surprisingly, some were dedicated to understanding a foreign language and culture; others were not. Many American officers in that period had attended an intensive two-week Vietnamese language course before deployment. Similarly, Vietnamese Navy sailors received some English language instruction.

For all of their deadly weaponry and ordinance, Swift Boats were not armored except around the small magazine located along the centerline under the main cabin deck. The skin of a Swift could be easily penetrated by small arms fire and the enemy version of the rocket-propelled grenade could blow out the insides of any Swift Boat while killing or maiming its crew.

* * *

Ens. William K. Boston came up to the pilothouse from the main cabin and pitched a towel at Lt. (jg) Samuel Buckhill Taylor. "I've put coffee on." Boston's tone was an invitation. By the time Taylor dried his upper torso, donned a fatigue shirt, and got coffee from the galley, Bill Boston had switched on a red chart light illuminating a map of the nearby coastal waters.

Vincent Pecorino, Engineman, 1st class, married, was seated at the wheel. Pecorino preferred driving at night. He listened to the engines and diagnosed possible maintenance to do in daylight when the boat was anchored in a river or tied up at one of the few fortified outposts established along the coast. The rest of the crew, four American enlisted men, supplemented by one Vietnamese Navy ensign, and three Vietnamese sailors-in-training were sleeping, stuffed in various berthing areas designed to accommodate a total of four persons.

As night watches changed according to a rotation established each afternoon, men would change sleeping places. In good weather, some of the men preferred sleeping on deck over the two engine covers. The engines transmitted a warm gentle hypnotic vibration up through the metal covers.

The sleeping system was specific only concerning the boat officers' bunk. At night, the boat officer or his Vietnamese officer-trainee took turns sleeping in one of the two berths in the main cabin. This practice was not founded in the privilege of rank, but for any nighttime emergency, everyone knew where to find an officer. This night, the boat was buttoned up against the rain, and those sailors not on watch were having a difficult time trying to sleep.

"That was a good ambush," Taylor's energy was up. "Three sampans between us. Did you get the report off?"

"Yeah, but I still want to go through the papers we found."

Taylor could saw Boston's finger tracing the course out of the Co Chien to the South China Sea and over to the rendezvous point and then into the Bo De. This gesture fixed the map and the operation orders into Boston's brain.

"Double, is the Bo De a waste of time tomorrow if this rain doesn't let up? The dry season supposedly began last month."

"It'll move on, Prevert."

Taylor, an older lieutenant (jg), relied on Boston's longer in-country experience for more than Delta weather.

Double and *Prevert* were two of the distinctive, personal, and unauthorized call signs used as nicknames within the squadron to identify particular individuals and to some extent, their peculiarities of habit or image. Boston's extended call sign was Double Bourbon. Some officers earned several such names, depending on the length and places of service. Taylor had three. *Prevert* was derived from the 1964 satirical film, *Dr. Strangelove.* Taylor never quite understood why this call sign was applied to him. Personal call signs today remain common throughout the American military.

"A typhoon crossed the Philippines last Wednesday, looking like it was bending south toward us," Boston continued. "Before we got underway yesterday, DivCom told me not to worry about it. That old mustang is never wrong about the weather."

The division commander in Cat Lo, DivCom, came up through the ranks and saw a lot of storms in his career. He had a sixth sense about the weather. Like many DivComs, he thought of these young Swift Boat officers and their crews as sons or nephews.

"He said it was going to hook north and move fast away from us." As Boston spoke, he drew a hooking arrow across the plastic laminated chart with his black grease pencil.

"DivCom said the clouds were moving in long, fat streaks back to the storm center. Somehow he knew that the storm would change directions." Boston scrawled a couple of long cigar shapes on the chart, each with a slight curve on their tail pointing northward. "He thought we might get some heavy rain, the wind kicking up, but that would be it. I thought the rain might come earlier and foul up our ambush."

Ens. Boston had been a compact, 155-pound wrestler at the University of Iowa. Since Officer Candidate School and later Boat School, he had put on ten pounds and begun smoking. Now in Vietnam, he restrained his college pugnacity. Fights came soon enough without looking for them. At twenty-three, fatigue apparent on his ruddy face, he was leading a two-boat patrol far from his comfortable, small-town life in central Iowa.

The river, Song Bo De, not connected to the Mekong River, flanks the northeast side of the Ca Mau peninsula on the southern tip of Vietnam. The top of the Bo De forms a "T" intersection with the Song Dam Doi to the right and the Song Cua Lon to the left. The Cua Lon is the main waterway through the Ca Mau and the U Minh Forest to the Gulf of Thailand. The Ca Mau is a tangle of mangrove swamps and small canals, a haven for communist forces.

"We'll be wasting time, alright." Boston was too cynical for his youthfulness.

Taylor's tone changed, "Bob Hampton's in charge; we'll be okay." He sensed his friend's worries.

Before responding, Boston looked at Taylor. He wondered why this older man had volunteered for the boats. Taylor was normally pensive and measured in what he said and did; he was rational.

"Prevert, stick around 'til we turn for the downriver run. Have your guys continue to station on me. We'll go over these charts and talk about the op. Maybe I'll feel better about it the more we work through this."

Pecorino injected, "Mr. Boston, the boat's in good shape. We're ready. What's the problem?"

"Vince, somebody thinks seven boats are better than three." Boston paused, running the fingers of both hands through his blond hair, again focusing on the chart that lay before him.

"Tomorrow morning we meet five other Sa Dec boats just north of the Bo De. We go in at 0800, inviting attack and hitting targets of opportunity. The mission is all right even if it is a little vague. With a smaller group, we have fewer maneuvering problems and can take better advantage of our speed."

"My engines will do their job," Pecorino declared. He was the leading petty officer on the boat. At thirty, he was the oldest man in the crew. His remark was not a reprimand for Boston's concerns, but Boston and Taylor understood the real message. *"As the boat officers, you guys do your job, and we'll do ours. Worrying won't help."*

"I know," Boston declared.

Pecorino had been with the 37 Boat when Boston first came aboard months ago. Boston knew how to take and give instruction and loved working with Pecorino on the engines. The crew was comfortable with Boston's leadership.

After Taylor radioed his boat to maintain station, the three men fell silent for a time and stared ahead.

Unlike Boston, Taylor had fleet experience before joining the boats, and he was older in many other ways. At twenty-nine, and in country a little over seven weeks, he easily accepted leadership from this twenty-three-year-old veteran. Boston came to the boats fresh out of OCS and an eight-week boat course. Taylor knew you didn't have to be a fleet sailor to know what you were doing out here. This blond-haired boy from Iowa proved himself time and again in the past eight months. Boston, like others off patrol, spent a lot of time in the bar at the base. He should have been working in the family business, building a life, and hustling girls back home instead of trying to keep his boat safe and his crew whole. He already had a Purple Heart and been put in for a Silver Star. Taylor recalled one of the stories.

* * *

Miraculously, Boston and his crew survived a particularly nasty morning in the Tan Phu Special Zone on the northeast side of the Co Chien River mouth. Special Zones, sometimes called Secret Zones, were coastal areas declared to be enemy territory and made off-limits for inhabitation. In other words, anyone found there was connected with and assumed to be the enemy. Such persons by day were ill advised to offer any military resistance to capture and removal from the zone. By night, sudden death could be the likely outcome of discovery. In either event, patrol boat officers-in-charge operated according to clear graduated rules of engagement. As the level of resistance increased, so, too, did the authorized level of response.

Boston, and his boat were leading a much larger and more heavily armed US Coast Guard Patrol Boat (WPB), *Point Marone*—call sign, Big Bear—and had already pushed through a couple of small firefights on the Rach eo Lon, a canal flanked by open fields with an occasional jungle fringe at the water's edge. Imagine a Mastiff plodding behind a small Bulldog. *Marone,* with much more firepower, was eighty-two feet long and had a higher vantage point than the PCF, moving fifty yards ahead. Boston reached the "T" intersection of that canal with the Rach Bang Cung to the left and the silted-over terminus of the Eo Lon to the right. A Forward Air Controller (FAC) overhead suggested that the 37 Boat alone might follow a small canal bending further to the right and into a very narrow, overgrown stream to see if it ultimately connected with yet another large canal running parallel with the Rach eo Lon and back to the Co Chien. *Point Marone* could not follow but swiveled in the open middle of the intersection while Boston advanced.

As the 37 Boat got well within the tangle of the mangroves and thick jungle, a Viet Cong homemade shaped mine was detonated high on the boat's port beam.

The FAC gasped into his radio, "Oh, God. Something's blown down there." The transmission was monitored in Vung Tau by the operational command for all these boats in the Delta. Its call sign was "Pastel."

"Airedale, this is Big Bear. I can't see him. Give me an idea where I should place some fire," Marone injected. Yellow and brown smoke wafted above the jungle.

The VC learned to fill a camouflaged container with explosives and pieces of metal, hanging the device from a tree to be command-detonated by wiring strung to a safer location, a homemade version of the American Claymore shaped mine.

The blast wounded everyone on board the 37 Boat. In the moment following the detonation, Gunner's Mate, 2nd class Raymond Huldy, the hulking gunner known as Gator, fired the eighty-one-millimeter mortar containing the infamous "beehive" or flechette round. When fired level toward the enemy, the beehive spews out fifteen hundred small darts in an ever-expanding deadly cone that chews through jungle vegetation and sometimes nails its human victims to trees or to the sides of rude fortifications. The flechette round can be the initial explosive American response to an ambush. It makes a statement about what life and death will be for the next several critical seconds of an engagement. Each boat might carry only one or two flechette rounds. It is regarded with awe.

"Pastel, this is Airedale. There's been another detonation, and I can see firing from your Elbow Golf unit." The pilot angled his small airplane in a tight bank to better see the action going on below. Elbow Golf was a call sign designation for Swifts operating on the Co Chien River.

"Big Bear, hold your fire. 37 is on the move," the FAC requested.

Boston's driver, Pecorino, jammed the throttles forward. The boat lunged along the narrow canal. The stunned and bleeding crew began firing everything they had with a trigger. It was unnecessary. The two young VC that blew the mine had foolishly been standing to see their handiwork. Now their bodies were a shredded mass from the flechette round.

So, too, was the 37 Boat. As it emerged into the open canal, the FAC saw a large gaping entry hole on the port side of the main cabin, wind-slapped debris still clinging to the damaged cabin. The main cabin had been unoccupied in accordance with standard general quarter's procedure. The effects of any explosion in the main cabin are multiplied by flying shards of window glass and boat metal.

"Elbow Golf 37, this is Airedale. Do you read me?" He repeated the message.

"Airedale, this is 37. I read you, but I'm having a hearing problem just now." The FAC began to relax. Even though he understood the probability that everyone on board might have impaired hearing after the blast, he also recognized the understated humor of the boat officer.

"What's your status? Need assistance?" The FAC saw the broad wake as the boat moved quickly west toward the river. Its guns had stopped firing, but the crew appeared ready.

"The boat is a sieve except below the waterline," a comment that all understood to mean that the boat was watertight and that the engines were sound. "No one needs to leave this boat, but all need attention." In this uncoded voice transmission, all American listeners also understood everyone to be wounded, but none required a medevac.

"Airedale, I'd like to get to the big river. By the way, the two canals connect, but I don't recommend using this way."

Jarred into speech, Pastel's watch officer in Vung Tau blurted, "Elbow Golf 37, this is Pastel. Permission granted. Two Ponies are coming," a reference to fixed-wing, rocket-armed Navy aircraft, OV-10s, stationed in Vung Tau, some sixty miles away. "Big Bear, this is Pastel. Exit your location and assist the Elbow Golf unit."

"Pastel, this is 37. Thanks. I'm almost clear. Don't need the Ponies." As Boston's boat lightly bumped over the shallow submerged sand bar found at almost every canal mouth down near the sea, he transmitted an unusual statement of elation. "Free at last, I'm free at last."

The after-action medical report noted that the crew suffered minor injuries, none requiring hospitalization. It could have been much worse. Shrapnel had peppered each man's flak jacket. The main cabin windows and bulkhead on the port side took the brunt of the blast, an indication that the mine's contents had not dispersed as uniformly as intended. Its pattern was still wide enough along that side to have put 138 separate holes in the boat, tagging everyone from the bow back to the mortar position. Boston's upper lip was cut by a small piece of shrapnel stopped by one of his front teeth. It had been a nasty day.

* * *

"It's a matter of scale," Taylor broke their silence. "Bob Hampton is in charge, knows his stuff, and keeps his head. We've all worked together, and there are no new kids. I'm going below for more coffee."

Pecorino and Boston then heard rummaging around the galley area. "You got any peanut butter? All I find is beer." Taylor had a red-lensed flashlight he used to search the little on-board refrigerator. More talking to himself, he said, "I found it. A guy can't live by beer alone, but with peanut butter . . ." They then heard Taylor's familiar whistle of the first bars of "Dixie."

On patrol the two-pound, dark green can with a pry lid was the fastest nutrition available. Most boats carried the peanut butter ration in their coolers. At room temperature, the contents were an oily mess. Refrigerated, it had the consistency of stiff dough.

Boston and Pecorino exchanged smiles. They knew Taylor was addicted to peanut butter, a habit acquired long before Taylor came into the division as a new kid.

New kids—new boat officers—had to prove themselves. Taylor had done just that a few weeks earlier in an introductory mission commanded by Frank Brooks. Seasoned boat officers were always skeptical of new O-in-Cs, especially older officers coming from the fleet. Occasionally, these men were arrogant and dangerous. A firefight got the new officer's attention; sometimes it took more. Boston had heard that Taylor had been a practicing lawyer and a prosecutor in Texas before joining the Navy. Rightly, he guessed there was a story. Taylor was an attentive student, but explosions, gunfire, and confusion affect people differently. Whatever the past, what mattered now was what a new kid did when things turned ugly.

Boston recalled one ugly instance. He, Taylor, and Brooks were on a daylight canal raid in the Tan Phu on the north side of the Co Chien. A B-40 hit Brooks' boat, killing his engineman. Taylor handled himself and his boat well when the rockets were flying. From that day, Taylor was trusted; his instincts were reliable.

Reeking of peanut butter, Taylor returned to the pilothouse carrying a fresh cup of coffee.

"You're right, Sam. Paranoia takes over when you've been here for any time. Before a raid, I worry about every detail of an operation and not so much about the boat and the men's ability to function. I worry about who is around me when it all turns nasty."

Taylor could see Boston's apology coming. "Sam, I'm sorry. I know you'll be there when things get tight." Boston felt sheepish that in expressing his anxiety, he had unintentionally implied that his own crew and his patrol partner somehow would not be up for the test the next day.

Smirking, Taylor ended the seriousness of the moment and Boston's embarrassment, "I'd rather not discuss it," a reference to an incident they witnessed in a Vung Tau bar. Remembering this, Boston grinned.

* * *

A communications officer Taylor knew from his sea-duty days was playing the role of the hard-bitten, disillusioned combat veteran despite the fact that he was assigned to a staff job at Pastel's headquarters, on the highest, most secure facility in Vung Tau, a hill about 600 feet above the city.

Seated with him at the bar were three young soldiers, who were new to the Army and certainly new to Vietnam; they didn't have the look. They were kids in their late teens and were learning about Vietnam and the war from this guy who only broke a sweat walking from the air-conditioned communications van to the air-conditioned mess hall. This fraud handled the general questions with an air of authority naturally gained from receiving and reading messages composed by others with direct knowledge. When the inevitable question was asked, "Sir, how is it out there?" he could not bring himself to construct a specific lie. "I'd rather not discuss it," he said as he looked down to his lap and caressed the rim of his beer can. Of course, the kids also looked down and at each other, embarrassed that they had somehow asked the wrong question of this morose hero. Boston and Taylor had been at a table nearby and close enough to hear the dialog.

As patrol partners, those two had done well. But in the periodic two days off between patrols, they were getting dangerously drunk and into trouble on the first night off patrol, and that night had been no exception.

"I'm gonna' go kick his ass," Taylor muttered. He had perfected a strategy of sitting absolutely upright while drinking. He thought that it kept others from noticing his intoxication and made him appear fully functional. Boston knew otherwise and was willing to stir things up, but this time he had second thoughts.

"Prevert, we don't need this. Got another way?" The young ensign was trying to keep the older officer out of trouble. The division commander had threatened to split them up as patrol partners if they didn't clean up their act off patrol. They would have a lot to lose.

"You're right. That asshole needs a dose of my gentlemanly resourceful legal training." His three years as a county prosecutor was training for Plan B. He got up and moved toward the bar, smiling and unsteady on his feet. Wondering what Taylor had in mind, Boston paused and then followed.

As his shoulder was warmly slapped, the talkative communications officer turned in apprehensive but dawning recognition; he knew Taylor.

"Hey, John Wayne, I haven't seen you since I was on the *Princeton*." The man's name was neither "John" nor "Wayne."

"Weren't you in Long Beach until a couple of months ago? Somebody said that you got a desk job here on the hill."

Taylor loudly pressed forward. "I'd like you to meet my patrol partner, Bill Boston. This little ensign has seen more crap than you and I ever passed."

Boston stuck his hand out, "Glad to meet you, Mr. Wayne," his blue eyes hidden by a grin.

"Naw, Bill, I was just kidding. He isn't John Wayne, you little butter bar," a reference to the single brass ensign bars on Boston's collars. "This is Ted Hake. He's a good guy." Taylor spilled beer on his own shirt, narrowly missing Hake. Hake, mumbled a half-hearted "Hey" and then, after a "Yeah," was speechless.

The three Army kids had warily gotten up and stood aside as Taylor and Boston approached their group. During and after the conversation, the boys saw something in these two Navy officers that they had not seen in Lt. Hake. In a few seconds of friendly banter, Taylor showed Hake for what he was. The kids nodded, shrugged, and turned away.

"Well, Ted, we gotta go now. Ens. Boston said we need to get back to our base. If you want to go for a little boat ride some time, let me know. And if you want to fire the guns, I'll get permission from Ens. Boston here."

Boston had difficulty containing himself. He pulled Taylor's elbow, and they both made for the street. Hake was relieved to see them go but then looked around to see if anyone else had been watching.

"Bill that was the most fun I've had in a long time. That jerk deserved it. He's the kind of guy who'll go back to the world and dazzle the ladies with his 'I'd rather not discuss it,' line and they'll never know the difference. They'll jump in the sack believing he's a hero, the SOB."

Further down the street, Taylor's anger was replaced by a more considered view. He shook his head, never breaking stride, and more talking to himself, he spoke.

"There's a truth here. When this is over and we go back to the world, a lot of his kind will play roles others lived, enhancing their significance here. In ten or twenty years, the jerk wad will run for Congress—who knows. If he's smart, he really won't discuss it. Still, voters won't sort out the phonies. They'll see a faded photograph, a uniform, and the fact of service here and probably ignore some decent, competent, and maybe better guy who never served or left the States. Worse, they won't look for the substance of either candidate."

Taylor was stone-cold sober. They headed for their borrowed truck to drive back to Cat Lo, a distance of about six miles.

Cat Lo, on the fringe of the upper waters of Vung Tau's harbor, was a fishing village before being turned into a full-service patrol boat base with lifting and major repair facilities. Home base for Coastal Division 13 (CosDiv 13), known as the Black Cat Division, its fuel pier was well away from the berthing piers. It had a mess hall, separate barracks and bars for officers and enlisted personnel, a transient officer's bunkroom, administrative offices, and a large docking area. A Vietnamese Navy command structure on the base maintained other barracks and a mess hall.

Swift Boats moving between other divisions put in to Cat Lo for fuel and provisioning. Cat Lo was a permanent, fair-sized, reasonably secure base even considering the poorly aimed one or two rounds of mortar or 120 millimeter rocket fire infrequently falling on or near the base. The firing often ended before boats could move to a safe location. It was from this base that Boston and Taylor had departed the previous morning.

The rain stopped. Dawn was a couple of hours away. The two officers hunkered over the chart table, making grease pencil notations on the laminated chart of the coast and the Song Bo De.

CHAPTER 5
Sa Dec

The central delta town of Sa Dec is west of the Mekong's split with the Co Chien River. Located on a large canal flowing parallel to and south of the Mekong's main channel, the Rach (canal) Sa Dec bisects the busy town. A Swift Boat detachment from CosDiv 13 berthed in the town center near a T-intersection of canals. Eight boats patrolled from Sa Dec, half the group normally underway at all times on any of its assigned rivers. Sometimes all patrol-ready units could depart for a major effort. Even at full strength, because of maintenance limitations, some boats were unlikely to sustain a protracted maximum effort. Minor maintenance and repair could be accomplished in Sa Dec, but engine replacement or battle damage required the unit to travel under what was left of their power or be towed by another boat downriver past My Tho and across Vung Tau's bay to Cat Lo.

The detachment's corrugated steel-sided barracks and mess facilities were located within a small, fenced compound further in town on the opposite side of the Rach Sa Dec from the boats' docking area. Despite the presence of US Army and irregular forces, Navy people felt less secure. They belonged on or very near their boats, not several streets away, across a bridge vulnerable to attack.

Lt. Robert Hampton was the officer in charge of the Sa Dec detachment boats. A twenty-eight-year-old Sacramento, California reservist just beyond his third year of active duty was recently promoted and extended his tour in Vietnam for six more months. His personal call sign was Pastor Bob.

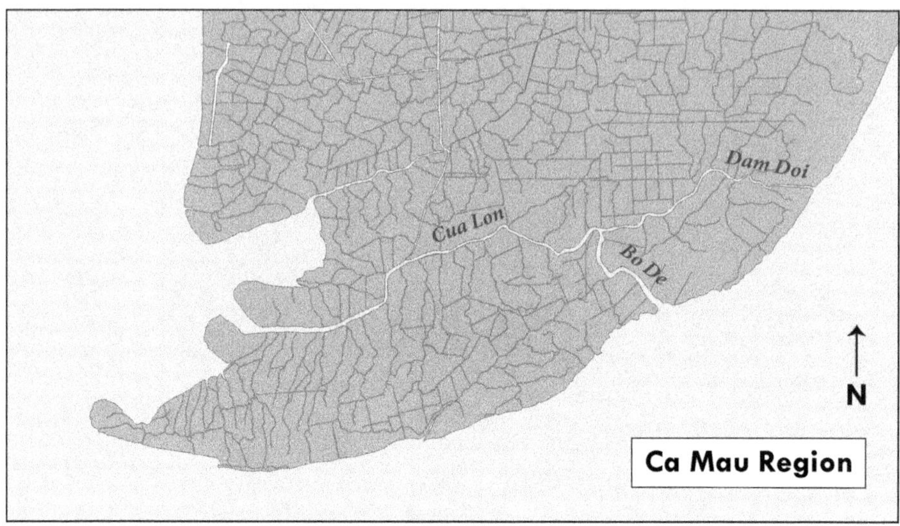

Hampton, almost six feet tall with short, dark hair, was well groomed in his fading unstarched green utilities. One reason for this was that he got a haircut every ten days from a local Vietnamese barber employed at the compound. That was one way of giving more order in this crowded muddy little delta town. Everyone understood that the only safe points of discussion in the presence of the barber involved sports or food. Like many of the men on the boats, Hampton had a deep tan from the waist up.

While on R & R in Hawaii three-and-a-half months earlier, he confided to his wife, Katie that he was considering the Navy as a career. The division commander in Cat Lo and the squadron commander in Cam Ranh Bay also believed he should stay in the Navy and thus had assigned him the important and sporadically dangerous leadership task in Sa Dec. That assignment was tangible evidence of trust and competence that would help him succeed in the future over contemporary Naval Academy graduates. He was an experienced fleet and combat junior officer, a valuable asset to the future of the Navy.

The makeshift detachment office was a small room on the first floor at one end of the barrack near the only gate into the compound. The unpainted plywood interior walls were otherwise covered with an area map, navigation charts, and thumbtacked sheaves of paper. Two desks, two chairs, one telephone, one field radio, and a PRC-77 were all behind a plywood countertop, bypassed through a swinging half-door. Stacked against an inside corner behind the desks were two so-called bulletproof vests, two steel helmets, two M-16 rifles with two slings of loaded magazines, one M-79 grenade launcher, and a sling full of forty-millimeter rounds for the launcher. This light, stubby, shoulder- or waist-fired weapon could shoot one forty-millimeter fragmentation grenade for distances up to four hundred meters. This sling, however, also contained special options for close-in or night work: two flechette and eight buckshot rounds. Boat officers and their crews recognized the compound's vulnerability.

Radioman 3rd class Mike Ringer, standing the communications watch until midnight, handed out paperwork for the pre-patrol briefing by Hampton. In addition to Ringer and Lt. Hampton, four junior officers lined up casually along the counter, some smoking cigarettes. Heavy rain was falling and prevented better ventilation. The group knew Bob's aversion to cigarettes. He wasn't a prude about smoking or anything else, but the haze got thick. As Hampton stood and turned to one of the wall charts, the smokers stubbed out their cigarettes.

Tomorrow was to be a long day. Off duty, these officers and their crews drank and seriously let loose. When a patrol was eminent, sobriety came quickly with equally serious focus on the details of the operation. No one wanted to go home in a bag.

Hampton's briefing got to the heart of matter. "Tomorrow we're going in the De at 0800. For the record, the typhoon turned north earlier today and is now tracking straight up the South China Sea and away from us. Tonight's rain is a leftover."

"Intel reports the North Vietnamese Army (NVA) moving a force to the Ca Mau, reportedly hauling B-40s—bunches of them. I don't know how they know these things, but boys and girls, it makes good reading. Fat chance of surprising them with this parade we're doing tomorrow, but who knows, we may get lucky. Our job is to see if we can catch anyone off guard, kill them, and generally disrupt their day. And if we attract a lot of attention, then we're to engage them long enough for Black Ponies to come in and slap them around. To avoid detection, the Ponies are to be hanging out some distance from the Bo De."

The Black Pony insignia of Light Attack Squadron Four (VAL-4) identified a unique aircraft used for reconnaissance and close support of the Navy's riverine and coastal forces. This short, fixed-wing-over North American Rockwell airplane resembled the World War II P-38 Lightening. Its Navy designation was OV-10, but it was also known as a "Bronco."

A single Bronco could deliver devastating firepower onto an enemy position. This firepower consisted of four 7.62 machine guns (M-60s), capable of firing five hundred rounds per gun, a twenty-millimeter cannon, eight to sixteen five-inch "Zuni" rockets with seven to seventeen pound warheads or up to nineteen rounds of 2.75-inch rockets, including flechette rounds for anti-personnel work.

Except for the ever-present M-60 machine guns, standard two-plane flights mounted these other weapons in a complementary arrangement to provide a versatile firepower package for most situations.

Ringer limped around the group, passing out lists of the primary and secondary operational frequencies, call signs, and checkpoints identified by map coordinates.

Hampton continued, "This operation is called 'Frisco Market,' and I'll be Frisco Leader. You'll be Frisco plus your hull number. Please avoid using personal call signs on the operational frequency." Hampton was careful to emphasize the words "please" and "operational."

"I will be the OTC," an acronym for officer-in-tactical-command of that day's activity. "Tomorrow, at 0745, our five units meet the 37 and 59 Boats coming off their regular Co Chien patrols. We rendezvous up the coast a sufficient distance from the Bo De River mouth and well to sea to avoid early detection, if we can.

"As we come together, the group will form into sections of two-three-two units with the usual intervals. We'll be in our tight, single-file formations before we make the turn for the river. Do your preparations during the transit. There must be no delays when we meet the two Co Chien boats. We meet. We form up. We go in. Simple as that.

"There are small canals branching off the Bo De, but watch for one that's off to the right as you enter. Boats got shot at from there one time. The last time I was outbound on the De with another boat, there was a sandbar that ran mid-channel for about a hundred meters parallel to the right bank. Tomorrow our inbound track should be closer to the right bank near that little canal. Since the tide will be up, this shouldn't be a problem. The boats still need to go in up on step," a reference to a speed high enough to lift up the keel, permitting a run in shallower water. "This sand bar is trying to become an island. We'll get announcements from the lead boats, but pay close attention to your fathometers until we are all in." Hampton paused while the others took notes and shifted their stances.

"The wind should somewhat mask our sounds until we are in the tangents of the river mouth. Double and Prevert, lead in as section one, and I will take the second section. Five-Buck Raider will have the last section, with Mr. Leyland to lead us out when the time comes."

Five-Buck Raider, Lt. (jg) Frank Brooks, was a slender, naturally hollow-eyed Naval Academy graduate. His fatigues always looked too big for his lean frame, but he was a thorough professional. Off duty, he never spent more than five dollars running around. He might have played cheap, but he was never a cheat on his wife back in Virginia.

Lt. (jg) Richard Leyland, a reservist from Texas, was also known as "Camel." He was tall, with a patient, unperturbed, and academic appearance. He was not given to speaking unless there was good reason.

"Also Five-Buck is the alternate OTC. Are there any questions to this point?"

The Camel spoke. "How long are we staying, and how far in are we going?"

"Richard, the operational message allows us to go the Cua Lon-Dam Doi intersection, but my present intention is to go only so far as the leftward bend of the Bo De, maybe not even as far as Tan An." Tan An was an abandoned village the Viet Cong destroyed.

"The objective is to cross the predicted track of the bad guys and see if we can provoke them. If that doesn't happen in the time it takes to get up there, I am not inclined to hang around. Even so, we should be ready for a whacking on our trip back out to sea."

The young men listened intently. They knew the rule: don't relax your guard until all boats are clear. There was nothing unusual about these instructions, including the designation of an alternate OTC. Theirs was not the laundry and dry-cleaning business. There were no other questions.

Hampton continued. "There's one sticky aspect." Boat officers don't like sticky aspects, and the officers' postures straightened.

"The OV-10s aren't exactly committed to us right now, and we won't know their level of availability until we rendezvous. The good news is that in the event they are not committed to us, we are not expected to stand and fight"—he paused—"very long. It could be a quick in and out. I'll make that decision." The group understood without comment the qualification, "very long." They also knew that Pastor Bob would make the right decision. They filed out, some talking about the movie about to be shown, purposely ignoring tomorrow's events.

Although Ringer would remain in Sa Dec the next day, his inner tension was ratcheting up. He survived enough firefights to believe his luck would run out some day. The closest he came to major injury that he was aware of was when a .51-caliber slug slammed into the side of his boat's engine cover on which he was standing. While shearing up the cover's metal, it also plowed through the side of the heel on Ringer's boot spinning his left leg behind and around his right leg. God blessed him that day as he tumbled down onto the deck. A second machine-gun burst mangled the after-steering station where he had been standing. Either from the impact of the slug or the twisting and falling motion afterward, Ringer had only seriously sprained his knee and ankle. Since then he had been unable to shake the jittery feeling he got during patrol briefings.

He was set to go home in less than a month. Mr. Hampton put him on light duty, he said, to give Ringer's leg a rest. Ringer would always believe, however, that he was given the break to assure that he went home alive. Pastor Bob was a decent man.

Robert Hampton almost never drank hard alcohol. He liked Canadian whiskey, but a fifth might last him a year. After lunch following a patrol, Bob would drink one beer before taking a nap. No one ever heard him curse.

Whether this moderate behavior was a consequence of spiritual conviction or just a way of taking care of himself, he came easily to his personal call sign, Pastor Bob. He loved his wife and was faithful to her. What came across to all who knew him was that Robert Hampton was comfortable in his skin.

Hampton sat at his desk, making a few notes. Ringer cleaned out the ashtrays and pitched the extra briefing notes into a burn bag. The wall map and charts were taken down and locked in his desk. Ringer knew quickly how the best of plans turned bad when put into motion. For him, it was time to focus on something else. He opened a worn, blue, cloth-bound book that he had started reading the day after his boot heel was shot away.

"Ringer, I'm turning in. Make sure your relief gets me up at 0100. Remind the security detail at the dock to be ready for us."

Hampton shoved the message board into his desk and locked it. His small red patrol notebook went into his chest pocket. Tomorrow the little book would be a ready reference to mission call signs, radio frequencies, and map coordinates. It would also contain notes for composing the after-action message. Pausing at the door, he turned back.

"*The Blue Max* is showing for the eighth consecutive night. Talk to Fogarty. Tell him to arrange a projector breakdown in about twenty-five minutes. Nobody going out tomorrow needs to be up late. Besides, all they want to see is George Peppard as a German infantryman, slithering around in a muddy World War I battlefield."

He saw Ringer's polite attention and continued, "In the beginning of the movie, Peppard rolls over onto his back to watch an aerial dogfight in the clear blue skies above. Right then he decides he's going to become a fighter pilot to fight a clean war."

Hampton understood the appeal such images had for boat officers and their crews. They had been imbued by their squadron commander's welcoming address with the dramatic notion that their job was similar to that of Spitfire pilots in the Battle of Britain, racing into harm's way to prevent German bombers from striking their homeland. He knew also that violent death was a part of both realities.

Hampton looked at Ringer for some additional reaction.

Ringer raised his right hand in acknowledgment. He continued to hold and look at the book in his left hand.

"Since at least half the group will be back tomorrow night, give *The Blue Max* to the Army and see what you can get in return," Hampton continued. "Also, in the morning, check my room for a letter."

Wordlessly, Ringer lowered the book, raised his left hand, and smiled. Ringer would not speak further this evening except to carry out Hampton's orders. He would escape into silence reading his worn, hard-back 1963 seventh edition of Webster's *New Collegiate Dictionary*. His Appalachian Mountain high school in Kentucky had not stressed a broad vocabulary. Ringer wanted to go to college. The interiors of his mind dreamed of higher pursuits.

The rain stopped. The air was clean and fresh. As Hampton walked outside the short distance to his second-floor room in the other barrack, he thought about some of the very skilled and bright people he had met in the Navy. Sometimes, too, they were a little strange. He thought, *Why would anyone read a dictionary from cover to cover?*

In his room, he switched on a lamp and floor fan, stripped off his sweaty fatigue uniform, and laid out a fresh one on a chair, topping the clean clothing with his wristwatch, a thin, small wallet, and his red patrol notebook. After wrapping a towel about his waist, he placed his pistol in the fatigue cap and carried that with his shaving kit along the second-deck outside walkway to the showers. Ten minutes later, he was back in his room. After putting on fresh skivvies and rechecking his gear for the next day, he sat at his desk and wrote a letter to Katie. He could hear music coming from the bar a few yards across the compound, but it did not distract him.

He wrote her almost every night that he was not on patrol. The letters were usually short, general comments about his day and upbeat statements about coming home. He was writing more faithfully since breaking the news to her that he added six months to his tour and was considering the Navy as a career. When she got home to Fresno, California after R & R in Hawaii, she wrote that while she was fearful, she knew he loved the Navy and approved his decision. One of her recent letters, however, revealed that she had become pregnant in Hawaii. He loved her so much that he often felt a nice weakness in his throat. Tonight he wrote more than usual.

After sealing the letter, he placed it upright against the wall at the back edge of the desk and turned off the light. He moved toward the cot but did not lie down. Instead, he got the pillow and placed it on the floor at the side of the cot. In the darkness he then knelt and quietly prayed.

"Dear Lord, God of us all, I don't know what tomorrow brings, and I can't change it or worry about its end. Please protect those in my charge, help me deal with my doubts and fears, and bring us all back safely. But if that is not to be, please protect our souls until the time of your coming. If I die tomorrow, Lord, please be with Katherine and our baby. Help her understand that I was doing what I thought was right and that I loved her and the baby to the end."

He always concluded his prayers with the same words.

"When I fall short as one of your children, Lord please forgive me. In all things, Lord Christ, your will be done. Amen."

Pastor Bob Hampton then climbed onto the cot, placed his pistol under the pillow, and lay on his back. For less than three minutes, he stared up into the darkness and listened to the music and the whirring of the fan. Then turning onto his left side, he went to sleep.

CHAPTER 6

South China Sea

Gloomy morning clouds draped the sea; a dull, green haze filled the air. Before dawn, Sam Taylor transferred back to his own boat. They stepped up speed to get to the Bo De area on time. Both officers caught some sleep during this part of the transit.

They learned that the force entering the Bo De would be twice that set forth in the original operational message. The OTC would not be Lt. Hampton, but instead was Navy Commander Edward Lewis Stroud, Pastel himself.

Pastel was the official call sign of the Navy's operational commander for the region. His offices were located high on the big hill above Vung Tau.

Taylor and Boston arrived at the rendezvous point fifteen minutes before the Sa Dec boats came in view on time. There was no sign of Pastel's group. They wallowed around in the long, gentle swells, keeping enough engine speed to maintain position. The boats were almost out of sight of land. Hampton's boat approached, and he stepped out of his pilothouse with a radio handset, gesturing with a circular motion over his head. That was a signal to Boston and Taylor to switch their PRC 77s to their informal frequency known as Bravo Sierra (BS). The boats had another radio, AN-URC-58, tuned to the prescribed frequency for this operation. Vung Tau, more than 120 miles away, monitored this raid through that frequency. What Vung Tau would not hear is that these boats had switched their smaller, shorter-range radios to a prearranged, Bravo Sierra frequency in order to have a reasonably private and often unimportant conversation. That morning Hampton's purpose was very important.

"Prevert, Double, this is Papa Bravo. I've already talked to my flock. Church is going to be crowded this morning with the Bishop presiding, and we don't want to be bumping into one another. Once we start the procession, be ready to pick up on Bravo Sierra on my signal or if anything doesn't seem right. Over." They acknowledged his message.

"This is Bob again. Most of the latecomers to this service are visitors, being led by a priest who's never been to this parish. Bless you, my sons. Out." With that, Hampton's 24 Boat swung around and ran north to see if his radar could find Stroud's group. All he picked up then was a small fishing boat moving toward the shore.

CHAPTER 7

Old Fisherman

Dinh Can-Than was fifty-seven years old, a fisherman all of his life. He had never traveled further from his coastal hamlet than the town of Bac Lieu. As a young boy, he remembered seeing Frenchmen in Bac Lieu. They hired men, including his father, to go across the sea as servants in the French army then at war, they said. His father never returned home. As Mr. Dinh grew older, he saw more Frenchmen, haughty and disdainful, always sweating. Later as a young man after the French had gone, Dinh sold fish to Japanese fliers who lived nearby at a grass-covered airfield. They were cocky but not arrogant, and they always paid for their fish. After the French tried to return, there were many bad times, and fishing was difficult.

His wife, Nguyet Thi Hoa, looked very old now; even though younger than her husband, she was always sad. They lost two sons. The boys helped them catch fish. The French wrongly accused their oldest son of collaboration with the Viet Minh. They shot him in the mouth as he cried out his innocence. Their next son, at the age of fourteen, helped the Viet Cong by reporting when he saw the South Vietnamese military or Americans coming near their fishing village.

North Vietnamese Army units came into the region. One night last year, NVA soldiers stopped the boy near their encampment. Worried that he was a spy, beating the truth from him proved useless. In the end, they, too, shot him in the mouth. The next morning Ong Dinh found his son in a field, and the NVA were gone. Hung around his son's neck was a sign, "Ke phan quoc," a *traitor.*

Now, Dinh fished alone. Fear killed his sons, and he wondered when fear would kill him. He knew only to do what he was told by anyone who held a gun. He was careful.

More soldiers from the north were now hiding along the banks of the Song Bo De. Local cadres of patriots controlled the area by night. They required people to bring food for these soldiers to a designated location in the jungle. Otherwise, no one was permitted near the soldiers.

Two weeks ago, Dinh saw these soldiers as he was motoring his small sampan down the Bo De to fish along the shore. He was called to the riverbank by the northern soldiers and taken to their Tieu Ta (Major). Phan Thanh Nguyen made him work and ordered him to take his boat along the coast to the north of the Song Bo De. There he was to fish and give his catch to a small group of Phan's soldiers living in the jungle. He was warned to look for American boats and to report their number and course of travel as quickly as he could get back to the beach. The soldiers had a radio.

By noon each day, he was allowed to return to shore if he saw no Americans. Maj. Phan said that marauding American boats would only come at night or at first light. Early in his assignment, a single American boat had stopped him. They returned his identity card and the logbook issued by the government office in Soc Trang when they saw that he only had fish aboard. The American officer gave him a tin of fruit, a pack of cigarettes, and a can of cold beer. The officer, who spoke some Vietnamese, smiled and said goodbye in a proper manner. Dinh did not share the gifts from the American officer.

When Dinh saw two boats this morning, he decided not to return to the beach right away. He was catching fish now and felt no special fear of Americans. Later he saw five more boats coming very fast from the north and meeting the first two boats. It was then that he decided to leave.

He beached his sampan and ran into the jungle and found one of the soldiers, a young boy, and told him what he had seen. He also said that the boats were not moving but seemed without purpose. He wondered what the Americans were going to do and whether his duties were ended. The soldier listened and then ran away further into the jungle. Dinh returned to his sampan to retrieve his catch. This had been the first really good fishing day since his arrival. Perhaps the soldiers would pay him this time. Maybe last night's rain had influenced the fish. Again, he wondered if his job was over.

CHAPTER 8

Long Journey

Maj. Phan, Sgt. Toh, and thirty men were all that remained of a special force of 160 North Vietnamese Army regulars who had made the long journey south from the People's Democratic Republic of Vietnam. Their mission was to come to this place, kill American men and boats, and seek revenge.

Sixty kilometers west of Hanoi flows the Yen River, far from the South China Sea, but similar enough in width and relevant terrain to the Song Bo De. The land near the Yen River is generally flat, but occasionally odd mountains seem to have been planted randomly in the surrounding fields and paddies. Further up the Yen River from the village of Duc Khe is a mountain trail leading to the Perfume Pagoda, a destination for pilgrims and tourists.

The soldiers, ignorant of their ultimate objective, spent nights in Duc Khe village and days training to accurately and consistently hit targets with shoulder-launched RPGs. They practiced coordinated rocket attacks, firing dummy warheads against painted moving targets whose silhouettes resembled the American boats. The soldiers learned to lead their target, accounting for its speed and to do so reflexively. From concealed positions, they shot as groups of three or four men, all aiming at the pilothouse or the engine compartment of the targeted boat. As soon as they fired a volley, they were taught to race along previously prepared trenches away from the first ambush site to a second firing position out of the direct line of responsive fire expected from the Americans, there to find another target of opportunity. With enough men trained in this tactic, fighting from several of these positions strung along both sides of the river, they might inflict truly heavy losses on the boats and delay their own deaths. The best they could hope for was two solid volleys before American airplanes overhead, if any, obliterated the shoreline.

Phan and Trung Ta (Lieutenant Colonel) Nguyen had studied maps of the area, intelligence reports of the patrol, and raiding habits of the Americans, including strengths and weaknesses of the boats and their crews. The chief weakness of these boats was their pilothouse; a well-placed shot could take out the driver, the commanding officer, and the gunner just above the pilothouse. They had no armor. The strengths were three heavy machine guns, a big mortar, speed, aggressiveness, and supporting aircraft.

Shifting launch positions was intended to avoid the firepower these boats brought to bear on an ambush site. Instead of running away, the Americans always pounced on ambush positions. Facing a sudden counter-assault required great courage, and often that was insufficient. The Viet Cong in the South died easily enough, but they lacked the discipline and training of this special force.

The year before, two American Swifts had entered the Song Bo De and surprised a convoy of sampans carrying almost a hundred Viet Cong and NVA. All of the sampans were either sunk or heavily damaged. Fewer than twenty soldiers survived, and many of those were wounded. For all practical purposes, that force ceased to exist. That was only one reason for revenge.

Afterward, the Americans moved their larger boats from coastal patrols to inland waterways. In combination with smaller fiberglass patrol boats and coordinated use of helicopters and airplanes, the Americans killed thousands of patriots and chewed up vital supply routes. The loss of all of Lt. Col. Nguyen's force would be a small price if they could destroy several of these boats in a well-planned, coordinated, and dramatic ambush.

Attrition of Nguyen's force was constant during the trip south. Nguyen was killed before they crossed into southern Vietnam. He died instantly from a Claymore mine, trip-wired along one of the many tracks of what the Americans called the Ho Chi Minh Trail. Little was left of his body when dragged off into the jungle. American B-52 bombers played their part in whittling down the numbers effectively entering the Delta. A bomb shard had sliced across Phan's mouth. Only now was it beginning to heal.

Malnutrition, mistakes, and disease killed many more of these young North Vietnamese soldiers and their junior officers. Recently, several men drowned, and equipment was lost during a canal crossing. Tieu Uy (Second Lieutenant) Nham had overloaded a sampan and paid for his mistake. As the starboard gunwale sank into the water, spilling out men and equipment, the opposite gunwale edge struck Nham's head. The survivors recovered some of the supplies but never Nham's corpse. Nham was the last junior officer in the force.

Then there were ambushes. Only the last encounter was a failure for the enemy. A village boy warned Phan that a party of local traitors, accompanied by an American officer, were waiting for his group further along the trail. Hiding his main force in the jungle with Sgt. Toh, Phan and six of his men moved away from the trail and around the ambush site identified by the boy. Phan estimated a likely course the traitors might take returning to their base. There they waited.

Just before dawn, Phan sensed movement. He could hear the slight rustle of leaves and the tread of feet on the jungle floor. There were ten men in the party. Toward the back of the group, one man was relatively taller and bigger than the others. All were clothed in black. He fired one shot at the big man and saw him fall.

For ten seconds, he and his men fired furiously, receiving only weak return fire. Then there was silence. He sent his men in to see what they had killed. Four bodies lay along a small path, and there were blood trails. Of the three blood trails, two stopped further in the jungle, indicating that the traitors had patched their wounds sufficiently to get away.

The third trail led away from where the big man had fallen. Phan's men reported finding an American well into the jungle, and they wanted permission to finish him off. He was too seriously wounded to take with them.

Phan ordered them away to strip the dead traitors of anything valuable, including food, weapons, and ammunition. This was the first time they had been able to strike back.

Before him lay this brute of an American. His cap had fallen away revealing his close-cut and thinning blond hair. The man was young, muscular, and broad shouldered; his chest was wide and deep like a water buffalo. Until he saw the man close like this, he did not understand how anyone could have moved as far as he did with his wound.

The man was unconscious, and Phan heard a gurgling sound. The hole in the right side of his chest from Phan's shot was satisfying, exactly where Phan had aimed. For the American, it caused a breathing problem, and he would soon die.

Phan found no papers on the man but did find a small pouch containing an un-opened package of cigarettes, matches, and a packet of what he believed was medicinal powder and one small tube of morphine. He knew what he would do.

Stripping the cellophane from the cigarettes, he placed the cellophane over the hole, then adjusted the man's right arm to cover the seal he had fashioned. Finally, he rolled the man onto his right side so that the hole was pointing downward. The man groaned but his breathing improved.

Phan sat on the ground and lit one of the cigarettes. He studied the man's face and wondered why he had come to die with these traitors. He looked like a Russian. He was handsome despite his hardened features. There was something noble about him. Phan surmised from the circumstances that this man was not like the French he had known as a child in the north. This man was not a mercenary or a dutiful and dedicated career soldier simply following orders. This man loved Vietnam and its people. Phan felt he had slain a knight.

Phan heard his men laughing and knew they were mutilating the traitors. He realized that he needed to get moving. Those who escaped would still cause trouble and bring others back. They would want to find their knight. He flicked the cigarette off into the jungle, stood, and pulled his pistol. He then fired one shot into the ground a foot from the man's head, turned, and walked away to rejoin his men. As he snapped his fingers at them, they fell silent, knowing how merciless he could be in matters of discipline. As he and his men trudged back along the trail toward Sgt. Toh's position, Phan searched for the packet of powder and morphine in his pocket, knowing he would need them later more than the man he left to die.

With all of their losses, there was more equipment and ammunition than soldiers to carry the burden. When they left their supply areas in Cambodia, each man had carried only two B-40 rockets with one launcher in addition to their packs, food, personal weapons, and ammunition. Now each man carried four or more of the rockets. They also carried a disassembled Soviet .51-caliber heavy machine gun and 500 rounds of ammunition.

Along the way, Maj. Phan persuaded villagers to feed his men and to help transport their munitions to the vicinity of the Song Bo De. Phan told these volunteers that his force was going on to the Ca Mau peninsula near the tip of Vietnam where the South China Sea and the Gulf of Thailand meet. He said that other men from the Ca Mau would meet them and take them further. He could not trust these villagers. Persuasion had been easy enough for the limited job of carrying their supplies a few kilometers. Besides, the villagers knew it was in their best interest to help these soldiers leave their area. He left a guard force with some of the supplies and forged on to his specific objective. Over the next two days, his men hauled the rest of the supplies down to the site in stages.

Before beginning the long journey into the Delta, Phan and Lt. Col. Nguyen were told to look for a specific but subtle geographic feature along the banks of the Song Bo De. The advancing Delta, long before man roamed the earth, had paused, creating a slight bluff at right angles to the course of the river. This bluff was no more than a meter higher than the terrain on either side of the bluff.

When Phan first saw this feature on the Bo De, he imagined it to be the remains of an elevated road, a hundred meters wide and two kilometers long. A casual observer would not have readily noticed the difference in elevation nor would they have appreciated the military opportunity this rise provided. Their fate had been well researched and planned.

CHAPTER 9

Site Preparation

When they arrived at the intended location on the lower end of the Song Bo De, Maj. Phan's first order was to send three of his men with a little food and one of the radios through the jungle to a place on the seashore four kilometers to the north of the river's entrance. They were to establish a concealed lookout for American boats. Based on intelligence reports, he discounted the possibility of a large force of boats approaching from the south.

Later that first day, Phan's sentries intercepted a man in a small, motorized sampan traveling downriver and brought him to the Major. He was a sad old man whose mouth smiled, but all else was pain. The old man, his eyes fixed on Phan's boots, answered all of the Major's questions with great respect and humility. He was a fisherman on his way to drag his small conical nets along the shore beyond the river. He carried a twenty-liter container of gasoline for his small motor. Phan pondered whether to take the sampan and kill the old man. Instead he put him to work.

The remainder of Phan's men was divided into two groups, working on either side of the river, with Sgt. Toh in charge on the far side. The old man and his sampan were used to ferry men and equipment between the sides. Before the final transit, Phan spoke with Sgt. Toh.

"Toh, what would you do with the old man when we no longer need him?"

"Tieu Ta, we never needed him, just his boat." Toh was a realist.

"We cannot allow him to leave us. Old men talk. Kill him when you reach the other side."

"Yes, Tieu Ta, but we can use him further. After all, he is a fisherman. We can kill him later."

"Trung-si (Sgt.) Toh, you haven't answered my question. What would you do when we no longer use him?"

"Our work here should remain a secret only until the American boats come. Then his death becomes unnecessary." Toh paused, stiffened, and then looked directly into Phan's eyes. "Tieu Ta, I would let him live. I came here to kill Americans, not sad old men."

Phan's torn mouth broke slightly into a possible smile. "Thank you. Before you finally cross the river today, send our youngest and fastest runner to me." Toh saluted and resumed his duties.

Ha Shi (Corporal) Vu, a seventeen-year-old boy from the mountains north of Hanoi stood erect before Maj. Phan.

"Young man, you go with the fisherman north along the coast until you find our comrades. From there, you identify a good path back to this area. Should our radio communications fail, you will run if there is trouble. Do you understand?" The boy nodded. He was frightened of the Major.

"The old man is to fish for the four of you and report the appearance and number of any American boats. He must go out before dawn and report to you by noon each day. If he fails to return or if there is any suspicion of him, you are to report this immediately. Is that clearly understood?" This time the boy nodded and mumbled comprehension.

"Tomorrow afternoon you will come here and take me along the trail you have selected. Together we will carry more food to your comrades. Again, do you understand?"

This time the boy spoke. "Yes, Tieu Ta." Vu's spirits lifted. The Major was entrusting him with responsibility. Also, this would be an adventure, absolving him from the heavy work parties.

The fisherman's sampan was barely seaworthy for the trip, or so it seemed to the young mountain boy. Within moments of their turn after leaving the river, the sea swells began rolling under the side of the little boat. Vu was nauseated, sometimes vomiting over the side until they beached at the expected place.

The two work groups dug shallow trenches behind and along the banks of the river careful not to damage the screening vegetation any more than was necessary. At certain points, they widened and deepened the trenches enough to hold four or five men crouching below the expected angle of return fire from the boats.

At the highest point of the bluff, a four-foot-deep command pit for Phan was built further in from the riverbank. Its floor and walls were lined with interlaced saplings. A shelf of limbs was fashioned along the side closest to the river. Phan kept his AK-47, the other radio, and his backpack there. On four tall posts sunk into the corners of the pit, the men constructed a flat stick roof layered with mud and sod from the jungle. A shallow access trench entered the back of the pit.

Phan had a 360-degree view of the river and the jungle behind him. Significantly, men in the firing pits could see their commander as action began. Theoretically, he was high and dry; the firing pits and trenches could fill with groundwater.

Rockets and launchers were stored in the jungle, resting on elevated pallets made from young trees selectively cut to avoid over clearing any part of the jungle near the river. Phan deemed the Chinese-made machine gun too likely to be put out of action early by counter-battery fire from the American 50s and directed that it be assembled but left protected in the jungle. Hauling this weapon had become more trouble than it was worth under the circumstances.

Phan's men were cautious. The removed soil was carried off into the jungle and spread. Likewise, they slept in the jungle away from their excavations and without fires. Each morning, they struck their small canvas shelters and packed as though ready for a march.

Until preparations were complete, they avoided all contact with the enemy forces. They worked but remained alert for engine sounds from helicopters, other aircraft, and especially American boats.

On one occasion, two boats came down from the Cua Lon River. Their diesel engines announced their approach long before they were sighted. With no more than these sounds, Phan's men on both sides of the Bo De quickly and quietly fell into concealed positions, carefully drawing vegetation-covered skids over their diggings. As the Americans passed, the men watched and studied these heavily armed boats, getting a feel for their proportions and speed relative to the ambush positions. The sailors on board also appeared alert but not menacing. Phan hoped his men gained confidence, seeing their enemy close and unaware. Passing safely out to sea, the two boats split up, one going north and the other south. Phan was after more than two boats.

Hanoi orders had been clear: attack only larger formations. In June 1969, the Americans placed a floating patrol facility on the Song Cua Lon west of Nam Can. It was therefore reasonable to allow one or two boats to pass safely from time to time. It was equally reasonable that a larger group might at some point come from upriver or from the north.

Once preparations were complete, Phan set a refresher training schedule for both sides of the river, timing their ability to gather and distribute rockets and launchers, along with AK-47s, ammunition pouches, and hand grenades at each of the firing pits. The groups were divided into teams responsible for sections of trenches and firing pits. It was all well-rehearsed. Phan's best expectation was a ten-minute warning of boats approaching from the north. His troops could be ready in four minutes. He could not afford to send another signaling party upriver without dangerously reducing the force within his ambush zone. Engine sounds would be his only warning.

Time and food were running out on them. The trek from North Vietnam had exacted a much higher price than expected. And now, though the rainy season ended, the skies began to fill with ominous clouds. Phan realized something unusual was going on with the weather.

They were limited in what food they could take from local people and still encourage their silence. Critically, the two radios he relied upon failed. Phan was reduced to using Ha Shi Vu as a runner daily to stay in touch with his lookout group to the north.

Vu came in late each afternoon, reporting on the efforts of the old fisherman and the lookout group. Phan decided to rotate the men to keep the lookout group alert, but Vu remained as the runner. Vu's trail was well selected and essentially direct except for a short detour to a footbridge over a small canal. That canal ran across the terrain between the coastal lookout position and the ambush site. Within four days, Vu also found a very small sampan submerged in the underbrush near the footbridge. Intentional sinking was a method of hiding an otherwise sound vessel. Vu refloated the small boat, fabricated a paddle, and took the boat down the canal to its juncture with the river.

It was easy enough to hear engine sounds of boats coming downriver, but to seaward, sounds could be deceiving. Before dawn each morning, Phan posted two men very near the river mouth to fire warning tracer shots if they saw or heard any American boats approaching. These men reached their lookout positions, using Vu's sampan. Except for warning, however, the lookouts would be useless in a fight.

Unexpectedly, rain clouds gathered. The potential for heavy rains worried him more than anything else. At this point beyond a light shower, the trenches and pits would fill with water despite the very careful site selection. Even without rain, Maj. Phan understood that soon they would all need to leave for food. They had no place to go; Lt. Col. Nguyen and Phan had never discussed retreat or escape. He worried how long they could stay undiscovered. He worried more that no boats would come at all, or worse, that enemy forces would descend on them from helicopters. His mind raced to think of contingencies.

Phan then ordered a detail to move the .51-caliber machine gun from the jungle, mounting it for defensive use on the other side of what he now called Vu's footbridge. The troops on his side of the river were instructed to gather at the footbridge in the event they were forced away from the river. Toh's escape, if at all, would be to go further into the Ca Mau.

CHAPTER 10

Readiness

That morning, Phan knew their endurance was ending. Hard rains during the night collapsed some of the pits, and virtually all of the trenches had several inches of water in them. Running would be slow and difficult. The roof and walls of Phan's pit were intact, although water covered the floor, having entered from the escape trench.

His men were hungry. They had no old fisherman to bring his catch. Only the rockets and ammunition were safe and dry. He resolved that afternoon to find a hiding place for the ordinance and the machine gun. That night they would travel by night until they reached food or the enemy. Their end would be no different in either case; they would simply disappear.

Phan was exhausted. From the beginning of this mission, he expected to die but not without purpose. The force, so strong in the beginning, now was starving. Five of the big American's cigarettes remained. He decided to smoke one of them for breakfast. He casually waved at Sgt. Toh on the other side. Toh was a professional soldier and a good man. Toh cared for his men but never let up on them when it came to duty and survival. All that would be a waste. Phan squatted near the riverbank and smoked, planning their departure.

As his mind drifted between despair and details of their withdrawal, Vu burst from the jungle yelling, "Boats! Boats!" Instantly, power returned to Maj. Phan's soul, body, and voice. He sprang to his feet. Other soldiers were already running to the pallets as trained. Vu stiffened when Phan approached.

"Detail," Phan demanded.

The young man recited, "Two boats first and then five more. The old fisherman came in and reported a total of seven boats far at sea." Vu gulped for breath. "But the boats stopped moving."

Phan's mind raced as he saw his men getting ready. The runner's final words sunk in. *Why did the boats stop? Why have they not rushed in as expected? This runner had to take twelve minutes at best to get here. Why stop?* He realized that his two men at the river's entrance had not fired any warning. *They are still stopped, or they are not planning to come here at all. There is another reason for the delay.*

"Did you actually see these boats yourself?"

"No, Tieu Ta. I did not. They were too far away. The old fisherman reported as I have said, and I ran here." Vu's breathing returned to normal.

Phan turned away to see his men's progress. Soon they would be ready. He might even have a little wait.

Then it struck him. *Wait! Wait! They aren't stopped; they are waiting.* He turned back to Vu and said, "Stand here until I tell you otherwise. Watch the opening of the river mouth. If you see tracer shots, tell me immediately. Do you understand?"

"Yes, Tieu Ta." Maj. Phan smiled for the first time that Vu could remember and struck the younger man on the shoulder with the open heel of his hand." Good," said the Major as he strode toward the riverbank. He cupped his hands around his mouth and commanded their attention. All stood where they were.

"Patriots, our brother has told us there are seven American boats coming to kill you. There will be more. The number does not matter. They do not know who you are. They do not know how hard you trained and worked for this day and how much you have suffered. Above all else, they do not know your steel as I do. I am overjoyed to be with you today, my brothers. Complete your preparations quickly, but we have time. Remember to shoot well. Show these invaders that we have courage."

Maj. Phan waived to Sgt. Toh. Now his hand formed a fist.

CHAPTER 11

Snapping Flags

Stroud's eight boats arrived eighty-five minutes after the planned entry time, their transit speed fixed by the slowest boat. He was angry. Already Stroud made three big mistakes. The 78 Boat on which he had made the transit was not fast enough and should not have made this patrol. The 78 Boat, working from Sa Dec, was sent to Cat Lo for an engine replacement and other long-overdue out-of-water maintenance. Ignoring the maintenance officer's report on the condition of the boat and its inability to sustain standard operational requirements, Stroud pulled this 78 Boat into the operation without the necessary work.

When the 78 Boat failed in moderate transit speeds at sea, Stroud made his second mistake in not transferring to another boat. He refused to release the boat. Had he released the 78 Boat and arrived at the rendezvous point on time, the day might have been different. He wanted to show that by his willpower and rank, he could force adequate performance from this defective boat.

Coastal Squadron One (CosRonOne) administratively commanded the Swift Boat force through various divisions situated at significant places along the coastline from the demilitarized zone (DMZ) north of Da Nang to the border between Cambodia and South Vietnam on the Gulf of Thailand. Administrative command covered training, maintenance, personnel, and force distribution. CosRonOne was based in Cam Ranh Bay, and its divisions were stationed at An Thoi, Da Nang, Cat Lo, Cam Ranh Bay, Qui Nhon, and Chu Lai.

Operational direction of these boats, however, often was exercised from different command structures on a regional basis. Pastel, in the person of

Commander Stroud in Vung Tau, directed boat operations in the Delta and some distance north of Vung Tau.

The officers and crews of six of the other boats in the Stroud entourage were experienced but transient. They came to Cat Lo for the purpose of manning rehabilitated boats for distribution to other divisions to the north. Stroud had commandeered these boats for this operation with just a day's delay, as he had told the Squadron Commander in Cam Ranh Bay. The seventh was the 69 Boat, also fresh out of overhaul.

The 78 Boat, eighth in the group, was drafted into the operation as an afterthought to bring the raiding force to a more impressive number: fifteen. The number of boats entering the Song Bo De was more important than whether all of the boats were up to operational requirements.

Stroud transferred to Hampton's 24 Boat and ordered the arrangement of the raiding group into three five-boat sections. He also designated Lt. (jg) Lester B. Wainwright as the alternate OTC.

Wainwright came into Pastel's command from one of the northern divisions where his sole boat experience was on sea patrols. This was Wainwright's first Delta patrol. He was an untested quantity.

"Commander, the 78 Boat won't be any help today. Better for all of us to leave her out here until we get back." Hampton knew that the 78 Boat was not up for the day. Stroud's anger, however, was in charge.

"No, Lieutenant, all boats go, and the 78 Boat goes in the first section. That way when Mr. Dhoge can't keep up, all the other boats will pass him. That ought to show that young man how important it is to maintain his engines." Stroud, in no mood for reason, opted for punishment.

Ens. Paul Dhoge, from South Dakota, twenty-four years old, looked like he just left middle school. Disproportionately large ears framed his broad, young face. Similarly, his hands and feet were large compared to the rest of his body, prompting jokes about what he would look like when he stopped growing. His personal call sign was "Puppy."

Dhoge was a good boat officer, performing his duties over the last nine months without getting his people hurt or damaging his boat or its tired engines. If the 78 Boat had gone in for overhaul instead of on this operation, Dhoge would have taken an R & R in Hawaii. There he expected to propose marriage to his girlfriend from Minneapolis.

"Commander, are the Black Ponies committed?" Stroud's face tightened with controlled rage at having to answer that they were not committed.

"Sir, what was their problem?" Hampton pressed on. Stroud did not respond. Moments of silence passed.

"Commander, these transient boat crews haven't been down here before. They're a tough bunch, but unfamiliar with our area. Give me permission to put some of my detachment boats in each section.

"Mr. Hampton, I came here to lead a fifteen-boat raid with or without Black Ponies, and I'm going to do just that. You can put boats wherever you like, but understand this," the muscles in Stroud's neck became taut, "I'm in charge of this raid, not you. For your information, however, I decided that we didn't need Ponies today unless we encountered significant opposition. And with a force of our size, that will not be the case."

Hampton long ago passed the point of intimidation by the very few senior officers he had met, who were more concerned about their careers than their responsibilities. "Sir, I understand who's in charge. That's why I asked for your permission. Our officers need to know that every boat meets operational minimum requirements and whether this operation is on its own or has effective outside assets."

Hampton realized how deeply embarrassed Stroud had been, riding the slowest boat in the group, and he wanted the 78 Boat's officer to pay for that embarrassment—and all the more Stroud wanted to ignore his own role in causing this delay.

"Very well, Lieutenant, position your boats, and let's get going." Stroud overlooked Hampton's firmness and moved to the afterdeck, gripping his hands behind his back.

Bob was thinking: *This is going to be a long day. Stroud is young for a commander and is doing this for his personnel file. There can be no other reason. He deliberately declined important air support just to look good at the end of the day. The man is a menace to be dealt with after today.*

Hampton picked up the URC-58 radio handset, ordering the units into three sections consistent with his original plan. The 37 Boat would lead in just ahead of the 59 Boat. The 78 Boat was spotted in the fourth position in the first section. The 24 Boat would lead the second section at the end of which was another Sa Dec boat. Mr. Wainwright was already leading the third section, but Hampton put Five Buck Raider just behind him and two Sa Dec boats in the rear. These two reliable boats, 28 and 54, would lead the way out of the river at the end of the raid.

All boats began moving to the Song Bo De at moderate speeds, shifting into tight sections. Hampton brought Stroud's freshly painted helmet, personalized flak jacket, and a small pack to him. Stroud wore jungle fatigues and boots like everyone else, but his were nicely starched and the boots had a high shine.

There was one other touch making the image complete. Commander Stroud reached into his pack and pulled out a wide leather belt on which was mounted a richly tooled holster. In Hampton's disgust with the pretentious holster, he saw the pistol it held, a nine-millimeter German Lugar, itself a symbol of particular evil. Stroud buckled the belt to his waist and donned the jacket and helmet.

As this was happening, Hampton's crew without flourish got into their sometimes greasy, unadorned flak vests and dinged helmets. They were uncomfortable with this loud, angry peacock and so kept to their business. On the bow, a small Vietnamese sailor climbed down into the peak tank to stand behind his M-60 machine gun. Both .50-caliber machine gunners jacked rounds into their guns and swiveled them back and forth expressing the feel of readiness.

As machine-gun rounds went home into their chambers, they separated from their links that clattered to the deck, a sound of attention much like the orchestra conductor's baton tapping the rostrum before the symphony begins.

On the deck just forward of the mortar box, a wool blanket had been laid out. Five mortar rounds, ready for firing, had been placed on the blanket and covered with a sheet of plastic. Each lead boat loaded its eighty-one-millimeter mortar with a flechette round. Other crewmen held M-16 rifles and were standing braced in various positions around the boat. Lt. Hampton slipped into his helmet and jacket and filled his pockets with M-79 rounds for the launcher on the chart table next to his driver.

Exhaust vapors rose in clouds behind each boat as heated engines responded to forward throttles. Speeds warped up; so, too, did the sounds. The deep, throaty roar of thirty diesel engines reaching their highest performance replaced the gurgling of milling about. Their large silk American flags now stretched out full length, snapped in the wind.

Commander Stroud stood on the starboard side of the pilothouse and yelled over the noise, "Mr. Hampton, have the boats reported readiness?"

"Getting that now, Sir." Hampton's upturned thumb put Stroud at ease while Hampton spoke into the radio handset.

"Frisco Market, Frisco Market. This is Frisco Leader. Report your readiness in sequence. Over." One by one, the boats checked in. Just as the last boat in section three announced its ready status, the 37 Boat called back, "Frisco Leader, this is Frisco 37. I am crossing the tangent at 1800 rpms. Out." The 78 Boat was already falling back. Frisco 37 and 59 never saw the tracers low-fired as they started the run.

"Commander Stroud, all boats are ready. We're going in." It was 0944.

CHAPTER 12

Last Instructions

Fear and self-doubt crowded Maj. Phan's mind. His men were in position, but had they trained properly? A fiery, confident speech did not ensure courage. Would the men have the discipline to hold their fire until the right moment and then not fire all at the same time but to shoot in calculated sequence? He reached for and lit another cigarette. Vu was still standing in the spot where ordered. Vu's youthful obedience softened Phan's anxieties. He got his field pack and walked to a point slightly behind the boy, quietly speaking.

Vu started to turn toward his Thieu Ta. Phan's voice stopped him.

"Keep watching for the tracers. Do not look at me. You have done well for all of us. As soon as you give the alarm, quickly return to the jungle. Retrieve our two men at the river mouth. Go to where you last saw the old fisherman and your other comrades. Do you understand?" Vu nodded.

Handing Vu his pack, he continued, "You and your comrades shall kill the fisherman. Next, gather your equipment, the packs, and provisions near the footbridge. Then cautiously return to this area if you can. Many of us will die today. My order is that you see what happened here today and report our success when you are safely away. The fisherman must die. Do you understand all that I have said?"

"Yes, Tieu Ta. I understand."

Vu might not survive, either, and if he did, his chance of finding some comrade with authority was remote.

Maj. Phan handed Vu his third remaining American cigarette. "Share this with the others this afternoon. I regret that I cannot do more." He turned abruptly and walked back to his command pit and waited.

When the tracer signals finally came, it was unnecessary. The winds from seaward and the deep rumbling sounds of the American boats announced the strength and firepower coming their way. Phan knew some part of the plan would succeed but also that he would die this day.

CHAPTER 13

Tense Moments

"Frisco Leader, this is Frisco 37. An empty sampan is tied up in the canal on my right. I see no people. The sand bar isn't visible. My track has plenty of water. No contacts ahead. No other boats and no people. Out."

Stroud and Hampton scanned the riverbank ahead. Hampton noted the sampan on the right bank of the little canal.

"Frisco Leader, this is Frisco 54. I'm in." The 54 Boat was the last boat in section three.

The 78 Boat moved well to the right as the second section began passing him. Stroud walked to the afterdeck to enjoy the results of his disciplinary orders.

Hampton hand-signaled to Ens. Dhoge to go to the BS frequency. "Puppy, this is Papa Bravo. Stay close aboard our sections, but if you get too far behind, let me know. I'll do something. Over." Puppy acknowledged. Hampton wasn't quite sure what he could do, but he was considering slipping one of his Sa Dec boats out of section three to escort Puppy to sea.

Stroud came back to the pilothouse. "Unfortunately, Mr. Hampton, nothing seems to be happening. We are nearing the place of last year's successful raid and the projected crossing point. I was certain that we'd jump some Victor Charlie today and go home with a good body count."

The clear relief in his face belied the suggested dejection in his words. Boat officers and crews knew to hold their hopes and emotions until the safe end of an operation.

"How much further do you want to go, Commander?" Hampton saw that Dhoge was now just abeam of Wainwright's boat. Stroud swept his binoculars ahead and then behind. He began to slowly shake his head. Hampton saw that Stroud was ready to come about, but then Bob felt that familiar tightening in his gut. The time was 0951.

CHAPTER 14

How We Got Here

Lester B. Wainwright spent his life consciously sucking up to superiors and taking delight, if not always advantage, in the misfortune of others. The background for today was no different.

Lester stopped active patrol several weeks before and joined Stroud's staff in Vung Tau as an assistant intelligence officer. He replaced a rebellious junior officer named Stone. Mr. Stone had incautiously muttered an opinion in Stroud's hearing, ". . . the Navy is screwed." As Stone intended, Commander Stroud took the remark personally. Stone was last seen in jungle fatigues boarding a flight to somewhere north of Da Nang. Assigned fieldwork with Marine units coordinating naval gunfire support, this was not safe duty.

Wainwright's patrol reputation in the Da Nang division was mediocre, but away from his colleagues, he had a keen talent for vividly coloring his exploits. Wisely, he also always paid bar tabs of senior transient officers and so had come to the attention of a friend of Stroud's. The friend, a man named Quinby, followed up on his suggestion to Wainwright that there might be a position with Stroud. Wainwright's division commander happily endorsed the move. The DivCom privately thought of his boat officers as fine legitimate sons, but for Wainwright, he reserved the concept of "the little bastard." His fellow patrol officers knew Wainwright as "L. B.," making the DivCom's term particularly appropriate.

If Little Bastard had left well enough alone in his new staff assignment, this day on the Song Bo De might not have happened. Intelligence reports over the weeks indicated that a force of NVA was working its way down toward the Ca

Mau peninsula. To correlate the reports into a line and time of travel that predicted an encampment on or crossing of the Bo De below the Song Dam Doi was simple enough. Lester presented the prediction to his immediate boss, Lt. Commander Delwood Shaw, Stroud's executive officer, who saw the possibilities that a well-supported small raiding force might catch these troops on the river.

Timing was critical. The most recent report of these suspected NVA regulars had been on the south side of the Co Chien River. A small ambush team from Coastal Group 35, consisting of reasonably well-trained and motivated local peasants, had itself been ambushed. Four men were dead and three wounded, the most serious of which was their American advisor, a Navy junior officer. He had been evacuated out of country but was not expected to live. Based on that contact and the force's estimated speed of travel, it was possible that the group had already crossed the Bo De and was hidden in the dark mangroves of the Ca Mau.

Still, Wainwright's boss reasoned, a quick little raid of no consequence would at least demonstrate effort if not results. A small force of Swifts could rush into the Bo De, go no further than the Dam Doi/Cua Lon intersection, turn around, and return to the starting point, calling it a day. Shaw would give the matter more consideration.

Lester Wainwright's reasoning was more cunning. During Shaw's intelligence briefing of Stroud and the other staff the next morning, Shaw pointed out the movements of the suspected force. Before Shaw could speak further, Wainwright interrupted, "Sir, isn't your projected crossing point in the vicinity of last year's very successful raid?"

Shaw confirmed.

As Shaw resumed his briefing, Stroud, too, interrupted. "Mr. Wainwright raises a good point, Del. We ought to plan another raid; see if we can catch them with their pants down." He looked around the room, smiling.

"Commander Shaw, you and the operations staff plan the event and get things moving," Stroud ordered.

The operational message was approved and transmitted that same day to the Sa Dec detachment. That afternoon Wainwright was summoned to Stroud's office.

"Mr. Wainwright, I am concerned about the welfare of your predecessor, Lt. Stone. He has a very dangerous job." Lester cleared his throat, a subtle habit indicating discomfort or caution.

"Contact the Marine Command in Da Nang and establish a relationship with someone up there, who can keep you informed about Mr. Stone. Make it very clear that this interest is not a pretext for special consideration. That sort of thing can hurt a young officer's career."

Lester knew the account of Stone's departure and understood the true nature of Stroud's instructions to him. He cleared his throat again. "Aye, aye, Commander."

"Got a cold there, Mr. Wainwright?"

"No, Sir. Thanks for asking."

Little Bastard still could not leave matters alone. He paused a bit. "Commander, I was wondering if this Bo De raid wouldn't be the kind of operation that you ought to personally lead and add a few boats."

Stroud chuckled. "Can't the Sa Dec detachment handle it, or are you trying to get me bumped off?"

"No, no, Sir. The Sa Dec boats can probably do fine. I thought that if the NVA are still there, this might exceed the detachment O-in-C's experience. Just a thought."

Wainwright liked the idea of planting doubt just to see how people reacted.

"Let me get back to my desk and call Da Nang concerning Mr. Stone. I'll report to you as soon as I learn something." Wainwright coughed two more times before he got to his desk and picked up the telephone.

Stroud's ego did the rest. Stroud could take credit for the concept and execution of the operation as well as any results. Wainwright, without ever leaving the base, would then be seen as helping Stroud look good. Wainwright hoped that he had not pushed himself too much or too early. Even so, Wainwright's scheme worked—almost.

Stroud readily understood manipulation and was particularly gratified when his staff manipulated things for his benefit. Stroud reasoned that one good turn deserved another. Just after midnight, Wainwright was awakened and told that he was to get his gear and assume charge of the 69 Boat and a transient crew for this one expanded operation. Wainwright was told that he would be the alternate OTC.

The 69 Boat was just out of overhaul. Its new crew, although individually experienced under fire, had been gathered from other boats. These men were waiting for the assignment of a new officer. Lester wondered how he might have avoided this predicament, but events moved too quickly for him. As he was leaving BOQ with his gear for the short walk to the Cat Lo piers, Lt. Commander Shaw came up out of the darkness and said he wanted to walk with him for a bit. What Shaw had to say did not take long.

"Wainwright, I'm telling you this once. I'm senior to you, and that means I do the manipulating. I calculate and contain the risks. I produce measurable results and try, if I can, to keep people out of body bags. Sometimes I protect commanding officers from themselves and your kind of behavior. You haven't earned the right to do what I do and from what I can see, you aren't smart enough. If you ever do this again, I will personally see to it that you relieve Mr. Stone up north. He's a good man, and you aren't. Think about that." He patted Wainwright's shoulder, smiled, and walked away.

Wainwright stood for a moment alone in the damp darkness, chastened but unreformed. Wainwright puzzled how he could win Shaw over or wait him out. Shaw's personal morality complicated matters. Since he didn't drink alcohol, he created no bar tabs. And so far as Wainwright knew, Shaw didn't mess with the women in town, either.

* * *

LB realized that the revised operational plan set only the outer limits of the incursion to the Cua Lon/Dam Doi intersection. Except for the size of the raiding force, Shaw had tailored the op plan for insignificance. If all worked well, they wouldn't be in the Bo De long enough to get into trouble. While Wainwright hoped this raid would be a nonevent, he was carried along with the intensity of the morning. Stroud's bad temper, evident before they began the run in, was unsettling; but Wainwright's anxiety was overcome by the sight and sounds of these boats revving up for the mad dash into danger. Out of all the noise of movement, Wainwright could distinctly hear the snapping of the silk American flag. He knew he had set something terrible into motion but was now powerless to influence its outcome.

Shortly after the 69 Boat entered the river, Lester began to relax. If anything happened, sections one or two would be engaged first. He was relieved when things happened to others. He always thought, *now it won't happen to me.*

Today there would be some fun out of all this. He watched the painful failure of the 78 Boat during the transit. Now he saw it slip from its position, first wide of the column and having steering difficulties from the combined wakes of the other boats and then attempting to come close aboard to starboard as it was being passed by the second section. Just now Ens. Dhoge's boat was coming abeam of the 69 Boat. Startling everybody, Lester hit his air-horn with two short blasts. He also grinned and waved at the helpless Ensign.

"What was that, Mr. Hampton?" Stroud's head whipped around at the unexpected sound.

"Sir, Mr. Wainwright is giving Ens. Dhoge a hard time."

Stroud grabbed the radio hand set from its clip above the helmsman. "Frisco Six-Niner, this is Frisco Leader himself. Cut it out." Stroud's hand was shaking as he returned the microphone to its clip.

Hampton started to thank Stroud but realized he was only angry because the sound had frightened him.

"Frisco Two Four, this is Frisco Five Nine. You might consider that we haven't seen any birds."

Stroud's anger started to reappear but was stopped cold by Hampton's eyes and gestured hand sign to halt. With the other hand he keyed the microphone and said, "This is Frisco Two Four, roger that."

Stroud then understood, and as he reached forward to steady himself on a little railing inside the pilothouse, Hampton saw both of Stroud's hands trembling. Hampton's driver saw it, too, and glanced at his boat officer. Hampton nodded his head forward as if to tell the man to watch the road.

Lester's prank with the 78 Boat distracted Lester and his driver. Stroud's rebuke brought them both back to business and the realization that the 69 Boat had lost its interval with the last boat in section two. Still puzzling over the message about birds, Wainwright reached over and slammed the throttles forward to regain position. As he did so, his boat, driven by its freshly overhauled engines, dramatically lunged ahead. The time was 0953.

CHAPTER 15
Deadly Beginning

Three RPGs from the right bank of the river flashed toward the third section. The first round arced lazily toward what had been open space now being filled by the 69 Boat.

Someone broadcast, "RPGs, starboard side." The 69 Boat's main cabin windows exploded. The blast mangled the interior and blew Wainwright out the portside opening of the pilothouse and almost overboard. He was saved from falling into the water only because a strap on his flak jacket caught on a strip of cracked metal framing.

This same explosion blew the rear hatch of the main cabin off its hinges. The hatch hit one of the men and threw him against the mortar box, breaking his neck, killing him instantly. As Lester's stunned and bleeding driver reached out to pull his boat officer back inside, the boat angled for the left, dropping its speed significantly.

The second and third rounds passed in front of the 78 and then the 17 Boat, commanded by Frank Brooks, detonating harmlessly in the water. The third section began turning toward the origin of these shots, their forward 50s opening up without command.

"Frisco Leader, this is Frisco One Seven. Section three attacking the right bank. Break. Frisco 19, this is Frisco 17. Can you go in with us?" To Hampton, Five Buck's voice was clear and distinct despite the pounding of the 17 Boat's overhead guns. As was common in these circumstances, though, his pitch and tone had elevated an octave or two. Brooks was unable to hear Dhoge's radio response but glanced across the water to the 78 Boat and saw Puppy's thumbs-up hand sign from the port side of the pilothouse. The noise of all of this firing was deafening.

Lester Wainwright was screaming for help.

This time Hampton grabbed the handset. "Frisco 69, this is Frisco Leader. Get off the net and stand by. Sections one and two, come about and engage." As he spoke, he motioned his driver to reverse course to the right. While acknowledgments came in, he could see from the corner of his eye that section one turned to port.

When Hampton realized he was acting beyond his immediate authority, he looked for Commander Stroud. He saw someone down in the main cabin. Stroud was sitting on the edge of the lower bunk staring into space. This was the most dangerous place for him to be in this fight, but at least he was out of the way.

Hampton grabbed the radio handset of the PRC 77 and began talking, "This is Papa Bravo. Who's up on this frequency? Over." One by one, the Sa Dec boats responded.

"This is Papa Bravo. The Bishop's indisposed, and I'm it. I smell a big rat on the left bank. Double, you and Prevert bring section one down on the left bank and hit it with your beehive if you get any sign of activity. Section two will do the same on the right bank. Five Buck, get the Camel over to Lester's piece of junk long enough to fire their beehive and see if anyone is capable of getting the boat back in action. I'm getting air support. Out."

Then over the din of heavy machine-gun fire, using the URC-58 operational frequency, Frisco 17 ordered the 28 Boat to assist Wainwright, whose boat was now slowly closing on the left bank.

A fourth rocket emerged from another point on the right shoreline traveling straight and level at the 78 Boat. That round struck the outside port corner of the pilothouse at eye level, instantly killing Ens. Dhoge and the driver. Steadied by the driver's dead weight over the wheel and throttles, the 78 Boat continued to move toward the shoreline between the two ambush sites. The gunner on the twin 50s above the shredded pilothouse, unaware that his officer and the driver were dead, directed his fire to the second site. The 17 Boat stood several yards off the bank and attacked the first site.

Five Buck called to Puppy to back down. The 78 Boat's radio was silent. Its inadequate engines, however, unremittingly drove the boat hard up onto the bank, tumbling everyone on the afterdeck. The gunner on the overhead 50s suddenly slumped to the side; an AK-47 slug had passed below his helmet just in front of his right ear and then tore away the left side of his face.

The two remaining boats in section three, without any specific orders, and sensing that there might be more sites on that side, began raking the entire right bank.

As the other sections came around, commands to individual boats were issued over the operational frequency, and Hampton, as Frisco Leader, requested assistance from Black Ponies anywhere as soon as possible, giving plain language coordinates.

Hampton stepped down into the main cabin to check on Stroud. Still rigidly seated on the cushioned lower berth, he had by then also covered his head with a gray Navy blanket. Pastor Bob left him there.

As section one bore down upon the left bank, their guns opened up early and at long range. Double ordered this tactic to force the hands of any aggressors in hiding. When he got closer, the beehive would be fired. Once attacked, never give the enemy any edge.

Just as the 28 Boat came alongside the starboard side of Wainwright's boat, a volley of five B-40s was fired from two locations on the left bank. Three of the shots spiraled wildly over the scene. One detonated against the high point of the stem of the 69 Boat, peeling up the deck and killing the Vietnamese M-60 gunner in the peak tank and Wainwright's already wounded helmsman. A second round hit the top of one of the 28 Boat's radio whip-antennas and exploded. The blast showered everyone below it but caused no injuries or other damage. The twin 50s on both boats continued hammering away at the enemy site.

No one was left standing on the 69 Boat's afterdeck. The rear gunner from the 28 Boat, Gunner's Mate 1st Class, William Bowers, leapt over to man Lester's silent mortar. He trained the gun around to his best guess as to the origin of the volley and pulled the trigger. Blessedly, the gun belched its deadly package. Bowers then worked forward to the pilothouse. He found the dead driver, but Mr. Wainwright was gone. Bowers shoved the corpse off the seat and tested the controls. All seemed workable. Bowers put the boat in reverse and started backing from the riverbank. The overhead twin 50s was still firing.

The 28 Boat also was backing in unison with Bower's maneuvers. As Bowers glanced across to his own boat, he saw his boat officer, Mr. Leyland, holding Mr. Wainwright and repeatedly pummeling his face.

When they got out to the middle of the river, one of Wainwright's dazed crewmen came forward and pulled the dead driver down into the main cabin. Another opened the ammunition magazine and began hauling out .50-caliber boxes for the overhead gunner and the deck 50.

Lt. (jg) Leyland probably was born looking old. Despite his twenty-five years, he was balding over the top of his head; the pockets below his lower eyelids drooped, and he had the beginnings of jowls. He was tall to be a boat officer.

Because he had to keep his head down when moving about the inside of the boat, he adopted a permanent stoop, his head pulled into his shoulders. The Camel's image of advanced age, however, concealed immense physical strength, particularly in his back and long arms.

Bowers saw Mr. Leyland hold the front of Wainwright's flak jacket with one hand so that Wainwright's boots barely touched the deck. With his right fist, Mr. Leyland repeatedly struck the other officer's face. As Wainwright began to slump, Leyland took the man's jacket in both hands and walked the body back toward the 28 Boat's afterdeck. As that same portion of the 69 Boat came parallel to Leyland, he launched Wainwright over to his own boat. As the body landed, there was a gurgling moan.

Wainwright's unconscious body sprawled in the midst of the bloody afterdeck litter of shell casings and bandage wrappers. This man had suffered no physical injuries beyond those administered by an enraged fellow officer.

CHAPTER 16

Rain of Fire

Sergeant Toh patiently watched the fifteen boats enter the river. He knew that his group should not be the first to fire. He promised to shoot anyone who disobeyed his orders or compromised their position in their private parts. "The first shots belonged to Tieu Ta."

During the initial firing, they kept their heads down. Only Toh had raised his head enough to describe damage results to the others and the approach of the injured 69 Boat. He hoped the Americans would believe that his side of the river was nonthreatening. This truly was a great victory, even if his men never got to shoot. He could see other boats turning to rescue their stricken comrades. Soon might be his turn to show courage. Once more, he looked up and saw these boats were indeed firing now at his side of the river. Toh heard the slap of the heavy slugs hitting mud thirty feet away. He rolled on his side and yelled to his soldiers to remain calm and that their time was approaching. He lifted his head again to better see that his men were safely crouched in their muddy, flooded pits. He smiled to encourage them. At that moment three .50-caliber slugs slammed into his body, the first taking off the front of his head and lifting his body several inches off the ground, the second shattering his spine and blowing out the front of his stomach, and the third hitting his right foot, which had become airborne from the impact of the first slug.

Sergeant Toh's men froze in shock, and some screamed. All forgot everything Toh had taught them. Five men in two pits immediately stood and shot their rockets. Others fired their AK-47s, and still others tried to run away. In an instant, the 69 Boat's machine guns found them. Shortly, there was another, somewhat muffled explosion followed by the wild chewing of ten thousand teeth. In a matter seconds, all of Toh's men were dead. Machine-gun bullets from section one and the steady fire from the 28 and 69 Boats' overhead guns continued to tear into their lifeless corpses until it became apparent that the big boats were safe.

"Frisco Leader, this is Frisco 28. I am moving Frisco 69 toward the mouth." The time was 0959.

CHAPTER 17

Rescue and Recovery

"Frisco 17, this is Frisco Leader. Ponies on the way." Hampton wondered why they were available at all. He vowed to find out the circumstances of this blessing.

To Frisco 17, "Can you close to Puppy's boat and get those people off? Over."

"Leader, this is 17. On my way. Frisco 54, keep my front and back door open." Five Buck understood that the Black Ponies were going to obliterate the 78 Boat.

Overlapping fields of fire from the American boats blanketed a wide stretch of shoreline on either side of the stricken 78 Boat. The 17 Boat wasted no time placing his bow hard at the port quarter of Puppy's shattered hulk. The driver held the bow firmly against the hull, permitting easy access to its afterdeck. Black smoke was billowing out the right side in the area of the 78 Boat's engine room but blowing away from the rescuers. Five Buck and three armed crewmen bounded onto the 78 Boat.

There was no priority or gentleness. The dead and the wounded were treated alike. They were laid out on the 17 Boat's engine covers. Triage would wait. As Five Buck gathered sensitive publications and small arms from the pilothouse and main cabin, he put pistol shots into the electronic gear. His crewmen transferred other loose weapons, the overhead and after machine guns, and what were left of the ammunition cans over to the roof of the main cabin of the 17 Boat. Not having time to empty the mortar box, they opened its lid. Five Buck ignited a thermite grenade, pitched it into the main cabin over the cover to the boat's ammunition magazine, and ordered everyone back to his boat. He then placed a second thermite grenade down the mortar tube and stepped onto the 17 Boat, yelling to his driver to back off. They had been aboard less than five minutes. Cooking ammunition then began exploding. The wind slackened and black smoke from the 78 Boat was drawn skyward.

"Leader, this is 17. We're clear. The Ponies should have no trouble identifying their target."

"We need Dust Offs," a reference to medical evacuation helicopters, "for no more than four people." All listeners understood that the others were dead and that some of the four wounded survivors of the 78 Boat might not make it.

"Frisco Market, this is Frisco Leader. Black Ponies are ten minutes out. Break. Sections one and two, get mortars in the air on your respective banks." A rain of mortar fire might block further escape.

"Frisco 17, take your section out of here. Secure a place on the beach. Have one of your units remain mobile and ready. Break. Unless responding directly to hostile fire, all units cease fire when the Ponies arrive." There was a slight pause. "God bless you. This is Papa Bravo. Out." There were no radio acknowledgments, but the units moved as assigned.

Within moments, mortars from nine boats were coughing out high explosives. The fall of shot varied between thirty and fifty yards in from the banks of the Song Bo De. The concept was to deny survivors an opportunity to leave before the deadly aircraft arrived.

"Frisco Leader, this is Frisco 54. I'm out. There's a sand beach on the left. We're going bow in. This is a good place for Dust Offs. The Camel will roam. Over."

"This is Frisco Leader. Roger, Frisco 54, start sorting out the passengers. We'll come after the Ponies strike." Hampton tried thinking if he had forgotten anything.

"Frisco Leader, this is Pastel. Two Dust Off units are outbound for your location. Request acknowledgment from Frisco Leader himself." Hampton recognized the voice of Lt. Commander Shaw in Vung Tau. Shaw, a good man, must have been the watch supervisor during this operation and would know why the Ponies were so readily available.

"This is Frisco Leader. Wait. Out."

Hampton looked down into the main cabin. He couldn't see Stroud. He then went below to check the forward cabin. Stroud was gone. As he came back up into the pilothouse, Stroud was standing on the starboard side, composed, and holding the radio handset.

"Pastel, this is Frisco Leader himself. Hurry those Dust Offs. These boats and their crews have performed magnificently."

"This is Pastel. Roger. Glad you're OK. Out."

"Mr. Hampton, continue getting us out of here. We'll talk later."

"Aye, aye, Commander."

CHAPTER 18

Survival

Before the shooting started, Maj. Phan had arranged his rifle and ammunition within his command pit and was assured to see his troops in their positions. He lit his second remaining American cigarette. He could not believe the value of his life came down to these next few minutes of anonymously inflicted death.

He removed a small, clean stick from his pocket and placed it on the shelf. During the trip south, Sgt. Toh had introduced him to the utility of this implement. When the ground is heaving from explosions or heavy automatic weapons fire is raining down, biting on the stick gives you something to focus on and may reduce the effects of concussion on the ears. Since then, he wondered if the stick would have kept him from injury when the shrapnel sheared across his mouth.

Corporal Vu yelled and ran into the jungle past Phan's position. Phan had not seen the tracers but now heard the sounds of the boats entering the river. He stubbed out his cigarette and looked to see if his men were ready. They knew to await his signal.

As the first group of boats passed him, he could see hull numbers and the men aboard at various stations. The man behind each big, deck-mounted machine gun at the back of the boats crouched slightly like a boxer ready to lash out at an opponent. Other men, holding automatic weapons were braced against the sides of the main cabin. All were intently looking at the riverbank. He felt threatened by their very sound and presence.

They assume we are here somewhere. I must allow most of them to pass before firing, he thought, *and force them to fight back through our positions. They will assume that the opposite riverbank is safe. Sgt. Toh understands this plan.*

One boat began falling back. The second group passed as Phan looked to his first firing team of three men and raised his open hands, his signal to fire at the closest two boats. He nodded at the soldiers' reciprocal gesture, and the three men stood. The loud blast of a horn startled their concentration. The soldiers looked back again at Phan; he, too, hesitated and then vigorously nodded his head. Each man fired a rocket, dropped launchers, and ran.

Phan agonized at the sight of the trail of these first shots.

They will miss the slower boat. My gunners have been deceived by the different relative speeds of that boat and the rest of the formation.

Inexplicably, another boat surged forward into the path of one of the rockets. Phan felt the detonation on his cheeks. The 78 Boat and one other began turning toward his shore, joining the firing of three other boats.

Phan crouched into his pit.

These American machine guns are all shooting at me.

He heard the clipping of trees, the slapping of mud, and the screams of his men. He quickly raised his head at the sound of another rocket explosion. The 78 Boat had been hit near its pilothouse but was still coming toward the shore, firing its two forward machine guns somewhere off to the right. He could see the hull numbers on the bow.

Who managed that shot?

Major Phan, mesmerized by the advance of the 78 Boat, saw its forward machine gunner swinging his guns along the shoreline, firing where Phan's teams had huddled. Other firing began churning the mud around his pit. He ducked again, screaming, "Americans are fanatics," and thrust the stick between his teeth.

Through it all, he heard the 78 Boat's engines whining at a higher pitch as the firing abated. He raised his head and saw that the boat was beached to his right in front of the first firing position. The machine gunner was pulling at the side of his guns.

Are his guns jammed?

Phan grabbed his AK-47, carefully aimed, and fired. The gunner collapsed.

Men on the back of the boat looked stunned. Phan switched his assault rifle to automatic and emptied his magazine at them. He could not be certain, but he believed others of his men were firing as well. He went back down into his pit, groping for a replacement magazine. He removed the stick from his mouth and saw that it was covered in blood. His recent scars had torn. He heard more rocket explosions more distant.

Toh, my Sergeant Toh has joined the fight. He would not shoot without targets. Toh is going . . .

Gunfire overhead became intense. Two of the posts supporting his mud-covered roof disintegrated, the whole structure collapsed on Phan.

Whether he was unconscious for a few seconds or longer, he did not know. His first awareness, though, was the sound of American voices, urgent and sharp. He forced his back up under the debris and guessed when he could safely open his eyes.

There, yards away, he saw American sailors moving bodies and other objects over to another boat. He could only see the top of the other boat. He saw a gaping hole in the right side of the 78 Boat. Smoke was spilling out and drifting downstream.

My men wasted a shot on this boat. Why, he wondered.

He heard machine-gun fire, but none was hitting near him. He then realized he was in a narrow safe zone between their fields of fire. The Americans did not want to risk hitting the rescue boat. He saw a man he thought was in charge of the Americans emerge from the right side of the 78 Boat's pilothouse and walk back to the mortar. He reached under the mortar and adjusted the tube up to the sky. He then raised his right hand in the air in a spinning motion, finally pointing to the rescue boat. Phan saw him pull the pin on a grenade, drop it down the tube and calmly walk away. There was no explosion, only billowing white smoke.

He's destroying the gun with an incendiary grenade.

As the rescue boat was pulling away, Phan heard the crackling of ammunition consumed by flames. Black smoke climbed in the air.

Surely there will be something left that we can use.

Except for engine sounds, he then noticed there was silence.

They stopped firing. Why? There is a reason for this silence.

Phan saw a lot of activity on the afterdecks of the other boats, and then his mind snapped to the enormity of what was about to happen.

Mortars. They are going to fire their mortars to block my escape. Then the airplanes will come. How much time do I have?

He stood full height, tearing away the roof debris, struggling toward the escape trench. Vaguely aware that smoke surrounded him, he grabbed his AK-47 and ran. Within seconds, eighty-one-millimeter, high-explosive shells plummeted into the earth around his former position. As he ran, he also heard airbursts.

Proximity fuses.

A nearby blast of one shell deep in the mud blew Phan into a smoke-filled, watery hole created by an earlier explosion. Without pausing, driven by fear, he jumped up and continued to run to the seclusion of the jungle. He would not stop running until he reached Vu's footbridge.

CHAPTER 19

Destruction

"Ponies, this is Frisco Leader. We bought it from both sides. One boat is dead on the north bank, and all personnel are evacuated. Please destroy that boat and paste the area. Over."

"Roger, Frisco Leader. That's a mess down there. I see blast effects on both sides of the river. What do you want on the opposite bank? Over."

"Roger, Ponies. The south side seems dead, but make a firing run on it anyway. The priority is for nothing useful to be left of our boat. Over."

The voice of the OV-10 pilot took a more respectful tone. "Frisco Leader, we'll take care of this, Sir. Out."

Bob Hampton replaced the handset to its clip and watched the two aircraft maneuver for their first run. Stroud stood on the afterdeck. All Swifts had moved to the center of the river below the sites to be attacked. They were spectators, standing a safe distance from a bonfire.

"Hold this position," Hampton ordered his driver.

The Ponies circled around to make their first approach from seaward. The lead aircraft came in on a higher track than his wingman whose course was offset and well behind his leader. Two five-inch Zuni rockets with ten-pound contact warheads streaked down from the lead aircraft onto the 78 Boat. The second Pony followed with a spread of four 2.75-inch warheads set with proximity fuses. These rounds erupted on and around the 78 Boat. With each ignition, the airplanes seemed to cease their forward movement as if momentarily forced back by the thrust of their own rockets. Rapid secondary explosions signaled the destruction of the mortar box on the afterdeck. With each explosion, crazy smoke trails streaked in different directions. Debris flew into the air, splashing with varying force out on the river. Softer popping sounds indicated the detonation of on-board grenades and other munitions. Ugly, oily smoke from the burning diesel fuel tanks piled up over the vessel.

Completing this run, the Ponies rose up over the river and banked to the left for the run on the other side. Again, both aircraft came in on parallel tracks, one behind and below the other, firing their machine guns in a moving wave of flame as any lingering human life on the riverbank ended.

They rose up and again banked and turned to the 78 Boat's left side. This eruption of fire began well below and continued well beyond the wrecked 78 Boat. More telltale secondary explosions on the riverbank indicated the extent of ordinance the enemy had left behind.

"Frisco Leader, this is Pony Leader. You want any more dropped on the boat or anywhere else? Over."

"Pony Leader, this is Frisco. The fire you started will take care of things. Sir, you are done. Thank you. Over."

"This is Pony Leader. Sir, you're welcome. Out." The two aircraft circled once high over the area and moved off on a return course to Ben Thuy.

"Frisco Sections one and two, this is Leader. Let's join Section three." All boats pivoted to the outbound course and throttled up. Turbulent flames formed a red shroud over the broken hulk of the 78 Boat. Living engine noises muffled the continued popping sounds of cooking ammunition. Black, oily smoke billowed up from that side of the riverbank. The raid was over. The green morning haze had burned away.

Commander Stroud stood beside the aft machine gun, watching the other boats pulling into crisp formation. Pastor Bob stepped from the port side of the pilothouse with his back to the driver, drew his sleeve across his eyes, and raised his head to the heavens. Tears streamed down his face.

"Please forgive us for all we had to do today."

CHAPTER 20

Side Trip

Lt. Hampton was unaware that Boston and Taylor had their own BS frequency.

"Prevert, this is Double. Let's drop back. Could you stick your nose into that ti ti, (small) canal where we saw that sampan on our way in? I'll cover." Taylor's only acknowledgment was to double-key his radio handset. They had worked together for what seemed a lifetime. As the larger formation cleared the river mouth, they were more than five hundred yards ahead of these two boats.

The PCF 59 leapt onto the water as it sharply turned into the canal. The 37 Boat stopped just outside. After a run of forty-five seconds at full bore, the 59 Boat brought its throttles back, wallowed, and executed a pivoting turn, throttling up again. As Taylor came out, passing in front of the Boston, Taylor stepped out of the starboard side of his pilothouse and gestured a thumbs down. The detour took less than three minutes from concept to exit.

As these last two boats came into the wider and deeper water of the river mouth, they passed the 28 Boat slowly executing a long figure eight, guns ready, and swinging at every turn to be trained toward the jungle three hundred yards away. As the two boats neared his track, the Camel stepped from his pilothouse and tapped his wristwatch and smiled. He knew Taylor and Boston had been sightseeing.

The rest of the force was beached along the sandy right bank of the channel. Taylor and Boston found two spots on the seaward end. They nudged in together, with only inches separating them. Everyone began taking off their flak vests and helmets, fatigue shirts soaked in sweat. Some hung shirts and vests on the stanchions. Boston disappeared into his main cabin, and Taylor stepped back to the afterdeck of his boat.

"All right, guys," speaking to both crews, "Get this mess cleaned up. Clear and clean your weapons and rearm. Get us fuel, ammo, and damage reports." Boston reappeared with two plastic cups of cold beer. Taylor raised his cup in toast. "I'll get the beer next time, Double." As they had at the end of previous raids, each took a generous sip and poured the remainder onto their heads.

Boston produced a canteen of water that they then used to rinse their hands and faces. The ritual completed, Bill Boston walked over to Pecorino.

"Mr. Taylor and I are going to find Mr. Hampton and report. When the boats are ready, your cups are down below. Vince, you and your engines did a great job today. Thank you."

Pecorino smiled and nodded his head. "You, too, Mr. Boston, you, too. We'll be ready when you get back."

The time was 1047.

CHAPTER 21
Sandbars for Dying

When Taylor and Boston jumped from their bows and walked toward the other boats, the sight was grim. Away from the cluster of boats, six occupied body bags lay side by side in the sand. Taylor wondered why some body bags were black but others dark green. He speculated that different contractors made them.

Just beyond the bags, a team of armed sailors were stationed in a semicircle around a probable helicopter landing area close to the edge of the water. All looked seaward for the Medivac helicopters.

Three young sailors sat quietly on the sand outside the semicircle. Blood-soaked bandages covered parts of their bodies. The young men looked detached from the world around them. One boy was rocking back and forth, and another was trembling. The other just sat, very still.

Further on were five stretchers containing the seriously wounded. Kneeling around two of the stretchers were four young men and Mr. Brooks. His face was close to the head of one of the casualties, nodding and speaking into the ear of the wounded sailor. The intensity of his efforts to comfort this fallen boy showed in Brooks' shoulders. Slowly Brooks' shoulders relaxed. As Boston and Taylor approached, Brooks stood, turning toward them. Blood covered his hands and fatigue shirt; immense anguish marked his face.

Brooks forced himself to take a long breath and joined Boston and Taylor as they continued walking toward a group of other boat officers.

"Who was he, Five Buck?" asked Double.

"I don't know. He was one of Dhoge's men." Pointing back to the body bags, he said, "One of them is Tubby, who was on Wainwright's boat."

As they continued walking, Boston unscrewed the cap of his water canteen and gestured to Brooks' hands. Without breaking pace, Brooks rinsed the blood from his hands. He wiped them dry on the seat of his fatigues. Behind them, two more body bags were now filled and carried to join Tubby and the others. Taylor placed his hand on Brooks' shoulder. Boston, wiping his own tears with one hand, took Brooks' other shoulder. In silence they reached the other group of officers.

Above the horizon, a couple of miles at sea, two unarmed Army UH-1D helicopters approached the landing site. Whapping sounds of their rotary blades caused those on the shore to turn away in anticipation of blowing sand as they landed. One at a time, the helicopters came in well up on the beach, maintaining power but reducing the pitch of their blades to minimize rotor wash and the expected blizzard of sand. Stretcher cases and the ambulatory wounded were loaded in the first helicopter. As the second helicopter landed, eight body bags were quickly placed aboard. The security and loading teams backed away, shielding their eyes for the departure. The aircraft commander increased pitch and power. As the skids left the ground, everyone on the beach turned and stood erect.

CHAPTER 22

Pep Talk

Stroud spoke as Hampton stood to the side. Wainwright was further behind the group. Lester's face was bruised and pulpy red. Blood trickled from his nose. His hand trembled as he daubed blood with a handkerchief. To the other boat officers, he did not exist.

"Gentlemen, despite our losses today, you can be proud of your accomplishment. They were ready and waiting for us, but I suspect we wiped them out to a man. Those secondary explosions along both sides of the river indicate what they brought to the party. That's ordinance they won't use elsewhere. I am very proud of you.

"Mr. Hampton, if you have the draft after-action report, show it to me before transmission." Hampton nodded. Then turning to the group, Stroud said, "Mr. Hampton will have some details for you. I repeat that I am proud of the way you handled yourselves." Their faces were masks of disinterest. Stroud smiled broadly and stepped back.

Proud? Accomplishment? Party? Taylor seethed. *This guy's a clown! Eight dead, and he's smiling?*

Hampton stepped forward and handed Commander Stroud two sheets of paper. The group adjusted its stance, ready for instructions.

"I'll take the Sa Dec group back home up the Co Chien. The 37 and 59 Boats will follow to the Bassac River mouth. Stay just inside there tonight. You can mooch fuel from that Thai gunboat stationed there. I'll send relief boats to you tomorrow. Do nothing fancy. I'll drop two more boats in the Co Chien."

"You transient boats will escort Wainwright's boat along the coast to Cat Lo. Commander Stroud will determine which of your boats he'll ride. Before you get underway, pass any spare ordinance to the 59 or 37 Boats. We wouldn't want them to be short of anything. That's it." LB was ignored.

As the group dispersed, Hampton's radioman trotted up. "Commander Stroud, Pastel is calling for you, Sir." Stroud waved the sailor back to the boat and followed.

Hampton's eyes told Boston and Taylor to hang back. He had something in mind.

"Five Buck, could you walk with us?"

Hampton relaxed. "Okay, boys, I've got more important things to do than wonder why I'm smelling beer on this beach. What did you find out during your little sight-seeing tour up that ti ti canal?" Hampton was like a mother. Eyes in the back of his head, he knew when you misbehave. There was no point to evasion.

"Bob, I wanted to know more about that canal and asked Sam to run in there. It was clear; that little sampan was gone. They had lookouts posted as we came into the river this morning. They di-di-ed when the shooting started. They knew we were coming and set up on us." Boston was back to business.

In the Vietnamese language "di" (phonetically, "dee") means to go.

Taylor recited his observations without passion. "I went in as far as the leftward bend of the canal. It's skinny, but there's plenty of depth for my boat. From that point, it runs for a straight five hundred yards at a forty-five-degree angle from the course of the river. Then it narrows more and appears to turn to the right. I'll bet there's a crossing up there." As Taylor spoke, he drew his foot through the sand, marking the canal's observed course.

"Write that up when you're off patrol. At least we'll stick it in our navigation log for the future." Hampton dragged his boot across Taylor's depiction.

"We're blessed they didn't get more of us. The watch supervisor at Pastel, Commander Shaw, helped a lot with the Black Ponies and the Medivac. Cong hasn't been reading our mail, Bill. We were spotted hanging around up north, I'm sure of that. As late as we were going in, they had plenty of time to set up."

"We needed blessings, Bob. What happened with the Commander? Something wasn't right. I felt it over the radio." Taylor had a sixth sense. Narrowing his eyes, he waited for the answer he had already guessed.

"This isn't the time for that. We have to get everybody back in place. We may not have seen the last of those shooters. Some are bound to be alive and dangerous. My guess is they are high-tailing toward the Bassac, so keep your ears open and check with Coastal Group 36." Each officer knew the terrain and distances that could be reasonably covered by an enemy on the run.

Hampton paused. "Five Buck, can you find a clean shirt? You'll feel better. If you are up to it, I'll leave you in the Co Chien with one other boat, maybe with the Camel." Brooks nodded.

Taylor had been patient. "Well, Pastor, if you're passing on my first question, what happened to Wainwright? He looks like he, too, had a very bad day."

"He says he tripped and fell when the shooting started."

"Maybe so, but if I had to guess, he fell on a bunch of knuckles."

"Like I say, my son, we haven't time for that."

CHAPTER 23
Seawolves

"Lt. Hampton, two Seawolves are coming up from Seafloat to take me to Ben Thuy for a flight to Saigon. Moosehunter wants to discuss this operation." Seafloat was a floating anchorage and landing pad for patrol boats and Seawolves in the Cua Lon River. Established in June 1969, this facility was in the heart of the enemy's mangrove swamps of the Ca Mau peninsula.

Symbolized by a fire-breathing Lowenbrau wolf painted on the nose of the gunship, Seawolves were the Navy's light attack helicopters. Early Seawolves were cast-off US Army helicopters when they became available. These gunships were repainted black or navy blue and refitted for the flying requirements of the Navy's mission to support surface assets. Four Seawolves were assigned to Seafloat.

Stroud, in the main cabin of Hampton's boat, was jamming things into his small pack and wasn't looking directly at Hampton. He had an odd look on his face. His scalp was taut and his eyes apprehensive. Hampton saw this before on other men, more often just before a raid rather than when it was over.

The commander of all US naval forces in Vietnam, COMNAVFORV, was Admiral Elmo Zumwalt, call sign Moosehunter. This was not to be a discussion. Zumwalt had a special affection for Swift Boats and the men who fought on them. His son was a boat officer on Swifts. Whatever gloss might be spread on today's events, nothing could hide the deaths of eight men and the effective loss of two boats. Hampton surmised there would be a reckoning.

"Can I do anything before you leave?" Hampton sensed he was seeing a man about to go to the guillotine and felt little sympathy for him. He tried to fill time to give Stroud an opportunity to think.

He continued, "We should transmit the after-action report to Vung Tau. Commander Shaw has been the watch officer for this raid. He will be looking for our report." Certainly Shaw's fine hand was all over these developments. Hampton mentally reconfirmed his intention to talk to Shaw.

Stroud was not in the reality of the moment but managed a reply. "I trimmed your draft to a bare-bones statement. We went in, got ambushed by a superior force, and responded vigorously, destroying all of the attackers. You can send this." Stroud handed the draft sheets back to Hampton and turned to complete his packing.

Significant entries had been marked over. Event times and all mention of the 78 Boat's operational difficulties were stricken. One sentence was added: "The O-in-C of PCF 69, despite injuries sustained in the initial phase of the ambush, saved his boat from certain destruction."

Hampton's outrage boiled inside, displacing any momentary compassion for this sorry excuse of a senior officer. Before he spewed his anger, Stroud spoke further; he had been thinking all along.

"I have news for you, Lt. Hampton. You're going with me. Get your gear and tell Mr. Wainwright to take charge of your boat."

Hampton's self-control returned. "No, Sir!" His tone was firm and flat. "Wainwright is in no shape to take charge of anything. One look at him will tell you that . . . Sir." Hampton's words were barely respectful; his tone was hard.

"Wainwright," he continued, "has a crewman with enough wits left to follow the other boats back to Cat Lo, and when I go with you, my LPO can take care of my boat."

Stroud's head snapped around at Hampton's refusal, but then, seeing Hampton's eyes and the set of his mouth, he froze. Stroud could not afford a confrontation here; he knew this young officer was not to be cowed.

"Suit yourself, Mr. Hampton."

Hampton considered continuing to challenge Stroud but decided that going to Saigon would be an opportunity to discuss more than anyone expected. Until then, his personal views could be put on hold.

"Mr. Brooks should be designated OTC for now, if that is agreeable with you, Sir. He's one of the toughest men we have, and he always keeps his head." Stroud nodded consent.

"I'll give Mr. Brooks the news and the after-action report for transmission. The tide's running out soon, and we need to get into the channel before we're stuck here. I'll send the transients on their way." Stroud again nodded.

"When the Seawolves get here, we'll run in long enough to jump off at the bow." Hampton's dangerous tone had subsided, but he was clearly making the decisions.

After briefing Brooks on the change in plans, Hampton gave him the draft report. He watched Five Buck's face contort as the muscles of his jaws began to work. They both heard the engine sounds of the transient boats pulling out for the trip back to Cat Lo.

"Take it easy, Five Buck. You've had a long day." Pastor Bob's tone was firm and steady. "After we leave, transmit this to Pastel as it is edited, but I am ordering you to omit this crap about Wainwright." He got a pen from Brooks' chart table and drew a single line through the false language, careful not to obliterate the writing. He then initialed that change.

"Keep this draft safe until you personally deliver it to Commander Shaw. He will understand what this is all about."

Brooks and Hampton were close friends and had been through a lot together. A slight smirk formed on Five Buck's lips. "I'll do just that, Pastor Bob. Have a good trip."

CHAPTER 24
Resting

As Maj. Phan crossed the footbridge, he saw Vu, the two soldiers from the coast, and the lookouts at the mouth of the Bo De. These men looked fresh and alert, but they were shocked at Phan's appearance. He looked awful. His mouth was bleeding, his uniform was filthy, and he was exhausted.

Saying nothing, Phan leaned his back against a tree and slowly eased down to a sitting position, trying to regain composure.

Phan was pleased that his men had taken time to surround the machine gun with sandbags. The gun was ready for any attack from the direction of the river. Under large bushes, the men had neatly stacked their weapons and packs. Unlike his clothing, their uniforms were in order. Phan's pack was two feet from the others. His men were aware of his appraisal but continued to stare down the path from the river, wondering if anyone else got away.

Reaching for the last American cigarette, he pulled out the soggy pack and remembered falling into the shell hole during his escape. "Vu, do you have that cigarette I gave you?"

Vu smiled and pulled the slightly bent but dry cigarette from his shirt pocket. He handed it to his Tieu Ta, struck a match, and held it carefully for him. Phan drew heavily on the cigarette and then passed it to Vu, turning his hand in a circular motion for the others to share. All remained silent.

As sounds of the OV-10s came overhead, they all stiffened. When the air attack began, their imaginations filled in the sights evoked by the sounds. Everyone but Phan and Vu backed further into the foliage.

Faintly, another sound caused them to grab their weapons. Phan rolled over onto his stomach and sighted his AK-47 across the footbridge and trail from the river.

"Tieu Ta! Are you safe?" A voice came from the jungle. "It is Ha Shi Tang. I am coming in. Please don't shoot." Phan saw the man on the path with his arms held high and without any visible weapon. Phan relaxed and arose from his prone firing position as the others came out to greet Tang. Tang was shirtless, his torso covered with blood. His hat was gone, and the hair on his head had burned away. Except for his burns, Tang seemed uninjured. They knew no others would come.

Phan stood and turned away. Pouring water slowly from his canteen onto his forehead, he was careful not to disturb the new scab forming around his mouth. He removed his shirt and vigorously shook it and put it back on. As he became more ordered, he spoke to the others with his usual but now tired firmness, requesting reports.

The river mouth lookouts said a gravely damaged second boat was escorted down river. From what the lookouts saw before they fled, Toh's group was likely all killed.

Phan's gaze then fell on Ha Shi Tang.

"Running to our next firing position, I fell. The machine guns found us. No one survived. When you left your pit, I knew that I should also run. Many bodies lay around me. When mortars began falling, I fell again." Tang's shirtless body looked frail. He was shivering.

"How did you lose your shirt, and why is your hair burned?"

"I don't know, Tieu Ta. When I woke up, I heard airplanes and knew that I must try to come here, away from their rockets."

Phan paused and turned to Vu. "Where is the old fisherman's body," assuming that Vu had carried out his orders.

Vu cast his eyes to the ground. "Tieu Ta, the fisherman was gone when I returned."

Phan then looked at the soldiers, who last saw the old man. The older of the two spoke.

"The old man vanished before we heard shooting. He took his boat." The second soldier nervously affirmed the story with a nod.

Phan knew these men, like Sgt. Toh, did not come here to kill old men. Besides, what threat was the fisherman now?

Hearing helicopters in the distance, Phan worried that they carried American soldiers for a counterattack. He had six reasonably fresh, well-armed men left and the heavy machine gun, but the best he could do now was to run away.

"We will leave this area soon. Get something to eat and be ready to move at my command." Exhausted, he had no energy to do more than sleep. Other helicopter sounds he heard were different; he could not determine their direction. He ordered Vu and one other man to be ready at the machine gun to cover the trail and the bridge.

The Americans could be very tenacious in searching for them. Phan tried to focus on the best way to avoid contact. Instead, he drifted into sleep.

CHAPTER 25

Aviators

Lt. Ronnie Lee Porter had been in the Navy seven years. He loved helicopters and the physical aspects of flying them. The UH-1Bs he had been flying with Helicopter Attack Squadron (Light) 3, nicknamed the "Seawolves" (HAL3) for the past five months had become a part of his body. He knew the meaning of its sounds, vibrations, and movements. He could make the airship dance. Porter was well qualified as an attack helicopter aircraft commander (AHAC). His new co-pilot today, Steve Carell, was good but not nearly as good as Porter.

Ronnie Lee was raised in the Texas Panhandle. A skinny farm boy, he was a track star and captain of his six-man high school football team in New Home, one of the many small communities that dot the high plains region of West Texas. To everyone's surprise, he took a chance and decided to go to Rice Institute, as it was known then, instead of enrolling at Texas Tech University in Lubbock or Texas A & M University in College Station. His desire for a first-class engineering degree from Rice located in Houston, Texas overwhelmed his easy inclination to remain a good ole country boy.

On his orientation visit to the Rice campus, he discovered that the Institute had a Naval Aviation ROTC program. The Navy was a great opportunity, a chance for a kid raised in the scrub brush of West Texas. In those years, America was at peace. Surmising that his life should be vastly different from that of his high school teammates and everyone else in New Home, young Porter fit in well with the academic and military discipline his choices required.

In those early years, Porter took calculated risks, with favorable results. Well before graduation and commissioning, Ronnie Lee's nickname, later his personal call sign became "Roulette."

* * *

Today was an urgent mission, but not without its perks. Porter was the Fire Team Leader of the two aircraft. He and his wingman, Lt. (jg) Gary Woolston, personal call sign "Stripper," were to pick up an O-4 and an O-3 for transport to Ben Thuy. These were officer pay grades, denoting a lieutenant commander and a lieutenant.

The urgency of this mission was clear. Seawolves, as gunships, did not act as taxis. Porter was ordered to carry two officers to catch a plane. This significance did not escape him.

The perk would come afterward at Ben Thuy. Dropping the passengers for their connecting flight to Saigon, the two crews could have a good late lunch, refuel, and be back at Seafloat before nightfall. Ben Thuy was just another Delta town, but it was a big city compared to Seafloat and in many ways safer.

From twenty-five hundred feet on this partly cloudy day, they could see most of the Delta and the beach near their objective. Their destination was marked by a tall spire of black smoke, pointing down like a finger out of the heavens. As they got closer to the Song Bo De, Porter considered the relative safety of his approach to the beach. He had two choices. He could drop down now to just above the jungle canopy and move fast over land, never presenting much of a target for ground fire until he came in for landing. Coming in from the sea, however, could allow a shooter at the jungle's edge with a good aim to get off shots at the face of the approaching helicopter. Takeoffs were always dicey.

He chose to approach from the sea. The patrol boats below could screen his arrival and departure. While his wingman maintained altitude, Lt. Porter's ship dropped dramatically and came in just above the wave tops. If his two passengers were ready, he needn't be on the sand longer than sixty seconds. Then he would go back out to sea and up to join his colleague for the rest of the trip to Ben Thuy. This was to be straightforward, simple, and smart!

Unless they were directly engaging the enemy, Navy helicopters in Vietnam normally flew at two altitudes, high above the potential of ground fire or on the deck. Other services called this the nap of the earth, traveling low at a speed over the ground so fast as not to present more than a momentary target for ground fire. Take offs and landings could be dangerous. The airspace between high and low was also known as the dead man's zone. For this pick-up, Woolston remained at high altitude, providing cover for Porter in the event the VC wanted to try their shooting luck.

As Lt. Porter approached the beachfront, he saw one of the patrol boats move toward the river mouth shoreline. Two men jumped from the bow to the sand, and the boat pulled back. Porter brought his ship in and landed on the wet, compacted sand close to the water, maintaining power and enough pitch to stay light on the skids. The two passengers hunched over, trotted forward, and climbed aboard.

Before lifting off, Stroud reached forward and pulled at Lt. Porter's shoulder.

With his open hand, he pointed up river. "Lieutenant, go out over there," he yelled. "I need to see this site from the air."

Things were getting complicated. Porter started to tell this guy, "No, we're not doing it that way," but then calculated he could gain enough speed going up river to give the man a quick look and then break right gaining further speed and altitude for the dash out over the jungle. From what Porter had seen, the ambush site was already badly shot up. Besides, this O-4 was important to someone, or Seawolves wouldn't be there. He nodded his head and switched on his intercom.

"Dobby, you and Tiny stand by your guns. This is going to be fast." Aviation Mechanic's Mate 2nd Class, Dobby Wallis, the crew chief, acknowledged. Roulette was about to spin the wheel.

Woolston had remained out and high over the water's edge, completing a long oval pattern parallel to the beach.

"Stripper, this is Roulette. I'll head upriver and break right just past the smoke and climb to altitude. Over."

Porter saw the smoke drifting now from the north, enhancing his chance to gain more speed when he altered course. Porter began pulling pitch and pushing the cyclic forward to lower the ship's nose.

"Roulette, this is Stripper. Roger. I'll cover off to your left."

* * *

Mr. Woolston had taken R & R in Australia. In a fit of exuberant intoxication, he pulled his clothes off in the Texas Bar in Sydney, a crowded hangout for American servicemen and Australian women. A tall, handsome, but rough-looking woman seated at the bar pointed and yelled to the crowd in a no-nonsense voice, "I'll take that one." She then climbed from her stool, gathering his clothes as she walked. She pitched him his trousers and commanded, "Let's go." The house cheered.

Six days later, she returned Woolston to the R & R center in Sydney. He was exhausted. All he could tell Roulette on the flight back to Vietnam was that she had some sort of a ranch-type property out in the countryside. He had seen very little of it, but she had taken good care of him. When they got back to Seafloat, everyone already knew his new call sign.

* * *

The Wolf lifted lightly and then nosed down to the left, picking up speed and direction. Porter felt the aircraft shudder as translational lift took effect. *This will not take long. The Oscar-4 better have his eyes open,* Porter thought.

CHAPTER 26
One Wolf Down

Stroud was near the starboard opening of the main cabin, Hampton on the port side. Tiny, the left side gunner, almost filled that opening. As the Seawolf streaked upriver, Hampton saw the left bank littered with broken, dismembered bodies and shell holes. When the Huey hard-rolled to the right, all Hampton could see was the sky and the other Seawolf offset high and tracking the same course.

Stroud studied the terrain as they flew along the river. He, too, saw smashed bodies and shell holes. When they passed over the still-smoldering hulk of the 78 Boat, Stroud saw there was little left of the boat above the waterline. Fumes from the smoldering ground below entered the helicopter's cabin. For a brief moment, Stroud was about to retch from odd smells mixed with the smoke. The sudden roll to the right surprised him, and he had a sensation that he was about to fall out of the gunship. Dobby Wallis, the crew chief at the starboard M-60, used his right arm, almost casually, as a brace against Stroud's body. As the helicopter straightened out and lifted on its new course, Hampton relaxed; Stroud did not.

Twenty-two seconds after the turn, the cockpit and main cabin were hit by 7.62 slugs. The burst of gunfire could not have been more precise in its track or more lethal. One slug hit the co-pilot on the underside of his left thigh, broke through, and continued into the man's chin and up into his brain. His body jumped and went immediately limp. Another round narrowly missed Porter's armored seat and coursed up the right side of Lt. Porter's chest inside his rib cage and protective jacket. A third slug broke up, coming through the deck of the main cabin. A larger piece hit Tiny's hip. He collapsed onto Hampton's lap. A second piece grazed Hampton's right shinbone and stopped in the fleshy part of his calf. The fourth round burst through the deck one inch from Stroud's left hand that he was using to stabilize his position. Heavy metallic sounds could be heard banging above Wallis's head. At that point only Wallis and Stroud were uninjured.

Porter seemed to be controlling the ship but was silent on the radio. The Seawolf leaned lazily to the left back toward the Song Bo De, filmy dark smoke wafting toward Stripper's position.

The starboard gunner in Stripper's ship poured fire on the site of the hostile gunfire hoping to break the shooter's focus long enough for a proper attack. Stripper radioed Seafloat while swinging around to see if he could assist Roulette and his stricken ship. He knew this was very bad; no transmissions came from Roulette. Thirty yards from the riverbank and another sixty yards upstream from that morning's ambush site, Porter's helicopter slid sideways into the ground, collapsing his left skid. The rotor blades whacked into the mud and broke up. The helicopter came to a rest with the right side tilted up at a twenty-five-degree angle.

Tiny screamed in pain; Hampton was gasping for breath under Tiny's weight. Dobby hauled Tiny out of the way. He momentarily looked at Mr. Carell but saw the man's bloody head was stuffed in. He then turned to Mr. Porter, whose left hand was still on the cyclic between his knees. He stripped away Porter's helmet and saw the dead stare in his eyes. Mr. Porter seemed to be looking to his left. Stuck to the inside of the windscreen was a small photograph of an owl sitting on a Collie dog. Flecks of blood ran down its gloss. Wallis carefully detached the picture from the windscreen and wiped the blood streaks from it, using a clean part of Porter's flight suit. He then tucked the photograph in one of his own pockets.

Damn, Mr. Porter got us down, Wallis thought. Porter's luck ran out.

Wallis grabbed and keyed the radio handset. "Sierra Whiskey 79, this is 23. My pilots are dead. Two others are down, and two are okay. Can you help?"

"Sierra Whiskey 23, this is 79. Roger that. Wait one."

Dobby Wallis turned to see how the others were. Tiny had regained his composure but was suffering, and the younger officer trying to stand was pointing to the right door. Commander Stroud was gone.

CHAPTER 27

Sounds of Death

The changing sounds of helicopter engines jerked Phan's mind into consciousness, two distinct and different sounds. Tang yelled and pointed, "Tieu Ta, there is an American helicopter up there. I hear another but cannot see it."

Phan instinctively knew one helicopter was flying low and fast. The sound was diffused by vegetation but increasing steadily. He looked toward his men, waving them into the jungle growth. Only Vu and the machine-gun server seemed not to see his motions. Vu was young, his hearing acute and his timing eloquent. Before Phan could react further to restrain Vu's clear intentions, Vu raised his AK-47 toward the treetops. The gun began spitting deadly rounds up through the trees and into what Phan thought was empty sky. In an instant, the dark underbody of a helicopter moved directly into the spewing trail of bullets. Vu swung around and kept shooting even after the helicopter had vanished.

Vu stopped firing and began laughing. They all heard the high-pitched whining engine sounds. Vu looked around a few seconds for confirmation of his skill but was almost immediately surrounded by a deadly cone of fire from the other helicopter. He and his server, in a cloud of heaving dirt and fluttering leaves, at once became shredded piles of bloody flesh draped over the useless unfired machine gun.

From the river came metallic crunching sounds and then silence. Phan motioned his soldiers to that sound.

CHAPTER 28

Return to the Bo De

"Any Frisco this net, this is Sierra Whiskey 79. Over."

"Sierra 79, this is Frisco Leader. Go." Lt. (jg) Brooks knew there was a problem. This untimely call did not come from the Seawolf that picked up Hampton and Stroud. The transient units were now well up the coast.

"Leader, my Foxtrot Tango Lima is down and out at coordinates Whiskey Quebec 310 660. Can your units get back in there and pick up our people? I'm covering. Over."

"Sierra 79. Roger, we're on our way." Brooks understood that the downed helicopter was the Seawolf Fire Team Leader. Without further command from Brooks, his group of boats raised speed and turned in column.

"Frisco 24, this is Leader. Do not enter with us. Maintain position near the mouth." The 24 Boat pulled to the side of the track of speeding boats. Each crew began scrambling into jackets and helmets, recharged their guns, and stood ready. The mood on each vessel was mean and determined.

As the group began again crossing the tangents into the Song Bo De, Brooks issued assignments. "Frisco 28, go in for the pick-up. Frisco 59 and 37, cover the flanks. With Frisco 92, I am standing off this time. Acknowledge. Over."

Orderly short replies crackled back. Brooks spoke again. "Pastel, this is Frisco 17. Have you copied what's going on here? We're going back for a pick-up; a Sierra Whiskey unit is covering. New assets may be needed if we don't get everybody. Over."

"Frisco 17, this is Pastel. Roger. We've got all that working." Brooks, too, recognized Commander Shaw's voice. Brooks and the others felt no pre-engagement tension this time, just grim readiness. The unspoken question hung in their minds, *What's Pastor Bob's situation?*

CHAPTER 29

Awaiting Rescue

Dobby Wallis eyed the jungle. "Roger 79. I copy. We'll start moving. There's a complication. The Oscar-4 has left the ship. Any instructions? Over."

Pastor Bob heard the expected answer.

"Roger Sierra Whiskey 23. Move to the riverbank and wait for pick-up. If Oscar isn't there when help arrives, get your men on board."

Hampton and Wallis helped Tiny out of the cabin and got him standing on one leg. Wallis detached his M-60 with ammunition and slung the load over his shoulder. With Tiny in between, the three men stumbled toward the riverbank. In three more trips back to the helicopter, they got the dead pilots, the aircraft logbook, and other documents as well as the rest of the weapons. As the other helicopter orbited overhead, they sat near the water's edge.

"What's your name, Sir? Mine's Dobby Wallis, and that's Anthony Gomez who squashed you like a bug. We call him 'Tiny.'"

"He did, Dobby. My name is Robert Hampton. Sorry to meet you. My guys will be here soon, and you'll be okay." Hampton seemed distracted.

After a pause Dobby spoke. "Why'd your skipper haul ass? I know it was a little dicey back there, but we're okay."

By then Hampton came to a standing crouch. "I guess he thought we were going to catch fire." Hampton saw the doubt in the young man's eyes. Self-sealing fuel tanks were intended to minimize that hazard.

"Look here, Wallis, I've got to look for him. You get aboard when the boats come. They will know what to do." He grabbed one of the M-16s and hobbled off toward the jungle. "I'll be back."

"Sir, don't leave. We're better off here. Please . . ." By then Hampton entered the tree line. Wallis lit a cigarette and considered following after him. Tiny Gomez passed out, sprawled over the M-60, unable to cover their position. If something happened before the boats arrived, maybe no one would get out alive. The rumbling sounds of approaching boat engines ended his debate. He would get his instructions from the boat officer. As he turned his attention to the approaching Swift Boats, he thought he heard small-arms fire.

CHAPTER 30
Other Assets

PCF 28 nosed against the muddy riverbank, twin 50s fully depressed and ready to rake the jungle. Bowers and two other crewmen swung over the bow to gather weapons and help lift Gomez and the bodies of the pilots onto the foredeck. Other crewmen hauled the materials and bodies to the afterdeck. Lt. (jg) Leyland then stepped to the bow and reached down to pull up his own men and finally Wallis. He and Wallis spoke briefly. Leyland moved to his pilothouse and keyed the handset.

"Frisco 17 and Sierra Whiskey 79, this is Frisco 28. Everybody is on board except Sierra Whiskey passengers. The gunner heard small-arms fire just before we beached. Over."

"This is Sierra 79; I'll take a closer look. Wait. Out."

The overhead Seawolf came back across the river on a lower track than before. As he got over the jungle, his rotor downdraft thrashed the trees and other vegetation.

Moments later, Stripper's voice went up an octave.

"Frisco, this is Whiskey. I have movement down here by a little canal. Four men are partially in the open, running for thicker jungle to the north. One looks like our man, arms bound behind him. I cannot fire. Over."

"Whiskey, this is Frisco Leader," Brooks asked the critical question, "Do you see any other Uniform Sierras?"

"Negative Frisco. They're in the jungle. I've lost them. I need to do some communicating. I'll call back. Out."

"Frisco 28, this is Frisco Leader. Follow me out of here." The afternoon sun was just over clouds on the western horizon as the small flotilla safely emerged into the gentle sea swells. The heat had gone from the day, and the sky was clear and clean. A slight haze still hung over the 78 Boat's hulk. The night would be pleasant.

"Frisco Leader, this is Sierra Whiskey 79. Special assets are en route from my home location. I'll remain until other units arrive. Expect Pastel will contact you ASAP."

The system was gearing up to try to find these lost officers on the assumption that one or both may have been captured. Assessment would be made to determine the feasibility and course of recovery. Messages would be sent, and various military and intelligence units in the region would be alerted to the task. For now, Brooks had to remove his group and the casualties to a position of relative safety.

Pastel, now Lt. Commander Shaw, transmitted the following message encoded to Frisco Leader for all Frisco units:

1. Detach two PCFs to standby near shore vicinity of Song Bo De for early morning extraction of Seal Team pair. Continue Frisco Market nomenclature and frequencies. Time and coordinates of extraction to be determined by Seal Leader, call sign Bright Light 6.

2. Detached units report safe completion of extraction and stand by for further orders.

3. Frisco 17 and other Frisco units are to withdraw and return to Sa Dec. En route, contact Coastal Group 36 for assistance with further evacuation of personnel from Seawolf 23.

Further orders to follow.

Brooks stepped out on the port side and gave a big slow wave to the 37 Boat, signaling for Boston to come alongside.

Brooks cupped his hands around his mouth and yelled across the long swell between the two boats. The cadence of his speech was slow and deliberate. "Did you copy that last from Pastel?" Boston raised one thumb.

To reinforce the message, Brooks went on. "Hampton and Stroud are on the ground. One of them may have been captured. We don't really know their situation. You and Taylor stay available out here."

Brooks continued. "Seals are coming in from Seafloat. Probably no drop off until after dark. Maybe they'll get lucky." Bill Boston nodded his head and gestured again with a right thumb up.

Brooks nodded back. "For the pick-up, do it fast, and get the hell out of there. We don't know how many bad guys are left, and today has already been too long and too bad. See you again in Sa Dec." He finished with a goodbye wave. As his and the other boats began pulling off to the northeast, Boston waved back.

Bill Boston hauled his boat back around toward the mouth of the Song Bo De for the third time that day, Taylor falling in behind him. The sun would soon set.

CHAPTER 31

Nighttime Search and Dawn Retrieval

Bob Hampton awoke to find himself in an awkward sitting position against a small tree. He could not move. His legs, splayed out before him, seemed detached from the rest of his body. The heel of his right boot was torn. His shirt was open to the waist, and he was numb from the chest down. He wondered if help would arrive before darkness. He drifted into unconsciousness.

* * *

Boston stayed off the radio since the Seals first checked in. He assumed they came in by helicopter, but he had no idea where they were now. Boston was anxious. "Bright Light 6, this is Frisco 37. What's your status? Over." His whispered call got a terse and whispered reply.

"Three seven, this is Six. We've checked the crash site and found no one. We're moving the pattern to the north and east. Out."

The Seal team leader's exertions had been audible through the radio transmissions, whispered words spaced by breathing. Boston correctly surmised they were between the right bank of the river and the reach of the small canal Taylor had briefly explored the day before. Little time remained before dawn. Local VC cadre, if any, would converge on the crash site for salvage purposes or to attack intruders. If need be, Seals were effective killing machines at night, but they were not equipped to stand and fight if discovered in the light of day.

* * *

Hampton stirred. His eyes popped open and then closed in anguish. *Oh God, help me, the pain. Can't move. This must be bad,* he softly cried out.

He lost track of time, trying to reconstruct events after leaving Dobby Wallis. He remembered following Stroud's direction of travel when he left the helicopter. Even as he looked for Stroud, Bob thought the jungle was beautiful, quiet, and peaceful, an example of God's hand in the world. The afternoon sun filtered through the trees. Overhead, he heard the orbiting Seawolf's rotors and felt no special danger as he moved through the vegetation.

Beyond the opening in the jungle canopy was a cluster of trees and then another span of thicker jungle. As he entered the small grove, he saw Stroud sitting on the ground in the same rigid manner as he had seen during the morning's battle. In his compassion for this broken man, he knelt down to quietly encourage Stroud to return to the riverbank.

"Commander, come back with me. Our boats are coming in to pick us up. We can be out of here in a few minutes." Stroud's face was contorted in pain although Hampton could see no physical injury.

He placed his hand on Stroud's shoulder and whispered, "Sir, come on. We'll be all right." Stroud's tension began wilting under Hampton's compassionate touch, voice, and words.

Hampton, focused on Stroud, failed to hear the tread of the North Vietnamese soldier who blundered into the grove. The soldier and Hampton were so surprised at first that they just looked at each other. Hampton thought how strange the man appeared; he was shirtless and the hair on his bare head was scorched. In slow motion, it seemed, he began to raising his rifle. Hampton, instead, fired first from the hip; his three-shot burst slammed into the soldier's bare chest and face. Stroud sprung to his feet and backed away from the bloody corpse. Then other firing came from the jungle, and Hampton was hit. He remembered feeling crushed as though something very heavy had fallen on him. He slipped from consciousness, hearing Vietnamese voices.

* * *

"Three-seven, this is Bright Light 6. Nothing so far. There's a clump of trees further away less than a hundred meters. We're going to check that out. Over."

"This is Three-seven. Roger. Break. Bravo Sierra." Boston's whispered response told Taylor to come up on the BS frequency.

"Prevert, start moving toward the river mouth. Over."

"Double, I agree. Charles cleared the area. Just a feeling."

Their engine sounds changed from a low gurgle to a deep, soft purr as the two boats lined up and started toward the darkened river mouth. Their crews got ready.

* * *

Hampton tried to ignore his pain and suppress his fear. His breathing became shallow. He sensed the nearness of sunrise.

Dear Lord, does it end like this? Why did I go after Stroud? Katie deserves better. The baby deserves better.

His mind drifted, and his breathing stopped momentarily. He began panting and seemed to choke back his sadness.

"God, thank you for being here. Will the baby be a boy or a girl? Care for them. Bless them and give them your grace. Forgive me . . ."

Tears welled.

"When I fall short . . . Lord, your will be done."

* * *

The partial light of dawn streaked the sky, but the jungle remained dark. Two shapes rose slowly out of the underbrush. They moved quickly into the trees. With hand signals, one of the Seals cautioned the other. As they moved forward, one drew his knife and came very close to slitting Hampton's throat. A moment later in a whisper, he reported, "This one's ours; he's dead. See anybody else?"

The other man moved across the grove. "A body over here. The face is gone, but it's a dead Charles. Looks like our guy took him out. Which one do you have?"

"He's not the Oscar-4." Stroud had a mustache; this corpse did not.

"That's Hampton." Both men knew their job was over for a time; they rested.

One of the Seals reached for the radio handset. "Three-seven, this is Bright Light 6. We found someone." He passed on the coordinates. "Frisco, can you pick us up at the riverbank just above the crash site? Your Oscar-3 did not make it."

There was a pause. "Bright Light, Roger. We're on our way in. Thanks for getting our man. Out."

They sat on the ground, forming a small circle with Hampton's body. The top of the sun moved above the horizon, its light showed first in the treetops and then began spreading down toward the ground. In the distance, the Seals heard faint engine sounds of approaching Swifts.

"How you want to do this?" one Seal asked.

"I don't know, let's split the carry. I'll go first; you help. This guy's had a long night."

"So have I. Why don't you carry me and let him help?"

Dark humor shielded them from the sadness of the moment.

They stood and moved to hoist Hampton's body and paused. The faint light now framed Hampton's face. "Look at his cheeks. The poor bastard's got tear streaks running through the dirt on his face." One Seal moved his hand to Hampton's face. "The poor bastard."

As they trudged back toward the river with their load, they wondered how long before they found him that he had died. His tear streaks were damp.

Boston made the pick-up with Taylor standing off protectively. As these Swifts left the Song Bo De for the last time, they sailed past the visible sandbar at the river's entrance.

Sam Taylor thought, *in a few hours, that sandbar will be covered through the next tide cycle. In months to come, the river will change the bar's shape and location. It may disappear altogether, but who will care one way or another?*

Softly and slowly, at almost a whisper, Taylor whistled a little bit of "Dixie."

CHAPTER 33

The Present

Boston had spent enough time in the past. Clearing the tears from his eyes, he carried the photographs to the Suburban. Placing them in an accordion folder on the front bench seat, he reclosed the house and his memories. He had another stop before going to the office.

CHAPTER 33
Ho Chi Minh City

The Lockheed C-141B Starlifter roared down the runway, increasing its speed as it climbed through the ugly, yellow afternoon smog around Ho Chi Minh City's airport. David Armstead reviewed that past day's work.

These flights, once significant to the American public, although never frequent, were now barely noticeable. In 1988, they had been front-page news but now rated slight space in back sections of few newspapers and virtually no television news. The results of these flights were often inconsequential except an occasional family getting final answers to an old loss. This flight was an afterthought in that history, coming as it did in the waning months of the president's first term. Competing candidates jockeyed to see who might take the reins of power, if at all, next January.

This version of the aircraft was configured with thirteen passenger seats forward of the cargo area in which were seven aluminum caskets, covered with netting and strapped to the deck. This was a substantial recovery.

Flight noise made conversation inconvenient but allowed Armstead the solitude to sort his thoughts. Soon, from something resembling a large briefcase, his aide prepared Armstead's usual double hit of Wild Turkey with two ice cubes. The bourbon and the aircraft's ventilation system eventually eliminated the unique smells of Vietnam from the cabin but not from his mind. His mood was reflective.

He wondered if his mind was tricking his present senses with the smell of death from his violent past. The caskets were the trigger. Lands of war smelled the same, a blend of expended ordinance and burned fuel, clothing, equipment, and human flesh.

Lands at peace have different, more natural, appealing smells to some. The Vietnamese Mekong delta blended the odors of decaying vegetation, cooking oil, wood smoke, salt air, and soy sauce. The protein made some difference, too. Cooked fish and pork were added smells.

Armstead remembered the smell of freshly slaughtered sea birds. One afternoon decades ago, he accompanied the Coastal Group 35 ambush team and village militia for a bird hunt in an egret rookery south of their fortified hamlet on the Co Chien River. The shoreline at the rookery was softened up by low bursts of .30-caliber machine gun fire before a defensive team was inserted to secure the rookery borders at rice fields beyond. About two hundred birds out of thousands were shot for hamlet consumption. Armstead recalled a white powder hanging in the air. As dying and wounded birds flapped down through the vegetation, dried bird droppings were knocked off the leaves. He remembered, too, the screeching sound of frightened birds puzzled by the noise of gunfire in a place that should have been their sanctuary.

Armstead loved the unique tonal sound of the Vietnamese language, its people chatting in their markets, and water taxis on the rivers. The private theater of his mind saw the grace and dignity of the Delta people and their patient tolerance of outsiders in their land.

Colonial France had come and gone; conquering Japanese had come and proclaimed a form of freedom dictated by the emperor who knew little about the Vietnamese people and their history and cared even less. The Japanese, too, had departed. The men of the north had come to dictate the lives of those who lived in the Delta. They were invaders of a sort, disrespectful and violent to change life in the Delta that had been changeless.

Then the Americans came, clumsy and innocent in their way, so terrible and brutal in warfare. The puzzle of American presence in Vietnam was that they alone never came to stay. They came to win, as was their spirit, but they never came to conquer. Their young men drank and whored, but they never intended to spoil. They often cried over the results of their own or others' violence and sometimes prayed quietly for forgiveness for what they had done.

War is evil, but that fine generation and the ones lucky enough to come home were branded in their homeland as evil, a scar that never healed.

Americans also died; some too surprised by the matter to make much of a sound, some miserable and noisily fearful of the end, with others too busy and determined in their work to notice that death was overtaking them. Even the dead were not to stay, returning to America and grief-stricken hometown cemetery farewells. Where their lives ended, families' pains continued. All, Armstead thought, were egrets.

Jet engine whines were an incantation for these memories swelling in Armstead's mind. He had to think of the present. Peacefulness in this land was unlike any other he had seen in his trips there after the war. By April 1975, physical fear and exhaustion marked the people. Afterward, a spiritual exhaustion set in. The Vietnamese people, north and south, were tired of the drab dispiritedness of a communist state. They waited for the dying off of old leadership. Proletariat revolution was not in their blood. Patience and the Vietnamese sense of entrepreneurship eventually could trump politics. Waiting was easier than revolution.

Armstead could never express, much less acknowledge to himself, the sense of heartbreak he now felt at this final trip. He imagined leaving behind the place of his birth of understanding; leaving home for the last time. He could never erase his memories but had to move on.

"Sir, would you like another drink or something to eat?" the aide inquired. Air Force Major Barrett Johnson knew Mr. Armstead never had second drinks in flight and would also decline food.

"No, thank you. Check ahead to make sure the medical center people are ready for these caskets."

"Yes, sir."

"I'll speak with the senior on the ground." Armstead pulled out his cell phone and thanked Johnson again, a signal for the major to get on about his business.

Johnson was never accustomed to Armstead's selective intensity. He could stare out the window for hours almost motionless. He would not eat, sleep, stand, or walk around. Johnson long ago concluded that during such apparent trances, Armstead's mind boiled with activity.

Maj. Johnson spent about three minutes, using the aircraft's secure telephone to speak with the US Joint Casualty Resolution Center, a bureaucratic umbrella over the US Army Central Identification Laboratory on Oahu. He verified their readiness at Hickam Air Force Base for the arrival of their special cargo. Johnson returned to his own seat behind and to the far side of his charge. Johnson's intent was to read and wait. He, too, could not relax.

* * *

For almost three years, Johnson was detailed to travel with David Armstead as an aide and protector, although in his estimation, his charge could do quite well on his own. Johnson was selected for this job because of his lethal skills, demonstrated personal courage, and efficient intellect. Most striking was his veneer of harmlessness that made him look like another over promoted wimp from Washington. As elements in his survival, he knew and enjoyed all these qualities. He also studied Armstead from the beginning of his assignment.

Armstead's background was acceptable to the Naval Academy, but it was uncertain as a boy that he would rise above his family circumstances. When David was barely sixteen years old, living in Houston, Texas in one of its then numerous ordinary and crowded post–World War II apartment houses, his father walked out on him, his mother, and younger brother. A report in his security file recited that young David came home from school one day to see his father packing and announcing that the boy was on his own. Soon thereafter his mother gave up and left town with David's younger brother. Armstead refused to go, insisting that he had to finish high school where he was, if he could.

For the rest of that school year, David worked at a local grocery store and sometimes a bicycle shop, sleeping at the homes of classmates. His great fortune was that he was smart, and his grades showed it. He had a sense for dealing with danger, avoiding a predatory pedophile's offer of residence. Things improved.

An English teacher at his school learned of his circumstances and began a discrete campaign to find David a stable situation. As if from a storybook, a Protestant minister offered the couch in his modest home and the security of a decent family environment. As important was the small yet anonymous financial support that came for Armstead. New clothing that fit suitably for the season always timely appeared in a box at the minister's front door.

In his junior year, the teacher worried about the boy's college education. She and her husband were already supporting a daughter away at college. Young David mentioned a desire to go to the United States Naval Academy, but that was, as everyone knew, a long shot.

She mentioned the dilemma to the mother of another student. The mother immediately volunteered the services of her husband, himself a Navy veteran. In a brief and intense marketing exercise by the husband, David acquired a congressional sponsor for the academy. In the fall of his senior year, David was accepted, pending his successful high school graduation.

A higher security clearance investigator some years later attempted to find out the identity of the anonymous donors of money and clothing. The Protestant minister was a pleasant fellow, but clueless, and not the sort for even the most harmless intrigue. The teacher, by then a widow and retired, politely refused to disclose any knowledge she had or speculation about the benefactor's identity. She was proud of having helped the boy and warmly smiled at the wonder of group effort that put him on the path to be a subject of intense security interest. There was something in her eyes that told the investigator that there was nothing sinister in whatever truth she knew. She had promised never to disclose the identity. The teacher was a lady of honor.

A snapshot of Armstead submitted with his application for academy appointment showed a mildly grinning high school kid, posing for the backyard photographer. Obviously fit, there was little to indicate the powerful man that would emerge four years later. He gained bulk, muscle, and a nickname, Bruno. He was not a fast runner, but he had power and stamina. He also had what the French called *élan*, a cheerful seriousness in the face of evident danger. His one noticeable loss was his hair. In the snapshot, his hair was, for that generation, full and blond, but over the years had become short and was growing shorter and receding.

He graduated in the top twenty-five percent of the Academy's class of 1964. Following an appropriate tour on a destroyer, he volunteered for an assignment as an intelligence officer in Vietnam. What he recognized to be an obligatory, hazardous in-country tour of duty for an Academy graduate became a compulsion that followed him throughout his life.

Twice wounded, the last almost took his life. He completed four tours before the collapse of the South Vietnamese government in April 1975. After the American pullout in 1973, he volunteered to remain as an embassy staffer. When the South Vietnamese military crumbled, he was not eager to escape. As two North Vietnamese medium tanks growled at the gates of the presidential palace in Saigon, Armstead, a recently promoted lieutenant commander, was motoring out the Co Chien River on a Yabuta junk filled beyond safe capacity with Vietnamese allies. He kidded himself into believing that the junk's fuel consumption would lighten the load and decrease its instability. The reality was stark; unless they found a friendly vessel before their fuel ran out and the seas freshened, the otherwise sturdy boat would founder, and they could all die.

At sea, within the screen of US ships rescuing the remaining Americans after the fall and the few Vietnamese lucky enough to escape, he located a Thai gunboat on its way home. In addition to his Vietnamese language fluency, Armstead was passably competent in the Thai language. David could easily move beyond political questions to human need, so he persuaded the captain to take all but nine souls to Thailand. Topped off with Thai fuel, Armstead sailed east. He wanted to save the boat and especially the nine Vietnamese men and women who had been a critical part of his final operation. He did not want them to disappear into miserable and often dangerous circumstances of a refugee camp. He steamed for the Philippines.

As he moved eastward with his nine friends, he was observed by the heavy naval traffic moving to and from Subic Bay. The journey became a story in the Western Pacific. His Navy superiors chose not to order him to abandon the junk. Without message traffic specifically addressing the issue, various US Navy ships regularly crossed his course, and in doing so, Armstead acquired additional fuel and provisions.

Twelve days later, the junk chugged into the US Navy Base at Subic Bay. The narrow neck into the bay opened into a large and storm-safe harbor. On twin halyards, the junk flew the American and South Vietnamese flags. A harbor patrol boat directed the junk to the destroyer piers where a mercifully brief welcoming ceremony occurred. That night Armstead got drunk alone in his temporary quarters.

There the glory ended. He spent the next three months in Subic Bay making special arrangements for his people and debriefing other Vietnamese refugees who became the flood known later as boat people. The war was over, and for Armstead, as for others, there seemed no further reason for a naval career. His request to be released from active duty status was granted in 1976.

Maj. Johnson had access only to his charge's security clearance file as that related to Armstead's military background. For Johnson, the story stopped there until 1987.

In the intervening years, Johnson learned Armstead had married and had begun raising a family, including two sons by birth and three adopted children. The adoptees by age and national origin partially tracked Armstead's civilian career path: a girl was Vietnamese, a boy was Afghan, and the third was a girl from Bosnia. The two sons by birth bracketed those by adoption. His oldest son was a first lieutenant in the US Marine Corps, and the youngest was finishing his junior year in high school.

Armstead's outside interests did not appear to be particularly political, but by the time of Johnson's introduction to Mr. Armstead, things had changed. Armstead became an Assistant Secretary of State for International Security Affairs, a lengthy title for a former spook now legitimized with public stature. How this came about and what Armstead had done to merit the title were unknown to Johnson.

To speculate was worthless, but he could engage in estimation, a spook's way of evaluating information in order to deduce an answer to a mystery. Secrets, distinguished from mysteries, were specific answers to particular questions. Do they have the bomb or not? Do they know a special technology or not? These are secrets requiring someone on the ground or something in the air or under the sea that reveals factual answers. However, what someone will do or say, or how or why they react to a set of circumstances is a mystery to be learned at a distance by estimation based on more-or-less tangible information. Despite their formal relationship, the two men were also friends. Maj. Johnson deferred that analysis to another time.

CHAPTER 34

Iowa Late Morning

"Good morning, Mr. DeeBee." The call sign variation had stuck with him even into business with the mere addition of "Mr." No employees knew or cared about its origins.

"You had calls; I put them on your desk." Shana was protective of him. She liked the way he treated his wife and his kids, sharing the opinion with other women in the company that Bill was one of the few real gentlemen around these days.

"A Mr. Armstead called. He said he was sorry he missed you. He left no number but said he would call again later today. Tommy wants you to stop by his office." The office environment did not require formalities of address.

"He's getting the fever. You need to plan your times in the Northwoods."

The annual decision needed to be made as to which family member would get what period of time at the summer home in northern Minnesota. Bill had been stalling his older brother and the other family members, waiting to get firm commitment from David Armstead.

* * *

"Hey, Tommy, Armstead called. I missed him. I assume he's letting me know his schedule for the summer. He will call again."

"Where were you? I called your house. Your bride said that you went early to the farm." Tommy assumed a grumbling fatherly tone with his two younger brothers, less out of condescension than out of a genuine and long-standing sense of responsibility for them.

Bill had been married for almost twenty-eight years. He and Virginia had two beautiful daughters out of college and one strapping son about to graduate from high school. Still, Tommy often referred to Ginnie as Bill's bride. That she had taken on Bill was, in Tommy's mind, a delightful blessing to them all.

"That's right. I went out to get some old photographs to be cleaned up, copied, enlarged, and framed. I stopped by Tech Graphics to have them do the work."

Bill paused. "I'd forgotten how messy the house was."

"Good," Tommy said flatly. "It should be forgotten."

Tommy Boston, the responsible older brother, was too young for the Korean War, too old for the Vietnam War, and probably could not have served in any case because of vision and back problems. He was a decent, honest, and astute businessman.

Tommy was also a worrier. Their kid brother, Cooper, had been a Navy fighter pilot in Vietnam. Tommy worried what their mother would do if anything happened to either of them. Unspoken was his own fear for his brothers' safety. Both brothers drew stateside tours as the war wound down. When Tommy realized they were coming home without injury, he said a short prayer of thanks. He might have prayed for their future if he had realized that his brothers were returning to Middle America with raging and deliberate infections of recklessness. Bill's case was also dangerous.

Tommy remembered the period that Bill was rarely sober and only occasionally clean-shaven. He also remembered the reported fights Bill got into during the time following his return from the Navy.

Before Vietnam, Bill Boston had been an open book of good looks and hearty laughter. He, like his father, was fascinated with motorcycles. On or off the bike, as many girls as he chased pursued Bill. In the spring following his graduation from the University of Iowa, Bill applied for Navy Officer Candidate School, mostly on the belief that going to sea was an appropriate adventure for a young man from Iowa. The politics and protests of the war were irrelevant to him at the time. Bill would do his duty. Six months later, Bill was off to Newport, Rhode Island for OCS.

Cooper was a year younger than Bill, but because of his exceptional academic skills, skipped two semesters before high school graduation. He actually graduated from Iowa State University one semester ahead of Boston. Cooper's participation in the university's Navy ROTC program earned him a commission and orders to flight school. There was no question that Cooper would be flying attack aircraft from a carrier off the coast of Vietnam.

Thus was established a higher level of competition between these brothers. Under these circumstances, Bill applied and was accepted for training as a Swift Boat officer; still junior in rank to his younger brother but sooner into combat.

Within weeks of Bill's homecoming and separation from active duty, he put away his uniforms and medals and began working at the company offices as an assistant sales manager. In his personal life, Bill opted for seclusion at the old family farmhouse. There, with typical energy, he turned the place into a bachelor flat complete with a well-stocked bar and memorabilia from the service. The good looks were still there but matured. The laughter remained but only when he was drinking. In time, Tommy thought his brother would lay aside the past and whatever dark images had changed him.

Then several weeks after Bill's return, Tommy learned from one of the shop employees the details of a rumored incident at Alice's Bar and Grill, a dump in town that was more bar than grill. Bill had become a regular, Tommy supposed, because Alice's place was so different from Bill's more respectable haunts years before.

A big guy from Newton, Iowa came in alone one evening and started knocking down double shots of Canadian whisky and following that with chasers of Old Grain Belt beer. He engaged other patrons in conversation, but not Bill who was seated at one end of the bar. Bill chatted with Alice while she tended the bar. To her patrons, Alice was addressed as Miss Alice, but behind her back and without ill will, she was known as Fat Alice. Bill had gone to high school with her son Jack. Jack, a Marine, came home from Vietnam in a body bag.

The man from Newton drifted into comments about former President Nixon and the Watergate break-in. Silent tolerance hung in the air when he referred to the president as a "tricky little bastard." Alice concluded it was time to have him move along back to Newton. As she dried her hands in preparation for a quiet word with the man at his table, he launched into another claim about the president.

"That Quaker asshole was no peacemaker. He kept us in Vietnam for politics, and a lot of dumb kids died because of him."

Alice didn't wait to approach his table. "Mister, you're getting out of hand. You need to take your opinions on out with you."

"Fat Alice, you can screw yourself before you'll shut me down." He stood and moved toward her and the bar on a line to pass behind Bill.

In less time than he took to say those words and move, Bill reached over into the tending side of the bar and grabbed a nearly full bottle of gin, spun around, and slammed the butt of the bottle against the back of the man's skull. The bottle broke a couple of inches below its neck as the big man collapsed to the floor, drenched in gin. Bill rolled him over onto his back and sat astride his chest holding what was left of the broken bottle close to the groaning man's face.

"Miss Alice, this gentleman is going to be okay. Would you please get me another bourbon? Put the gin on my tab."

Alice smiled. "Sure Billy. I'd be happy to, but don't worry about the gin."

The other patrons were stunned to immobility and silence. Bill was half the Newton guy's size and had never shown any inclination to violence in his hometown. They all knew that Bill had been to Vietnam but not much more than that.

Soon the man recovered his senses and realized his predicament. Bill addressed the man with a measured tone.

"Sir, I have some questions for you. I suggest you answer me truthfully. Nod your head if you understand and don't speak quite yet." The man began nodding.

"Have you ever served in the United States military, Sir? Speak now." The man croaked out a weak but audible "No."

"Sir, do you now apologize to Miss Alice for your unkind words and threats? Speak your answer loudly." The man's eyes had rolled back in search of Miss Alice standing about three feet behind his head. This time the man's yes was yelled.

"One final question. Sir, am I correct in believing that you will never return here?" The man closed his eyes, nodded, and yelled his response.

Silence still gripped the barroom as Bill allowed the man to rise and leave. Alice put Bill's glass of bourbon on the bar, took the remnant of the broken gin bottle from his hand, and pitched it in a nearby trash container. She then put her ample arms around Bill's neck and hugged him. She did not see the tears streaking Bill's cheeks. The other patrons returned to muted conversations.

Bill stopped being a regular patron and over the next year or so kept pretty much to himself. The myth of the crazy Vietnam veteran had already taken hold in America, and Bill wanted no part of it.

Bill had a tough time getting back into the world as Tommy knew it. For Bill Boston, the real world—of good men trying to do and be their best—was what he had left in Vietnam. Now he was expected to set aside his insights and settle down to a peaceful oblivion of disconnection from the reality and nuances of evil and good. In time, Bill stopped coming to work with any regularity.

Tommy was shocked the day Bill returned clean-shaven and dressed for work.

"I moved into an apartment yesterday." He paused. "I don't need to go back to the farm. Could you help me with that?"

"Sure thing, Billy." Tommy knew Bill had turned a corner.

"One other favor, Tommy." His voice had a warm certainty. "Please accept my apologies for the last year. I shouldn't have left all the work to you."

Whatever it was that caused Bill to change and stop his destructive behavior, Tommy would never understand. A year afterward, Bill met Ginnie while on a business trip to Denver, and they married six months later. A couple of years after that, he and Ginny had two daughters. Their son was born in 1986.

Bill's lifestyle became thoroughly Midwestern. He devoted himself solidly to his wife and children, the family business, and his community. The community never really understood his behavior in the first place and forgot the problems he caused before he left the farm.

Well before Miss Alice's death three years ago, Bill helped her sell the bar. A Chinese woman from Des Moines set up a successful restaurant in the old joint. The income from the sale helped Miss Alice live comfortably at the assisted living center on the outskirts of town.

* * *

"Look, Billy. We've got to make some kind of a decision. The bottom line is that I'm not getting a damn thing done in this office. I'm up in the air about when I'm going to get up north. We're all in the same shape."

"Calm down, Tommy. I'll get a decision in the next day or so. It will work out just fine. Don't worry, please." Bill talked to his brother in a manner that always had a calming influence. His brand of kindness and patience was infectious. Tommy's face relaxed, and a smile crossed his lips.

"Okay, I'll wait."

CHAPTER 35

United States Federal Courthouse

Houston, Texas

Aloof, insulated silence typifies a United States district judge's chambers. Generals of armies and leaders of great nations have powerful mandates. But a federal judge's power is derived from Article III, Section 1, of the United States Constitution. The language is simple and direct.

> The judicial power of the United States shall be vested in one Supreme Court, and in such inferior courts as the Congress may from time to time ordain and establish. The judges, both of the supreme and inferior courts, shall hold their offices during good behavior, and shall, at stated times, receive for their services, a compensation, which shall not be diminished during their continuance in office.

The good intentions of the framers of the Constitution were to create a judiciary free from political frailty and without fear of losing their jobs simply because one of their decisions might be unpopular with a president, the Congress, or the citizenry. The underlying belief was that honorable judges, wisely selected, would act soundly according to the highest calling of the law and in the best interests of the country. In short, these appointments were made for life and "good behavior," sometimes an elusive standard.

As often happens, however, differences exist between thought and reality. A few judges believe their powers also come from God or alternatively from their own intellect, if any.

Casually seated at one end of his dark brown leather couch, sucking on a cigarette as though it was his only source of oxygen was one of these princes of the American Constitution.

"George . . . George, I'm simply not going to do that. You may be right. But who knows what the hell is right? Anyway, I don't care. I'm not signing the order!"

Between drags on his cigarette, a strong sound of air being pulled in and blown out punctuated the judge's speech. An odor of alcohol mixed with the burned tobacco.

George Lindsay, a lawyer of earned and family credits, ignored the obvious, waiting for an opportunity to reason further with the judge. The law clerk, seated in a hard-back wooden chair a discreet distance from the judge and the attorneys, appeared indifferent to the scene being played out.

Lindsay and his partner, Sam Taylor, together with the government attorney, Mike Charbonneau, had come to the judge, seeking a discretionary order not subject to appeal either way the court ruled. But for bureaucratic policy reasons within the US Attorney's office in Houston, Texas, Charbonneau could have acted properly without the order. As an accommodation to Charbonneau's bureaucratic timidity, Lindsay and Taylor sought the judge's written approval to keep things tidy. To no one's surprise, now that the judge withheld that approval, more time and client money was going to be spent to accomplish the goals that all the lawyers and their clients had agreed upon. Such are the day-to-day realities of the legal profession.

Clearly, these lawyers had made an error in judgment. The informal hearing should not have occurred after the judge's lunch.

"I know you fellows would like me to sign this and make things easy for everyone. I'm just not going to do it. I don't want to. I'm sure you understand; well, maybe you don't understand, but I'm not going to do it, anyway." His mind seemed to be wandering. The lawyers remained silent, waiting for the judge to find his mental place.

"That's the way it is. The Circuit can reverse me if they want to. Hell, you know they ain't going to do that, anyway." The judge was more talking to himself. Lindsay's opportunity never came.

Other than to exchange initial greetings, Sam Taylor said nothing during the conference. Knowing the futility of any gesture restrained Taylor from leaving the room. He wanted to smash the judge's drunken face and be done with this charade of fealty. Instead, he forced his mind away from attention to the conversation and adopted the law clerk's indifference. Taylor put his brain in neutral.

His Honor continued to breathe heavily, chain smoking as he went along, and dropping ashes on the couch and his dollar-green carpet.

"This election year, the president may be out on his ass next January, but not me. I worked my tail off every election year and kissed my share of asses, too. I knew our senators, and now I've got this job for life if I want it." Since he had no trial in progress, lunch had been longer than usual.

Taylor's mind clicked inward. *Why am I here,* he thought. *Have I done anything wrong or evil to have to sit in this room and listen to this person? In my other lives, I knew what I was doing was right even if I was not in control. Besides, who cares what he thinks about the president's re-election chances?* Reincarnation was not a part of Taylor's belief system, but he did see his life in distinct stages.

A cloud of blown smoke brought Taylor's thoughts closer to the surface. An urge began stirring within Taylor to leave the room and to keep walking from all this and other things about his present life. At that moment, however, Lindsay's voice, with calculated cheerfulness, broke through.

"Judge, we appreciate your time in visiting with us." Lindsay stood.

"George, any time. You're a good lawyer, for what that's worth."

"Well, thank you, Judge." Lindsay resolved that "any time" would never include the afternoon. "Mike and I will work through this. Thank you again. Sam, are you ready?"

Taylor's protective mask fell away. "Yes, Judge, it is nice seeing you again," the forced cordiality unnoticed only by the judge.

At that point, the three attorneys left the judge, who by then had risen from his couch, dusting ashes from his trousers. The law clerk, a silent eunuch, remained behind as the lawyers left the chambers. The lawyers then passed through the secretary's office into a secure, nonpublic hallway that further isolated this judge from scrutiny.

Taylor barely listened to the ensuing discussion between Lindsay and Charbonneau. They were embarrassed by the judge's behavior and decided to work the matter out quickly. Lindsay and Charbonneau wanted to erase their mental tapes of the unpleasant meeting. They wanted to distance themselves from the spectacle.

Each man lost something in the process of trying to use the judge. Charbonneau came off as a wimp in front of his colleagues for not doing what he had the authority to do. Lindsay saw his cultured variety of manipulation and pandering powerless against this drunken creation of the Constitution. Lindsay rarely questioned his method, just his timing. Taylor lost interest in the present.

CHAPTER 36

Hickam Air Force Base

Hawaii

Hickam Air Force Base, always beautiful, extended a respectful welcome as the airplane landed. An honor guard manned by representatives of each service unloaded the seven caskets.

Each casket had been marked discreetly with coded sequential numbers. A Navy doctor, a lieutenant commander assigned to the US Army Central Identification Laboratory carefully compared the coded numbers with the prospective identity files. His was a politically sensitive job. From a pathologist's point of view, however, the task offered challenges. Recent shipments had not been without surprises.

"Be certain of your results. These may be the end of it," Armstead pointedly ordered. The Navy officer precisely understood Armstead's meaning.

"Where is Doctor Moore? I was hoping to see him."

"He's off-island. He went to a prosecutors' conference in San Diego. He was to speak on cold-case forensics."

"Track me down next week with your preliminary findings," Armstead continued. "Start with A-790. That's the one that might not be genuine. Tell Capt. Moore I missed him and that I am buying the next drink."

The US Joint Task Force Full Accounting Center on Oahu had a sterile title, intended to gloss its gritty mission examining human remains and matching, if possible, those remains to missing American servicemen. Armstead knew the technology had greatly improved over the years, and he expected the Center to use every measure to support its conclusions. The technicians at the Center were well aware of Hanoi's past feigned disappointment at having "misidentified" a Vietnamese national for a US serviceman. Those incidents had been occasional in the early years.

Armstead assumed the Vietnamese would keep the American government suspicious to the end, meticulously checking the remains, such as they were, to ensure that military pomp and ceremony was not wasted on a Vietnamese peasant. The Americans early on assumed that carelessness or the supposed Asian view that life was unimportant caused the occasional erroneous assertion that a particular body, or what was left of it, was American. In reality, the decayed remains of an "Enemy of the State" now and then were sent as a gesture of humor. When mistakes were reported and accompanied with a request for disposition, the usual response, without apology, was, "Dispose at your option." Routinely, the option was cremation and burial in Hawaii.

From 1962 until the collapse in 1975, a little more than twenty-five hundred Americans disappeared in the Southeast Asian war. Neither the news media nor, it seemed, the US government ever quite agreed on the exact top end number. Today, the Pentagon lists all such casualties as presumed dead, with one symbolic exception still carried as "missing in action." As to the exact number, anti-war activists; some veterans' organizations of dubious reputation and motivations; ill-informed, opportunistic politicians; and quick-buck journalists, profiting from the war and their shabby treatment of American servicemen, still do not agree on those missing or unaccounted for. Some still argue that POWs are hidden away in remote regions of Southeast Asia.

David's personal belief about the number really didn't matter. He was certain beyond any question they were all dead.

There were 78,000 MIAs in World War II and 8,100 in the Korean War. The national fetish over Vietnam's American MIAs was now only of academic interest to Armstead. His job was to assist the identification and the return of such bodies as were consented to by the current government of Vietnam.

What disgusted him were the shoddy flea-market peddlers hovering around Washington's Vietnam Veterans Memorial Wall, selling trinkets and t-shirts for their own profit and none to the cause they trumpeted. Unlike other monuments in and around the District, the Wall was a place of sadness, attracting families and comrades of the fallen, along with a host of frauds and wannabees claiming veteran honors to which they were not entitled. To Armstead the

Wall, conceived and touted to cherish the lives lost, perversely dishonors those who made the sacrifice and the nation that produced a generation of men and women willing, if not fearlessly, to go in harm's way. The Wall was just another symbol of protest against that particular war. Many veterans of the last sixty years sense this dishonor and having once seen the Wall, vow never to return.

"Barrett, tell me when we are ready to take off. I'm making a couple of personal calls to the Mainland."

Midafternoon

CHAPTER 37
Houston, Texas

Lindsay and Taylor left Charbonneau in the federal building and walked back to their offices beyond the east side of Main Street. Summer was still several weeks away, but Houston's heat and humidity were already rising.

"Sam, what the hell is the matter with you? You haven't said a word since we left his chambers," Lindsay snapped. His patrician manner had been reserved for the judge and Charbonneau, in that order.

"It's better than the alternatives," Taylor responded in a carefully measured voice.

"That's well and good, but I felt alone. Damn, your face was icy. What were you thinking about?" Lindsay wanted a plausible answer, not necessarily the truth.

Taylor dodged the question. No purpose would be served by screaming out his rage and frustration to someone who wouldn't understand how Taylor came to that point.

"That's easy. I was thinking about pleasant surroundings. This summer we're going back to my friend's place in Minnesota. It should be an interesting gathering."

Taylor saw that Lindsay now was trying to reconcile Taylor's answer with what he had seen on his face in the judge's chambers, something dangerous. He was not interested enough in the topic of summer vacations, however, to ask why the gathering would be interesting

Taylor and Boston had exchanged telephone calls during the last several weeks, figuring how they could get Armstead and a small group of former boat officers together. David now was often mentioned in news reports as a "State Department representative." Curiously, he was sometimes called a Department of Defense spokesman. Taylor and Boston exchanged contrasting news articles. Armstead agreed to the gathering only on the condition that they avoid discussion of the current political environment or his present job, especially in light of the upcoming national nominating conventions.

Their lives took different tracks with less in common now than they had almost three decades before. Nevertheless, many Swifties remained friends with a bond of trust and understanding beyond other relationships.

"Maybe the judge didn't notice you daydreaming," Lindsay fussed.

"Screw him. He was in no condition to notice anything." Taylor enjoyed the effect on Lindsay of his irreverent language.

Lindsay winced and continued grumbling back to the office, his way of signaling his essential acceptance of Taylor's explanation. He was in no mood to argue. For Lindsay, grumbling purged his anxieties.

* * *

Now in his late fifties, Samuel Buckhill Taylor's education and profession bound him to a world of restraint, reason, and order. That world had been less happy and successful than he had hoped. In his view, however, success and a quirky kind of happiness had been found in his prior world of violence, irrationality, and chaos. Since leaving the Navy, his self-image seemed to be measured by missed aspirations. All his life, he tried to do what he thought was right and proper. He felt empty. A person of outward cheer and amiability, inwardly he was alone and detached from everyone except his wife, family, and closest friends. Since Betsy had passed away nearly three years earlier, he was more angry and hostile with everyone. He saw no way out.

Despite being out of shape and overweight by thirty pounds, Sam Taylor projected a self-assured, restrained passion in a manner that reduced client tensions. His résumé was commendable. A local assistant district attorney both before and after his naval service, he became a federal prosecutor in the Houston office of the Southern District of Texas. Entering private legal practice, he also prowled around local politics.

Professionally, he had a strong reputation for careful evidence construction and was particularly effective at building or attacking circumstantial evidence cases. He compared such cases with connecting the dots to form a picture of the truth or lack of truth of a matter. In recent years, he found satisfaction in being known as a white-collar crimes litigator. Taylor had a special understanding of the dark side of man's nature, almost reading a crook's mind.

His marriage a year after leaving the Navy had produced fine sons, Little League involvement, and a pleasant house in a pleasant community. He dearly loved his energetic, outgoing wife. She brought a sparkling dynamic to everything she got involved in. God sent her to save him. Now, their sons, young men in the world, could each be trusted with any important decisions about his life, and he told them so.

Part of Sam was never fully attached to the present. At this time in his life, Sam had played all the cards dealt to him and had no control over, or even much interest in, the outcome of the game. As unhappy as he was, he realized trying to control everything was a formula for controlling nothing. Some of his colleagues in the profession still played the game even though their personal lives were often in shambles. Today Taylor vowed to change directions.

* * *

Arriving in the law offices of Lindsay and Taylor, LLP, they retrieved the usual stack of call slips and went to their respective corner offices.

"Mr. Taylor, you have a personal call holding on line three," Mary Jacobs whined. She had followed him in from her desk.

"Right. Enlighten me on the identity of this caller." The officious bitch had a way of needling Taylor.

"It's Mr. Boston. He always uses those stupid Navy codes." She regretted the unnecessary comment immediately.

Ms. Jacobs, in her forties, was technically skilled and mildly attractive and had normally good qualities for a stable office environment. Her face, however, had a permanent wince etched around her eyes and mouth. Taylor ignored his instincts and hired the woman on the recommendation of one of Lindsay's clients and a glowing reference from another lawyer in a similar business litigation firm across town. Clients can be forgiven, but he should have been suspicious of praise from another attorney.

This kind of employee gets passed around from job to job because no one wants to risk a lawsuit to get to the heart of a bad attitude. Taylor decided to find out what her problem was to see if she was salvageable. She was up for review.

"They're known as personal call signs," he corrected. "Thank you, Mary. I'll speak with him. He shouldn't fool around like that." Taylor's tone was cool but cordial. Mary dreaded those times when Mr. Taylor became polite. She correctly surmised that it was dangerous to criticize anyone close to Taylor. She had seen his kind before. She may have gone too far. As she left his office, closing the door behind her, Jacobs suspected this job might not last beyond the summer.

* * *

"Whiskey—Tango—Foxtrot—my man. How are you doing DB?" Sam Taylor's voice was warm again.

"I'm okay, Prevert. What's wrong with your secretary?" Boston seemed genuinely concerned.

"In case the word hasn't reached Iowa, such ladies are now called executive or administrative assistants, and here we refer to them as 'Legal Assistants.' But right now I am thinking that she's a constipated bitch. Her work is good, and she's a decent enough looking person, but maybe she's blown a fuse. Somebody in the past pulled her chain. One day she is rude, and then on other days she's just pissy. She makes pretty flaky pronouncements about politics, the military, and the presidency. I haven't heard her laugh or seen her smile since she got here. I may fire her." Taylor stopped talking, but Boston remained silent, sensing there was more.

"I knew my luck ran out when I lost my two prior secretaries." Taylor was wandering from the happy subject of the call but knew this helped him formulate a plan about Ms. Jacobs.

"Are you talking about the Sioux Indian woman and that hottie that moved to San Antonio? Didn't you say that the Indian lady is working at some Christian Mission in the Dakotas?" Boston met both women when he visited Houston on previous occasions.

"You got it, Double, although fortunately I never allow myself to think of any of these women up here as 'hotties.' Every now and then we get a corporate client or a small business where they failed to realize that mixing business with pleasure in the workplace often leads to lawsuits. I'm candid and graphic with them about the consequences of ignoring my advice. Guys straighten up when told that while they are planning how to get into some female employee's shorts or thinking about a little light groping, they need to review their financial statement, update their résumé, look for a good divorce lawyer, and fish out their checkbook. It's a threat to their inflated egos." Taylor liked venting to his friend.

Ms. Jacobs had become worse. When Taylor was talking to his service friends, she became particularly sour. With all of that, so far as he knew, she was single and void of a social life. Still, she could turn out the work of four legal assistants, factors that would make the nastiest woman valuable.

"Just so you know, I'm taking notes to share here in our office and the plant. We haven't had any problems and can't afford to have any now."

Taylor was more interested in Boston's news. "So DB, what's the schedule?"

"I don't know yet. I made the pitch to him earlier and just got off the phone. He called from Hawaii, of all things. He's concerned about getting away long enough for all of us to really relax."

"I wish we were that kind of busy," Taylor injected.

"Anyway, I've given him some dates from which to pick, and the rest of us can fall in line. What's your vote?"

"Bill, the way things have gone here today, I'm ready to leave right now. What about Camel and Five Buck?" Richard Leyland and Frank Brooks would be good additions.

"They're in for now. I'll send you the dates to keep open. Got to go now, Prevert. Bye."

"I appreciate your call. Later!" Replacing the receiver, he drifted back into depression. Something had to change.

The day slipped by as a blur despite its emotional ups and downs. In the past few months, Taylor would have knocked down several drinks between leaving the office and bedtime. Alcohol was no solution. He now looked forward only to long walks, the kind he enjoyed with his Betsy. They would briefly discuss business, but more often, they chatted about their sons and their wives. Without that wonderful intimacy, Sam Taylor believed he would perish. They had dreamed of a day when they could spend more time together. That day would never arrive.

CHAPTER 38

Approaching Northern California

After the Navy, Armstead worked in Dallas, Texas for a wealthy businessman, considering that life still offered excitement, reward, and commitment. The work was less in the business world and more in the tangled web of his employer's involvement with the CIA. The Dallas martinet was financially successful, but Armstead concluded he could become one of many drones if he remained with the company. He returned to California. In 1978, he met and married a tall, attractive girl from Casper, Wyoming. Alicia towered over Armstead.

At a friend's cocktail party, a man named Mr. Brady approached Armstead for "an activity not unlike those performed in military service." At subsequent meetings and in the company of others, this gentleman was always addressed as "Mister." His cordiality was ingrained.

"Mr. Armstead, your talents and interest in the welfare of the United States and its missing servicemen are well known. In one little matter, I feel you can provide valuable assistance through your contacts here and in the former Republic of South Vietnam. Are you interested? Of course, you will be compensated."

Armstead had wondered how this refined and precise gentleman could be interested in the murky world of soliciting intelligence operatives. The implications sparked David's interest, and he agreed to "one little matter." He had been well compensated. As time passed, Mr. Brady invited Armstead to work on several little matters not limited to Southeast Asia. His monetary compensation had been substantial, as had his risks.

David and Alicia Armstead maintained a long-distance marriage. Because he traveled so often, they decided to keep their home in California and a stable environment for their growing family rather than enduring the frustrations of living in the DC area, a region that held no charm for her. He kept a small apartment in Washington, DC, and she maintained their home in San Anselmo, California.

Alicia Armstead had an undergraduate degree in civil engineering and a master's degree in architectural history. After the birth of their first son, she aggressively started a building preservation business, specializing in renovations of architecturally significant structures. As the family grew, she sold that business and incorporated another entity, known as Prestoration Consultants. There on a less-demanding basis, she consulted with property owners and third-party contractors to restore anything from an old home to a waterfront warehouse. She was charming and elegant but not a woman to mess with. For Armstead and Alicia, this may not have been the best arrangement, but it worked for them and their children. As it turned out, Armstead was home more often than one might expect, and it was a real home, not a rented apartment or a townhouse. When he had to go to DC, he told her that he was going back in country.

Mr. Brady asked Armstead if he would like to become more directly and publicly involved in advancing the interests of his country. Such vague remarks were predicates for specific intentions. Given Mr. Brady's style and new title, there was little doubt of the importance of the question. David Armstead became legitimized, a term that did not diminish his bastardy, but simply put a civil service general schedule (GS) number to it. He was Secretary Brady's man and not part of entrenched bureaucracy, willing to please only if there was little career risk.

C. Dunham Brady, too, had become directly and very publicly involved in advancing the nation's interests. A tall, portly, white-haired man of intensely honed intellect, he had an exact memory for detail and nuance of the spoken and written word. His speech reflected his analytical skills and was well considered. His voice was strong, deceptively tinged with a Louisiana accent. His manner was always patient, cordial, and correct.

A graduate of Rice Institute in Houston, Texas, he had earned his law degree from Tulane University, quickly becoming successful within the legal profession. The considerable personal wealth he had gathered along the way was incidental in his mind. His profession did not limit him, and in time, he found himself in the relatively small circle of elites whose views are quietly sought by both major political parties and others. His advice was sound and always worked if one was smart enough to follow it.

For years, he shunned overt government service, electing instead to offer advice when sought and occasionally to execute some of his ideas quietly or as a special envoy. In this, he was limited only by his nonpartisan sense of duty to the nation and his personal code of honor. His Senate confirmation as secretary of state had been remarkable only in its genuine unanimity.

Brady's achievements were obtained in spite of and in part because of a progressive blindness that afflicted him in his fifteenth year. He completed his formal education with the help of readers. Today he might ask someone to read a particular document for him. With one eye, he discerned faces, colors, and his environment. With the help of a magnifying glass, he read documents held no more than two inches from his "good" eye. The other eye was gone and covered with a black patch. At a glance, a person might conclude that he was either a diplomat or a retired pirate. In some respects, he was both.

"Go to Paris and meet a back-channel representative of the government in Hanoi, a fellow named Phan. I have in mind an informal discussion concerning alleged un-repatriated American prisoners of war and the recovery of more American remains." Mr. Brady and Armstead understood this assignment was supplemental to protocols worked out with the Vietnamese government in 1988 and acted upon over the next dozen years. "You possess special qualities to help us."

Back-channel conversations were useful and deniable. Brady brought Armstead to the State Department for just such work. He was neither a political hack nor a career drone steeped in the peculiar vagueness and duplicity of diplomacy. Brady wanted Armstead's moral and practical reliability as an offset to State's often narrow, self-serving positions.

Armstead agreed to the trip. Mr. Brady enjoyed the benefits of a menagerie of mirrors and sources of information. David understood that he was told what Mr. Brady correctly sensed he should be told.

Despite muddled and wishful thinking of some interest groups and their practiced and welcomed deceit upon the American public, Mr. Brady knew the mythology of the war in Vietnam had become a public truth for most and a political opportunity for many. He, too, understood there were no un-repatriated servicemen left alive in Southeast Asia. Bringing home American bodies was another matter. He encouraged a broadened mission of our government to make the fullest possible accounting of all Americans missing as a result of our nation's previous conflicts.

Armstead was an advance man for closer relations at a more official level, if appropriate. Brady explained it was unlikely that Phan had any more independent authority than Armstead, and so the two should simply have conversations. Mr. Brady was interested in relationships rather than details.

* * *

Phan Tran Nguyen was a small man with an emaciated appearance. The sparse dark hair on the top of his head was cut short. His facial skin was stretched tight. His forehead was oddly smooth, showing no lines but suggesting prior surgery instead of a worry-free appearance. The scar on his left cheekbone ran to the corner of his lips. Teeth were missing on the front upper left side of his mouth. That side of his face was flatter than the other. His left earlobe was gone. Although not unpleasant at a conversational distance, awareness of the possible circumstances that caused those scars aroused memories for Armstead.

The frail and battered appearance was deceiving. His handshake was strong, and his skin lacked the dryness one would have expected in a man in his late sixties. Despite Phan's loose-fitting Western-style suit and the scars that Armstead could see, it was clear Phan was mentally and physically tough. Like other postwar communist Vietnamese officials, Mr. Phan presented the image of a man that earned his position of power. Phan was neither a professional politician nor fawning bureaucrat.

Armstead's initial impression of Phan in Paris was that he was a hard negotiator. Armstead was told what to expect from a physical standpoint and spotted Phan within his entourage before the two were formally introduced. Phan had a determined look on his face to impress the American representative. The North had won the South, reunified Vietnam, and politically beaten the most powerful nation in the world with a persistent public relations campaign aimed at American civilians. Phan intended that message to dominate their talks. If concessions and advantages for Vietnam could be obtained in exchange for words and a few corpses, hardly more than debris, maybe there were other victories to be won from the Americans.

As Phan and Armstead were being introduced, Phan's manner changed. A peculiar smile crossed his face, and Phan's body visibly relaxed. Armstead believed this to be an act.

Their discussions had been cautious and cordial. Phan specifically denied his government had any American prisoners. At the same time, he implied the possibility that there might be some Americans who elected to remain in Southeast Asia under the protection of unreformed military units not controlled by his government. Armstead knew there were a handful of Americans, not necessarily rogues, who intentionally dropped from sight after the war. Their own families would not have welcomed these individuals home, nor did they count as MIAs.

Phan earnestly stated that his government could help locate more American dead "in order to end the pain of uncertainty experienced by their families." More active cooperation easily folded into the existing program. Armstead hated the duty and tried to maintain formality. Phan maintained his smile.

CHAPTER 39

On the Ground

"Mr. Armstead, we'll be on the ground at Travis in thirty minutes. I've arranged transportation to your home," Maj. Johnson announced.

Armstead's shift in thought was immediate. "Thank you. A low-key civilian car, I hope. It's a little over an hour to San Anselmo. Call the secretary's office and tell them I'll check in tomorrow."

"Yes, Sir. How long before we go back to Hawaii?" Johnson's first ex-wife here was hoping for a few days' visit.

"We'll see. It depends on telephone calls," Armstead muttered. This was a stop of convenience; Armstead needed some down time.

This base was not much different these days with the war in Iraq than it was in the Vietnam period. Civilian contract carriers hauled live men back and forth from the war zone. The dead came home in Air Force transports, usually early in the day to avoid any unfortunate exposure to live traffic.

Armstead looked forward to seeing Alicia and their family. Near the top of Fawn Drive, their home boasted a spectacular view of the surrounding hills and the Pacific Ocean in the distance.

His oldest adopted daughter, a Vietnamese named Justine, was thinking about marriage weeks after graduation from California State University at Fresno. Armstead grumbled about any mad rush into marriage but realized he was no longer as important to her as her boyfriend, a tall former basketball player at Fresno State, now in medical school. Despite the tensions and importance of his public life, David Armstead's private life was unremarkable, and that was how he and Alicia liked it.

As he climbed into the back seat of the dark, full-sized Buick, fatigue overwhelmed him. Sunset was two hours away—perfect timing. He was asleep before clearing the front gate at Air Base Parkway.

CHAPTER 40

Washington, DC

Department of State

"How was your trip? Any obstacles?" Secretary of State Brady began peppering Armstead with questions even as he gestured to a comfortable chair near the window.

"Fine, Mr. Secretary." Armstead had developed a habit of answering one of multiple questions. This tactic allowed him to compartmentalize his answers and allowed him to avoid unnecessarily subjective answers. "We flew out of Vietnam with seven caskets, but one was a ringer. Six came home."

"So I have been told."

Armstead waited for Mr. Brady's next question.

Brady studied the younger man's posture and replayed in his head Armstead's voice tone. "David, is there a problem?" Armstead knew the wheels were turning.

"Yes, Sir, there is. My counterpart, Mr. Phan, is odd. He keeps talking about more bodies but isn't specific. These six we came back with are a good result, but if he has a big revelation, he's not showing his hand." Armstead described Phan's manner.

"Phan has a sense of humor, not like yours or mine. I haven't made light of identification errors, nor have I made any fuss. I've played this straight and accepted him at face value. We could keep dancing like this for the next decade, but there's more. May I tell you my perceptions?"

Brady began packing his nasty-looking pipe in preparation for Armstead's comments.

Armstead, accustomed to this process, knew he should pour out his observations, relying that the secretary recorded every word, inflection, and tone. Armstead also knew this was a predicate for another step by Mr. Brady. Within the upper structure of the Department of State, this other step was called "retreating into Siberia," in which the secretary became essentially unavailable for other business. As the period of retreat lengthened, some would add that he was hibernating in his cave. The result of this activity was always decisive, if not at first appearance cryptic.

"From our first meeting, I've had the disturbing feeling that I met or saw Phan somewhere in the past. Phan has done nothing to dispel that feeling. The Vietnamese language, like others, has several levels of formality depending on the age, gender, and status of the speaker and the listener." Armstead explained what the secretary already knew, but David needed to state clearly his steps of logic.

"Phan is always cordial, but his word choices have been inconsistent with our relationship. For example, when I left him last fall at Noi Bai Airport in Hanoi, Phan invited me to return. He addressed me as a friendly brother, 'Ahn,' you should return again. Perhaps I will have some real bodies for you.'"

"I ignored the familiar and used the most formal term of address, 'Ong Phan.' I asked him if the bodies I was transporting were not real. My word choice implied neither friendship nor brotherly regard, but formal respect."

Mr. Brady slightly raised his hand, "So I am clear on this, you men had been enemies, and although you were fluent in each other's language and in French, your relationship, at least from your point of view, while amiable, is and continues to be built on official distrust."

"You distilled the essence of my feelings. Phan went on to tell me that time changes all reality to illusion and that we might someday find an important reason for truth. He suggested our next meeting, if any, should be in Vung Tau."

Clouds of smoke like that on an outdoor grill rose around Mr. Brady's head.

"I flew in and out of Saigon this last time. We had lunch one day in Vung Tau and it was a nonevent, discussing the weather and the remains of a wrecked ship rusting on the shoreline just north of town. As we parted, he suggested that our next meal should be in the Delta. I told him that I hoped we would continue to discuss truth and reality rather than illusion. All he said was, 'Perhaps.'"

Mr. Brady messed with his pipe. "David, tell me about the ship?"

"I have no firm understanding about it, but it foundered as a consequence of weather and rough seas north of Vung Tau. My belief is that this grounding was not a part of the war, at least not my war."

Armstead continued, "Sir, here are my issues. After all these years, it doesn't make sense to hint of some final truth. Phan knows well that our attitude has cooled concerning any live POWs. We know that is fluff. The prisoner of war issue is now a subject only for fiction and fantasy. A magazine article reported allegations of a North Vietnamese defector that some four hundred US bodies were stored in a Hanoi warehouse, awaiting some appropriate use. That report was made back in 1980. Now, twenty-plus years later, from the Vietnamese view, there could be no positive purpose served by a massive repatriation of dead Americans. That just isn't going to happen. Phan's game is something else."

"David, today it is sufficient that six American families have their own answer." Mr. Brady set the pipe aside and brushed ash debris off his tie and shirt.

"In the climate of this year's campaign, it's not likely that anyone is going to show much interest in Vietnam's MIAs. This war in the Middle East and 9/11 are the big-ticket items."

Poking at his pipe, he continued. "I appreciate what you're doing, and I understand the difficulties that this poses for you. I may ask you to go back, but let's reserve that. Tell me about number seven." Pathology intrigued the secretary.

"Hawaii called me last week, confirming their preliminary analysis. The seventh wasn't a match—not even close. What they gave us were the remains of an oriental male somewhere in his sixties, dead only about four years by their estimation. He probably died of a gunshot wound behind his left ear. Both leg bones had old multiple fractures. The best guess is that he was probably the victim of extended torture followed by execution."

Armstead paused as he watched the secretary slowly move his head from side to side. The secretary had detractors since taking office, but cruelty was not one of the criticisms; it was foreign to his nature. Armstead decided to omit additional details.

"Mr. Secretary, the bait-and-switch game doesn't bother me. But I am still trying to fit together what Phan is implying. If he's got anything worthwhile, I would like to induce disclosure before it is too late." Armstead understood the realities of national elections and memory limitations on passion. There were no guarantees that a future president or secretary of state would be dedicated to the repatriation of those who fell in an unpopular war thirty years ago. Both men examined their private thoughts.

"Maybe you and Johnson need a change of pace. Get your mind off of Southeast Asia. I might find something for you to occupy your time. Your trips over there are grim events, to say the least." Mr. Brady already decided that David was going back and very soon. The break he clearly needed could wait.

"When I took this job, I had plenty of people, including security types, to handle sensitive assignments. I didn't want operatives from prior administrations trying to shape me only to their views. I needed someone that I trusted to be unselfishly candid. You're that person."

Brady continued, "I've kept you away from this war on terror. Middle East conflicts will continue well beyond this presidency. The outcome is doubtful but will stain many reputations. I don't intend for yours to be one of them. The country is in safe hands now, but who knows the future?

"Frankly, this business with Phan has been a welcomed distraction, a puzzle from a no-longer-volatile region. Keep at it."

"Thank you, Mr. Secretary." David wanted to change topics.

"What's your estimate of the campaign?"

Brady lightened his expression. "The president will prevail in November. The Marquis of Queensbury rules aren't much good in politics, and we'll see a lot of shots below the belt. What concerns me most is the role of the news media. When they appear to take sides in a partisan issue, they become only a bulletin board for that side and not a watchdog for the nation. It is unhealthy."

Armstead jumped in, "Is there anyone who bears watching?"

Without a pause, Brady answered. "There's this fellow, Stroud. He did all right in a couple of early primaries, but I don't think he's a serious candidate this time for the top spot. Maybe he wants to be the number two person in the race. Watch and listen to him carefully. His voting record has been careful to avoid controversy."

"He's introduced other candidates from high-dollars-a-plate events to hot dog-and-chips fundraisers. He gives a good speech without obviously beating his chest. He gives the impression that he's not especially advancing his personal political goals. You two served in Vietnam at the same time." The secretary seemed to expect a comment from Armstead.

"Yes, Sir. I know him. He had a nickname. The ordinary guys on patrol boats called him 'the Shroud.' During the time he was in charge of a couple of boat operations, they had high casualties. He was captured during the last op and later escaped." Armstead avoided stating his personal point of view. "The high casualty rate was explained by saying that tough men going into harm's way are going to get hurt."

Brady nodded. "The senator has certainly made progress with his party. He's kept his distance from the rest of the field except for his introductory speeches.

He knows how to get folk's attention with his war record. He never brings it up but has surrogates do that for him"

Armstead resisted temptation. He had no liking for anyone who risked human assets as Stroud had done and later used his military service to further a political career. Stroud grew in prominence in his home state following his escape. He parlayed that into a congressional seat for two terms, and after that, the Senate. Stroud shaped an anomalous image. He was old enough to carry off the role of pensive seniority, and yet he had served with a younger generation of Americans. His political views never drew critical public analysis. Staying behind the crowd kept anyone from looking closely at him. Maybe these years of free passes would someday end.

Mr. Brady sensed David's thoughts.

"David, he's a United States senator. He can't be all that bright, but folks are afraid to attack him because of his war-hero status. The man does seem to have color, and he talks closer to the middle than anyone I've seen around here in years. Senator Stroud is dangerously eloquent in his speeches, something that supports my reservations about him."

The secretary might have said more but caught himself. Glancing over at the huge clock on his credenza, he said, "David, time is getting away from us. Thank you for coming by."

Armstead stood quickly. "Yes, Sir. Thank you for your interest in what I'm doing. Here's a copy of my extended report for you to read, if you wish."

"That will be fine, just fine. You know if I read every paper that came through this office, I'd be totally blind."

Armstead always enjoyed their meetings. This man saw more with his brain than most people saw with two eyes.

When Armstead left, Mr. Brady keyed his intercom to speak with his secretary.

"Judy, please come in here to get this report left by Mr. Armstead. She was through the door immediately.

"Ask Captain Quinby to come by in the next couple of days. I want him to research some casualty statistics in the Navy during the war in Vietnam. One other thing, find out when it would be convenient for Maj. Johnson to visit with me."

Judy was the woman who made things happen. "Yes, Sir. I'll take care of this."

CHAPTER 41

Washington, DC
Senate Office Building

Edward Lewis Stroud acquired the visible trappings of power and influence that drive some men. His wide desk was situated in the corner most distant from the outer reception door. Large windows flanked wall space in that corner. Any visitor, humble or otherwise, was required to cross an open space to greet this man. If the window blinds were open, with their host's back to the sunlight, the visitor's journey was intentionally disarming. The surface of the desk was clean except for a telephone, a legal pad, and a pen set. On a credenza behind the desk was a pedestal-mounted bronze reproduction of the official seal of the State of Indiana.

A door to the left of the desk, normally closed, led to a small private, windowless office and working desk. That desk had a telephone, computer, and a wired printer and was covered by stacks of files and binders. A leather couch was situated so its occupant could not be seen through the open door.

The walls of his public office were crammed with carefully selected mementos of Stroud's every human contact from prep school onward. The images portrayed the owner as an athlete, scholar, warrior, hero, statesman, and politician.

Photographs were everywhere, but of particular prominence was one depicting Stroud's post-captivity return to the United States in early 1970. Stroud was one of the highest-ranking, nonflying officers to be captured by the enemy. His escape, also rare, had drawn national attention for its daring; no less so did the photograph, for it showed Stroud in dress whites emerging from a military transport aircraft, gaunt but smiling. The composition of the photograph, placed over the small credenza, was superb. Most disturbing were Stroud's eyes. That photograph touched all viewers, regardless of their politics about the war. He was, for all observers, an immediate and haunting national hero.

To the left of the photograph was a carefully mounted front-page newspaper headline with text and photograph from the Indianapolis Star. The headline read, "Terre Haute Hero Escapes Cong." Further to the left of the headline, was a dark-framed display of Stroud's military service medals and ribbons including a Silver Star, two Purple Hearts, and the POW medal.

On the right side of the haunting photograph, as it was often described, was a four-pronged brass, free-standing coat-and-hat rack. On the inside hook was a faded dark blue baseball cap. The front of the cap in gold lettering, equally faded, read "*USS Vance* 63–65." Stroud had been reassigned to a new duty station several weeks before Lt. Commander Marcus Arnheiter took command of the *Vance* in Hawaii. The cap remained packed away until after Stroud's election to Indiana's Eighth Congressional District. Stroud was happy to unpack the hat and explain that he had been fortunate in that reassignment to avoid the scandal that later erupted and embarrassed the *Vance* and the Navy. Explanations aside, the hat symbolized one image of Stroud as an "old salt."

On the outboard hook hung a fur-collared, brown leather Navy flight jacket, complete with a gold-lettered sewn breast patch saying, "CDR E. L. Stroud, USN." Nobody ever questioned why or when he, a non-aviator, got the jacket. The jacket had a slightly roughed-up appearance. Two other photographs, one in the office and the other in the reception area, showed him wearing the jacket. One had been taken at a 1987 Fourth of July celebration in Washington, DC, and the other at a 1994 Indianapolis 500 race. Colleagues in the Senate never saw him wearing the jacket at casual cold-weather events.

Also prominent was the photograph of Stroud being sworn in as a United States senator. Conveniently, an American flag fluttered in the background. First elected to Congress during President Carter's administration, Stroud served two terms in the House of Representatives before ascending to the Senate.

This crisp, patrician patriot had managed to make a neat transition, as circumstances required, to becoming a man of the people. He acquired the semblance of a populist. On a small table beside a tastefully upholstered high-back chair were two contrasting black-and-white photographs. One showed the short-sleeved, open-collared Stroud talking with factory workers in Terre Haute, and in the other, conversing with a singular and stoic Muncie area farmer. The chair's fabric was itself a statement of unintended contrast with the two photographs, a field of small white fleur de Lis over a midnight blue background.

Stroud had painted himself suitably for all occasions. Fools would attribute his success and outward power to hard work, merit, and God's blessing. The truth was less lofty and rested squarely on ambition, ego, and a fluke of timing.

As the door from the reception area burst open, two distinctly different men entered. One was Senator Stroud in a well-tailored, two-button navy blue suit, a white long-collared starched shirt, and a power red tie. Stroud was tall and handsome. His brown hair was touched with streaks of gray.

The other man, Billy Fern, was quite different in both appearance and behavior. He was short, fat, and his cheap clothing was disorganized. Physical unattractiveness was not this man's only distinction.

"Senator, I can't believe this. You're whipping their ass every day, and you're not even considered a real candidate. Those polls I've commissioned are beautiful. While those assholes are out there, kicking each other around the block, you're the guy going around the country introducing those jerks with your 'Heal America' speech. Not one of those toads realizes what's going on." Fern's rants were salted with expletives.

The Senator ignored Billy Fern's remarks as he strayed to the corner of his desk and shuffled through some mail. Billy Fern was one of the best campaign mechanics in the business. His appearance and foul mouth concealed a crafty kind of generalship that candidates need but don't like. Stroud tolerated Fern's foul strings but finally raised his hand.

"Billy, don't get carried away. If I'm brokered properly, I know I should remain in the shadows."

"That's true, Senator . . ."

"Look, Billy, you're right."

Fern plunged on. "Stay in the shadows, but we have started opening the shades to let you out and be seen by the general public in a different light. More the statesman, more of, you know, a healer, like this 'Heal America' thing. It's just great!"

The phone rang. The senator picked it up, turning his back to Billy. Billy amused himself by wandering past the various photographs.

"Yes, dear. That's all right. Yes, I know. That's good. Are you sure? I see. I hope you feel better later in the day. All right. Yes. Goodbye."

As he hung up the phone and turned toward Fern, Billy wheeled around and said, "Was that Mrs. S.?"

"Yes, Billy, it was."

"She on the sauce again, Senator?"

"Yes, Billy, she is."

"Senator, you need to take that lady to the Betty Ford Center or something because if you don't, she'll be a disaster."

"Billy, we talked about this before. Mrs. Stroud is quite ill, but if I put her under treatment, that is going to get out."

"Senator, it's okay. People say it's a disease. So why not do it?"

"I can't afford that, Billy." Money was not the barrier.

"Jesus, Senator! You've got to send her some place because if you don't, she's going to die or hurt herself or hurt someone else. She's unstable. Give it more consideration."

"Okay, Billy. Thanks for your point of view." Fern knew he was being blown off again.

As Stroud's public prominence increased, his wife increased her isolation and drinking. It had been a tough job to showcase her only briefly in public appearances. In this particular campaign year, Billy was more than concerned. The senator was holding out on Billy as to the problem, not the problem that she drank or that she was unstable, but why.

Fern knew Elaine Stroud's health was a sensitive subject and resolved to find a facility she could go to that would be more private and less known to the public. Billy had, despite his coarse exterior, a respectful admiration for Mrs. Stroud. She was a kind and beautiful woman, who came from a refined, sheltered background. She inspired kindness and civility in Billy. Elaine Stroud wasn't the strong personality needed for the rough-and-tumble political campaigning that Billy's kind of clients and their wives often got into; she deserved better.

"Hey, these pictures here show you with some guns. Were you a good shot or were these just poses? I remember seeing these when we first met but forgot to ask you about them."

Without pausing for an answer, Billy went on. "What are these?"

"Billy, uh—yes, I am a good shot. My father gave me that small pistol in college. It's a Colt .32 Automatic. It's hammerless, or at least the hammer is inside the mechanism. The other pistol on the right is one my father got in Germany in the last days of World War II. It's a Parabellum '08, 9 mm."

"Looks like a Lugar. So your pop fought the Nazis. My grandfather got smoked in Dachau." Fern's brusque speech hid the deep pain of never knowing his grandfather. He saw his father's lifetime of grief, but like other Jews of Billy's generation, he was angry that so many had gone passively to their deaths in Hitler's concentration camps. In Billy's fantasies, he imagined that he would have made them pay, resisted to the death.

"You might say that. Father was a civil administrator during the war. After the Army rolled through a town, his unit would come in and restore order and public services. By war's end, he was a lieutenant colonel. He came home in 1946."

Stroud's biographical sketch did not include that his father looted furnishings, silverware, and artwork just about every place he went. He also quietly took bribes only in US dollars. Years later back in Indiana, his father, laughingly told business colleagues that he was given the art objects as a commission for his services; after all, "that's what is meant by being a commissioned officer." Senator Stroud did not respect his father but marveled that he got away with corruption all his life.

"You don't see guns like these around today. They look old." Fern never touched a firearm of any kind. He thought the only people who had guns were the cops, the military, rich guys like Stroud, and crooks. Still, the photographs fascinated him.

"Have you still got the German gun?" Fern imagined that this pistol had been taken from a dead Nazi, perhaps one of the men who murdered his grandfather. He wanted to actually see it.

"No, it was stolen in Vietnam. I keep the other one at home if you would like to see it sometime," Stroud responded absently; his mind was refocused on how to delay dealing with his wife's issues until after the convention.

Billy wasn't interested in little pistols—they looked like toys—but he was captivated by the idea that he knew someone who openly owned firearms.

"What do you do with pistols like that? I'd think if you were shooting a burglar, you'd want a big gun."

Stroud thought he was hearing a child. "Billy, I don't really want to shoot anyone. Scaring them with the possibility of being shot can be a pretty effective deterrent. On the other hand, the Colt is a simple thing to shoot." Egged on by Fern's wide-eyed wonder, Stroud added, "That Colt belonged to my father before the war. I keep it hidden in the hallway of the house in Georgetown."

Billy pondered for a moment what it would be like to shoot any pistol, for any reason. *Maybe shooting a Nazi would be good,* he thought. Time and reality came rushing back.

"Damn! I've got to get out of here. I'm working on an invitation for you to speak at the National Press Club. It's a great opportunity. If those poison pens like you, they really like you. So far as I can tell, not one word out of your mouth for the last five years has been negative about the First Amendment. Those jerks don't mind it being abused as long as they are the sole abusers. Check you later, Senator. Please think about Mrs. Stroud." Fern lumbered to the door.

When the door closed, Stroud was pleasantly alone. He reflected for a while on the course by which he had engaged Billy Fern's services, almost as a man would reflect on doing a deal with the Devil or engaging a prostitute for the first time.

Fern got things done, made things happen. Despite his coarse and simple language, the "Heal America" speech had been Fern's concept and substantial writing. Its universal appeal had been Fern's creation. Billy got paid for letting his clients get the glory. Fern was never openly criticized for his appearance or obscene vocabulary. Many candidates had used him successfully. Few publicly acknowledged his help.

Billy's attitude about party lines and special-interest groups was truly nonpartisan. One tenet of Fern's philosophy was that the average party loyal pays little attention to detail. They have no energy for that. What they want is for their candidate to resemble an ideal and not that he or she actually be ideal; public imagination would do the rest.

Another Fern philosophy was that no group wanted a candidate to surrender his principles except with respect to their own special interest. Only a small, sweet bell need ring to get a special-interest group's support. Fern liked sweet bells. These views equipped Fern to shape his clients' image for the greatest appeal.

When he first met Fern, Stroud felt like a horse at auction. Fern looked at his teeth, checked his feet, and the sway of his back. Fern's perception was very close to the truth. Fern made a detailed study of Stroud's background and found no blemishes. In fact, he perceived Stroud as a thoroughbred that could be packaged as a winner, a decorated war hero, a prisoner of war, an escape artist, and capable politician.

The tactical problem that Stroud faced was that Stroud's party had too many candidates, too many so-called front-runners, too many in the pack, and they were too eager to destroy each other before getting the opportunity to destroy the opposing party's candidate. If Stroud had run with the pack, he might have been hurt. No thoroughbred should have to do so.

Instead, with careful planning for three years, Fern packaged his thoroughbred, keeping him in the second tier of runners. Through this device, he became almost better known than any of the individual members of the first tier. There he was less subject to scrutiny. New York's former governor had played it cozy and coy and had stayed out of the pack also. But the word was out on that fellow. They would eat him for breakfast if he came forward.

Stroud was different. Stroud's oldest campaign poster was displayed prominently in the outer office thanks to Fern's perception. Stroud's first campaign for Congress played upon Stroud's military career with the slogan: "We are Proud of Stroud." Stroud's campaign stumps harped on the evils of the Vietnam War and the wrong of being involved in it at all. This sold at a time when America was also preoccupied with the myth that veterans were all crazed, baby-killing, pothead losers.

Later, Stroud gave scant support for the war in Iraq, just enough room to change his mind if that war ended favorably. He was agile in his positions.

Stroud was a vocal supporter of women's issues. Every two or three months for the past several years, Stroud spoke to nationally recognized women's organizations. He didn't really care which side of the political spectrum they represented; he found his place in bemoaning any injustice suffered by women.

If all worked according to Fern's plan, Stroud would arrive at the convention, leading his state delegation amidst the bloodletting of the pack during the primaries. Even if there was a clear leader before the convention, accompanied by the usual kiss-and-make-up press conferences in the name of party unity, there would be a sense that Stroud had been a popular party loyalist without enemies all along. That, coupled with the delusional euphoria of a united convention, would set the stage for Stroud's elevation.

The party's good old boys and girls, the mechanics and pragmatists rampant in both national political parties, would once again point the way. Stroud's party wanted to win in November and would believe that Stroud presented their best opportunity to do so as a vice-presidential running mate to the leader, whoever that was.

This plan was an incredible long shot, a back door to the White House without objective vetting by the press or the revelations of the grueling primary process.

While preaching strains from his theme speech, "Heal America," Stroud, the media would bleat, cleaned and reconciled the political field of battle for the leader. Qualifications, temperament, integrity, and the future of America might all be sacrificed in quest of victory.

CHAPTER 42

Fern's Analysis

Beyond the party convention, Fern had clearer visions. Image was more important than candor, principle, and substantive capability. Perversely, anything questioning one kind of flawed behavior of a candidate challenges everyone's flawed behavior in that category. Thus, such challenges had to be squelched and avoided. Everything was fair play to nourish and defend the suspect behavior—lies, distortions, and false piety.

Billy remembered his father's bitter observation that some people float only in troubled waters. Stroud would never have been in the game without the country being angry and divided over many issues. In Senator Stroud's case, America's guilt over its treatment of its servicemen in Vietnam could be directed to support one of its decorated veterans, an act of voter self-absolution. A candidate generously calling for a healing rather than for an examination of personal responsibility would play softly on the ears of the guilty, attracting in the process some unhappy veteran votes.

Sculpting Stroud as a populist, an admittedly difficult task, would appeal to voters who incorrectly think public and commercial corruption is rampant in our country. A man with the right message laced with impossible promises can make any voter ignore whatever passes for principle and never trip on logic or common sense. Carefully executed, these manipulations can translate into votes. The readiness of the people to accept the words and images of politicians and to make heroes out of mere men and women were all parts of Fern's vision. America's taste for clever nonsense could be a tool at the polling booth.

Billy took this pompous minor aristocrat and made him into someone that the entire public might vote for, if not this year, four or eight years from now. If some Stroud skeleton jumped out of the closet, Fern wasn't worried. He correctly believed that the voting public ignored most kiss-and-tell exposés and memories of a candidate's past indiscretions, unless they were prodded to do otherwise. Condemnations by the other party were accepted as part of the political opera performed every two years. The fact that there had been an earlier Mrs. Stroud, who divorced him soon after the war, was irrelevant. Half the damn country had been divorced, and a hundred percent of those never honestly questioned their role in failed marriages.

A little troubling was a single report that Stroud, supposedly among friends, had bragged that it was important to marry rich girls. Both Mrs. Strouds had been women of substantial inherited wealth. That did not bother Fern too much. Elitists were understood to marry within elite circles and not the girl next door teaching in the public schools. For this reason, Fern was unconcerned about any disclosure of Mrs. Stroud's alcoholism as long as Senator Stroud correctly orchestrated the disclosure. An understanding public sympathy would allow voters to move on and not wonder who or what brought the poor woman to her compulsion for alcohol. Fern was embarrassed to admit that he was actually motivated by a personal and honorable empathy for Mrs. Stroud's well-being.

Fern's analysis was flawless. Stroud, properly packaged, would carry a universal message. The flaw was not in the analysis but in Stroud himself.

CHAPTER 43
Georgetown
Stroud's House

Flanked by a tobacco shop and a small, used bookstore at the end of the block, the townhouse in Georgetown was attractive and unassuming on the outside. Entering the house on one side was a formal parlor and across the wide entry hall, a study. A plain, narrow mahogany table stood to the side of the hallway near the front door.

The parlor was decorated with a mixture of authentic colonial furniture and neo-classical artwork. The large front window facing the street was draped in such a way as to obstruct outside light. Although there was no door into the parlor, that entry might as well have a theater rope slung across it. The room presented a cold, sterile feeling.

The study contained a large working desk of simple lines, two guest chairs, a small sleeper sofa, computer, a combination printer-fax machine, and a small television set. Its large front window, facing the street from the study, was covered from the inside with a finished wooden panel. The same heavy drapery used in the parlor obscures the front of the panel facing the street. A floor-to-ceiling walnut bookcase concealed the inside of the panel. A thick door blocked visual access from the hall into the study. Solitude had been added to cold sterility.

Elaine Stroud knocked gently on the study door. She was wearing dark tailored slacks, low heels, and a cream-colored, long-sleeve blouse. Short, dark hair framed her delicate face. Her make-up, carefully applied, signaled readiness for the outside world. This slender, correctly attired forty-seven-year-old woman had been dressed since 6:00 p.m., and now she waited for a few more seconds before knocking again. A voice responded.

"Enter." Stroud waived her to one of the guest chairs as she came through the door. He still had on his dress shirt and tie. He closed his computer screen and swiveled around to face Elaine. He waited for her to speak.

"I feel better. I know it's late, but aren't we going out to eat?" Her tone was submissive and gentle.

"No. I ate before getting home. Besides, I have work to do." He looked toward a small notebook next to his keyboard.

"I thought you wanted to go to dinner. I am sorry that I wasn't feeling better this afternoon." She began to rise, her eyes now avoiding his.

"You thought wrong. I am sure you'll find something in the kitchen. Doris normally prepares something for you before she leaves."

"You're right. I'll find something and then get ready for bed. Will you be coming up soon?"

"Probably not; I'll sleep down here." Stroud paused. "Elaine, you should remember that I have very busy days and don't want you to call me unless it is truly important. Do you understand?" Stroud spoke quietly but without feeling.

"I understand. I was wondering if I could go back to Indiana to see Mother for a while. That would give you time to work. I would love to see how our house is doing."

Her face brightened with the thought of their rambling Craftsman style home on two shaded acres just outside of Terre Haute.

"We'll discuss that another time. I'll have Lester check on your mother and give me a report." The audience had ended; he turned on his computer screen.

Elaine Stroud quietly moved to the doorway and, looking back, softly spoke. "Good night, Edward. Maybe I'll see you in the morning." As she closed the door behind her, she heard only the clacking of the keyboard.

CHAPTER 44

Emails from Iowa

Bill and Virginia Boston lived on an elm-shaded cul-de-sac. Most afternoons, when Bill arrived home, two dogs of uncertain heritage greeted Bill's Suburban. The short-legged shaggy dog named Dusty usually rose up from a hole he had scratched in the corner of the backyard near the attached garage. He barked mildly with a repetitive cadence as he advanced toward the truck. His linear movement, however, was not fast because he stopped every now and then to chug around in a little circle before moving on.

The taller dog, Budweiser, was shorthaired, with a resemblance to a yellow lab, at least in the face and head. He was fat and out of shape. Even his long tail was fat. Budweiser's chief endearing quality was his bark. Actually, he had never been known to bark in the normal sense; his universal sound was a continuous wooing, lasting as long as five or six seconds at a time. Budweiser would stop walking briefly when his breath ran out, either from wooing or the exertion of walking. Eventually both dogs were able to gather at the driver's door, tails wagging. The dogs were aging.

Their home, dogs and all, was a two-story over a basement and a three-car garage. The house was a 1950s adaptation, reminiscent of a Frank Lloyd Wright design. Ginnie had one car space, and Bill had two. Bill's second space was occupied by a 1970 Red Corvette convertible with a 350-cubic-inch motor, his 1951 Indian 80-cubic-inch Black Hawk Chief motorcycle, and a 1997 Softail custom, 80-cubic-inch Harley Davidson. All three vehicles were carefully positioned in the space and separately covered with properly sized tarps. The convertible had forty-three thousand miles on it.

When Bill stepped up into the home and closed the door, the two dogs stood looking at the door, waiting and wondering what their options were. Finally, Dusty retreated to his hole and Budweiser to the cooling influence of the concrete driveway apron that was added to accommodate their son's beat-up old truck. Budweiser apparently believed his best way of knowing when Tommy got home was to sprawl across his parking space. Risk wasn't in Budweiser's calculations.

"Let me help you with the chopping." Bill dried his hands on the kitchen towel.

"No, set the table. I'll have this done in a minute. Don't worry about Tommy. I'll put some of this aside for him when he gets in." Both knew Tommy would mow through whatever was placed before him and then dive into the refrigerator, looking for more. They enjoyed watching Tommy and his two sisters grow up but with a different joy.

"Pour us some tonic, and we'll sit for a bit while this stuff simmers." Virginia moved quickly in the kitchen. She had arrived home twenty minutes earlier. She was a great cook but not given to dawdling in the kitchen during weeknights. Bill set the kitchen table, put a slice of lime in each glass of tonic, and disappeared into their den. He sat on the couch, slipped off his shoes, and propped his feet on the coffee table just as she entered the room.

Grabbing her glass, she too settled into the couch and placed her bare feet next to his. "Okay, Billy, what went on today?" These little gatherings just before dinner were common, although sometimes it was his turn to ask first about her day.

"I heard from Armstead. He said he thought he could be at the lake from June 26 to maybe the June 29 or 30. If everyone else can make the same schedule, it will be great." Bill paused to eat his lime slice. Ginnie never knew that Bill started eating lime slices in the service bars in Vietnam where the only safe fresh citrus was in bar fruit. Ginnie knew there was more on Bill's mind.

"With you and Tommy coming up on the first or second of July, I was wondering if the girls are coming in?" Bill paused. "Anyway, would you mind if we extended our invitation to include the guys and ... ?" Bill liked using his index finger to stir the ice.

Ginnie smiled at Bill's youthful enthusiasm and waited to hear his other rationales.

"They won't all accept, but it would be wonderful if they did. There won't be a space problem. We can always put one or two couples over in the Petersen cabin." Bill and Ginnie purchased the Petersen cabin five years before just for such occasions and for guests their kids invited when they were in high school and college. Neither girl was married yet nor feeling compelled to hurry their biological clocks. Their son, Tommy, could sleep anywhere, even in the old Grumman aluminum outboard boat tied to the dock.

Bill had been running the numbers and had in mind precisely where everyone would sleep if everyone accepted. He probably even accounted for the possibility that the girls might also bring boyfriends. She felt his excitement.

"And I promise, we'll have the war all talked out before the wimmin arrive."

"Gee Billy, what am I to do? You have it all worked out." She grabbed their empty glasses and started toward the kitchen. "Billy, this is why we have the place. Best of all is to be with our friends and kids. Thanks for asking, though. Of course, go ahead, invite everyone."

Bill also headed for the kitchen. "I need to send an email tonight. I want this settled." Virginia had their food on the table.

Later that evening Bill sent emails to Sam Taylor, Frank Brooks, Richard Leyland, and David Armstead. Blind copies were sent to Boston's two brothers.

OK, guys, Bruno has responded. He can be at the cabin by 26 June. I'll drive up there on the 25th, and we have the cabin to ourselves until Wednesday, June 30. If any of you are flying into the Ely airport, let me know your arrival time, and I can pick you up. No problem. The real problem is getting a connection to Ely. Northwest hasn't yet published its summer schedule. An alternative is flying into Duluth. Keep in mind that Prevert is driving up from Texas. Let him know. He's telling me he's driving through Duluth around 3 p.m., so he can pick up anybody flying in around that time. Save yourself some money. He has one of those big damn Ford Excursions. Pack pretty light; bring a sweater and a swimsuit along with your other casual stuff. Hopefully we'll get good sun during the day and cool nights. If it gets too cold, we can get a fire going. Prevert has been coming up here a lot over the years, and he could get here blindfolded. He won't even run aground, so I suggest that you take him up on his offer. Any of you newbies who insist on finding your own way here, let me know, and I'll fax directions.

The other thing I want to tell you has to do with the 4th of July long weekend. Ginnie and I want you to stay longer, at least through the 4th and bring your wives in on or after July 1. We have plenty of room and a guest cabin 500 feet down the lake. We'll make sure the ladies are picked up at the airport(s) or whatever. If it helps, let them know this is not primitive living. Besides, my brother Cooper has a real house 700 feet the other direction. Rowdy guests and family get to stay there whether he's there or not. He's a former Navy pilot who flew off the Shangri-La. Of course, I'm the mature brother.

There's one condition. We've got to have the war all talked out by the end of the day on the 30th. I look forward to your responses.

Bill had trouble sleeping that night. He was excited to see his friends and open their wonderful Minnesota retreat to these men and their wives. He hoped everyone would accept. His brothers had been great to juggle this with their own situations. As Bill began thinking about food, beverages, and menus, he drifted off to sleep. His last thought was to follow up with Tech Graphics and the copy work he wanted.

CHAPTER 45
Responses

Bill's emails generated responses.

Dear Double:

I'm flying into Duluth on Friday. Got a good deal special. Will talk to Prevert about a ride on Saturday. Mrs. Brooks claims that she will be too busy to take off before the long weekend. That's a crock, so I made NW reservations anyway for her to Duluth that next Thursday. Got a good deal for her, too. She always talks like this, but I know what she really wants. She hopes the women don't get stuck doing all the cooking. I said before there's a reason the Navy gave us our own boats. She thinks it would be fun to see what kind of women married us. I heard three operative words: stuck, fun, and see. And they say men don't listen.

Five Buck

The Academy graduate, Frank Brooks retired as a captain. His wife was thought to be a ball-buster as an effective director of public works for the City of Lexington, Virginia. She knew how to relax when the time came and was particularly good at that when they were out of town. They had one married son, a brilliant man by all accounts.

Bill:

Coming into Duluth Saturday, Northwest Airlines. Flown them before, sometimes sketchy on arrival times. Prevert sounds pretty good. I'll firm up with him.

Carol says she wouldn't miss it. She never met any of the people I knew in the Navy, but she thinks she might have gone to college with Prevert. She knew a Sam Taylor but didn't think of him as particularly perverted. Boy, if her Sam and our Sam are the same, she's in for a big shock. The same flight for her the next Friday. Let me know if I can bring anything. Do they have liquor stores in Ely? Attached is a copy of my business card with all my contact crap if you need it.

Richard

Richard Leyland, Camel, was an accomplished litigator in Dallas, Texas. Although wealthy, he never bought into the social pretensions that characterize that city. He was working on his second master's degree at Southern Methodist University just because he wanted to. This degree was in tax, and the earlier degree was in construction management at Texas A & M in College Station, Texas.

Camel had two special passions: his synagogue and cricket. He was known to decline food, sleep, trial settings, and even clients to attend cricket championships anywhere. At a genteel party one evening, Carol shocked the other guests by soberly and dispassionately announcing that Richard, who was absent, would decline even sex if the option was cricket. They had been happily married since before he served on the boats.

Dear Mr. Boston:

I am Mr. Armstead's assistant. When your email came in for him earlier this week, he was unavailable. I contacted him today about your message. He asked me to pass on to you his thanks for the extended invitation and that he would talk to his wife, Alicia. He will get back to you about her plans ASAP. He expects to be in the municipal air terminal in Ely at eleven a.m. on Saturday, June 26. Will it be convenient for you to pick him up then? He is looking forward to seeing you gentlemen again.

Our family vacationed one summer in Ely years ago on Lake Burntside. It was beautiful. My dad remarked that the whole area looked like a Hamm's Beer ad.

Please contact me if there is anything I can do. It is a fair statement that I have better contact with Mr. Armstead, given his active schedule.

Margaret Lokey

At the time of Ms. Lokey's conversation with Armstead, he was in Ho Chi Minh City, soon expecting to fly out for the States. Armstead told her to respond but not to make any commitment to the extension. He said Barrett would make the specific flight arrangements to assure Armstead's presence in the Ely terminal by 11:00 a.m. He confided that he didn't know if he could be gone that long, just relaxing. She told him that it sounded like a great opportunity to do just that among friends; these people were genuine friends. She suggested that he and Alicia could use this as an opportunity for a getaway time.

Ms. Lokey liked and respected her boss and the seriousness of his work but ended their call with, "Get a life once in a while."

Taylor did not respond. He and Bill spoke frequently enough on the telephone. Sam mentioned the possibility that he might not be able to stay through the Fourth of July. A man in Long Island, New York, Taylor's most consistently lucrative client, was thinking about having a big house party over the long weekend but had not yet made up his mind. Taylor understandably was holding that date open. The client insisted on paying Taylor's full hourly rate, portal to portal, and transportation costs just for Taylor to attend the party. The man was always in trouble over one thing or another and wanted Taylor around as often as it was possible, even when it wasn't really necessary.

Taylor hoped that the client's party would be shifted to Labor Day. Besides, he liked the thought of seeing Ginny and the family. With genuine affection, they called him "Uncle Sam."

CHAPTER 46
Ho Chi Minh City

Armstead and Maj. Johnson had flown commercial in from Japan. Johnson, traveling in civilian clothes, booked himself in coach, but Armstead in first class. Armstead meant to get that economy changed if he could.

Phan sent a young man to the airport for the drive to the Mondial Hotel on Dong Khoi Street. It was two blocks north of the passenger dock on the Saigon River. For reasons not fathomed by Armstead, Phan had not booked them in the nicely renovated Continental Hotel further north.

Dong Khoi, meaning "general uprising," at the end of the war replaced the familiar name to American military and journalists, Tu Do or "freedom" street. Tu Do had been the spine of the red-light district of Saigon.

In the war years, better hotels of Saigon's center became a symbol of American presence. Senior and transient officers, junketing politicians, and journalists teemed. As with all of Saigon in those days, the hotels and the surrounding streets were bustling, crowded with uniforms.

Senior military officers abounded. As with their civilian equivalents, most military executives were well groomed and studied in their manner. Some, but not many such officers, as in every war in every age, had advanced in their careers without risking more on a decision than a wrinkling of a shirt or pair of trousers. These people and their bosses moved singly or in groups of twos or threes. Such men were different from second-tour officers who had "faced the tiger." Combat officers in any uniform, in any land, have a certain look.

Executives required clerical and support personnel to disseminate decisions. These people, too, had a sheltered but cautious look. Job performance normally did not involve physical risk.

Tired, sunburned young men, oddly out of place and uncomfortable in their clean, starched khakis or utility greens, walked the streets in clusters of five or six, feeling safer. In from the field, these clusters would exchange places in the numerous bars or pause a bit, waiting for one of their members to deal with a peddler or prostitute. A cluster might shield one of its own from the attention of the US Military Police or the rough military police of the South Vietnamese Army, the QC. A cluster would move on when threat abated.

Visiting politicians and U.S. government functionaries never quite dressed adequately for the country's weather or street environment. Always sweating through their clothing as though they had been plucked from their offices in Washington, DC and dropped into Saigon with little more than a toothbrush, they always had a harried look.

With the end of the American War, as the victors called it, so ended the names of many of the streets and their character. Gone were the prostitutes and wandering soldiers and civilians; gone were the aggressive vendors, pimps, and noise. Today's Saigon was far different. The only uniforms were those worn by the few police seen from time to time, hotel bellmen, and school children. General Uprising Street was now a quiet, somewhat shabby, though pleasant downtown avenue.

Armstead's room at the Mondial was better than that provided for Johnson. Johnson's was smaller with one window facing a grimy wall of the building next door. Armstead had two windows facing the same grimy wall. Armstead's double bed was firm and comfortable. Johnson's was not. Other furnishings in these rooms were testaments to central committee planning. During their travels in Vietnam, virtually every *khach-san*, or hotel, where he and Johnson stayed had the same styled chairs, upholstered or not, convenience table, and credenza, the finished wood of which had a deeply polished red hue. Television sets, if they worked, presented fuzzy, oddly colored images.

Hotels like the Continental and Delta Caravelle and lavish resorts, particularly the Furama in Da Nang, a joint venture between the Vietnamese government and Chinese investors in Hong Kong, were exceptions. Central committee wisdom had withdrawn in favor of commercial appeal required to attract business and tourists.

Electrical service in Vietnam was subject to failure. Nicer buildings had back-up generators and important equipment, like air conditioning and elevator systems, and they were newer and better maintained. The Mondial was not so blessed. Two acceptable circumstances in these lower-end inexpensive hotels, in the event of air conditioner failure, were old ceiling fans that mostly worked and private bathroom showers. There was always cold water and less often, hot. If the elevators failed, one could wait for repair or try the stairwells, an option that presented its own safety hazards.

Wisely, Phan booked them on the second floor from which a wide, carpeted, attractive staircase led down to the lobby. There was an added benefit to the second floor; across from the head of the stairway was a clean, mostly empty bar with complimentary Internet connections. Internet cafés were found in most big cities of Vietnam, and even if one was suspicious that dark forces monitor every computer, a user could still access Western news sources, search engines, and email providers.

Armstead recognized this critical predictor of Vietnam's future as more powerful than any political, social, or economic policy of government. The erosion of oppressive power caused by access to outside information was obvious. Central committees of a totalitarian state notwithstanding drab or otherwise calculated sameness could not long stand against abundant creative images from the world beyond. Armstead sensed a patient waiting by the younger, energetic generation for the older to move on.

David walked down the hall and rapped on Barrett's door. It was five in the afternoon. "Are you ready?" Armstead for the first time saw into the room that had been allocated for Johnson. "I'm buying."

Both men had changed clothes and were wearing chino slacks and short-sleeve cotton shirts. Walking into the hotel bar, they presented an interesting contrast to the two barmaids. The older, shorter man was burly and powerful, his thinning hair cut short; the younger was slender and fit, his longer hair neatly combed. Armstead heard the girls agreeing that the bigger man was Russian and the younger man possibly was French. They also wondered about the sexual preferences of each.

One of the girls approached the small table the men selected, smiling but not quite sure what language to use. Armstead's Vietnamese language skills had been honed thirty-five years earlier in the bars of Vung Tau on the coast and in the thatched huts of rural villages of the Mekong Delta.

The young woman's eyes widened and chin dropped as Armstead spoke with unmistakable Delta tone and clarity. "Young miss, may I assure you that we are Americans and are both men who admire and respect pretty girls. Now if you will, please bring me some Japanese whiskey, and my friend would like Cuban rum, if you have it. No ice, please."

The girl was stunned but quickly recovered. In Vietnamese, she called back to her co-worker saying, "They are Americans. Really." Her smile and the tone of voice also confirmed the men's gender preferences. Turning back to these men, she spoke gently in slightly accented English.

"Gentlemen, may I bring you anything else?" Both men shook their heads in the negative.

Barrett's Vietnamese proficiency was much more cultured and came from the service language school in Monterrey, California. He and Armstead had been pulling this routine regularly. It was a game for them and a sweet entertainment for all barmaids. Barrett remembered Armstead's delicate rendition of a Vietnamese love song in a bar in Da Nang. Barmaids were always pleased to learn that Armstead was not Russian and Johnson was not French and that neither man was gay.

The girl delivered the drinks along with mixed nuts, including green and red pistachios. She proudly but softly advised, "My cousin lives in Cincinnati." Seeing the smiling reaction of the men, she retreated to the bar, joining her friend in muted conversation, wary that these men might also have special qualities of hearing.

"Barrett, your room is a dump. There's not much to be done about this until tomorrow. As usual, I expect our friend to call me around eight for breakfast." Proper names were avoided in such places. The Suntory whiskey was a good Scotch knockoff.

"David, I'm sure your room isn't much better. Don't worry about it."

Johnson liked Cuban rum, but then he liked all rums. He also liked vodka but had sworn off the nasty stuff in Vietnam. On one occasion, he bought and opened a locally made, cheap bottle from which came a sweet, odd aroma that nearly gagged him. The little bottle was awful even as mouthwash, a reasonable substitute in Third World countries.

"I don't know what he has planned tomorrow. I only know we were told to come here and see what happens. One thing for sure, we're moving to the Continental."

Mr. Brady's instructions had been more specific. "David, get a message off to Phan, asking if you could continue your farewell discussions of last month. Be accommodating but push him—firmly."

Brady had been in Siberia, assessing Armstead's report and now had a clear view not completely shared with Armstead that he wanted to put an end to the games and get solid information from this meeting. He told Armstead, "With the campaign season in full swing, I don't want to be distracted by some foreign government's little games."

They finished their drink. "Let's go to the restaurant at the end of the block. It looks new. Did you see it when we drove up?" David fished cash out of his pocket.

"Yeah I did. Looks promising. Truth is, later let's find that little Mexican restaurant from the last time we were here. They have pretty good stuff."

David agreed. The restaurant was almost authentic Cal-Mex. The wait staff wasn't Hispanic, but the décor and food at the place matched the joints in and below San Diego. The Vietnamese beer also was very cold, the food spicy hot. *Between the Internet and Mexican food, the commies haven't got a chance,* he thought.

As they passed near the girls behind the bar, Armstead gave the girl at the cash register more than enough money to pay for the drinks and gratuity, a 50,000 Vietnamese Dong bank note with two hands and thumbs over. As he did so, he spoke again in Vietnamese, "Young Miss, thank you for the drinks and comfortable table. We will come again." The note was worth a fraction over $15.00 US.

Barrett smiled, and David bowed slightly as the girl accepted payment. When the Americans were in the hall, moving down the wide stairway, the girls launched into loud and happy chatter, delirious over the charm and politeness extended to them in their own language.

Out on the street, Armstead enjoyed the peaceful feel of new Saigon, the shallow curbs and wide sidewalks, the Pedi cabs, and little shops. The buildings had a faded, gracious look. Colonial France had left its mark on the architecture and street design of Dong Khoi.

Old men in baggy shorts and loose-fitting, short-sleeved shirts strolled in twos and threes, softly talking about the things old men everywhere discuss. Even the silent, single old men, hands held loosely behind their backs, moved with a pensive unhurried pace. The puttering of a small motorbike driven by a helmeted young man broke the evening quiet.

Occasionally, a young woman passed, her head and chin held slightly up, her *Ao Dai* gently fluttering with her fluid stride, her long clean black hair rustling like a beautiful horse's tail. The *Ao Dai*, with some design variations, is a traditional long form-clinging gown of slacks and long-sleeve jacket. Although women wore a variety of colors, most often the combined garments were black, white, or mixed. Shoes might be sandals or heels, high or low. Sometimes they wore a conical straw hat or a delicate silk scarf. If the sunlight was strong, these girls might also wear gloves to protect their small graceful hands. David saw them as beautiful, gentle butterflies gliding around the strolling old men. Tonight they were delicate black butterflies.

Barely had they entered the restaurant, when Johnson and Armstead realized their choice was perfect.

CHAPTER 47
Mondial to Caravelle

"Good morning. I hope I am not calling too early. Did you have a good night's rest?" Mr. Phan was cordial and always punctual. The time was 7:59.

"No, no. Thank you. I did have a good sleep. Where would you like to meet?" Armstead actually did sleep well. The air conditioning had not failed. He had been up exercising in the room and had showered.

"We haven't been to the Caravelle before. I thought we could meet there at the rooftop in an hour."

Except for Phan's form of address, the conversation had been in English. Armstead noted the continued improvement of the correctness and tonal quality of Phan's English diction. "That will be fine. Nine o'clock?"

"Good. Mr. Johnson can join us. Chao Ong." Phan was gone.

David wondered about the unusual invitation for Johnson. He dialed Johnson's room. "Meet me at your door."

Johnson was ready for the day. "You're joining us for breakfast at the Caravelle. Can we leave here in forty minutes?" Armstead folded his hands back and forth as though shaping a hamburger patty. Johnson merely raised his thumb and closed the door. Armstead returned to his room.

Armstead and Johnson ritually avoided substantive telephone calls from their rooms and said little more than was necessary when talking in hotels. Johnson understood also that he and Armstead were to be packed before the short walk to the Caravelle.

Both the Continental and the Caravelle hotels along with the Rex had been haunts of military transients and the press corps of the Vietnam War. Often the press correspondents were content to get their stories at the military briefings and the cocktail bars in these hotels.

Garbed in reporter chic, floppy jungle hats, jeans or khakis, and lightweight L. L. Bean fishing jackets festooned with film canisters and armed with tape recorders and Nikon cameras, some ventured into the countryside to get the real stories and report their version of the truth. Hotel bars beckoned the journalists, not only with their cheap alcohol, but also with a ready audience to hear what the war was really about. By war's end, these hotels and bars had been worn down to a dilapidated state.

Today's Continental Hotel, also on Dong Khoi, was a classic example of French colonial design, built in 1880. This four-story, elegant structure had been remodeled and now presented a clean and unexpected opulence that included dress shops, a beauty spa, and three attractive restaurants. The lobby of the Continental was charmingly and creatively furnished.

The clean modern lines of the Caravelle were a contrast to its colonial companion across the square. It was now composed of two structures, the original ten-story hotel with a rooftop bar and restaurant and the twenty-four-floor Caravelle Tower.

Two other buildings of note shared the square: the Notre Dame Cathedral and the Municipal Theater, both built by the French before the turn of the nineteenth century. The French completed the sprawling twin-spired, red-brick church in 1883. While now open for Mass on Sundays, the government did not encourage attendance.

The Municipal Theater, originally designed as an opera house for the French and other Western inhabitants of Saigon, was completed in 1900. This neoclassical building, a smaller copy of the opera house in Hanoi, was painted a bold yellow. A sweeping marble stairway led into the spacious theater. In 1955, the theater was transformed into the home of the National Assembly of the South Vietnamese government. With the collapse of that government in 1975, the building deteriorated. In 1998, the theater was restored to its colonial grandeur.

The morning air was mild and only moderately humid. The streets were busy, but as the men reached Lam Son Square, there was almost no vehicular traffic. Shade had yielded to bright sunlight.

Passing through the Caravelle's contemporary lobby, they found a waiting elevator to the tenth-floor restaurant known as Saigon-Saigon. In the evenings, this place was more a bar than a place to eat and overpriced. Recently the hotel had begun serving light Western-style breakfasts, a touch appreciated by both Armstead and Johnson.

Phan stood as they approached his well-chosen table, somewhat distant from the other patrons and comfortably shaded. Still, the table offered a view of the square and its prominent buildings.

"Chao cac Ong." The men, also in Vietnamese, acknowledged Phan's greeting.

Phan continued with his niceties but now in English. "Your flight was comfortable and your accommodations adequate?"

A waitress brought a single-sheet breakfast menu and a pot of French roast coffee, pouring some in each cup. Real cream, not powdered, was already at the table. She wordlessly retired.

"Yes, the flight was fine, and we found a very good restaurant near the Mondial. A real treat." Armstead's pointed praise ignored the quality of their rooms at the Mondial.

"I suspect you were disappointed in the hotel, but I had my reasons and want to make up for any inconvenience the Mondial may have imposed for either of you."

"Thank you for your concern, Ong Phan. This is only a passing matter. I am more interested in our plans for the next few days." Armstead was eager to get on with business.

The waitress returned and took their orders. Even Phan ordered bacon and eggs with croissant.

"Yes, I understand." Turning slightly, Phan looked out over the city to the north. "Vietnam is a beautiful country. It is sad that its past has been so difficult. As a small boy in the North, my family dreamed of driving the French away from our land. We had no idea that it would take so long and be so costly to do that and then to rid ourselves of you Americans." There was no bitterness or anger in his words or tone.

For the first time, Phan was showing these Americans his private thoughts. Johnson and Armstead remained silent, not wanting to interrupt this moment recognized by both as rare.

Phan paused. "I would like for you to see my country, to see it as I have and to know that its people are as good as any on Earth."

David decided to speak with compassion. "Ong Phan, we too did not realize how long it would take for us to leave, but I assure you, we never came to stay. It was costly also for us, almost beyond our understanding. Even today there is a smoldering hostility within my country over our involvement in Vietnam. Sometimes I feel burdened by that as much as I suspect you feel sadness within your country."

Johnson was uncomfortable with the intensity of the dialog between these two former enemies. Relief came with the waitress: food and fresh coffee.

Phan, too, welcomed the interruption.

Johnson took his opportunity to speak. "Until I traveled with Mr. Armstead, I had never been to Vietnam. It's a beautiful land. I was too young to serve here, but from my perspective, the war had upsides. We have some great Vietnamese food in the United States, and my ex-wife can't stay out of Vietnamese salons."

Armstead was surprised at Johnson's shallow view of the consequences of war, but Phan saw the irony of Johnson's train of thought and laughed.

"Yes, we gave you café and salon workers, and you gave us half-American children. Then the Russians came to 'help' us. Not a good trade."

Barrett laughed. "That makes us family, of sorts." He tipped the last of his cup toward this Vietnamese gentleman. David smiled and joined him.

The moment retreated.

"I have a proposal and a request of you both." Turning to Johnson with a steady look, he said, "Tieu Ta, would you forego your bodyguard duty for two of days? David needs to accompany me to Can Tho so that I might show him something. If you will permit this, I assure his safety. Besides, I know him to be capable of protecting himself if need be."

Johnson raised both hands slightly but said nothing.

"David, if you will go with me, you will find what I have to show you very engaging." This was the first time that Phan ever used Armstead's given name. Armstead thought the word *engaging* seemed unusual in the context of their discussion. Maybe he would not have to push Phan as much as Mr. Brady had thought.

"I would be happy to go with you, but what about my caretaker here?" Armstead gestured at Johnson with his thumb.

"He might move to one of our nicer hotels. I did not want your mutual privacy intruded upon as it might be at more prominent places. Our ordinary hotels attract little attention."

As a practical matter, placing listening devices in every room of every ordinary hotel in Saigon was impractical. That they avoided talking business or schedules in unsecure places did not diminish Phan's thoughtfulness.

"Barrett, find that Mexican restaurant tonight and tell me all about it. Stay here or across the street. I'll find you when I get back." Turning to Phan, "When do you want to go? I'm packed."

"My driver from will pick you up at the Mondial in thirty minutes if that is enough time. Be down near the door to the place you ate last night. We have a long drive, maybe five hours or more."

Both Americans realized these were private arrangements; Phan was not interested in anyone knowing where they were going or why.

Mr. Phan picked up the check, and they left the cafe. In the Caravelle's lobby, Phan walked away without further farewells. Barrett left his room ahead of

Armstead but checked out of the Mondial after Armstead. Johnson had been in the second-floor bar and logged onto Yahoo sending his "sister" a quick note.

Dear Rachel:

Just to let you know, your bro got here safely and had a wonderful dinner last night. Shopping around today to find what you asked for. Got plenty of time today and tomorrow. My buddy has struck off on his own. That's OK; there's a Cal-Mex place here that's almost as good as the Mexican Village in Coronado. I'll eat there tonight. Saigon really is beautiful, seductive.

BJ

As Johnson stepped out under the hotel awning, he saw Armstead near the end of the block as a light-gray, four-door Toyota Corolla drove up, stopping long enough for him to get in. Johnson wondered if he should have acquiesced to this plan. Armstead wasn't a man to go unnoticed in Vietnam, much less any other place. Barrett walked in the opposite direction toward the river, eventually working his way back around to the Caravelle. Saigon-Saigon reportedly had very good Cuban rum even if it was pricey. The next time Johnson used Yahoo email was to send a message to yet another "sister", Sue.

CHAPTER 48

Drive to Can Tho

When Armstead entered the Toyota's front seat, he saw that the driver was a lean, clear-faced, well-groomed young man about twenty years old. David greeted him in Vietnamese, but the boy responded in nearly perfect English.

"Good morning, Mr. Armstead. My name is Vu. My father has spoken highly of you and the work that you have been doing." He placed Armstead's bag in the back seat.

"When I pick up my father, you can sit in the back where it is more comfortable." David's mass was more appropriate for the back seat.

"Where did you learn your very good English?" David was surprised. This boy had the shape and general appearance of the motorbike operator he saw the preceding evening.

"In school and from my father. Actually, we have you to thank, in a way. My father's English improves every time you visit here.

Vu turned northeast onto Le Thanh Ton and pulled over to the curb. Armstead stepped out and moved to the back seat just as Mr. Phan came up to the passenger side. Vu moved the car into the traffic with reflexes common to his age.

"Father, I have your valise in the trunk. We were just talking about our English lessons."

Phan smiled and looking back at David, said, "Those are valuable lessons. Do you suppose you could remember your driving lessons as well? We are not in a rush. You may slow down, and maybe Mr. Armstead and I will be more comfortable." Phan and Armstead met eyes in the universal understanding of fathers about sons.

Vu complied and moved more with the flow of traffic. Saigon's streets, while there was a pattern, were not laid out on a grid. Again, the French had left their mark. Moving out of the city center, Vu raised the windows and turned on the air conditioning. A short time later, to the southwest, they connected with National Highway One. Can Tho was 165 kilometers away, a little over a hundred miles.

Vietnam's National Highway One runs from the country's northern border with China to the Ca Mau peninsula, flanked there by the South China Sea and the Gulf of Thailand. From Saigon, the highway meanders along the north side of the Mekong River past My Tho to a point opposite Vinh Long near the Mekong's intersection with the Co Chien River. The road, not a highway in the Western sense of the term, is long and bumpy, including two ferry crossings: one just west of Vinh Long and the second across the middle Bassac River. The drive, including ferry waits and other stops along the way, can take four to five hours. Everything from foot traffic and ox carts to noisy, smoke-belching trucks uses the roadway. Traffic stops even for waddling groups of ducks and geese or to drive around piles of rice drying near the shoulder of the road. Progress had, however, come to the Delta.

After a light lunch in My Tho, Armstead settled in for the more difficult part of the drive to Can Tho. The air conditioning was working, and the stops so far had been minimal.

"David,"—again the address by Phan was familiar—"you will be surprised with what you will see shortly."

Armstead had decided to relax and play the tourist. The region, so familiar to him, was always interesting. He felt energy within that did not always accompany him on government trips. He leaned forward in the back seat to look out the windshield. His breath stopped for a bit, followed by a whispered, "I'll be damned."

A huge suspension bridge had been built across the Mekong, its towers and large, blue, drooping cables now visible for miles. It looked like a gigantic inchworm crawling over the flat landscape. The southern landing of the span is between Long Binh and Sa Dec to the west.

The driving surface of the bridge is well above the river, almost 125 feet at its highest, accounted for masts of large commercial vessels traveling to Phnom Penh, Cambodia. Although its over-water span is slightly under a mile, the built-up road surface on either side leading to it adds another mile to the profile of the bridge.

The My Thuan Bridge opened in May 2000 and was built at a cost of fifty-two million dollars US. One-third of the funds came from the Vietnamese government and two-thirds from Australia. The bridge is not only a substantial commercial opportunity for the investing nations but will dramatically change the cultural, social, and economic fabric of the southern Delta. Time will tell if that is a positive change for its people.

Armstead felt old as he remembered the primitive, isolated Delta of his past. He remembered the cheerful wrinkled old Bas on the water taxis and their easy closeness with the rivers. No *Ao Dai*s for them. They wore sandals, baggy black pants, and light cotton short-sleeved blouses. If their heads were covered at all, they wore the conical straw hat or a common cloth scarf. There were no gloves and no other protection for their skin as so carefully observed on the butterflies in Saigon.

Armstead recalled visits to village schools during the war and the clusters of laughing kids that surrounded him. He supposed these children would grow up, marry, work, and die without ever seeing the lands beyond the southern Delta, or for that matter, without even caring if such lands existed. He now questioned how much of that would exist in years to come.

"I knew you would like this. If we share much in common, it includes not liking ordinary tourist sights and memorials to the American War." Phan massaged the scar on his cheek.

"I don't want Vu to forget what this was like before that bridge, before I came here from the North, and before you came here from America." Phan, too, seemed to be gaining energy as they now passed Sa Dec and moved on toward a ferry crossing. They had been traveling a little over three hours.

CHAPTER 49
Can Tho

The town of Can Tho faced the Song Can Tho, an elongated loop of the Bassac. Its riverfront consisted of small shops and a few squat old hotels and restaurants. Can Tho's tourist attraction was the floating market on the Bassac River, a few kilometers to the southeast.

Phan and Armstead checked into separate rooms at the Quoc Te Hotel while Vu found a good place to park and unload the Toyota.

The Quoc Te or International Hotel fronts on a wide street that parallels the river. The whitewashed building's exterior was simple in its lines. The tiled lobby, without air conditioning, was comfortable as ceiling fans slowly circulated the humid air. The rooms were clean and adequate for the locale.

Armstead washed up and returned to the lobby, joining Phan and his son.

"Let's take a boat ride before dining." Phan seemed the ever-cheerful tour guide. They stepped out through the wide, doorless entrance into the street. Beyond them was a quay wall and periodic landings to the water. Just south of the Quoc Te, Phan walked down one of the landings where a man in his mid-forties was sitting in his motorized sampan.

In Vietnamese, Phan negotiated for a short sightseeing ride. The local Central Committee was not as stringent in its control and extortion of local commerce as in My Tho and elsewhere. Boatmen were allowed to supplement their meager incomes by hauling tourists in competition with the committee-sponsored services.

The sampan engine resembled a large Briggs and Stratton lawnmower motor mounted on the stern in such a way as to pivot and swivel. Protruding from the engine was a six-foot-long steel shaft to which was attached a four-bladed propeller, approximating the diameter of a salad plate. The boatman could lower the shaft of the spinning propeller into the water and adjust its depth as required by the water below the hull.

In the war years, David Armstead had seen and ridden in many of these long-shaft sampans. They were fast, light, maneuverable, and capable of safely carrying heavy loads. The VC often used these slender boats, ten to twenty-five feet long, to move themselves and supplies across and down the rivers and canals.

On one occasion, David recalled having found and destroyed a twin engine long-shaft sampan, a real gunrunner. As the concussion grenades blew out the bottom of the boat's stern, sending the two shafts and motors spiraling away in separate directions, he thought of whiskey smugglers and their high-speed boats used during the Prohibition era in America.

Armstead respected these boats and their skilled drivers. He often wondered what it would be like to import one of these into the United States or to make one for pleasure boating or fishing. He assumed government and Coast Guard regulations would spoil the fun.

Bargaining concluded, the four men boarded the sampan and sputtered out into the channel. Phan spoke in English. "My friend here neither speaks nor understands English."

Safely away from other traffic, the driver brought up the speed to move down the Can Tho and onto the Bassac. Within ten minutes, he made a sweeping left turn into a small, jungle-arched canal. His speed dropped to a gentle glide along the stream, no wider than twenty feet. The banks were thick with brush, and though sundown was still a little less than two hours away, the shade was significant. Periodically, the jungle would thin as dappling light covered the boat and its passengers.

Phan, Armstead, and the driver instinctively slouched into the boat, eyeing the canal banks. Only Vu remained upright. Phan talked with his son about his own memories of Delta canals thirty-five years before.

The driver stopped twice to drift under two footbridges and between the narrow, crossed pilings supporting them. The walking width of each bridge, four feet above the water, was no more than eight inches. Further into the canal, the jungle opened, and the canal widened another ten feet. Small mud-walled, thatched-roof huts were visible on either side. On closer inspection, the tops of the canal banks were marked with footpaths. A local woman was seen standing in her doorway. Two small children playing on the bare ground in front of her home stopped and looked at the passing sampan. Further on, two young boys and an older girl ran along a parallel path, chattering and calling to the driver.

"Those are his wife and kids," Armstead ventured a guess. Phan nodded.

This is a world far away from politics and government and raw power, wherever it comes from. These are people as good as any on Earth, David thought.

Still further, the canal widened to forty feet, and the jungle retreated. Fields opened, and more homes could be seen. Three small houses, much newer than the traditional huts, fringed the field on one side. These houses had high-peaked, smooth-metal roofs. Each had a porch across the front, shaded by a smaller, slanted corrugated metal roof supported on the outside by posts. Each was only different in its vivid color: blue, yellow, or bright green. These little homes were not unlike Cajun shanties found along bayous of South Louisiana. They could not have had more than two rooms, another product of central committee thinking—a standardized house kit.

On the other side of the canal was a dilapidated dock, thirty feet wide and clearly unsafe for any purpose. Nestled in a grove of tall rubber trees a hundred yards from the dock and surrounded by crowding vegetation was a two-story French colonial plantation house. A rooftop extension over the upper deck sheltered another full-width porch down below. Six tall, matching shuttered windows were on the front at both levels. Similar shuttered windows were on the side of the house. Paint had long ago peeled and fallen away. The front door was gone. The second-story roof showed a large hole at one end. Some of the shutters were missing or hanging crazily. Time and the jungle were eating this mark of past French presence even as the Vietnamese themselves were building new homes with a Gallic flavor.

Other sampans were tied up along the sides of the canal, some to primitive docks. The distinct smell of wood smoke drifted in the air. Ahead a hundred yards, another rubber tree line rose from the land, and the canal bent to the left. Passing between the tree line, the canal suddenly spilled into the Bassac River with its broad ponderous flow to the sea, miles downriver.

The passengers looked back and knew they had passed through a kind of paradise. Perhaps the driver did not think of his little stream as paradise, and the older men certainly knew the savage hell that had once surely exploded there. Only Vu seemed innocently enchanted.

"I think he's taking us back to Can Tho. The sun is getting tired, and we should eat." Phan smoothed his wispy hair and massaged his scar.

"Mr. Phan, all we do is see sights between meals. Life here can become simply an activity to pass the time until the next meal." David was being pushy. However, he would always remember this little trip through paradise.

The driver dropped them off at another landing just across from the Mekong Restaurant, an open-air cafe not far from the hotel. Their table was close to the sidewalk and the street beyond. A short distance south along this boulevard stood a large statue of Ho Chi Minh. Passersby took no notice of the tall statue.

Phan and Armstead ordered beer. Vu ordered Coca-Cola. In the half-light after sundown, the four remained silent for a time, enjoying the beginning of evening.

Delta food had not changed through the years. The men ordered interesting soups with a mix of greens and chopped-up things that swim or live near the water, salad rolls, steamed vegetables, and hot rice. Small portions of cooked pork or chicken blended with different sauces were offered and ordered from the worn-out menus. Other beers and Coke appeared as the food was brought to the table. The conversation had been pleasant and light. Armstead felt comfortably at home.

When the dishes were cleared from the table, Phan ordered a large warm carafe of local rice wine, Ba Se De. Vu cleared his throat and spoke. "Father, you and Mr. Armstead may want to talk, and I would like to wander about."

Phan responded, "Remember this isn't Saigon, and we have an early morning." Vu smiled and was gone. David shook his head, knowing that parents aren't so different after all.

The other patrons, mostly Vietnamese, were seated in the back of the café near a television set and the bar. Television was more interesting to the locals than the tourists. Two tables somewhat nearby had only Western tourists, two German university students hitting the beer with enthusiasm, and a table of three Italian girls with their delicious burnished skin and long, dark hair. They too, were drinking beer, but without the zeal of the young men. Both groups wore light-colored, loose-fitting pants or shorts and shirts. David and Phan assumed the two groups would join sooner or later.

CHAPTER 50

Mekong Restaurant

From long experience David Armstead knew the culture of serious conversation in Vietnam. It was rarely to the point, always predicated with insignificance and never rude. Real conversation must be unhurried and relaxed; mutual trust was essential.

When David was first assigned to Coastal Group 35 as the junior advisor and only other American, it took six weeks before any meaningful conversation with the village and hamlet leaders occurred. Quiet conversations did not just happen. Sizing up the participants took time, maybe days or weeks. Sure, one could function and communicate during this ambivalent period, but real understanding always took time, and not everyone was patient. Americans especially were not frequently geared for patience. Even now Mr. Brady, known for his tolerance and courtesy, could not afford the patience needed in this land.

David remembered his first real conversation that occurred in a small deckhouse of a solid Yabuta junk, a tough, Japanese-constructed wooden boat that could absorb a lot of punishment from the enemy. The junk was tied up to the dock on a side canal beside the Coastal Group compound. Three headmen in the village invited David to join them for beer and other refreshments. A light breeze from the nearby sea filled the deckhouse with salt air.

The men gathered, sitting cross-legged or comfortably squatting on the deck. They could not do otherwise; the ceiling of the deckhouse was at most only five feet high. On the deck in the center of the gathering was a large, shallow, enamel-covered bowl with a block of ice sitting in its middle. A case of half-liter bottles of beer was nearby. A young woman, the daughter of one of the headmen, opened and poured five bottles over the block of ice and withdrew. Next to the case were five ceramic coffee mugs that a headman handed to his companions. In order of age, each man dipped his mug into cool beer and drank. The fifth mug, prettier than the other four, was set aside.

As they drank and refilled their mugs, they began talking about the conditions of the perimeter fortifications and the safety of those living within or working the fields beyond the wire and the mud-walled, steel-roofed bunkers. They agreed on procedures for moving people into the relative safety of the compound and protecting the children. They spoke of the availability of Swift Boats and air cover to help them in time of attack and when the boats might bring a Bac Si, or doctor, to look after them. More often, this was a Navy corpsman and sometimes an informed and helpful boat officer. All this occurred as more bottles were opened and poured over the diminishing block of ice.

The young woman returned with small bowls, big spoons, and chopsticks. She also brought in a large bowl of pho, Vietnamese noodle soup with cooked fresh greens, and a smaller bowl containing a reddish curdled mass. Armstead never blinked when he learned that this was congealed chicken blood, a delicacy.

When darkness fell, the woman returned with two candles and a small chunk of ice. More beer was poured. Then the oldest of the headmen took the fifth mug and dipped it in the beer. He gave a toast and handed the full cup to another headman, the person he had toasted. That man drank and then dipped the mug and presented a toast and the mug to another.

Finally, the oldest headman took the mug, filled it, and toasted David. The gist of the toast was to express gratitude that David had come from his land and safety to help them and that he shared their risks to fight the communists. From that point they were brothers.

Even today, Armstead remembered the feeling in his stomach and his throat when the mug was passed to him. He was almost speechless, but protocol demanded more. He drank from and then dipped the mug reaching out to pour some beer into the other mugs. His toast said that he was honored to be there to share their lives. He hoped to prove worthy of their friendship.

Likewise, Armstead's memory was clear today that there had been no discussion that theirs was a civil war, a righteous war of unification, or any invasion by the United States. He knew then and now that the men around him were fighting for their own freedom against what they considered invaders from the North, and he was there to help them fight for that freedom.

Not everyone was patient or tolerant of the cuisine. One day, David invited Bill Boston to go with him to a large island in the middle of the river. There they joined one of the headmen and his other guests for beer and refreshments. After the beer had taken its toll on the young American, the chicken blood nailed him. Boston did not remember leaving the small hut or his trip to the outhouse and his irrational damage to the structure. As he was stumbling back to the hut, David met him and took one long swing at his jaw. Boston dropped like a sack into David's arms. Armstead hoisted the limp body onto his shoulder, bid goodbye with apologies to their host, and delivered Boston to the deck of his Swift Boat, ordering his crew to bed him down and patrol out in the middle of the river until the next morning.

A few weeks later, Armstead invited Boston's new patrol partner to a deck-house event. Sam Taylor handled the whole affair with more charm and tact.

CHAPTER 51

Later Mekong Restaurant

"You have a fine son, Ong Phan. You should be proud. Do you have other children?

"My wife lives with me in Ho Chi Minh City; we have no other children. You have children? If so, you are blessed."

Mr. Phan never used any language intimating a spiritual awareness.

"Your boy seems very intelligent and quick. I have three sons myself and believe they are fine men. I also have two beautiful daughters."

Phan nodded.

"Yes, Vu reminds me of another young man I knew many years ago. They could have been brothers. The world needs young men like that."

The men paused. The German students stood and moved toward the Italian girls. The Germans had silly, hopeful grins on their faces, and the Italians smiled and slightly lowered their heads.

"Today you said that you wanted Vu to know what it was like here before you came south. How did you get here?"

"I walked. Sometimes I ran and often crawled here first in 1969. There were 160 of us, but by the time we got to our destination, there were few left and no junior officers. My Trung Ta died in Cambodia."

Armstead needed to be careful about the past. He did not wish to intrude or provide an opportunity for anything but useful candor.

"I assume from your present age, that you then led this group. Were you successful?"

"Yes, maybe so. I survived with two others, obviously at great cost." Phan absently touched his scar, seemingly lost in his memory. "We captured an American officer, but he later got away."

Armstead hoped his face and eyes did not betray his private pleasure in that result.

"After our victory in 1975, there was no reason to return home. I remained in the South, working in the new government. I relocated people and reeducated them. Maybe I helped them." He drained the wine from his small glass.

Looking steadily at David, Phan continued, "My first wife and two daughters in the North died while I was gone."

Armstead resisted the impulse to shift in his chair. "Did we do that?"

"No, David. They died in 1974 from a disease, an epidemic. The People's State was not a healthy place, even without American bombers."

The familiar address and the answer relieved Armstead. David ignored the implied cynicism concerning health in North Vietnam.

The Germans now seated with the Italians, probably dreamed of greater companionship. More beer was brought to their table. Now no one was near the American and his cordial guide.

Phan straightened in his chair and poured more rice wine for them.

"David, you did not come ten thousand miles to be a tourist and to hear about my past, although I have enjoyed showing you today's Vietnam, and I don't mind talking about the past."

"Ong, while it is my job to be here and to listen, I am honored that you would spend your leisure time with me rather than your son and your wife."

"The past can be very important for what it tells us to do and to avoid in the future. You and I are getting too old to fight wars. We have come to the point of thinking about greater purposes. I met a man in Paris early last year, who told me that older men should have perspective. I have studied that English word and think it is a good word, capturing what my language says in more words."

One of the German boys moved around the table to a position between two of the Italian girls. Although neither Phan nor Armstead spoke of this, they both thought they were witnessing a mating ritual.

"Now to business." Phan's tone noticeably changed. "I tell you with all certainty, Vietnam has no American prisoners of war, nor do we know of any held elsewhere. I have known this since before we first met; you know this also."

"That is true. Thank you for saying this. In my country for many reasons, some people want to believe otherwise. They are victims of their heartbreak and the greed and ambition of others, little more. Others thrive on that lingering natural sadness and suspicion of the American government. These became steps in their path to higher public office. It has always been so with people like that. Maybe you have those in Vietnam?"

"Yes, we do. As for your soldiers who are missing in action, you and I can continue to visit sites and go through the procedures of sending them home, but the numbers will be few. There is no secret hoard of Americans, living or dead, despite what people may say or suggest."

Phan was speaking with absolute honesty. Armstead's experience and his heart told him this.

"I agree. My government tacitly recognizes the reality of all wars that despite our best efforts, some never come home. Soon we will see a shift in my government's emphasis from Vietnam's missing to all Americans missing in action wherever they may be. Again, thank you for saying this."

Phan understood tacit recognition often was all there could be. These mutual representations cloaked a deeper understanding between the men.

"Your remarks are particularly appreciated when I consider that in the range of three hundred thousand of your soldiers are missing. The word *perspective* comes to mind."

This time, David reached for the carafe of wine and poured the last of it for them. Phan smiled. Armstead had been listening intently.

"Mr. Phan, do you believe we should continue these missions, you and me?"

"Possibly, but I may no longer be involved after this trip. My superiors believe that I have too long enjoyed this assignment."

"No offense intended, but I wish mine would."

Again, Phan smiled. He liked Armstead's dry humor.

"David, is your country having a national election this year?"

Armstead knew damn well he knew, but he nodded.

"From what I have studied and Vu has told me, your country's political selections are made differently than here. In Vietnam, elections are less important than being selected for candidacy. Here, election is a conclusion; candidacy is not. In your country, both are important and uncertain until the people have voted. Your candidates publicly make dishonorable and coarse statements that we avoid, even in private."

Armstead wondered where all this was going and what sources Phan had consulted to have this understanding.

"Vietnam handles failure differently. In your country, a candidate who fails simply regroups for another day or quietly retires from politics. In Vietnam, political failure of any kind means humiliation, isolation, and sometimes death. Our way has too many consequences and yours too few."

"Here, we know the bad persons will not get far, and if they do, there are ways to soften the damage they may cause. In America, the bad ones have a better chance to succeed, and you don't seem to have much to prevent the damage they do except to wait for the next election."

"I should call you Giạo-su; I'm in a comparative political science class. After this, maybe you can find a position as a teacher." Armstead's light remarks were also serious. He decided not to get into America's constitutional requirement for separation of powers.

"How do you perceive your courts and the law? Do you trust them, and do they work for common good?"

The professor pressed the student.

"We need more wine for me to completely answer, but I can give you a short answer."

Phan crossed his arms in interest.

"Men and women are a problem everywhere. America is no different. Our people's representatives make the laws. The people sometimes select judges. More often, small groups or individually powerful officials do this. Many of our laws are passed with good intent, but we have lost perspective"—he paused on that word and smiled—"on common good. Today common good may mean pleasing only the most voters, rather than what is objectively good for the entire country, poor and rich. We are divided and not equally so." David had long held these beliefs.

"I have another word for you to study: *idolatry*. We have a lot of that in America, and it shows up in selfish ways. When I say that men and women are the problem, no laws or courts are going to work well for the common good when an attitude of selfish idolatry prevails. Do I trust the courts? Sometimes. Do I trust the laws? Mostly. Do I trust the wisdom of the people? On that one, I pray."

"David, we both should teach. It is late, and I have another adventure for you tomorrow morning. At 6:30, the boatman's wife will be in front of the hotel to take us to the floating market. Is that acceptable?"

Phan dug in his pocket, but Armstead put his hand forward in the universal stopping gesture.

"Ong Phan, please allow my country to pay this. I have so thoroughly enjoyed the evening's conversation and meeting your son. Please."

Phan conceded. Armstead deftly produced his MasterCard as the waiter approached the standing men.

"David, you will not have a problem waking in the morning. The city begins moving quite early. We'll talk more."

The Germans and the Italians by then were also standing and gesturing for their checks and laughing.

CHAPTER 52
Washington, DC
Senate Office Building

"Senator, Captain Quinby is on line two. When you get off the phone, remember you have a 10:15 haircut appointment."

Mrs. Baxter was efficient to a fault. She was also the kind of mature woman about whom no one would suggest that she had her job based on anything but merit.

Stroud punched the speaker button and propped his feet up on his desk. "Duane, how are you this morning? Is the Navy treating you right?" The Senator and Duane Quinby had known each other since before Vietnam.

"Yes sir, they're treating me fine. I'm on temporary additional duty (TAD) to the Secretary of State's office. I came across something that might interest you."

Stroud picked up the receiver. Over the years, Captain Quinby had been a source of information about naval matters and delicate personnel issues. He was nearing the end of a dull career and was hoping that Stroud would take him on in some capacity. Stroud, on the other hand, knew their relationship would end as soon as Quinby could no longer be his snitch.

Stroud put his feet back on the floor, sat erect, and listened carefully.

"Any idea what this is about or where it is going?" He paused and listened.

"Good work, Duane. Let me know if you get any clues. Goodbye." Stroud punched another button.

"Mrs. Baxter, get Lester in here right away."

* * *

Lester B. Wainwright never married but in all appearances was a gentleman who could be a corporate executive, a talking head on a news show, or an engaging and mature television actor, touting sex-enhancement drugs or the virtues of investment planning. He worked hard to hide his ordinary background and stunted concepts of morality. Lester bluffed his way through most of his fifty-seven years with an uncanny sense of just when to suck up and when to shut up. He had some administrative skills, but his chief asset was that he looked the part of an administrator, a manager. Smaller minds in positions above him improved their own self-image just by having him around. With these traits, he found a home for the past nine years as the dean of men at Claridge Academy in the State of Washington, an expensive boy's prep school.

An even more perverse version of Professor Kantorek in Remarque's, *All Quiet on the Western Front,* Lester distorted his military service, painting the view that in Vietnam, he alone was a hero among losers.

From that safe cubical of life, he was rediscovered by the senator two years earlier. Stroud needed an administrative aide and thought Lester would be an exacting servant.

Stroud, with the help of Duane Quinby, arranged a little reward for Wainwright in the form of a grossly belated Purple Heart for Lester's injuries on the Bo De operation. The award ceremony was timed to occur the day after Lester started work. Stroud planned to encourage a level of respect for Lester by the other members of his staff.

There were two problems with the senator's plan. First, with the exception of Mrs. Baxter, the staff was composed of people just like Wainwright and Quinby, calculating suck-ups who knew Stroud just as well as he knew them. Second, in a short time, Wainwright's behavior squandered any respect the ribbon might have provided.

Lester entered Stroud's office with his usually guarded smile, hoping to learn why he had been called in so abruptly. Stroud was standing and seemed ready to walk out.

"Lester, I have a job for you. I've been told that the secretary of state is asking questions about my service in Vietnam. Why, and who is causing his interest?"

"Why don't you give him a call, Senator? Sometimes a direct call does the trick." Lester was always reluctant to revisit the war and his ignominious part in it.

"Wainwright, don't you understand that's the last thing I should do? I get information from my contacts precisely because they are close to their sources. A direct call could blow that."

Stroud was becoming impatient with Lester's lack of aggressive imagination. Lester was good when he was the person thinking up some scheme, but he was slow to see the possibilities of someone else's ideas. Stroud often showed anger just to get Lester's attention. He now saw that Lester was prodded into thought.

"David Armstead is the secretary's fair-haired boy when it comes to anything in Southeast Asia, but I have no idea what he's up to right now. When do you need this?" Lester placed his hands in his trouser pockets, and a relaxed collegial look drifted over his face.

"Damn it, Lester. What is that old man doing? It never means anything good as far as I am concerned. That blind old fart sees more than most men, and I don't want him looking at me. Do you understand me, Lester?"

"Yes, Sir," Lester muttered. The hands came out of his pocket. "If it's okay with you, I'll speak with Billy Fern and see if he can help. He's got contacts. I am sure Armstead is a part of the answer. May I ask you who gave you this information?"

Stroud didn't like sharing his sources. He worked hard over the years to insulate them. Stroud's motto was *share and lose.*

"All I will say is that my man is a military officer, working temporary duty at the State Department."

Lester wasn't stupid. His brain conjured a name: Quinby.

Without further attention to Wainwright, Stroud looked at his watch and walked out through the reception area and past Mrs. Baxter.

"Mrs. Baxter, help Lester find Mr. Fern."

CHAPTER 53

Bassac Floating Market

Armstead's second-floor corner room window overlooked the street and the quay wall, with a small grassy park in between. The side window permitted a downriver view. He had asked to be awakened at 6:00 a.m. The desk clerk seemed puzzled but did not question his guest's desires.

The headboard of his bed backed up to the side window. What David did not know was that on the other side of this peaceful corner room was a pair of very large loud speakers, one pointing downriver and the other across to the park.

At 5:00 a.m., a blast of martial music brought Armstead bolt upright in bed. Even louder, it seemed, was the male voice proclaiming a greeting to all, urging the listeners to arise for the good of the people.

Armstead rolled over to the bedside facing the front window. Placing his hands over his face, he wondered if this was a dream made worse by last night's beer and rice wine. It was just reality beginning a new day. He shuffled to the front window.

On the street and in the park, groups and individuals were briskly exercising, tossing soccer balls, or doing Tai Chi. Popular with elderly Vietnamese, Tai Chi's slow fluid movements resemble a dance.

The music moderated while the male voice did not. The announcer turned to news and propaganda. By 5:30, the noise ended, and the people scattered. As Armstead headed for the shower, he thought, *I better get my lazy decadent capitalist ass moving.*

In the lobby early, he had a cup of coffee, a bread roll, and a piece of fruit. Phan and Vu showed up just as he pitched his trash.

"You came down early; the public-address system encourages early rising," Phan said as he and Vu each pocketed a bread roll and a boiled egg.

At the nearby landing, they saw two additional passengers: a young girl, maybe nine years old in little black pants and a faded white pullover shirt, and her younger brother of five or so, in shorts and t-shirt. David remembered them from last evening. All three were barefooted.

Their mother had a wiry frame, large hands, and wide feet. She wore the common black pants and a white, worn-out, short-sleeved shirt. Her face and arms were tanned from the sun, and it was clear that she had very strong muscles. Her invisible legs were no doubt strong as well because she managed to hold the boat steady with one hand on the landing, her legs pumping from one side to the other as the men climbed aboard. Her dark hair was pulled back and covered with a straw hat. Spaces showed where teeth had been as she smiled broadly and greeted her passengers. Armstead, careful in his best Delta Vietnamese, thanked her and praised her children. She was typical of Delta women.

As they settled in and the boat moved downriver, the children scampered to the seat on the bow. The children, too, were developing wide feet, almost prehensile. Armstead sat at the next seat back, with Mr. Phan facing him. Vu occupied the last seat and engaged the woman in inquisitive conversation. In English, Phan told Armstead that her only language was the Delta dialect and accent he had used in his courtesies to her.

The sampan picked up speed, going downriver into the wind. Conversation was difficult given the engine and wind noise. Only Vu talked to the mother. This was good for Vu to know the simple people of the Delta.

Twenty minutes down the Bassac, a cluster of movement appeared. The sampan veered left toward the movement, easily crossing a slight chop across the water. The cluster became a teaming mass of sampans and junks, large and small, spread over about four hundred yards. Boats slowly moved in all directions at once, with only minor differences in speed. Armstead guessed that as many as three hundred vessels were milling about. David envisioned schooling fish frothing the water surface. Slowing, their sampan moved into the mass.

Merchants hung from their masts examples of the wares on board. Smaller vessels mounted temporary poles hanging particular vegetables, fruit, fish, a chicken, or a pig in a stick cage. One junk offered sauces and other condiments, another clothing and shoes, and another cages of small birds. Smaller sampans darted among the crowd, offering bottled drinks and fruit to vendors and shoppers alike. One sampan sold hot pho, a meal on the run.

Sampan tourists, mostly Westerners, milled about. Many boats contained river women, old and young, often traveling with their children. Occasionally a Vietnamese man accompanied the women. Quiet bargaining between vendors and shoppers were suppressed by eruptions of lively talk when friends passed by. Traffic control was unusually cooperative. David saw no collisions or frayed tempers, only cheerful people enjoying an early trip to market. Thirty yards away, he saw a large sampan containing five passengers: the Germans and the Italians.

He and Phan bought fruit and vegetables and a cage containing two chickens. Vu bought a Coca Cola and looked at the two men in puzzlement. *How could they take those things back to Saigon?* As the sampan moved out of the mass and back upriver, Vu realized that Mr. Armstead and his father were going to give the boatwoman the things they purchased. His father then offered his boiled egg to the girl who quickly placed it in her pocket. Vu, seeing his father's intent, gave his egg to the woman. She nodded in thanks but said nothing. As they left the market, Phan asked the boatwoman to take her time getting back to Can Tho. With that, speed and wind noise dropped, and serenity returned. Phan relaxed onto one elbow, stretching his legs along the side of the boat. Armstead, facing him, did the same thing. They remained silent in those postures for a short time. Vu resumed his quiet conversation with the boatwoman.

As though last night's conversation had only paused, Phan spoke first.

"Men and women are the problem everywhere. Man's stated high purposes aren't always joined with good deeds. During and for a time after the American War, I believed the harsh measures I executed were necessary for the good of my people. After the war, I trusted that our struggle would end because our foreign oppressors were gone. We would enjoy peace and freedom from outside threats. But threats come in many forms. I now see this clearly."

"This looks pretty peaceful," Armstead said. "What's wrong with all this? The roads are improving; the bridge near Vinh Long is fantastic. Last night, I saw homes close to the water that forty years ago would have been unthinkable as well as unsafe. Vietnam is not at war. That seems to be a much better way."

"David, our people are still not safe. The way of the North is cheerless and unproductive, while here in the South, there is a feeling of good expectations, and I ask, why? At least one answer," he continued, "is that the people in the South saw something we of the North could not see in the same way. We reviled American bombers and captured pilots, but in the South, Americans genuinely wanted to help Vietnam's people. The French helped themselves, and certainly the Russians were no better. I have come to believe that America being here was a good thing for all of Vietnam."

Damn, I never believed that I would hear something like this from anyone, David thought, *much less a Vietnamese communist.*

"Ong Phan, do you know that many Americans are still angry that we came to Vietnam at all, that not only were our purposes low, but that all of our deeds were bad? Even today some Americans only see my country in a dark light? These people thrive only in darkness." Armstead was surprised to have made this candid admission.

"Yes, I do know this. We took advantage of the spirit of protest in your country to turn it against you, to affect your politics and the war. It is ironic that at the same time in my country, death would have been the outcome of even peaceful protest. That boatwoman and my parents in the North would never have thought that protest against any government was anything but very dangerous business."

Armstead could see beyond Phan to the bow where the girl and her brother were sitting. The young girl retrieved the boiled egg, now was carefully cracking and removing the shell, piece by piece. The brother watched with quiet patience.

"Why do you think your people are not safe now? With all of the foreign invaders gone, the French, the Japanese, the Americans, and the Russians, why are you worried?"

David was curious. Weren't the Vietnamese people directing their own lives even if that direction came from a maze of central committees all over the country?

"David, there are dangers all over the world—angry and ambitious people, too. Selfishly for Vietnam, it is important for America to be strong and to be able to trust in its higher claims. Trust is an important word."

The depth of Phan's thinking and candor caught Armstead by surprise. Phan had been learning more than English: he wanted to go beyond the confusion of partisan rhetoric and political ideology. Armstead's mind paraphrased part of a Tsun Tsu principle: *Know yourself, and you need not fear the result of a thousand battles.* Ong Phan Tran Nguyen knew himself in a way few men ever enjoy.

"America plays a dangerous and thankless role. It is the only world power able and willing to maintain the peace, even at a high cost for its young men and women and always hounded by critics from within and those in the shadows. I fear then for America and its people. If the leadership of your country falters and turns from its role, the rest of the world and my people will be in more danger."

"That's an interesting proposition. You need us to spill our blood, so you can be safer and be criticized for doing what you cannot? You want us to spend our money so that you are free to spend yours on more peaceful pursuits?" Armstead looked away, not wishing to show his deep resentment of the concept.

"Remember this; the present government of Vietnam has not been a critic when other countries in the West and in other parts of Asia have freely done so. Vietnam will remain a poor country for many years, but its people are strong and patient in spirit. I cannot change the darkness that lives in the minds of your countrymen. We have such people, too. In time, their ways will be seen as evil."

Armstead's hostility subsided. He knew that Phan was speaking from his heart and as a friend.

The men shifted in their postures. The little girl finally broke small pieces of egg and fed them to her brother, taking none for herself. The boy smiled at the gift.

CHAPTER 54

Bassac Revelations

"It is time to tell you why you came ten thousand miles to this wide river. This little sampan is far from the ears and eyes of dangerous men of low purposes."

All Armstead could do was to murmur thanks, "I hoped for this day."

"First, I have known you for a long time, longer than you think. Now I also trust you. You are a man of high purpose, trying always to have your deeds conform to your purpose. Many men are not like that." Armstead bowed his head slightly.

"In 1969, I came to the South with my comrades for a specific mission, to kill many American patrol boats. Their aggressiveness hurt our cause. Many areas were turning to the southern government for safety. We needed to show that we could destroy Americans, that the people were foolish to trust the southern government, and show the American people that it was foolish for them to trust their own military and civilian leaders. We succeeded."

"Ong Phan, you get no argument from me. America was defeated in the streets from within and not militarily. Protest was fashionable, and even today it is fashionable to criticize anybody working to solve difficult problems. The political landscape in America is not very inspiring." Armstead gave no further insights to his cynical thoughts.

"I assume you did not intend for this to be a review of geopolitical strategies thirty-five years ago. Did you succeed in your military mission?"

"Yes, but not in the way we hoped. Our tactics were correct but only briefly. We completely destroyed one boat and severely damaged another. Later, we destroyed a helicopter and killed many Americans. Your forces made a devastating response. Only three others survived that day. Today I cannot think that such victories were worth our great effort and losses. Whatever our strategy, what happened on the Song Bo De that day made no difference in the war at all."

"You went all the way to the Bo De? I know that river. It was some distance from where I worked, but I know it. When in 1969 did this happen?"

"Early December. What we never accounted for was a typhoon."

"A typhoon? I didn't know a typhoon hit the Delta. That would have been terrible."

"You're correct, David. The typhoon came from the east, but then abruptly turned north. All we got were heavy rains, but that was enough to make our job almost impossible."

"What about the helicopter? There had to have been two of them."

"One of my soldiers shot at the first helicopter as it passed us low and overhead. I heard it crash, but we never were able to see it. As we rushed there, another of my soldiers found two American officers alone in the jungle. My soldier was killed. We returned fire and captured one man, but the other was dead. I had just enough time to search the dead American, bind our captive, and run away from the other helicopter as it searched for us. We ran until after darkness."

Armstead's mind could see these events as they must have unfolded.

"What happened to your captive? Was he repatriated in 1973?"

"No, he escaped. He simply walked away. I had him for about six weeks, trying to move north. We were all exhausted. He likely loosened his bonds and crawled away. I later learned that his repatriation was very dramatic."

Armstead wondered. Successful escape is not often dramatic but a matter of chance, fortuitous timing, or just dumb luck. The fact of repatriation, of coming home to your own forces, is always dramatic.

"Do you know who this officer was? I'll be curious to find out what became of him."

"Oh yes, but I must tell you more about what I saw the day we captured him. My soldier who found them had been seriously burned earlier in the day. He was not alert. When the shooting began, we came to a clearing seconds later. My soldier was down. One American was on his knees but bent over with his head in the soil, like he was in prayer. Behind him, the other officer was standing with his hands in the air, holding his pistol only by its barrel. He was crying out in English. I did not understand his words, but his meaning was to surrender. He was tearful and begging for his life."

David's brain was scorched by the implications of Phan's statements. He needed to be very cautious and precise in his questions.

"From what you saw, who killed your man?"

"The dead officer on his knees."

"From what you saw, who killed the dead officer?"

Phan lingered and then locking his eyes with Armstead's, said, "The other American officer."

Armstead's stomach tightened, his jaws clenched, and rage welled. He was rescued only by his need for focus.

"Did you see the rank held by the dead American?"

"I turned the man over and set his back against a sapling. His collar markings were those of an American Dai Uy, and on one side of his collar were the two small silver flowers, the Vietnamese Dai Uy insignia. I searched his pockets. The man we captured was a Tieu Ta," Phan volunteered.

Armstead was being drawn into a murder case. Part of him wanted the matter to end there, to write this off as just another sadness of wars. In combat, good men can fail themselves and others around them. Why should this matter to Armstead or Phan or even to Brady? These thoughts were only passing. If Phan was telling the truth, one American son-of-a-bitch murdered a fellow officer. That is what matters.

"Who was this person?" He chose now not to call him a man.

Phan took in a deep breath. "His name is Stroud. You call him Senator Stroud."

Armstead fought back his nausea and the burning sensation on his face. He drew his legs up, centering his body on the small seat. He looked out over the water and then to the two children in the front of the sampan. He closed his eyes and become transported into Stroud's presence. *Stroud murdered to avoid a fight and save himself,* he thought. Armstead was almost overcome with helpless rage.

As Phan similarly changed positions to maintain the boat's balance, Armstead spoke. "How do I know you are telling me the truth?"

"You don't know this. Prove me wrong. You are right to think that my country might repeat our successful strategy of thirty-five years ago, to interfere again in your domestic politics. In your thinking, ask yourself what my country can gain by doing this. Our relations with America are improving. Why should we complicate those relations with a distracting accusation over old events and meaningless deaths?"

David was not ready to answer.

"When you say that Mr. Stroud's repatriation was dramatic, what did you mean?"

"Did I use an incorrect word? In 1970, a comrade translated a story written in your military newspaper, *Stars and Stripes*. Mr. Stroud said that he escaped from a large group of soldiers and killed many in the process. He said many things that were not true. He walked away in the night and left us sleeping. He spoke eloquently of the fallen officer with great emotion saying that he and the Dai Uy fought until the last and were overwhelmed by many soldiers. Mr. Stroud told a story that was better for a theater or a play."

"Dramatic was close, but not precise. Stroud's escape had been fictional." Phan was relieved to tell his story. Armstead's anger was washed by skepticism and disbelief. This was just a story without any proof, an accusation made by a former enemy against a hero, a national political figure. Still, Stroud was not a man Armstead ever respected. Phan, on the other hand, was different.

"Why have you told me this? What do you expect me to do?"

"A coward with a pistol is dangerous. A coward with a country can be a disaster. I planned to humiliate this man to his death. He killed one of his own because he was afraid to fight. He got away from me. He will not escape from you."

Armstead saw angry determination in this man. This was not an act manufactured for his benefit. He and Phan had been enemies but were brothers in this matter.

"David, you are an intelligent and discrete man. You know your country's laws, its courts, and your people better than I do. You will know what to do to prove or disprove what I say. Until the first day that we met in Paris, I did not know what I could ever do with my secret. From then I knew the purpose in our meeting and would someday have my opportunity."

"You may have known of my military service or the work I have done as a government employee but nothing about me personally. Certainly, you were told that I spoke the Vietnamese language, as I knew that you spoke English with good skill. Why would you think that I was any opportunity for you?"

"Until this morning, you had no knowledge of what I have told you. Correct?" Armstead nodded.

"You were not in Vietnam at the time of these events either. Correct?" This inquisition was purposeful. David nodded again.

"You were in hospital, perhaps in Japan or America, recovering from a grave wound to your chest. What do you remember of the time you were wounded?"

David's left hand moved up to the right side of his broad chest.

"Not much. Just before daylight, I was returning from a night patrol, and we were ambushed. I remember nothing until I woke up in a hospital in Sasebo, Japan. I awoke again on an airplane returning to the States and the third time in a Navy hospital in California. Then they told me I was going to live. I was very lucky."

"True. Anyone shot where you were hit has almost no chance of living without immediate attention." Phan paused. "I am the person who gave you that attention. I am also the man who shot you."

Grinning, he extended his hand toward Armstead placing his index finger exactly on the spot where the bullet had entered David's body.

Poking at the spot, he said, "That is why I knew I would have my opportunity. It is a good thing, too, that you were a smoker then."

Phan leaned back, pleased with his disclosures. David believed this part of the story to his core. When he woke in Sasebo, he remembered being asked if he knew who saved his life. He did not. He was told that someone had done some quick thinking. They covered the entry wound with a cigarette package wrapper and rolled him on his side so he could breathe and not drown in his own blood. His peasant soldiers would not have been aware of this method of field treatment for lung shots. He, too, was glad that he had not given up cigarettes at the time.

The sampan swerved to the left, picking up a speed toward the Can Tho River. When Armstead looked back to the stern, he saw Vu no longer speaking with the woman. The engine noise increased, and Vu smiled, giving David a little wave. David looked forward. Phan had turned to face the children. What Phan said could not be heard, but Armstead saw the eyes of the children, their shy smiles reacting to Phan's words. To them this old man spoke gently as a grandfather.

CHAPTER 55

The Quay Wall at Can Tho

At the landing, the boat woman called to her daughter to hand up the things the men had purchased. Phan declined, saying that they had no room for those things in the rest of their journey. He asked if she would not mind taking those items and using them so that he would not feel foolish for buying them. Armstead joined in the request, saying it had been their pleasure to ride to market with her and her beautiful children. Would she consent to keeping the food and the chickens? She consented and smiled. As she drove away from the landing, she looked back and waved.

"You understand my people. I told you they are as good as any on Earth, and proud."

They walked along the wall. Vu was ahead of them.

"Anh Phan," for the first time David used the familiar form of address, loosely translated to mean "brother," "you have provided much information but little I can use as proof of what you say. And truly you are trying to interfere with American domestic politics, but this may be for a good reason. My burden now is to decide what I do with it."

"The fast boat back to Saigon will give you time to ponder your burden. It makes a short stop in My Tho, but without a breakdown, we should be in the city by midafternoon. It's a Russian hydrofoil. They left it behind. It leaves in one hour. I have tickets, and I thought you would want to rejoin Tieu Ta Johnson.

Can you be ready? And don't worry about Vu. He will take the car back to the city."

Phan knew David's mind; a reply wasn't needed. There was no longer any reason to stay in Can Tho or Vietnam, for that matter.

Phan quickened his pace and joined his son. Armstead saw him match his son's step and place his hand on the boy's neck. Fatherly instructions were being given and understood.

After they checked out of the Quoc Te, Phan and Armstead walked over to the nearby Mekong Restaurant, buying two beers and two orders of salad rolls. There they waited for the hydrofoil to arrive. It was twenty-five minutes late. Just as the boat off-loaded its passengers, Phan passed David's ticket to him and walked briskly toward the embarkation line. Before David could get aboard, Vu called out to him. He stepped out of line and approached the boy.

"Mr. Armstead, I feel the same respect my father has for you. Here is a gift for you to take to America."

The young man reached into a bag and produced a box about the size of a large, hardback dictionary, carefully wrapped in a dark blue paper.

"Would you accept this as a token of your trip to Vietnam? If you will give me your email address, I would like to stay in touch."

"Anh Vu, I would like that very much. Thank you."

On the back of his hotel receipt, Armstead printed the Hotmail address he only gave when necessary to divert junk mail. As he shook hands with the boy, Phan called out for him to board the boat. When the hydrofoil pulled away from the dock, Vu got in his car and drove off. Armstead placed the gift in his leather travel bag. As with all gifts, David was curious about the ratio of size to weight.

Air-conditioned and comfortable, the hydrofoil could carry maybe sixty passengers. Half that number was on board today. To Armstead's surprise, the course taken by the vessel was through canals that had previously been too dangerous for any American or South Vietnamese military.

The boat's engine cooling system relied on great amounts of river water sucked through large intakes. Periodically, the boat would stop dead in the water, back up fifty feet, and then resume its normal speed. After two of these stops, Armstead realized that the maneuver was the only practical solution for clearing the intake chutes of accumulated water hyacinth. Great tangles of the stuff could overheat the engines. Russian design never contemplated the choking vegetation of Southeast Asian rivers.

Armstead spent the trip to My Tho, marveling at the sights; he knew these waters better than the streets of his hometown of Houston. Phan sat with their bags and read a book. After taking on many more passengers at My Tho, Armstead joined Phan in the small forward cabin.

Speaking now in Vietnamese, "That was very kind of Vu to give me the gift. Should I open it now?"

Phan put his book aside and responded in Vietnamese.

"Maybe you should wait until you get home. My son likes to write long notes, and you want to have time to enjoy it. Have you enjoyed this trip?"

"It has been like no other in my life." Armstead knew the quarters were close to other passengers. "You have been kind to take your time to show me all this."

When the hydrofoil docked in Saigon, the two men shuffled off the boat with the other passengers. Cabbies crowded in to entice fares. Phan got the attention of one and asked Armstead if he would like a ride to wherever he was going. Armstead declined, saying he needed the walk after all the riding, and the hotels on Lam Son Square were a short distance away. During their brief conversation, the people on and near the dock dispersed. Only two or three remained anywhere near the men. Street traffic rolled by. Phan then drew Armstead behind the trunk of a cab and extended his hand in farewell.

With what passed for a smile on his scarred face, Phan spoke English to Armstead for the last time.

"Vu will call you in the morning to see when you need to go to the airport. The gift contains the pistol and some other items. It also contains a statement in Vietnamese I wrote after I learned that our friend was becoming more important than he ought to. Your diplomatic passport should get this through without difficulty. I hope this helps you. We will not meet again. Goodbye."

Without waiting for a response, Tieu Ta Phan Tran Nguyen got in the cab and rode away. Pressed into Armstead's right hand, Phan had placed an American military identification tag, a dog tag that bore a service number and the name Robert Hampton, USNR, Prot.

CHAPTER 56

Caravelle's Saigon-Saigon Bar

The midafternoon sun shaded the rooftop bar. Armstead entered with his small travel bag. He spotted Johnson at a table for two, having a beer. Walking up, he took a seat.

"Say, Boss, I see you're safe. How was the trip? You want a drink?"

"Yeah, a beer. It was fine. I'll tell you about it later."

When the beer was brought to the table, Armstead removed his light jacket.

"Barrett, you need to do a few things. Take my bag to your room. I'll get it later."

As he said this, David's left hand formed a fist, the signal that Johnson was never to let the bag out of sight.

"My oldest daughter's graduation is next month, and Alicia is planning a family dinner party. So, I'm going shopping for nice table linens I promised to get. Afterward, I'll check in here. Get us on the Air Vietnam flight to Bangkok tomorrow and then back to the States. Screw coach for you. Book us both in first class."

Johnson gestured a thumb up.

Armstead took a long pull on the beer, stretched out his legs, and relaxed.

"You need to see where I've been. A huge suspension bridge spans the Mekong near Vinh Long. Below Can Tho is a floating market on the Bassac, like nothing I've ever seen. I felt lifted up around the people out there. I'll never forget it."

"Damn, David. You sound like a travel agent. If they have Mexican food, I'll go with you the next time."

Armstead called him a shallow cretin. They finished their drinks, paid out, and left the bar. As Johnson got off the elevator on his floor, he told Armstead his room number. David continued down to the lobby.

On a small side street across the square, he located a gift shop containing figurines and other decorative items. The proprietress stocked an extensive selection of table linens. David picked a nice-sized white cotton tablecloth with eight matching dinner napkins. These had beautiful handwork and embroidered detail.

Armstead enjoyed shopping in Vietnam, particularly Saigon. He admired the cordial manner of the mature, often attractive women who ran all the good shops. These women were charming and businesslike.

Women in the American South along the lower Mississippi River shared a trait in common with the ladies of the Saigon dress and gift shops. Despite tonal differences in their speech, they had a polite, almost intimate softness to their voices.

David and this lady spoke Vietnamese. David used a more refined speech than the bar and countryside variety. She responded approvingly. He requested gift wrapping for this present to his wife. She selected a box that David rejected as too large and bulky. She was trying to avoid too many folds in the cloth. She then produced a smaller box to David's satisfaction. He said that would be more convenient for the flight back home. She then offered a selection of paper for him to consider. He wanted no ribbon.

"Co, this dark blue paper will be excellent."

She put the wrapped gift in a rope-handled, heavy paper bag, and David left the shop.

Checking into the Caravelle, he went to his room to freshen up. He left Alicia's gift on top of the television cabinet but folded and carried the rope bag down to Barrett's room.

As Johnson opened his door, David walked past him to his leather travel bag. Removing Vu's gift, he handed the rope bag and Vu's gift to Johnson.

"Thanks for holding my suitcase. I assume you'll be using room service tonight. I'm eating at the Continental tonight and will turn in early. Did you make our flight arrangements?"

"Just got off the phone. No problem. Are we taking a taxi to the airport?"

"I don't know that yet. We'll see in the morning. Can I get you anything while I am out?"

"Nope, I did all my shopping while you were gone. See you in the morning."

David took his time at dinner, returning to his room shortly after dark. He was not surprised that his wife's gift had been opened and carefully rewrapped, but not carefully enough.

With all this moving around today, it must have been hard for anyone to keep their eyes on the ball, pleased with his precautions.

Vu called at 7:59.

"Mr. Armstead, if you are checking out, what is your flight time? May I give you and Mr. Johnson a ride to the airport?"

"Thank you, Ahn Vu. How about 11:30? We'll be out front." The less said, the better.

Clutching his Alicia's gift under his arm, David joined Johnson in the lobby at the cashier's counter. On time, the two men walked out of the hotel and stood briefly under the portico. Vu arrived as scheduled. Johnson got in the back seat with both travel bags, and David took the front, his daughter's gift tucked under an arm. Once into the noon traffic, Johnson moved Vu's gift into Armstead's carry-on bag. Both men carried US diplomatic passports that would get them through security and customs almost anywhere with just a wave of the hand. Authorities were less likely to challenge the senior member of the pair, if at all.

Both pieces of luggage went into overhead storage, with David taking care to wedge Alicia's gift on top. Bangkok was a forty-five minute flight.

CHAPTER 57

From Bangkok

Their flight home through London's Heathrow Airport was scheduled to leave Bangkok before midnight. He and Johnson had plenty of time to find Internet connections to check messages and make phone calls. Margaret Lokey sent David a copy of her email response to Boston's message. David regretted making even a tentative commitment to the Ely trip. He decided to postpone a final decision.

David had a lot of emotion wrapped up in Vietnam and needed to clearly think through what he had learned and what he could do with his knowledge. Whatever his gut feelings were, all Armstead really had was a pistol and a dog tag, if genuine, of an officer he had known in Vietnam. He also had an interesting story from a former enemy.

Until yesterday, he had not even known that Hampton died. David remembered Bob stopping by the Coastal Group one afternoon, following his R & R. Bob was happy to have seen his wife. She supported his career plans. After David's evacuation, he lost track of a lot of people.

Armstead made two preliminary decisions. The first was to say nothing of substance to Mr. Brady or to Johnson. Neither needed to be compromised by David's new insights. If Phan's motives and truth were to be questioned and tested, David had to do that and take responsibility for the outcome. It was part of Johnson's job not to speculate about David's activities. Maybe a little further along, David would tell Barrett what was necessary.

The second decision was prudent and practical. He needed more information and trusted advice. Steps beyond that were unknown.

* * *

The telephone rang at 3:30 a.m. in Sam Taylor's bedroom. Years of law practice made Sam no stranger to late-night calls. Such calls required an ability to listen as mental focus returned.

"Good morning, Sam. Sorry to call you so late. This is David Armstead."

"Damn. Mr. Armstead, it's been a long time. What can I do for you?"

"Forget the 'mister' crap, Prevert. I need some of your time. I woke Double Bourbon and got your number. Can we talk now?"

Switching on the lamp on his bedside stand, Taylor was alert. "Sure, go for it, Bruno." They understood some friendships require little cordiality.

"I need a short course on exhumation. What's the fastest, easiest way to get one, and how do I find a lawyer to help me? I need someone to do a good job and keep their mouth shut, not some grandstanding publicity hound. I can't tell you why I need this or much else, but a man like you can give me the quick answers."

"Okay Bruno. This is easy. You need three things: cash for the lawyer—always take care of the lawyer first—consent of a next of kin if you can get it, and third, a court order from a judge where the exhumation is to occur. I assume you want an autopsy. I will help you with all this if you give me more information. As a practical matter, arrangements need to be made and paid to get the body out of and then back in the ground, a mortuary service, and you need a forensics person ready to do the autopsy. The mortuary service may be able to help on that. Am I correct that you're contemplating an autopsy?"

"That's right, Prevert. What about Fresno, California? The widow may be there if memory serves me right."

"If the body is there also, that will be better. As for Fresno itself, I can help you on a lawyer there. I represented a Texas client in an insurance fraud scheme investigated by the Justice Department there, using a federal grand jury. My guy never got put on trial, but I researched local counsel. I can look into it tomorrow. I'll give you my office number."

"Don't need it. I got that from Double, too. How much cash are we talking about?"

"Bruno, just for you, I'm free; but I'll have to find out what the Fresno lawyer expects. I suspect you would like this to be a back-channel deal as much as possible. If you will allow me to engage the attorney, I can insulate you more from the proceeding. You can take your time paying my firm for the Fresno lawyer's fees. Again, this is a tomorrow thing."

"Somehow I knew your craftiness would come in handy. What sort of time frame am I looking at?"

"That's the one thing I can't know yet. Courts are different in different places. Some judges work, and others don't; that's just the facts of life. What I can do is explore with local counsel whether there is an ethical way to get the best judge or at least the best judge for this special matter."

"It's refreshing that a lawyer is really talking about ethics. I thought all of you were slimy crooks." He laughed.

"Screw you, Bruno. I resent the word 'slimy,' and the crooks are fewer than you think. Give me a fax number, and I'll send you something tomorrow, showing you the essentials of what an exhumation order should say and what supports granting one. I'll get a mouthpiece in Fresno, who'll put up with your bull and make arrangements for billing to come to me, if that meets with your approval."

"Forget the fax. I'll call you when I'm back in the States. Are you going to Minnesota in June? I'm only tentative at this point."

"David, please see that you make it. The whole damn gathering is so that we can see you again after all these years. Nobody is going to talk your kind of shop, and it will be a wonderful opportunity for us see our old friends."

"I'll see what my wife says and check the schedule. What about your wife?"

Sam paused. "Glad to see you feel obliged to get permission from your wife. I miss that. Betsy died three years ago."

David's tone changed. "Sorry, Sam. We'll talk more. Go back to bed. I have a flight to catch."

As they boarded their flight, Johnson thought it odd that Armstead still carried Alicia's gift package under his arm. After dinner, drinks, and the first movie, the lighting in first class was subdued. Passengers drifted off to sleep. Armstead stood up, briefly looked around, and then shifted his wife's gift into his carry-on luggage with the other blue-wrapped box, as yet unopened.

"You want to tell me what's in the other box?" Barrett's curiosity had won.

"It's a gift from Mr. Phan. I haven't seen what it contains," avoiding a direct lie. "Whatever it is, I thought it best to confuse its contents with the other gift. I'll open it back in the States."

I'm getting my leg pulled, Johnson thought. *He's holding back on me. I guess he has his reasons.*

Armstead settled in his seat and went to sleep.

CHAPTER 58
Heathrow to Washington, DC

Armstead awoke refreshed as the airplane landed in Heathrow. They had an hour to catch the next leg of their flight to Washington, DC. Johnson saw Armstead's energy rising. His boss was eager to get back to Washington.

"I don't know what's planned for me, but I need to be in town for a few days at least to get some balls rolling. Do you know about this small reunion some friends are having? It's in late June."

"You got an email on that while we were in Saigon. You want me tagging along?

"I don't know that, either. While we've been screwing around in Vietnam, my home life has been getting away from me. My daughter's graduation from Cal State, Fresno is a couple of weeks off, and before that, I'll need to move her crap back to San Anselmo. There's no time for a personal life, much less vacationing in Minnesota."

This was the first time in Barrett's assignment that his boss spoke of ordinary domestic concerns. Barrett actually enjoyed seeing David grumble. Johnson's marriages had fallen apart because of the peculiarities of his duties, always at someone else's disposal. Wives came second. Emotional and physical fidelity weren't the problem. He simply was never home enough to sustain a marriage.

"You need time off. We spend a lot of time in the air and spooking around on the ground. It won't hurt you to get away from all this and go home."

Armstead's primary anxiety concerned the exhumation effort. He planned to call Taylor when he got to his apartment. Nothing could move fast enough to suit Armstead.

"You're right, Barrett. I need to talk to the secretary and see if I can deal with these other matters. I'll stay in touch."

Another movie came on, some sort of chick flick. Both men wondered what kind of idiot selected these films for captive audiences. Barrett dozed off, and David's eyes glassed over. Ever since his conversation with Sam Taylor and their exchange about ethics, Armstead had been examining Phan's revelation in the competing light of ethics and pragmatics.

CHAPTER 59

Armstead's Apartment

Armstead's one-bedroom apartment in Addison Heights was near Reagan National Airport and Boling Air Force Base. David selected the little place for conveniences of flights, particularly back to California. The apartment, modestly furnished, had a neutral feel to it, almost airless. Sometimes instead of telling his wife he was going in country, an oblique reference to Washington, he would tell her he was staying at the Budget Inn.

Today, Armstead was grateful for the seclusion the apartment offered. He never entertained there, and everything was in its place—quiet, simple, and unassuming. On the way from the airport, he stopped at a grocery to pick up some fresh milk and vegetables. He placed his travel bag on the end of the bed, removed his coat, and returned to the living room. At the end of the sleeper sofa he kept if any of his children visited was a telephone and note pad. He picked up the phone and dialed Sam Taylor's office in Houston.

"Have you got something to tell me, Prevert?" He didn't waste time with hellos or greetings of any kind—just business.

"You bet, Bruno. Get something to write with, and I'll give you the name of a lawyer in Fresno. She's got cojones but keeps a low profile. You ready to copy?"

"Of course, I'm ready, Prevert. Go for it."

"The lady's name is Sandra Tobyn. I've retained her and explained what I have guessed are your needs. She'll take care of the practical stuff, hiring the mortuary service and getting an order signed by a judge. I told her you would handle getting the consent form signed and lining up a forensics person. Is that about it?"

"You're good. What about a timetable and how fast the court will act?"

"On the first question, that's really up to you. She's ready to talk to you and thinks she'll get the order following a ten-day notice requirement."

"Hold on there. What is this notice requirement? I thought we could get this done quickly with a signed consent."

"This is quickly, in legal terms. You haven't told me anything to support urgency, and most judges, Bruno, understand that the subject of an exhumation isn't running away. So they may want a public notice."

Taylor often expressed legal advice in basic language.

"This notice is posted somewhere in the judge's courthouse and in a publication of general circulation. For you elitists, that doesn't mean the *New York Times* or the *Washington Post*. My recommendation is that you should let this go down as an ordinary filing and notice in Fresno. Unless someone with special interest knows enough to look in the Fresno paper, this isn't going to cause even a ripple."

"Okay, Sam. Give me her number, and what's this going to cost?"

"About five grand for the total. I sent her half that for a retainer, and the rest she estimates for the digging and replanting. I'll cover all that and bill you."

As long as no one was likely to be offended, Taylor often depersonalized somber events to help others avoid being hung up on their emotions. He gave David the Tobyn details and suggested that Armstead work out the schedule directly with her. He also suggested that Armstead get guidance from Tobyn on the necessary content of the consent document.

Years of law practice taught Taylor when to ask questions and when to remain silent. He respected Armstead's need to keep this close to his chest, but bells were going off in Sam's head, and he never ignored those bells. They kept him alive in Vietnam and prudent in the practice of law.

"David, you need to tell me what this is about. It stays with me. I have the feeling that you don't trust resources normally available to you. You wouldn't be calling me for this kind of work if you trusted the people you work for. I didn't come to town on a potato wagon, Bruno."

Armstead fell silent.

"Bruno, are you there?"

"Yeah, Sam, I'm here." More silence. "Do you know anything about a big raid on the Bo De River sometime late in 1969? I got wounded before then and was sent back to the States. I lost track of everything except staying alive and didn't return to Vietnam for two years."

"I know," said Taylor. "We got our butts kicked, lost one boat, and another was heavily damaged. We lost good people, too. What's this got to do with anything?"

"Who got killed?"

It was Taylor's turn for silence.

"Our boats lost eight, including Paul Dhoge and Pastor Bob. A helicopter was shot down, killing the two pilots. Hampton was killed after that. Turns out we were facing well-armed NVA."

Armstead resisted asking about Stroud.

"The bastards set up on both sides of the river. They had dug-in positions that allowed them to run from one to another, staying ahead of our return fire. Multiple volleys from different sites. A very bad day."

"Who was on that raid?"

"Fifteen boats. It was too big an operation. Pastel scrounged up some transient units passing through CosDiv 13. Besides Pastor Bob and Puppy, there was me, Double, Five-Buck, and the Camel for sure. I don't remember the other guys. Say, if you want to know more about that day, get your ass to Minnesota. Four of us who were there will be at the lake, even if you aren't."

"Maybe I will." Armstead wondered how much he would have to disclose to get these men talking.

Armstead was kidding himself if he thought that Sam Taylor had forgotten his original question.

"I didn't know the guys on Puppy's boat, but Puppy was from one of the Dakotas. Hampton was from Sacramento, and his wife was from Fresno. Do you want me to go further?"

"Not right now, Sam. Give me some room."

"Okay, Pal, if we're talking about Katherine Hampton, then you might want Mrs. Tobyn checking marriage and death records there and in Sacramento to track her down and where Bob is buried. She can find Katherine through voter registration and driver's license records even if she has remarried. Tobyn shouldn't have a problem with any of that, but it may spike the bill a bit. Talk to her and leave me out of it if that makes you more comfortable."

"Thanks a lot. I'll let you know about Minnesota. Will you keep this to yourself with Boston and the others?"

"You gotta be kidding. It's called attorney-client privilege, Bruno. Without your consent, I'd face jail if some judge tried to force me to tell anyone as long as you aren't planning to do something crooked. Call me if I can do anymore. Let me find some client that I can actually bill."

Taylor knew he'd pressed Armstead enough. It was time for Armstead's turn to decide on more disclosures.

Armstead appreciated Taylor's gruff manner. He got his points across without sounding like the empty-suit lawyers in the State Department. They would cut and run when their personal future was threatened, but Taylor would fall bloody to his word.

Armstead unpacked. He checked the alarm setting for 2:30 a.m. Most nights in Washington, he called Alicia just before her bedtime. The four-hour time differential began his new day with the call home. This practice also forced him to bed and into his office early.

It was still daylight outside. David had one more task before turning in. He got a kitchen knife and carefully cut away the wrapping paper. The box he found had been wrapped twice. The inner layer was a cushioned paper. Inside was a varnished wooden box. Cheaply hinged and hasped, the box was never meant for security, just for containment.

Inside were oily cloth wrappings covering a pistol, an empty magazine, seven nine-millimeter cartridges, one empty shell casing, and a leather holster. Taylor was surprised. This was a vintage German Lugar complete with Nazis markings and the Eagle of the Third Reich. Its grip was unique. It was in good working order but had been a long way from home.

Time had not damaged the holster. David inserted the pistol in it, a smooth fit. The leather inside formed around the shape of the pistol and the working edges of the slide. Whether this really belonged to Stroud or not, the pistol and the holster belonged to one another.

Two other items were in the box—three sheets of very flimsy, fading unlined paper that had been folded once and a red notebook. Armstead felt like he had opened a tomb, its treasures hidden for centuries. He went to the kitchen sink and washed and thoroughly dried his hands. He returned to the table.

The handwriting was Vietnamese. The writer frugally and neatly wrote on one side of each sheet as though lines existed, a thin reedy quality made more so because the ink was fading.

My name is Phan Tran Nguyen, Tieu Ta. I write this to record certain events in 1969. Following a successful attack on American Imperialist patrol boats, the remnants of my force captured an American Navy officer, a Tieu Ta. This American surrendered without fighting. I took from him his pistol and ammunition, including a very beautiful holster. He was not injured in any way at that time. He was tearful and frightened. He fell on his knees after I disarmed him. This man surrendered after shooting another American officer, a Dai Uy, who looked dead when I saw him. I removed from the dead officer a metal strip used for identification and a small red book with American writing.

Helicopters searched for us, and we ran away. For 32 days we kept moving toward safety and Cambodia. Exhaustion overwhelmed us. One night, the prisoner slipped from his bonds and walked away. Because of my negligence, he was able to escape. I never reported this.

In 1978, I saw an American newspaper showing a photograph of this Tieu Ta, who was now a political person in his government. A comrade translated the words for me. The newspaper said that the Tieu Ta escaped from our soldiers after killing many. He spoke of valiantly fighting beside the dead officer before my soldiers overwhelmed them. All this was many lies. This man dishonored his uniform and all brave men of battle.

Phan Tran Nguyen 11.6.78

Armstead went to a cabinet and got a half bottle of Wild Turkey. He nearly filled a juice glass, adding ice. Returning to the table, he stared at the notebook. He had seen many of these pocket notebooks, red vinyl covers with three rings at the top of the fold, made in the United States.

David slowly turned the pages. The rings of the notebook were rusting. Dampness and the owner's sweat caused deterioration of the rings as well as the writing on the pages.

On the first page was a typewritten list of phone numbers of military liaison offices in various Delta towns. The second page, also typed, contained flight schedules of military transports from Vung Tau to Saigon and Saigon to Cam Ranh Bay.

He also found a page that listed Armstead's fleet post office address and title when he was assigned to Coastal Group 35. David remembered writing that for him before Hampton went on R & R in Hawaii. David's handwriting was clear.

Further back were twenty-one sheets of Hampton's writing. Each page contained militarily significant information that might have been useful if captured, past SEALORD mission numbers, dates, and units as well as checkpoints and call signs. One page contained a list of discontinued ordinance, known as suspended lots, for safe disposal. Armstead was reminded that good officers sometimes make mistakes. On the other hand, the legitimacy of this notebook might have been doubtful had Pastor Bob removed the earlier sensitive material.

On the next-to-the-last sheet of writing was a SEALORDS mission number and the words "Song Bo De." Written along the left margin were the words, "more units—15 all." On the opposite margin was printed, "Sinful FUBAR." The closest Pastor Bob could ever come to using foul language was to write the familiar acronym.

On the backside of that sheet were written Robert Hampton's last notes. Fifteen small boxes drawn in a column contained a number. The numbers were not sequential. Armstead recognized these to be Swift Boat hull numbers organized in three sections. Boston's 37 Boat and Taylor's 59 Boat were at the top of the column. The last sheet contained a printed list, Pastor Bob's final written words: "Stroud clutched—Puppy died—going to Moose—Seawolves—see LCDR Shaw."

Armstead had wanted to disbelieve Phan, to ignore his story and write off all this to some elaborate hoax. The papers were genuine, and Armstead was no stranger to complex deceptions. Even if this was all true, how did Phan know the importance of this material and have the presence to make this statement twenty-six years ago before Stroud was even a minor player in politics? Those answers could wait.

David drained the juice glass and poured a second round, now without ice. He found the digital camera Alicia had given him for his last birthday. Returning to the dining table, he took pictures of the individual items, adding Hampton's dog tag. He attempted close-ups of the pistol, showing its identifying information and the backs of the bullets and expended round.

He then got two Ziploc bags, putting the notebook in one bag and Phan's statement in another. Both bags and the camera were placed in his briefcase along with the dog tag, the pistol, the holster, and the bullets and shell casing.

He placed the wooden gift box neatly in the center of the dining table.

Wild Turkey and travel fatigue overwhelmed any further need to think and plan. As he climbed into bed, he purposely shifted his thoughts to Alicia. Alicia knew so little about his work, and now she would know even less.

Tomorrow morning, they would discuss her workday and their plans for his next return home. What their kids were doing was always a topic. This time he wanted to talk about graduation and the proposed trip to Minnesota.

CHAPTER 60

Washington, DC
Secretary of State's Office

"Good afternoon, Mr. Secretary. I apologize for not being in earlier." Armstead had gone to a local Kinko's and his bank safe deposit box before traveling into the District.

"Quite alright, David. You've had a busy time lately. Tell me about your trip and our friend, Mr. Phan." Brady was relaxed even for a Friday afternoon, but Armstead worried that his inner tensions would show through. Withholding information from Mr. Brady was not in David's nature. He needed to be careful.

Brady sat behind his desk and gestured for Armstead to take a seat across from him.

"We took a sightseeing trip into the Delta. Maj. Johnson was left out of the journey at Phan's request. His revelation was that they had no hidden prisoners of war. He thought we should continue looking for MIAs but didn't think he would be the person assisting us. When I said goodbye in Saigon, he said we wouldn't meet in the future. He gave no further explanations."

Secretary Brady was tediously fussing with his pipe, seemingly mindless of Armstead's report. Now clouds of smoke billowed up from the pipe along with debris from his efforts.

"So that's it, Mr. Armstead? Nothing we didn't already believe and he's now out of the picture? Damned pipe! Nothing comes easy."

Brady placed the uncooperative pipe in a large glass ashtray.

"Well David, let's move on. What else is on your mind?"

"Sir, I need some time off. My daughter is graduating from Fresno State. On top of that, in late June some Navy friends want Alicia and me to join them for a vacation in northern Minnesota, about a week. I have a box load of personal business and obligations to take care of. In short Mr. Secretary, all of this worldly important stuff is depriving me of a real life."

David Armstead was never a complainer, but hearing himself brought inner shame. Deceiving Brady also embarrassed him. If he stayed in Washington for the next six weeks, he would never be able to do anything about Phan's disclosures.

Brady chuckled.

"Domesticity can be daunting. I received your invitation to the graduation and have no doubt that a vacation in the North Woods with your wife would be good for the nation. Do what you need to do."

"Thank you, Mr. Secretary." Armstead stood.

"Extend my best wishes to Alicia. Unfortunately, Mrs. Brady and I can't be at the graduation."

Brady paused. "This may be an opportunity for that fellow Maj. Johnson to have some time off, but that's up to you. Stay in touch."

As Armstead headed for the door, Brady picked up his pipe and banged its bowl on the ashtray. "Damned pipe."

CHAPTER 61

Houston, Texas

Law Offices of Lindsay and Taylor

Sam Taylor left the firm administrator's office. His conversation with Iris Suttle took twenty minutes. Mary Jacobs was near her ninetieth day as a probationary employee. She could be fired for any reason as long as the basis was nondiscriminatory in a legal sense. If she was a member of a protected group under the law, bad attitude might not be enough.

Jacobs was Caucasian in a multi-ethnic staffed office. There were two male partners, but the majority of associates and staff were female. Taylor and Lindsay were planning to create two more partner positions at the end of the year. Targeted for promotion effective January 1 were the senior female associate, a strong litigator, and a workhorse young man, who was building a lucrative wills, estates, and tax practice section for the firm. He needed to be a partner to supervise other associates, a valuable revenue multiplier for the firm. The partners wanted to lease vacant office space next door to be remodeled for that new section. That space had two special advantages for the young man: a private toilet for him and proximity to the elevators. The man was wheelchair bound.

The firm's procedure before any termination, including a probationary employee, was to review that employee's personnel file and discuss potential grounds for claims that might lead to the courthouse. From this analysis, a termination of Ms. Jacobs would be clean.

Something was nagging Taylor's mind. Iris told him about negative comments Jacobs had made about her work assignments and about Taylor's friends. Iris said that, oddly, when Taylor was out of the office or when Jacobs was in the break room, she was almost pleasant. Iris and Taylor agreed that a carefully constructed counseling session might clear the air. The only question was to decide whether Sam or Iris would do this. Sam decided to handle the job. Iris was tough and effective, but compassion was not her highest quality.

As Taylor passed the reception area, he instructed the young woman to hold his and Mary Jacobs's calls until he said otherwise. It was 3:05 p.m.

"Mary, could you step in here? I want to visit with you for a while. I've asked that our calls be held."

Mary Jacobs stood. She knew this was going to be unpleasant. She had done this before.

"Do I need to bring anything?"

"No. I just want to talk."

Taylor did not go to his chair behind the desk but instead moved to one of the two comfortable client chairs facing his desk. He gestured for her to take the other chair.

Mary braced for termination. *They always take a comfortable chair to seem caring and concerned before they chop off your head.* She closed the door behind her. Taylor saw her tension.

"Ms. Jacobs, I have a decision you can help me with. It affects you, so I thought I ought to find out what you think."

Suspicion crept into Mary's mind.

"What do you mean, Mr. Taylor?"

"I've been concerned for several weeks that I've done something to hurt or offend you. It's to the point that I don't feel relaxed around you and want to see what needs to happen for this not to be a problem for either of us."

"I don't have a problem. Are you going to fire me?"

She did not want to have this talk. She preferred to be given her walking papers and just leave. This kind of meeting always happened on a Friday. This was Friday, and the departure of one employee would be less disruptive at the end of the day and the week. There would be no time for tears or outbursts or even much in the way of goodbyes. Office workers prefer to suspend their enjoyment of gossip and get on with weekend plans. Reactions to a termination can be deferred. Mary's mind raced with the scenario she had seen and been a player in before.

"Don't kid me on this, Mary, and I won't kid you. Firing you is one of the options, but not the only one. I go back to my original concern. Have I done something to hurt or offend you? That's a simple and straightforward question, and I must have your answer."

She looked first to the side and then at a spot behind Taylor's desk. She seemed frozen.

"Not really, Mr. Taylor."

Sam had learned long ago that "not really" often meant "yes."

"You're an accomplished worker. Your technical skills and efficiency are equal to the best people we have here. And, you put in the time needed to get the work out. I don't want to move you, and I sure don't want the firm to lose you. That's the reason for my major distress. Now, tell me what's going on."

Taylor decided this third demand, if deflected, was his last. He waited. In the void of silence, the person who truly wants to talk will speak first.

"Plaques" was all she said.

"Plaques? What do you mean? The stuff hanging on that wall?"

He pointed to the careful array of professional plaques and certificates prominently displayed above his credenza. Virtually every lawyer's office in the country uses similar displays. Beyond showing a license to practice issued by the state governing organization, there would be undergraduate and law degrees, certificates of admission to practice before various courts and other items commemorating special service as an attorney or community volunteer. For some egos, the more displayed over bigger space, the better their projected image. Sam Taylor had his share.

"No, Mr. Taylor. Those over there."

Sam followed her eyes to the small area next to a built in bookcase. There, almost hidden were five items. First, was a ship's plaque from *USS Princeton* (LPH-5) on which Taylor had served as the legal officer before volunteering for the boats. The second was the plaque for Coastal Division 13, and the third was the squadron plaque, showing his subsequent service on the staff of Coastal Squadron One in Cam Ranh Bay. To the side were two more wall hangings, a framed eight-by-ten-inch photograph of Taylor's boat, PCF 59, underway on the Co Chien River, and below that, a three-by-eight-inch lacquered painting of a Vietnamese woman in a traditional *Ao Dai*. Two Vietnamese officer trainees who appreciated Taylor's special interest in their people and culture had given this painting to Taylor. This version was more popular in Hanoi than in Saigon and elsewhere in the South. These men had also given Taylor a Vietnamese-English dictionary, now specially placed on the nearby bookcase. Sam often wondered what happened to these men after the fall of the government in the South.

"What's wrong with those? I've had them in every office since leaving the Navy. I never thought they would be a problem for anyone, least of all offensive. I have more regard for these few items than all that crap over there."

A sad little smile showed on Mary's lips. Taylor could be blunt, but she had never heard him use off-color language. He was stung.

"I was opposed to that war," she said. "It was wrong and unnecessary, and we shouldn't have been there. We destroyed their country for our own political reasons."

Taylor heard this kind of talk, a mantra of the past, but not in many years. Arguing with her points would be like spitting in the wind. The infection in her thinking was too deep to be changed by any argument he might attempt.

"Mary, I was and continue to be opposed to the idea of any war. It's always tragic and destructive for everyone; that's what wars are about, and why they are always bad. I don't argue any of that with you or anyone else."

Taylor needed to get them past this wall. "But why are you upset over these few little mementos? I saw your file. You couldn't have been more than fifteen years old when we left Vietnam. Is there something else?"

Mary's fragile defiance began to soften, and Taylor thought he saw tears brimming in her eyes.

"Were you particularly touched by the war?" He waited for her answer.

"My older cousin Darrell was killed there. He was only twenty-two. He was my favorite cousin. The last time I saw him was in a coffin at his funeral in Lake Charles. I never knew how it happened or why he died instead of coming home. He was just dead and . . ."

Tears began running down her cheeks. With her left wrist she tried to wipe them away. Sam could tell she was concerned about her make-up.

". . . I never got to tell him I loved him or to tell him good-bye."

She quietly sobbed.

"I'm so sorry, Mary. That must have been tough on you as a young girl. I can only guess what impact that might have had on you."

Sam's older brother flunked out of college his senior year and was drafted for the Korean War. The family was nearly paralyzed with fear for him that whole year. Eddie came home without any visible wounds. The only combat he saw was after the truce in late 1953. Racial animosities notwithstanding, the heart of matters between the combatants had to do with jealousies over prostitutes in a nearby Korean town. Caught in crossfire between black and white American troops, Eddie dove into a hole pulling sandbags over his body as fragmentation grenades were tossed between the angry soldiers. Sam, as a young teen, overheard the story told by his brother to one of his Army buddies who spent his draft service in Germany.

Sam never understood his older brother's attitudes before or after that war. He didn't see his brother as particularly heroic then and had worried that in combat, his brother would be killed, too busy fumbling with his glasses to defend himself. After several years, Sam stopped trying to find explanations for his brother's peculiar behavior. Not that Eddie had failed to be a good and useful citizen in society; he was just different.

Mary became composed but wanted to speak more.

"Darrell was in the Navy. He served on those boats. I've seen photographs like that one."

Taylor's concentration fractured. Up to this point he was making headway, helping this bitter woman be purged of decades of anger. He was still trying to figure what to do with her. He could draw people out, but this was different. Now this exercise took a high-speed turn.

"What are you saying, Mary? Your cousin Darrell was a Swift Boat sailor? When did he die? What was his name?"

Taylor sat up in his chair, tightness forming in his throat. Mary looked at the floor, lost in her grief.

"1969. He was my aunt's son, Darrell Tubbs."

Taylor slumped back, shaking his head.

"Engineman 2nd class Darrell Tubbs, from Lake Charles, Louisiana," he muttered.

Mary's head snapped up.

"Yes, how did you know?"

This time she saw tears in Taylor's eyes.

"I was with Darrell the day he died." Taylor removed his eyeglasses and rubbed tears away. "Do you want to know more about that? I remember it well."

Mary nodded. Sam stood and looked at the framed photograph.

"We were on a big raid. My boat was near the front of the string of boats going up a bad river; Tubby's boat was near the back. The bad guys shot first."

Mary smiled at her cousin's nickname. She called him that, too. Tubbs wasn't fat at all. He was tall and handsome. She adored him as a model of a man that might one day be her husband.

"I didn't realize Tubby had been killed until after the operation was over. I can tell you this; he did not suffer. He had on a steel helmet, but when he got thrown from the force of the explosion, his helmet hit a large metal chest at the back of the boat. The impact must have snapped his neck. He had to have died quickly.

"I didn't know him that well, but if you want more information, speak to Mr. Boston the next time he calls. He knew Tubby from boat school. You may have heard me speak of Frank Brooks; I call him Five Buck. Frank also knew him better than I did and can tell you more about that day."

"I never knew any of this. I was just twelve when he died." Tears brimmed, but she smiled.

"Brooks was shaken by Tubby's death. Guys don't talk much about things like that, particularly with outsiders. Mary, you aren't an outsider. By all accounts, Tubby was a fine man. We never forgot any of these men."

Mary stopped crying. She laughed softly for the first time that Taylor ever heard.

"I'm sorry Mr. Taylor. I must look a mess."

"I'm in pretty bad shape myself."

Mary nodded her head and stood. She absently smoothed the front of her slacks, sniffled a bit and shook her head.

"I can't believe this. I never imagined that I would ever find answers so close."

"I know. I'm beyond being able to rationalize these things. When they happen, they just happen. You won't ever hear me talking religion in the office, but this day was meant to be, and we should honor it."

"Mr. Taylor, I'm so embarrassed about the way I treated you and Mr. Boston. Can I call him to apologize? I feel terrible about this."

"Don't worry about it. I'm sure he'll call next week, even if you don't."

Taylor hesitated. His natural instincts within the firm were to avoid gestures that might be misinterpreted. Modern notions of office proprieties had throttled sincere compassion. So he kept his distance.

"Thank you for going through this with me. Are you going to be okay?"

She nodded and smiled, extending her hand.

They didn't really shake. He took her offered hand in both of his and briefly patted their grip.

"Now if you feel you're up to it, let's take a walk around to the library while I explain a project I'll dream up for you to work on next week. That should take care of the gossips in the office. As far as I'm concerned, what we said here today is our business. Agreed?"

"Agreed."

CHAPTER 62
Washington, DC
Department of State

Armstead's office was austere. Plainly framed eight-by-ten-inch photographs of the president and the secretary of state flanked a seal of State Department on the wall behind David's clean desk. Above a walnut bookcase on a side wall were framed photographs of Ens. David Armstead upon graduation from the Naval Academy and another taken of David and Alicia on their wedding day. There were no other hallmarks of his adult life of service in or out of uniform.

At his desk, he removed a white legal pad from the center drawer. Making a few brief notes, he picked up the telephone and dialed. He made four telephone calls late that Friday afternoon. The first was to Mrs. Tobyn in Fresno. She confirmed her readiness and the time frame from receipt of the signed consent to granting of the order. He disclosed the identity of the deceased and his widow, as far as he knew. Mrs. Tobyn assured him that she would have little difficulty in finding Pastor Bob's widow. David told her his plans to attend his daughter's graduation later that month. He expected to combine the graduation with this other business in Fresno. Mrs. Tobyn treated him with unusual warmth. He wondered what Sam Taylor had told her.

The second call was to Johnson's cell phone. Armstead believed that Johnson performed all life activities with a cell phone at hand. Additionally, Johnson, like Armstead, was almost never at his assigned physical office.

"Barrett, you and I are going to have a little break, up to six weeks. If I need you, I'll give you a couple of days' notice. It would be a good idea, though, for you not to leave the country."

"That will be easy. I need to visit with my second ex-wife. She has some honey-do work for me. Call anytime."

Understandably, Barrett's domestic life had paid a price for his work.

"I'm probably going to Minnesota in late June and may ask you to help out. Mrs. Armstead may join me, and it would be nice if you could facilitate our flying arrangements."

Johnson understood the code that he should have a small Air Force passenger aircraft available for their limited use.

"Boss, you have a lot going on back in California. Let me know, and I'll do what I can."

Despite their official relationship, Armstead and Johnson recognized their friendship. Armstead knew that Johnson would show up when needed.

The third call was to Navy Captain Whitly Moore at the Army's Central Identification Laboratory in Hawaii.

"Good morning, Whit. It's not too early for you?"

"Don't worry about that. We come in early for just that reason. You folks in Washington never seem to make your calls on our schedule, so we account for that."

"I missed you the last time. You were teaching prosecutors in San Diego."

"Right! But I was also eating at the Mexican Village over on Coronado. The food is still good, but the place isn't the same as the old days."

Before medical school, Whit Moore had been a Navy Intruder pilot, flying bombing missions in North Vietnam. The Naval Air Station and the Mexican Village at Coronado were landmarks for such men.

"I have news for you, Whit. None of us are the same as we were then. I took Alicia there last year, and she ragged me about our waitress, a stout burley woman named Sonya. Sonya had worked there since 1967. Alicia speculated that Sonya was, no doubt, one of my girlfriends. Since then I have decided to avoid old haunts, at least when my wife is along."

"David, did you get our report on the last bunch? You should have."

Whitly Moore was a detail man, especially in administrative matters. He had enjoyed general surgery early in his medical career and that coincided with the needs of the naval service. He was also a compulsive student and gravitated to pathology, now one of his driving passions. Unlocking secrets within human tissue and his dislike for loose ends fueled the fine quality of his present work, also dictated by the needs of the service.

"Yes, I've read it and briefed the secretary. I am actually calling about another matter, an imposition on you."

Whitly was born in Western Tennessee and understood that "imposition" vaguely covered a broad degree of inconveniences. Armstead posed the matter as though Whit had a choice to decline the imposition. Of course, Armstead's thoughtfulness and their long friendship compelled this Southern gentleman to accept the task.

"I have some confidential work for you, an autopsy on an exhumed officer here on the Mainland; he died in Vietnam and was buried here. I don't want to cut orders for you but was wondering if you had enough leave on the books to sneak out for two or three days. I'll pay for your travel if you can't bum a ride from Hickam to the West Coast. What do you say?"

"How much lead time can you give me?"

"You've got at least ten days, more like fifteen. After that, it could be on short notice, maybe one or two days. Will that work?"

"I'll make it work. Am I going to enjoy this or at least the objective here?

Doctor Moore liked people who enjoyed discovering secrets. He also liked the idea of getting off the islands for a while. Mainland Americans and particularly his extended family in Tennessee didn't understand how a man living in paradise looked on leaving every now and then as a good idea.

"Sure you will. Thanks for not asking for details. Please know this is part of our job. You might say it's doing the Lord's work."

Captain Moore never wore his religious faith on his sleeve, but Armstead's representation sealed the matter for him.

The fourth call was to Alicia, telling her that he would be home that weekend, ready for her list of his chores. He promised total availability until their daughter's graduation.

CHAPTER 63

Washington, DC
Stroud's Office

"What can you tell me about Brady or Armstead?"

Senator Stroud suspected that Lester Wainwright's efforts, if any, had been unrewarding. He believed Lester was less than worthless to him these days. Stroud no longer enjoyed demeaning Wainwright as a device to stimulate his finer qualities. Wainwright's corrupt brightness had dimmed with his laziness.

"Armstead is back in town, and the secretary leaves for the Middle East next week." Lester's hands sunk into his trouser pockets.

"Lester, what do you do all day? Maybe you should call that boys' school you worked for and see if they still have a spot for you. Brady's trip to Damascus has been in the papers for days." No incentives, positive or negative, would salvage Wainwright's performance.

"Armstead left town, probably late last week. I'm told he went to California and that he's expected to be there for quite some time. The story being put out is that he's taking off time for personal reasons. Nothing is innocent about Brady or anyone he likes."

Stroud saw Wainwright's mental gears moving. The hands came out of his pockets, a sure sign of actual thought. Maybe Lester knew something he had not reported to Stroud.

"Senator, that's the story of Armstead's public life. For a guy employed here in Washington, he spends most of his time being somewhere else. When he isn't working, he tries to be in California with his family. I found out he was back here and sat in his apartment building most of one morning. He went to a copy service and a bank and then to State. Armstead is not very social, and from what I know of him, he doesn't fool around. He's dull. Now you're telling me that Quinby says he left town that evening. Your answers aren't here in Washington."

Stroud's expression darkened at the mention of Captain Quinby.

"Lester, I never said anything to you about Captain Quinby. Where'd you get the idea he was involved in any of this?"

"Honestly, Sir, you collect people like me. Quinby is part of your collection. I do a lot of listening. That's how I put things together. Besides, I checked Quinby's status with one of my contacts at the Defense Department. He's on temporary duty at the State Department."

Stroud was pleased that Lester was showing initiative and some backbone, even to the point of snapping at him.

"All right, Lester, maybe I've been a little hard on you. I can see you are frustrated with this assignment, and you may need some help. Can you arrange for someone in California to keep track of Armstead and report to us?"

Wainwright nodded.

"This has the highest priority," Stroud continued. "Get the money out of my campaign account but keep the transaction clean."

Wainwright understood "clean" to be synonymous with "laundered." Early in Wainwright's career in the senator's office, Lester had developed a file of fictitious vendors with bank accounts through which campaign consultation fees were paid. This practice, fully known to Stroud, funded a variety of activities, not all of which were related to Stroud's political campaigns. Besides the obvious criminality of falsifying campaign expenditure records, some of these funded activities would have horrified the senator's ardent supporters.

"I'll take care of the bookkeeping issue and get someone good for the work in California. I know a man who was fired by the Bureau. I would never use him; he's too sleazy. But I can pay him to recommend good retired FBI agents to do straightforward surveillance work."

Stroud rocked back in his chair, placing both hands behind his head. "Despite my occasional irritations with you, Lester, I like the way you think. You often do your best work, using what I call the Rule of Opposites. Most of us ask honest people to identify other honest folks. You, on the other hand, go further and consult a crook to find out who is honest."

Lester's hands found their way back into his pockets, but then came out again almost immediately. He even cleared his throat, something he hadn't done in months, another solid sign of real thought.

"Sir, I need to change the subject. Mrs. Stroud called yesterday wondering if she was invited to your luncheon presentation at the National Press Club. I told her I would find out and called Billy Fern. He said to ask you."

"I'll deal with Mrs. Stroud. Did you get Fern to help you on the Brady-Armstead matter?"

"I tried, but he declined, saying that he was not an investigator. He said that your best use of him would be to tell him about the results of an investigation and not get him entangled in the details. He's right. We need to keep this in-house."

Lester, too, was reluctant to share much with anyone other than Stroud. He sensed that Fern shouldn't be in a position to identify an intrigue.

Wainwright debated pressing about Mrs. Stroud. Over the phone he could tell that her voice was swimming in gin. When he expressed his concerns about her to Fern, Billy shared his own worries about her and the impact on the senator's political ambitions.

"Fern and I are concerned about her health. She probably shouldn't attend the luncheon, but of course, that's up to you. When she called yesterday, she wanted to speak with Mrs. Baxter. I took the call because Baxter was away from her desk. Mrs. Stroud has been talking to her with frequency."

Stroud saw Wainwright's discomfort in trying to be tactful. This open secret within the office was threatening to go out on the street, and Elaine was getting out of control. Their housekeeper was paid to keep Mrs. Stroud from getting into much trouble on a day-to-day basis, but now Elaine was affecting the senator's working situation. Mrs. Baxter, an apparently loyal and honest employee, was also inordinately kind, a quality that encouraged Elaine to call even more.

Billy was right; hospitalizing Mrs. Stroud might be the best of all bad choices. Getting her out of Washington and into some isolated treatment center in Indiana would be an improvement over the present situation. Stroud was paying too high a price for marrying her money. He hoped she would drink herself to death before he had to act.

"You and Billy make quite a compassionate team. She isn't going to the Press Club or anywhere else in public. Tell Billy, however, I agree that Mrs. Stroud needs treatment, and I've tasked you with the job of finding some place for her in Indiana."

Wainwright's relief was palpable. Elaine Stroud had touched his heart, too.

"Lester, if we're done here, go to work on the California investigator. Take care of that before you do anything about Mrs. Stroud."

Stroud followed Wainwright out to Mrs. Baxter's desk. The senator apologized that his wife was burdening her with unnecessary telephone calls and asked Mrs. Baxter to keep a log of Elaine's future calls. He confided his sadness over his wife's condition, pleading for understanding. He was in the process of seeking help for her. Stroud's words elicited an expected sympathetic response.

CHAPTER 64

Fresno, California Federal Building

Fresno, located in the Central San Joaquin Valley, is surrounded by agricultural land. Its growing population is seventy percent Hispanic, ten percent Black, and twenty percent "Other," numbers that distort the visible ethnic diversity of the region. The city is blessed with wide streets and low-profile buildings; tall is defined by eight or ten stories.

The federal building on O Street is tall. It is unique only with respect to the large concrete planters conspicuously protecting the public entry. Explosives-laden vehicles could not penetrate the building. In addition to surveillance cameras, the security system consists of blazer-jacketed older gentlemen, contract guards, who work the metal detector, search bags and purses, and see to it that people get floor directions.

On the fourth floor is a district office of one of California's United States senators. Each such office is lightly staffed but always ready to receive the senator or her guests. Staff is prepared to schmooze the occasional voter coming in to complain or get information. Usually not very busy, these offices are often unnoticed by the general public.

A satellite office of the United States Attorney for the Eastern District of California is two floors further up. The main office is in Sacramento. By contrast with the senator's office space, this office is very busy and active, conducting investigations and trials, both civil and criminal. Except for the predominance of drug-related crimes, legal professionals nourished on both sides of criminal cases might regard this branch office as Sleepy Hollow. Nonetheless, people are always coming and going—not much chance for unnoticed discussion.

"Kate, this is Helen Morse in Senator Black's office. Could you come down here during your lunch hour? I have someone who would like to meet you."

Helen Morse was a polished, mature woman who made a point of knowing everyone in the building from the federal judges and their staff down to the old guys at the security desk. She was the senator's local gatekeeper. If you ever got on her wrong side, you had regrets. She had other contacts, as well. Senator Black used Helen Morse for sensitive and important situations that other senators might delegate to junior administrative aides.

Katherine Hampton McCullough worked in the US Attorney's office for seventeen years, first as a secretary in Sacramento and then in Fresno as one of its two victim-witness coordinators. Fresno was her hometown. When the opportunity came to move back, she took it. Her gentle nature and quick mind were a perfect combination for that particular work.

Kate and Helen had been friends of sorts for over six years since Helen's senator had won her seat. They rarely met socially outside the building but freely exchanged information about grandchildren and holiday trips. Neither woman was into mysteries. Each accepted the other at face value, but Kate would never question Morse's invitation.

"I've got some people to shuffle off to court and paperwork, but I can be there at 12:30. Is that all right?"

"Certainly, I'll have sandwiches ready!"

The morning was a blur of activity. Kate got caught up in her work and almost lost track of time. Hallway laughter from two of the attorneys brought her back at 12:21.

She walked into Senator Black's office on time. Helen was standing there, smiling and gesturing for Kate to enter the senator's private office. Helen closed the door without going in herself. Seated on one of the leather club chairs was a man Kate did not recognize. He smiled, rose, and extended his hand in greeting.

"Mrs. McCullough, I'm David Armstead, a friend of your late husband, Robert," he said. Locating this woman had been no problem for Mrs. Tobyn.

She was surprised at the poise and directness of this man.

"Yes, I know who you are. Bob wrote me about you. You're 'Bruno,' aren't you?"

"Yes, ma'am," he smiled, "although I'd prefer not to be remembered as 'Bruno' or any of the other names people gave me over the years."

He motioned for her to one of the chairs.

"Lone Ranger is another name, isn't it? We bought you something when Bob and I were in Hawaii on R & R."

Armstead was amazed by the accuracy of her recall. He collected several personal call signs. Nodding, he looked at the floor and at her for one long pause. "Yes, a big-flowered Hawaiian shirt. I wore it on special occasions. My Vietnamese friends liked that shirt."

"I bet they did. It was outrageous, even for Hawaii. Why are you in Fresno? It's a long drive from the bigger cities."

"Tell me about it. My daughter is graduating Saturday from Fresno State, and one of the reasons I came here was to move her junk. We live in San Anselmo, and she's moving home for a short time."

"Can't get rid of her, can you? Do you have other kids?"

David felt he had known this woman all his life. The senator's private office had become a confessional.

"Five altogether. I don't want to get rid of her or any of them, but she has a serious boyfriend."

"Who's the boy?"

"Frank Southard. He played basketball here until a couple of years ago. He's now in medical school. He's a good kid."

"Daddy, you need to relax. Your daughter is going to be just fine. I remember Frankie Southard when he was an undergraduate. He was a good player, a great student, and a decent boy. He organized a post-season youth basketball camp with his teammates. This city still has a small-town appreciation for good deeds."

Her warm smile infected Armstead. She reminded him that as his children got older, he needed to let go. There was an awkward pause for the unstated other reason for his visit.

"Katie, I need to ask you some questions." He straightened.

She had a steady lock on his eyes. Calling her "Katie" as Bob had, scratched at her heart.

"I understand," she said evenly.

David sensed her tension, but at the same time, he saw that she trusted him.

"Did Bob talk about people back then?"

"Yes, you and others. I enjoyed the letters. I enjoyed reading about Bruno or Animal or Five Dollar Playboy or whatever you all were called. He clearly liked you and had great respect for almost everyone he served with."

"Five Buck Raider was the name." He leaned forward slightly. "Did he ever write about anyone he didn't respect?"

"Not directly, but he did express disappointment and sadness about some people he knew. He said something in his last letter about being distrustful of arrogance, especially in other officers. He was conscious of his responsibility not to be reckless with his men."

"Did he indicate which officers he was referring to?"

"No. I do know Bob was proud of all the boat officers and crews he served with. He told me about one hot shot, a kid from Iowa who was always getting into firefights. He said that officer wasn't reckless, but he never backed down. After each fight, tears streamed down this kid's cheeks. Bob liked the fact that everyone was afraid and still did their job."

She paused, a little lost somewhere. "If you want a copy of that letter, give me a mailing address, and I'll send one to you. I can never part with the original."

"I understand. I know the painful journey you must have had after Bob's death." He spoke from his heart, and she knew it. "You apparently got on with your life, as you should. Some never did and never could."

Armstead saw her lips were tight and trembling. Her eyes were wet. Inside he hated dragging her back into the past, but he wanted her to know how he felt.

"I need your help. I have a consent form here for you to sign. I need Bob's body exhumed and examined. Also, here's the card of a lawyer you can talk to if necessary. Mrs. Tobyn, on Shaw Street, is available for you to visit before you sign this. She helped me find you. She is competent and confidential. The fee and other cost arrangements are taken care of, but she will do only as you direct or decide. I can't tell you much more." Armstead felt relieved to have come this far.

With a determined aura, Kate reached for the papers. "Give me that form!" The other hand dropped into her purse and retrieved a pen. Tears moved down her cheeks. She leaned over the table beside her chair and signed.

She said, "I see this needs a Notary. I'll get this taken care of in a few minutes." She wiped her tears.

"Katherine, I haven't wanted to push you on this. You might talk to Mrs. Tobyn first."

David was near losing control of his emotions.

"Bruno, my husband trusted you. So will I. I know Mrs. Tobyn's reputation. She's a good lawyer. Did you know that her son was killed in the Gulf War?"

Armstead regretted his ignorance. He wondered about the people one might casually see in a day, who were in some fashion touched by the personal sacrifices of men and women in the military. They moved along in life despite lost loves and hidden pains.

"No, I didn't. I only found her through the efforts of another former boat officer, now a lawyer in Houston named Sam Taylor."

She smiled and reached back in her memory.

"That would be Prevert, wouldn't it? I always thought that was one of the more intriguing call signs. You see, Bob did share his feeling about all of you—at least the good ones."

David respected this woman and saw what it was that made Bob love her. She was strong.

"Bruno, this is unfinished business. I know that, and so do you. Do what you must."

Armstead's throat was taut.

"Yes, Ma'am, it is, and I promise you, I will."

She relaxed and composed herself. "Give me your card. I'll return shortly with this consent notarized. Remain here." She knew he was better off staying in the senator's office.

As she walked out the door, she saw that Helen was gone, and there were no sandwiches. She looked back. "Tell Helen she owes me a real lunch."

Armstead's afterthought to ask her to keep quiet about this meeting wasn't necessary.

CHAPTER 65

Fresno

Senator Black's Offices

David was on his cell phone to Dr. Moore. "I plan to fly to San Francisco just after Memorial Day. I'll pick you up. A signed consent will be faxed to you within the hour. I'm taking the original to a lawyer here in Fresno. She'll take care of getting the court order. You order up the dead man's medical record for what that might be worth."

"The lawyer's name is Tobyn. Let me know your flight schedule."

Armstead was pacing. He was all business. His visit with Pastor Bob's widow had convinced him he was doing the right thing, so far.

"Can you do your work at a mortuary? That's what Mrs. Tobyn is suggesting; a funeral home on L Street."

"David, I can work on your kitchen table, but I'll make some backup arrangements with the Calstate Medical Center in Fresno. I can prevail on their administrator. One way or another, we'll get the job done."

"Thanks Whit. I'll put you up at the Radisson on Ventura. Nice place, a good bar, and it's less than ten minutes from the funeral home or the Medical Center. Call me on my cell if you want to talk."

Armstead was moving closer to more answers and the truth. He was thankful that he had always been cordial to Helen Morse and her senator, a real friend to the military to a certain level but a terror when spending dreams got out of hand. Like Helen, she appreciated unpretentious charm and class. Helen Morse knew David in other circles and would have helped him even if Black had not called her first.

Kate McCullough returned with the notarized consent, having placed it in an envelope with her business card.

"Mr. Armstead, I put my home number on the card. When you are able, let me know what you can. I'll speak with Mrs. Tobyn later about whether I should be around when Bob's grave is opened or when he is reburied."

After she left, Armstead printed thank-you notes to the senator and to Helen. He placed the notes on Helen Morse's desk and left the building.

Armstead counted on the autopsy to resolve most of his questions and doubts. If Whit recovered the expended slug, then David might match it to the other bullets and pistol Phan had given him. A legal education wasn't needed to see that he was closer to proving, at least to himself, the truth of Phan's story. What he would do then was unknown.

CHAPTER 66

Fresno to San Anselmo
On the Road

After Saturday's graduation ceremonies, David and Alicia checked out of the Radisson for the trip back to San Anselmo. Alicia rode with Justine in her six-year-old Toyota Tercel. Justine had a date with Frank that evening in San Anselmo. This arrangement left Armstead driving alone in the GMC Yukon, pulling the U-Haul trailer stuffed with Justine's things. He wanted a little chat with Justine's sister and brothers who were unavailable for her graduation. If at least one of them had come along, then he wouldn't be driving alone. He decided to kick his self-pity and focus on the road.

Thirty minutes out of Fresno, his brain pleasantly restarted. *God, I love being a dad,* he thought.

Armstead also loved and hated his cell phone. Everything moved much faster than before the days of telephone messaging services, faxes, and emails. The chief casualty of this progress was the loss of time for well-developed thought. Saved time became a commodity filled with other volatile accelerants.

Reaching for his phone, Armstead dialed Sam Taylor's home number.

"What are you doing this afternoon, Prevert?"

"I'm sitting on my can, waiting for your call, Bruno. Where are you? My caller ID says 'out of area.'"

"My daughter graduated from Fresno State this morning, and I'm driving home with her things while she and Alicia are in another car, probably breaking speed limits."

"Pal, that's an unstated duty you have when kids come into your life. I wouldn't trade anything for it. What else is on your mind?"

"Thank you, Sam. Tobyn is just what I wanted. I took the signed consent to her office yesterday. She already had the petition prepared and sent her runner off to file it. Her runner phoned in the case number, and the public notice time started running today. We are on schedule. She goes to the judge with a proposed order on the first business day after ten days is up."

"That's right as rain, David. I told you she'd be good. What about Katherine Hampton?"

"She's now McCullough. A wonderful person. I know why Pastor Bob married her."

Armstead hoped his remark had not pained Taylor.

"My wife used to say, 'It's all a gift—even the sad days. She was right. What else?"

"Pass on to Bill Boston that I am definitely going to Minnesota and that Alicia will join us on July 1. I can't commit to being there through July 4."

"Since I call myself your lawyer, Bruno, what in the hell do you think you're going to accomplish leaving there over a long holiday weekend? Get a life. Besides, your wife won't relax the first a couple of days there; no one does. It's kind of a detox. What else?"

"Am I keeping you, Sam? It's midafternoon on a Saturday; you couldn't possibly be going to court."

"It may be midafternoon for you, but here it's toward evening, and I'm going out. People keep trying to set me up at dinner parties, and I'm a little tired of it. The last woman they picked for me couldn't out-think a rock. All she could say between white Zins was 'Oh, really.'"

"Okay, Mr. Taylor, remember it's all a gift. I'll call you later."

If anyone else had been in the car, that conversation would have been impossible. Armstead enjoyed Taylor's abrupt manner and his discomfort with friends playing matchmakers. He decided to list Taylor's more colorful metaphors. How dumb does a person have to be not to be able to out-think a rock?

Highway traffic zoomed by while he was lost in the pleasure of talking with Sam Taylor. Further along California Highway 99 outside of Modesto, he noticed an older-model Ford Crown Victoria matching his speed some distance behind him. Other vehicles, in a hurry streaked around the Ford and David. His initial thought was that he and the Ford driver were the only law-abiding motorists on the road that day, likely another old guy.

Testing his suspicions, he pulled off the road and into a service station. He made a big production of checking the trailer and its hitch.

Returning to the highway, he noticed the Crown Victoria still following. David turned west on California Highway 120 for six miles and then onto Interstate Highway 5, resuming his northward track toward Stockton. The Ford still followed.

He thought, *whoever this guy is, he's just following. I'm no Steve McQueen, and this isn't the streets of San Francisco; so let's just see how long we play this game.*

Whether Armstead could have lost the Ford or not was irrelevant, considering the trailer tied to his tail. There was something constructive he could do. He dialed another number.

"Barrett, do you have anyone watching me or is that you driving the old white Ford Crown Vic on my tail for the last hundred miles?"

"Not my car, David. See if you can get a license and a look at the guy, and call me back."

Armstead clicked off just as McDonald's arches came into view. He pulled into a parking space reserved for long-haul vehicles and RVs. Inside he started toward the men's room, passing a large glass window adjacent to customer booths and saw the Ford moving by outside the drive-through lane. He got the plate number and a fair look at the driver, a bald-headed man wearing a suit jacket. Blazers and sport coats never looked so drab. David crossed to the other side of the McDonald's and saw the Ford driving back onto the access road, disappearing from view.

Armstead phoned Barrett after resuming his trip. He described what he saw and gave him the plate numbers. He also told Barrett that the Ford was no longer following him.

"What do you think, my friend, am I in grave danger of abduction and being held for ransom by this old fellow?"

"I don't think so, Boss. You're not pretty enough. This sounds like a classic retired bureau agent. Those old farts are everywhere and have a fondness for Crown Vics. They contract out for a little change from time to time. It gets them out of the house where they're driving their wives nuts. Often they have a handler, an ex-agent smart enough to manage a stable, no, a pasture of these guys, working private cases. They're generally good guys and are harmless. Someone has an interest in you. You want me out there?"

"No, I don't think so. He's not around now, but I'll call again if he reappears. I do want you around for my Minnesota trip, but that's a ways off."

"Don't sell these old fellows short. He probably broke off because he thought you made him. They're patient sorts. Don't be surprised if he's around a lot. On the other hand, they hate missing meals and sleep, so if you want to sneak out, do it in the evening during *Wheel of Fortune*."

They laughed and said goodbye. This adventure was ludicrous, revolving around old events and aging men. More than half the populations of Vietnam and America weren't even born when Bob Hampton was murdered.

When David pulled into his driveway on Fawn Drive, a drab white Crown Victoria was parked down the street. This man was an old bird dog.

CHAPTER 67
Fawn Drive

Over the next several days, the Crown Victoria maintained a discreet distance from the Armstead home. A faded green Malibu periodically relieved the Ford. When David left the house in his Yukon, either alone or with his wife, one of the lurking sedans would follow. Trips to the grocery were spiced with stops at the dry cleaners, a hardware, and a liquor store.

Armstead reported the Malibu plates to Johnson who later confirmed that the vehicles were registered to former FBI agents. Johnson concluded that these men were doing no harm. Given their natural instincts in favor of law enforcement, they could be relied upon to report any observed criminal activity in the neighborhood, an added value.

Another inclination, according to Johnson, was notifying local law enforcement of their presence in order to avoid being disturbed in their essentially benign activity. Such notifications were not always candid. Police officers in the area were advised that the two old men were working a domestic surveillance case on the neighbor's three doors down from Armstead's home. This, of course, cast suspicion on the marital fidelity of both occupants of that house. A routine pre-patrol briefing warned officers to be alert for a potential domestic call to that address. Neighborhood life moved on quietly.

Alicia was in her third-floor office, known as the Crow's Nest, when the mail arrived. She was sending emails before the long Memorial Day weekend. Their yellow Labrador retriever, Sluggo, lumbered to the front door when the brass mailbox flap clacked. On some occasions, the dog had been seen to intercept a second batch coming through the slot. He never learned what to do with the mail other than to stand motionless, waiting for someone to pat him on the head and remove it from his mouth. Today there was only one batch.

Armstead patted the dog's head anyway and picked up the envelopes that had scattered across the wood floor. Sorting the pieces, he walked into the kitchen. The home was pasted against a mountainside, with the first floor dedicated to children' and guest bedrooms and a large utility room. On the second floor were the kitchen, dining, and living rooms, as well as the master bed and bathroom. A large sliding-glass door opened onto a wide deck and panorama view of northern California beauty.

Only the crow's nest occupied the third floor. Alicia ran most of her business from that space, accessible by a narrow circular staircase. Sluggo generally guarded the foot of those stairs while maintaining a vigil on the mail slot.

"Bruno, is there anything for me?" Alicia called.

Early in their marriage, Alicia seized on that name as the embodiment of her affection for David. His protests hadn't worked, and he always felt intimidated looking up at her, pleading to be called David. Her smiles were withering.

"No, just the usual and a piece for me. I'm going out on the deck to read."

Katherine Hampton's smoothly legible handwriting caused a small pain in his throat as he carefully opened the letter. Besides her cover note, there were two items, two sheets of folded paper and a photograph. Her note was brief.

Dear Mr. Armstead:

The copy of Bob's last letter and a photo of our son, his wife, and my granddaughter are enclosed. You can see Robert's resemblance to Bob. That's been a blessing for me. Perhaps someday I will get to meet your wife—Alicia, is it?

Katherine McCullough.

Unmistakably, the son was a copy of the father. Bob Hampton always seemed comfortable in his skin; this young man had that same look. Staring at the picture caused David to think, *the peace of the Lord that passes all understanding.*

Placing the note and the photograph back in the envelope, David turned to the letter. He recognized Bob Hampton's careful handwriting, a deck-log quality that enhanced its clarity.

My Sweet Katie:

Thanksgiving came and passed with its usual strange, out-of-place feel here. The food was good, but we had to reach back for our memories of other Thanksgivings. I did that, but mostly I looked forward. I'll be home in 3 months and there for the baby's birth. And oh yes, I'll try to do that Lamaze thing with you. I love you so. By the way, when are you quitting at the school? I can't imagine how big you'll be around the tummy by then.

Going on another boat ride tomorrow morning with several other guys and expect to be back by late afternoon. I couldn't ask for better men.

This is a new kind of war for the Navy. Most, but not all, of the people I work for are good, trying to do the right thing under tough circumstances. Thankfully, only a very few are in this for themselves and little else. One of our boat officers thinks that someone will try to emulate Kennedy. He hopes whoever tries that will be decent, but that's in God's hands.

Well, Baby, let's think about names, about being together, and about Little League or ballet lessons and maybe more kids. I pray for us every night.

Love forever,

Bob

David felt embarrassed as though he had been standing in Bob and Katie's bedroom, overhearing their most private and vulnerable thoughts. He realized that this last writing had not left Vietnam before Pastor Bob; his dreams and aspirations for them were gone.

Vaguely he heard the glass door sliding and saw Alicia coming out with two glasses of water. She always looked clean, fresh, and full of energy.

"Why the glum look, Bruno? Did Sluggo chew up the mail?"

She placed one glass on the table beside him. A second look told her that David's sadness was deeper. She sat in a deck chair in front of him but scooted it closer and placed her hand on his.

"What's going on? You look sad and far away."

Armstead debated about how much to tell her but knew that it would be useless to conceal the immediate reason.

"The widow of one of the men I served with sent me a picture of their son and a copy of his last letter. It involves something I'm working on."

He handed her the contents of the envelope, knowing that she would ask no further questions. That it was something he was working on put the matter beyond other inquiry.

"I would like to meet her, too" she finally said. "I don't suppose the pain ever goes away. I can tell she must be a fine person. Was her husband a friend of yours?"

"Yes, he was."

David reclaimed the letter and took his glass of water draining it.

"Are any of the kids having dinner with us tonight, or is it just you and me?" he asked.

Alicia long ago accepted her limits in David's professional life. She understood that he served the best interests of the country and that her greatest kindness was to love and trust him.

"I can't answer that, Bruno, but either way, you're taking me out. Have you noticed those old cars down the street? Allyson says its detectives doing a stake-out on Gina and Ross. She thinks they're getting a divorce."

Allyson, the neighborhood gossip, had an uncanny knack for half-truths. Often the percentage was lower.

"No kidding. That's interesting."

As Armstead moved back into the kitchen, the telephone began ringing.

"Armstead family, can I help you," David answered. At home he felt like a receptionist fielding calls to others.

"Oh good, it's you, David. This is Whit Moore. I'm glad I caught you before the holiday weekend."

"Hey Whit, you might not know it, but being here at all is a holiday. What's up?"

"Your barrister lady called this morning. She said the order would be signed first thing Tuesday after Memorial Day. She said if I got over there ready to work by Wednesday morning that would be perfect. I ought to come in Tuesday to check on where we should actually do the deed."

"Great. I'll pick you up at the airport."

"Rethink that offer. I'm on United's flight 64, getting into San Francisco at 7:06 Tuesday morning. A man your age shouldn't be shuffling around so early."

"Watch me, Whit. This works out just fine. It's a four-hour drive to Fresno. Just have your tail waiting for me in the terminal. I'll find you."

Dr. Moore was three years older than Armstead.

CHAPTER 68
Georgetown—Memorial Day

"Lester, can't this wait until I see you later at Arlington?"

Stroud was to be among those photographed with the president as he placed the traditional wreath at the Memorial to the Unknown Soldier. Stroud had a full day of appearances. Billy Fern had prepared a tight schedule, including a speech to a disabled veteran's group in the early afternoon. With the Vietnam Wall in the background, Stroud was to present a somber, tailored version of the Heal America speech, pledging support in the Senate for any measure that would increase medical benefits for this class of veterans. Each of these appointments presented special photographic opportunities for Stroud and any other politician appearing to be a friend of servicemen. Actual voting records on significant legislation became irrelevant, compared with visual images of media campaigns.

"I'm sorry to call so early. I just got a faxed report from our contact in California. To refresh your memory, this is the honest guy recommended by my crooked buddy. I thought you would like a summary rundown."

"Make it quick, Lester. I'm working on a speech revision and have to get out of here in half an hour."

"Some dull stuff. Our man's people picked up Armstead at his home in San Anselmo about two weeks ago and followed him to Fresno, California. His wife went with him. They checked into the Radisson and almost immediately he left and went to a lawyers' building on East Shaw. There were at least five firms in the building, so they can't identify which one he went to. Afterward, he went to the federal building. Besides courts and judges, all sorts of government offices are there. Our people couldn't identify the office he went to. Anyway, he was there for about two hours and then went back to the lawyer's building where he remained for another hour. A woman, as yet unidentified, came out with him, said goodbye, and they parted company. He then . . ."

"Lester, you're crowding me with detail. Get on with it." Stroud's impatience was growing.

"I was about to say, he went to a cemetery and walked around. He was seen to pause at four different locations, but not close enough to determine which grave or graves he was interested in or if he was just sightseeing. He returned to the Radisson's hotel bar where he met his wife for a drink. There was nothing else of note until the next day.

"They attended Fresno State's graduation ceremonies and afterward drove to some apartments near the campus. He hooked a U-Haul trailer to the back end of his truck. At that point, his wife got into a beat-up white Toyota with their daughter and drove away. Apparently it was already loaded."

"Lester, while I don't have kids, sounds like he got stuck driving the trailer while the women dashed off."

"That's about it, Senator. They don't give any detail but say that the 'surveillance was compromised' on the way back to San Anselmo. They resumed later near his house."

"Anything unusual after that?"

"No. Our people discreetly followed him to several usual errand stops. I spoke with our contact. He said his men report that Armstead is easy to follow, stays within the law on the road, and is careful with his truck. They said his daughter drives like a mad woman. So does his wife."

"Okay, Lester, meet me at Arlington a little before ten and bring the report. Maybe we can see what he's up to."

CHAPTER 69

Fawn Drive

Armstead was in their bedroom, packing a small travel bag. Alicia walked in dressed for bed; he was fully clothed in khaki pants, a white pullover, and jogging shoes.

"Where are you going, David?"

"I need to be away for a couple of days, maybe three days, but I'll be back for the weekend."

Alicia laughed. "This is like the old times but better now. Three days then might have been three months."

Armstead zipped his bag and walked over to her. Hugging her, leaving or returning, was always special for him. His love for Alicia included her gentle tallness.

"No, baby. This will not be more than three days, or at least three nights." He paused, "maybe four nights."

She laughed again.

"When do you expect Justine home?" he asked.

Alicia climbed into bed, and he sat on the side near her. He wasn't in a hurry.

"She's out with her brothers and sister. They have a scheme cooked up. They're going to play a joke on Frankie but haven't shared that with me. Why do you ask?" They were happy that the whole family was together for now.

"I'm taking her car if she shows up in the next hour or so. She can use mine. You don't suppose she'll mind, do you?"

"We do have five cars; why not take mine or one of the boys' cars? They're bigger."

David ignored the questions. Alicia knew David well; what he was up to had to be important. He never surrendered his Yukon to anyone. Interrogation was pointless. Instead, she pulled him down to her lips.

"She knows not to be late. We're going shopping in the morning. I'll bet you're thrilled not to have to tag along."

"Good point."

A little before eleven o'clock, Justine's Toyota bounced noisily onto the long driveway. They all got out of the car laughing. David saw and heard this from the bedroom window, kissed Alicia, grabbed his bag, and went to the kitchen. He told the kids he was going on a short trip and said that Justine could use his Yukon for the next few days. He said she needed a bigger car for errands. Giving her his keys, he kept his empty palm before her. She reached into her jeans for her Toyota keys. They grinned at the thought of their big burly dad carrying a key ring decorated with a little pink teddy bear. They, too, knew not to interrogate him.

David's last words were, "Justine, please don't hurt my car."

Armstead backed out the driveway in his best imitation of Justine's driving. When the rear bumper scrapped the street, he knew that his effort was accurate. Before he was fully straightened on the road, he punched the accelerator and wove away from the house. The Crown Victoria a short block away, remained motionless.

Fifty-eight minutes later, he checked into the Vagabond Inn on Bayshore Highway, five minutes from San Francisco International Airport. He set his alarm for 6:00 a.m.

CHAPTER 70
SFA to Fresno

Doctor Moore, dressed in slacks and a sport shirt, poorly concealed his disappointment at Armstead picking him up in the beat-up old Toyota. Given his tall lanky frame, he would have preferred more legroom.

"Moving up in the world, David?" he asked. "Bet it gets good mileage, too."

"Cut the crap, Whit. People have been watching the house lately. I can best ditch them using my daughter's car. It looks a wreck but runs great, and the mileage is better than my Yukon."

The two men remained silent until Armstead settled in on US Highway 101 South.

"Did you get any sleep on the plane?" Armstead disliked red-eye flights.

"I can sleep anytime there's an opportunity. When you have us in the Radisson, I'll take off on my own for a while. I told Mrs. Tobyn I would stop by and decide on the work site."

Moore had his own style. He was moving into his game-day mode. It was Moore's call about the conditions under which he would work. Armstead was actually grateful that his friend was taking charge of the program.

"If someone's watching you, maybe you want to just hang out at the hotel bar."

"Look, Whit, I do things other than drink. Maybe that's your pastime on the islands, but I have some calls to make, and the hotel has an exercise facility. I'll be okay."

"Good. Wake me when we get to Fresno."

Adjusting the seat and folding his hands across his stomach, he muttered, "That pink teddy's a nice touch, too."

Before noon, Moore left the hotel in a cab. He needed more space and convenience than was offered by the Toyota. Armstead worked out and placed a call to Barrett Johnson.

"I'm in Fresno for the next couple of days. Could you track down a Navy Commander Shaw? His first name is Durwood or Delwood, and he's retired if not dead by now. He was in Vietnam in 1969. I don't know what's become of him."

Finding people for Armstead without knowing why was part of his job.

"No rush. Just locate him. Don't contact him. I'll take care of that if need be."

David had made other plans while on the treadmill.

"Next, take care of flight arrangements to Minnesota for me and Mrs. Armstead. Bring us into Ely from San Francisco before noon on June 26, and Alicia needs to show up on July 1. Book us commercially and separately into Minneapolis or Duluth, Make sure that our ultimate destination isn't known."

"I'll take care of this. My service has Guard and active duty units in that region doing training flights consistent with our needs. Did the old guys follow you to Fresno?"

"No, I enjoyed giving them the slip the other night." He paused. "Last item: I intend to drop off the scope with the Minnesota trip. The bottom line for you is that this may be a good time for you to go off the scope as well. It's going to be a busy late summer, considering the frenzy of the political conventions. Your choice."

"I appreciate that, Boss, but I'll still have my cell phone on."

Three days later, Johnson saw Navy Captain Duane Quinby in the State Department and asked his back-channel help in locating Commander Shaw. Quinby was more than happy to assist.

CHAPTER 71

Medical Center, Fresno
Physicians' Lounge

"What can you tell me, Whit?" David stretched back in an upholstered chair. It was 10:30 a.m., and no one else was in the lounge. He listened intently to Dr. Moore who alternated between pacing the room and leaning against the back of a large, comfortable sofa.

"This is going to be quick and dirty. Tell me if you want more detail." Armstead waived his right index finger in a circular motion pointing up and outward, a flight deck signal to take off.

"A nonfatal wound sheared the side of your man's right heel. In other words, this man's heel was raised at the time he received that injury. Perhaps he was running. Another possibility is that he received this wound from below. You mentioned that a helicopter crash was a part of the circumstances of this man's death. This could be the result of ground fire. However this happened, Mr. Hampton did not die from this injury."

Mentally recording this recital, Armstead closed his eyes.

"The fatal wound began near the top of his right shoulder blade. I can't tell if it was a contact or near contact wound at this late date, but I can estimate, based on the angle of the bullet hole in that bone, a possible position of the body at the time of the shooting.

"With the blow to his foot, I'm certain he was unable to move without pain and then with a significant limp or hobble. He had to have been determined to move any significant distance on that foot. Clearly, he would not want to stand upright very long. At some point, he would have gone down either to a sitting, kneeling, or crouching position. My belief is that at the time of the second wound, he was doing one of those."

"I base that on several findings. First, the entry wound coursed downward from the top of the shoulder blade at a slight angle. The bullet then struck a bone in the front of the chest and was deflected backward, somewhat deformed, and tumbled down into his body cavity. Two points are significant here. The bullet was not a heavy, high-velocity round from a combat rifle. If the bullet had been fired from one of those weapons, there's a possibility that this second wound could have been, with luck, less than fatal as well, assuming timely treatment. Instead of being deflected by the bone, the slug might have punched on through to exit just above the man's rib cage. Not to say that he wouldn't have been seriously wounded, but more to suggest that he was not shot with a shoulder-aimed military rifle."

"This deflection lowered the velocity of the slug and caused the tumble through Hampton's body. It stopped near his rectum. You never know where a bullet will go as it slows down. A critical issue is whether any organs or vessels were hit and how much leakage he suffered."

"Under these circumstances, if he did not die quickly from shock, he could not have lasted more than a few hours without treatment."

Whit paused, and David opened his eyes. Armstead's jaw worked in concert with his mental images of Pastor Bob's passage into death.

"Back to my belief about his posture. As I explained, it's improbable that he was standing. In a prone position, the angles are also wrong. He could not have stood long unassisted in a fully upright position. He would have been bent over and almost falling down in that position to have taken the shot at the angle I found. As a practical matter, the person who shot him was either in a tree or standing above or behind his victim."

"Here's my best estimate: the man died from the second wound inflicted while he was in a sitting or kneeling position, perhaps crouched, shot from a pistol as the shooter stood behind him."

"Do you have the bullet?" Armstead cut to the chase.

"No, there is an incision and stitching in his groin where I suspect the slug was removed when the corpse was brought in from the field before being flown back to the states."

"Can the slug be located? Did you take photographs and make tapes?" Armstead unsuccessfully tried to avoid peppering Moore with questions.

"Not likely and yes. These things happen. Field mortuary work isn't focused on forensic precision, either then or now, despite all the crime shows we see on television. It would be nice, but that isn't the reality of combat deaths—never was and never will be."

David's spirits sank.

"Do you have any idea what the slug was?"

"Hard to be specific. Judging only from the entry hole in the shoulder blade, anything from a .38- to a .45-caliber, or similar round."

Armstead knew that a "similar round" could be a nine-millimeter.

"When you get back to Hawaii, write up this quick and dirty and develop your film. Then find a confirmed identity MIA/KIA with a record date of death as near to Hampton's as you can. Place all of these records in that file and put it away."

Armstead had given this thought. "Seal all of that with a label saying, "not to be opened except on your written authority" and tell me if anyone asks. Be cautious about this."

"Okay, what's happening here, David?"

"I am going fishing. As I asked, did you bring A-790's file with you?"

"Yes."

"What's in its place in Hawaii?"

"A duplicate with a note that the original is checked out by me for your review."

"Fine; let me know if you get any inquiries about this." David paused. "Let's get lunch and a beer. If we are done, I'll call Mrs. Tobyn to get Hampton back in the ground."

Disappointing as the absence of the spent slug was, Armstead had answers and was ready to move on to the next stage. He needed to know more about what happened the day Pastor Bob died.

CHAPTER 72

Washington, DC

Senate Office Building

"You're a blithering idiot, Lester. Your people in California lost Armstead, and when he shows up again, they have no idea where he's been. The bill's outrageous for what we haven't learned."

Stroud was fuming and losing his patrician control. Wainwright swallowed and waited for the rage to end. If his men lost Armstead, he wanted to be lost. That's important.

"Do I have to lick the stamps, too?" Stroud raged. "You didn't have enough people on this and weren't thinking at all about the objective. Keeping me happy is the objective, and I'm not happy."

Apparently Stroud heard his own venom and pulled back. Lester saw his chance. He had to get the senator further calmed.

"You're right, Senator. I didn't use enough men, but I do have a recommendation. Armstead could not have been sightseeing at the cemetery in Fresno. The first report said he stopped at four different general locations in the cemetery. Why not send people there to list all the names in those areas, or if need be, get a list of everyone buried there? Those guys wouldn't recognize a name, but we might."

"Good idea, Lester. This time I require results, not just a bunch of boring crap."

Stroud's anger was wearing thin on Wainwright. Although the door from the senator's inner office was closed, Lester was certain that Mrs. Baxter and anyone else out there heard Stroud's rant. He wasn't sure how much longer he could handle this job. Claridge Academy certainly has insidious aspects, but its elitist self-image forbids emotional outbursts.

CHAPTER 73
Minnesota
Northwoods Arrivals

For twenty-six years, the Taylor family spent more than half of their summer vacations at Bill Boston's cabin in Ely, Minnesota. As the family grew, so did their wonderful memories of the beautiful Northwoods. Sam's sons were now married and following their own lives. Sam's family contraction completed with the death of his wife.

Clinging to old habits and with an expectation of renewed energy, Sam had serviced the Ford Excursion for the fifteen-hundred-mile trip from Houston and packed lightly. He stocked a small cooler with tonic water, club sodas, and fruit. Sam left the provisioned truck in his garage and drove Betsy's small Mitsubishi to the office on Thursday morning. When Sam left his office that afternoon, he detached from his usual routine. Arriving home, he ate a light meal, took a brisk walk, showered, and went to bed at 7:00 p.m. Waking at 1:30 a.m. Friday, Sam was on the road a half hour later. He would stop only for gasoline and to pass tonic and soda until he reached a motel in Ames, Iowa, sixteen hours later. Timetables were less stringent and more fun when Sam was not alone.

Lindsay, Sam's law partner, never understood why he enjoyed long road trips, especially with a wife and kids. Lindsay's idea of a vacation was to fly somewhere exotic with his pouting, leggy wife. There the two would spend several days ignoring the scenery, eating too much, and staying mildly drunk.

For Sam, this trip was the best opportunity for him to think through what he needed to do for the rest of his life, to change that which he could, and to accept that which he could not. Every journey into northern Minnesota conjured images of a weary, searching pilgrim struggling up into a cool and gentle wilderness. Leaving behind the Texas heat and humidity and the frenzy of big city stress and traffic was a powerful metaphor and motive for getting away after midnight.

Sam left the motel after a light breakfast on Saturday. As in the past, he calculated his timing to avoid any traffic problems posed by the Twin Cities and adjusted his speed to arrive at the Duluth airport just before 3:00 p.m.

Frank Brooks' flight from Virginia came in Friday night. Taylor had no idea what Brooks would do with his time until Sam picked him up the next afternoon, but Brooks insisted that he would be waiting in the terminal and looking also for Richard Leyland's arrival from Dallas. The Camel had declined Taylor's offer for the two of them to drive to Minnesota, preferring instead one more billable day in the office and a cocktail party he and Carol were invited to Friday night.

Sam fully understood the typical Northwoods scenario that would play out for the next forty-eight hours. Newcomers and repatriate pilgrims took two days to wind down physically and to relax emotionally as a predicate for deeper rest over subsequent days.

The first night involved greetings between new and old friends and settling in. A simple dinner was washed down with good wine, and as the evening wore on, stronger alcohol was offered.

Summer sunset is late in Northern Minnesota, between 9:30 and 10:00. It is in the light of late dusk that hosts and visitors join in a first-night tradition. Casually clothed, or not at all, depending on the circumstances, ages, and gender of the participants, those who are able make a running jump from the boat dock into the cold waters of the lake. Warm towels and whiskey was ready for the keyed-up swimmers. Significant conversations were deferred for another time.

Day two involved walks in the woods and sightseeing around the lake. Fresh air, light food, swimming, and maybe casual reading would induce interesting discussions into the evening. It was this pattern and more that Taylor anticipated as he made his first pass through the passenger pick-up area of the Duluth terminal.

Both men were standing at the curb as Taylor stopped. Brooks was dressed as though he had just stepped around the corner to his neighborhood market for a morning paper, casual pants and a golf shirt, unshaven, but rested.

Richard Leyland had on tailored khaki pants, an open collar, long-sleeved, dark blue shirt and a rumpled pale blue seersucker jacket. Each had small travel bags, but Leyland also had a soft briefcase hung from one shoulder.

Sam Taylor had not spoken to either man for several days since they decided when he would arrive at the Duluth airport. For Sam's part, he expected they would be standing there when he made this pass, and they fully expected he would appear on time. None of these men had seen each other in over thirty years. Despite their advancing ages, they were the same reliable men he had served with that terrible day on the Song Bo De.

"Dallas has ruined you, Camel. I wouldn't be surprised if you brought a dinner jacket. Ditch that briefcase. Bill assesses fines for anyone doing business up there."

"Gimme a break, Prevert. This is the way we travel casually from Dallas and the briefcase contains some perfect Cognac I brought to share with you oafs when the time is right."

"I like the way you guys say hello. It's only been thirty-five years," Brooks said. "How long is the drive to Ely?"

Leyland grinned at Brooks in the back seat. Hellos were not a part their relationship.

"We'll be there in a little over two hours. Start enjoying this part of the trip. You'll notice that the further we go into the area north of Lake Superior, the more removed we become from all the BS, unless Camel brought some in his briefcase."

They laughed as Taylor found his way out onto US Highway 53 North.

* * *

David Armstead's Friday morning trip to the Oakland airport had been entertaining. He was first followed by the Crown Victoria and then later by the Malibu. He thought they were trying not to be noticed, but their changeover was obvious. He imagined that the first old guy had to make a sudden pit stop and called in his buddy from somewhere behind him. Armstead then took a Southwest Airlines flight to Seattle, where he caught Northwest Airlines into Minneapolis, staying at a hotel near the airport.

Very early Saturday morning, Armstead boarded an Avroliner, a stubby seventy-passenger Northwest Airlines regional flight to Duluth. Barrett Johnson, in uniform, greeted him in the terminal and quickly escorted him through security to an Air Force C-130 on a training flight from Polk Air Force Base, North Carolina, engines turning. When he deplaned in Ely, the pilots walked with him into the small terminal. Armstead had a few words of thanks for the pilots, shaking their hands. They then stepped back and threw Armstead casual salutes, more like waves, and returned to their aircraft. Five minutes later, Bill Boston drove up in his blue Suburban.

The solitude of the region folded around Armstead from the beginning of the drive out from the airport. Boston purposely avoided going through the village of Ely in order to enhance for David the feeling all newcomers have: peace and unhurried isolation. He entered Echo Trail, a nicely paved road three miles north of town. The road's winding length is about twenty-five miles, ending very close to the Canadian border. Thirteen miles up the trail, near one of its many substantial curves, Boston made a right turn onto a gravel road through the woods. Trees and heavy brush filtered the sunlight and obscured any view of the lake that Bill had so often talked about. Just over the second rise of the road, a slash of twinkling blue water showed through the trees. Boston brought the Suburban to a halt in a clearing behind a large house, strangely referred to as a cabin.

The property had been in the Boston family for over seventy-five years. Bill's grandfather and his friends in return for its availability built the original cabin over a period of years. That structure had been subsumed into a much larger residence with a modern kitchen and conveniences, indoor plumbing, insulation, and central heating, all surrounded by a deck.

A large stone fireplace dominated the living and dining room, the walls around which defined the size of the original cabin. There were now six bedrooms or sleeping areas, depending on relative needs for privacy, and three bathrooms, hardly a cabin by any definition.

The lake was sixty feet beyond the leading edge of the deck. A gravel pathway softened by pine needles wound down to a large square, floating dock. Local regulations required all such docks be removed each winter. The lake, screened by tall pines along its shores, is five miles long and no more than a half-mile at its widest point.

The Boston cabin is located along the lake's north side and is one of three properties owned by the Boston family, sharing a thousand feet of shoreline. Only twenty-three homes are on the lake.

After lunch, he and Boston took a lake tour on *Cooper's Coot*, Cooper Boston's pontoon boat. The environment was much different the last time they saw each other on the Co Chien River. As they headed back to the dock, three men came out from the trees and waved. The years had not changed their recognizable shapes and relative heights. These comrades were again together.

CHAPTER 74

Day Three—the Lake

On the deck after breakfast, the men enjoyed coffee and speculated on the wind's arrival on the lake. A solitary fisherman worked his way near the shore from the east. Boston grumbled that he preferred for fishermen to give his little lagoon a wide berth. He did not begrudge a man's fishing opportunities but thought the guy should respect Bill's privacy.

"He'll move on, Bill," Armstead said. "He looks harmless from here. When the wind comes up, he'll be gone."

"He's not a local." Boston continued to be mildly offended. "That's a rented boat he's using. Probably rented the whole rig. He might even rent some fish long enough to take his picture." Bill liked fussing about intruders in his peaceful domain.

Taylor joined the commentary. "Did any of you ever think that the VC used to watch us going by, wondering what in the hell we were going to do?"

"You're right, Prevert. They didn't shoot at us all the time, just when they thought they could get away with it or when we messed with them. The problem was that we messed with them a lot."

Brooks also kept his eye on the fisherman; none of the men looked at each other. They watched the angler's casting style.

"I'm glad those years are behind us." Taylor stood and walked to the rail. "We are a bunch of lucky mothers to be here at all and not under the grass somewhere. And the last damn place I wanted is for my name to be on the Wall."

Armstead remained silent after the conversation moved from the weather, the fisherman, and the Wall. He watched his friends carefully. They were as good as any men he had ever served with anywhere. They were strong and reliable. His mind conjured the word *faithful.*

The Camel came alive. "What's bothers me even today is that Wall is more a symbol of sadness than honor. Politicians go there to make speeches. Television crews get footage for specials about the war, and not one of them really gives a damn about the men who died or anyone who served there. It is not about celebrating the fine men named there."

Leyland said what most of them thought. People back home got pretty loose with their accusations about the war and the people who fought in it. They avoided bringing up a former Swift officer who built a political career on lies about his and the service of others in Vietnam. House rules for Armstead's visit prohibited discussion of present or even recent political events.

Brooks played the realist. "We've got to go beyond all that. We know the truth even if the rest of the country doesn't. It's not healthy for us to focus on that part of our past. We need to focus on not having that happen again."

"Five Buck, I've done the best I can over the years not to focus on my negative feelings when I came back to my own country, my own damned people. The only time I can ever talk about how I felt is with guys like you." Leyland stood and moved next to Taylor.

"I know that. We all know that," Brooks quietly responded.

Boston spoke next. "When I came home to Iowa, I tried to fit in again. Everyone had changed. My oldest brother will tell you that I got into a lot of trouble, but the truth is I didn't want to be around anyone. Rather than be a problem, I retreated to our old family farm."

The men waited for Boston to continue. Taylor watched his friend's eyes, knowing that this was heartfelt stuff coming out of him.

"What pissed me off most was being branded with the home-front image, a crazy, dope-smokin' typical Vietnam veteran, messed up by the war. I was proud doing what we did. We did nothing dishonorable, but we were the only ones who knew that. If I was embittered at all, it was because of assholes back home."

The men shared a common belief that many guys coming out of the war screwed up were that way before they ever heard a shot fired and probably were no more so than the average for the population of America at the time. Still, the distorted public perception remained.

"So Double, what happened then?" Taylor had known his answer for years.

"One morning, I decided the one who'd changed was me."

He paused contemplating his next words. "God didn't bring me through all this for me to sit on my tail, being drunk and angry the rest of my life. You could have blown my brother Tommy off his feet when I showed up ready for work two days later."

He paused again. "Since then I focus on the present and the future. When I think or talk about the past, it's the good stuff: the funny things and the really great men we served with. That's the way I look at the past."

Boston joined the others at the rail. Taylor turned and addressed Brooks and Armstead.

"So now that the Reserves have been heard from, what do you Academy types, Regular Navy pussies have to say for yourselves?"

Brooks chuckled. "First, the man in the fishing boat is to be commended. Renting, in the long run for an occasional user, is cheaper than buying."

The others smiled or winced. Five Buck wore his frugality like a badge.

"As to the past, Vietnam and the home front of those days were just part of my Navy life and not necessarily the most difficult part. The post-war years were tough on the military and tough on those trying to do good jobs for their service. All I can tell you is that my time on the boats was the best, and I'll always remember the people we sailed with."

Brooks looked at Armstead.

"I agree with my classmate," Armstead said. "I've been too busy to think about what America thought about me or what we did in Vietnam. Although I wasn't a boat officer, I've surely made a mistake by not staying up with you fellows over the years."

Armstead continued, "The Reserves haven't been fully heard from. Prevert, what's your view on our past?"

"Double Bourbon made my speech. None of us wanted folks kissing our ass or any kind of big damn parade, but I never expected to be miscast. This country seems to be flopping around in smoky views, religious and otherwise, that take people off the hook of self-examination and personal responsibility. There's a bubbling political and social divisiveness I don't recall ever seeing in my life. Forget about the big-ticket controversies like race, gender, and AIDS. If we don't do something about this angry schizophrenia loose in the land and trade it in for big doses of hope and unity, we'll be in deep trouble. Maybe I'm just a tired old guy venting. "

Sam looked toward the woods and then turned back to his friends. "The best thing that ever happened to me was serving with you guys." His eyes brimmed with moisture. "I'd do Vietnam all over again but maybe better." Agreement with Taylor needed no words.

It was 10:30 in the morning. The conversation had been too serious for the setting and maybe too long for a beautiful day on this lake. Now Brooks and Armstead moved to the rail. The fisherman drifted from their sight.

Boston broke the silence. “I wish Pastor Bob was here. Maybe he could have given us some answers,” he reflected.

“I agree,” Leyland said, “but remember, I always called him Rabbi Bob? Let’s suit up and head for the dock.”

CHAPTER 75

The Dock
Minnesota

Beer, soft drinks, and pink wine were chilled in the cooler on the dock. Only Boston liked the wine. For a while after lunch, the men ragged Boston about his horrible taste in wine. Its low-alcohol content and the crushed ice he packed in each refill of his plastic cup he defended, made the drink hardly more than flavored water. He promised to serve good stuff that evening at dinner and very good stuff when the ladies arrived. The afternoon passed in restful quiet, interrupted only by the fisherman motoring to the lodge on the east end of the lake. This time he cruised along the lake's midline. Sunset was five or six hours away.

Armstead had climbed out of the water and toweled his torso. Getting a beer from the cooler, he sat on one of the Adirondack chairs. The old scar was visible on the top of his chest. Boston tinkered with a filtering device used for piping the lake water to the house. Brooks dozed in another chair, and Taylor stretched along one edge of the dock, reading a paperback book. Leyland paddled an aluminum canoe around in the lagoon, periodically slowing and peering into the water.

"Prevert told me you guys were all on the operation when Hampton got killed. What happened? I was in a hospital somewhere, and I never knew how he died."

"We heard about that, Bruno. You were shot up badly, and the next thing we knew, you were gone. None of us believed you'd make it." Brooks spoke without opening his eyes. "Pastor Bob was OTC on a hugely bad raid on the Bo De."

Taylor put his book down, rolled over and came to a sitting position. "The thing started out as a small raiding force, but by the time Pastel finished screwing around with it, we had fifteen boats committed to the deal and no reasonably available air cover."

Boston stopped working on the filter. "Better than half the boats on that raid had never been in the Bo De. They had been working in the northern divisions and somehow got pulled into the operation on the spur of the moment."

"Bob told us we were trying to intercept an NVA force that was moving toward the Ca Mau," Brooks added. "Later we were told that was the bunch that shot you. Turns out, that group was gunning for us all along, and we sailed right into them."

"Puppy Dog's boat got hit, beached at the ambush site, and was hit again with at least two more B-40s. Puppy, his driver, the man in the overhead fifty and at least one other man on Dhoge's boat were killed." Brooks could have been reciting commodity market prices.

"One other boat got plastered but survived the day. Three or four men on that boat were killed, but not the O-in-C, Lester Wainwright."

"Never heard of him. Who was Wainwright?" Armstead asked.

"There's a phrase that describes him," Taylor injected. "Dipshit. That kind never knows the damage they cause. He came from another division where he got people hurt. Then he was sent to the Hill in Vung Tau where he'd be less trouble. Pastel put him in charge of the 69 Boat for this operation and made him the alternate OTC. Wainwright was inept."

Boston resumed working on the filter. Armstead saw the others smirking about Wainwright.

"Wait a minute, back to Hampton. What happened to him?" Armstead pressed.

Taylor scooted over to the cooler and got a beer. "It was a very bad day. Except for the two boats and eight dead at that point, we had done a pretty good job of killing the killers. We later found out they had come to the Bo Do for the specific purpose of ambushing a large force of Swifts. They were dug in on both sides of the river and had devised a running attack to avoid our typical reactive fire. When it got down to it, they were pretty much wiped out. OV-10s came in and mopped both banks with rockets and machine guns and, in the process, turned Dhoge's boat into a pile of junk. What was left of us rendezvoused on a sand spit out from the river mouth. The tide was low, and it was a good place to sort things out."

Taylor took a long drink from the can and continued. "When Double and I got there, Stroud was finishing some sort of BS talk to the group about what fine young men we were and all that horseshit. In the meantime apparently COMNAVFORV ordered Stroud's ass to Saigon and sent two Seawolves to pick him up."

Brooks continued the story. "Stroud ordered Pastor Bob to go with him, and the two of them took off on one of the wolves. By then, the transient boats were heading back to Cat Lo, escorting the 69 Boat and Lt. (jg) Dipshit. Our group was going back to Sa Dec. The wolves hadn't been gone five minutes when we heard gunfire and an explosion. The lead helo with Stroud and Bob on board had been shot down. Stroud went off into the jungle for some reason, and apparently Bob went looking for him. Camel went in later and picked up the two surviving crewmen and the dead pilots. One of the crewmen told Camel that he heard a firefight in the jungle just before Camel got there. Seals later found Bob. Bill and Sam brought Bob's body and the Seals out the next morning. There was some report that Stroud had been captured."

Their collective and individual memories of the operation were as fresh as if it happened that morning.

The narrative stunned Armstead. "Was there anything good about that day?"

"Maybe one thing," said Taylor. "Camel got to express his deeper feelings." Taylor waived for Leyland to come over.

Leyland had eased the canoe closer to the other men. When he saw Taylor's gesture, he gently stroked the canoe alongside the dock. Taylor steadied the gunwale permitting Leyland to climb out of the canoe. He got a beer, drained it, and looked around, wondering why he was called in.

"We were just telling David about the Bo De and Pastor Bob's death," Taylor said matter-of-factly.

Leyland's face darkened.

"Bruno asked us if there was anything good about that day. I told him you might have an observation about that."

Brightness returned, and Leyland grinned. He held up his right hand from which was missing the last two fingers.

"Do you know how I lost those fingers, Bruno?" Not waiting for Armstead's answer, he said, "They got shot away during a firefight two weeks after the Bo De. That was my ticket home, but do you know what the last good thing I did with that whole hand before the fingers went away?"

Armstead knew he would get an answer the others already knew.

"I got to use that hand and the other one to beat the crap out of a miserable little bastard named Lester Wainwright. When his boat got hit, he lost it. We pulled alongside to help him and his crew. Two or three of his guys were dead, and Bowers went aboard to fire the beehive and get the boat back in the game. Wainwright, that little asshole, ran over to my boat to get away from the carnage. He wasn't hurt at all. I grabbed his worthless ass and pummeled him with this hand and then the other. I threw that bag of dung back on the deck of his boat. I was pissed, and he deserved it. I'd do it again today."

He walked to the cooler and got another beer and turned back. "Where's that SOB? I'm still pissed."

"Is that how you talk to juries, Camel? I always wondered what real trial lawyers said to juries."

"Screw you, Prevert. This was different."

"Whatever happened to Bowers?" Brooks asked. "He was a good man and a hell of a gunner."

Leyland sipped his beer. "He's my law partner in Dallas. He got out of the Navy, and we both went to law school together. We'll be together until we both drop dead."

"What about Stroud? Did people search for him?" David knew the routine but wanted to hear their views.

"Once they got him into the jungle that was pretty much the end of it. At some point I read or was told that he escaped. He and Pastor Bob are supposed to have fought them until they were overwhelmed." Brooks was searching his memory.

Leyland, still fuming about Wainwright, found distraction in talking about Stroud. "He's a senator now; you know that. That's another thing that pisses me off. Why do we elect these pretentious bastards? As soon as they get into office, they play like God put them there. Puffed up assholes."

Food was in order, Boston decided. "I'm grilling chicken breasts and corn on the cob tonight. There are about fifty jumbo shrimp ready for one of you to put on the grill before then. If Sam will do the salad, we'll be in business. Besides, there is something I will show you before the light gets away from us this evening."

Empty cans were thrown in a bag, and the dock was put in order for the evening. As the others trudged back up toward the cabin, Leyland took one long leap into the lake, swam out for thirty feet and back, climbing out he emitted one long "hooo-aaah."

CHAPTER 76

Northwoods

Dinner on Deck

The grilled shrimp were demolished with the help of garlic and horseradish-laced red sauce. As the last of a crisply chilled white wine was poured, Boston went back into the house. When he returned, he was carrying four long, white mailer tubes and a thin package about fifteen by twenty inches. As he stripped away its brown paper wrapping, he began talking.

"I went to our old farmhouse two months ago and found a framed photograph hanging on the wall of the parlor. I took it to a graphics place in town and had them reframe it for preservation and made blown-up copies for framing. Those tubes contain your copies."

As he stripped away the last of the wrapping, he held the photograph up for them to see.

"I didn't know if anyone still had a copy. Mine disappeared a long time ago." Richard Leyland's three-fingered right hand moved out to touch the frame.

"I've got the original back home, but this one is the blown-up version, and I thought I would hang it up here."

"We looked like a bunch of Mexican bandits. That's a great photograph." Taylor leaned forward in his deck chair and squinted at the picture. "There's Bob Hampton and Paul over in the corner. Double, you look like you were in the bag."

"I was. We'd been up all night, and I had a couple of beers before we got to Cat Lo, but I remember you having more than two."

Taylor smiled.

Armstead bent over, studying the picture. "I remember this deal. Five Buck, is that your skinny ass I see next to that Trung Uy?"

"Sure was. That was a good haul. Everything worked right for us that night."

Boston enjoyed the reactions of his friends. "David, it was your reports that got us all that stuff. There were a lot of other pictures out at the farm, but I couldn't find any with you in them."

"That's okay Bill. Thanks for the copy. Time has sure done you guys in. Camel, you were losing hair back then."

"Truth be known, I wouldn't trade anything for being there," Taylor said. "Like I told you, I'd do it again right now."

Over the next twenty minutes while the chicken was cooking, they talked about the other people in the picture, Vietnamese and American, officers and men. They rehashed the simultaneous two boat night ambushes set at different points within the Long Tuan Secret Zone and their triumphant return to Cat Lo.

When dinner on the deck ended, the group moved inside to the plywood-topped table, handmade by the original builders of the cabin. The table had been host to more than seventy years of board and card games, meals, and conversations. For the Boston family and their guests, the table was the centerpiece for new and restored relationships.

Richard Leyland emerged from his bedroom, carrying his briefcase. Curiosity got everyone's attention. Leyland opened the case and pulled out two bottles carefully wrapped in newsprint saying, "Only the *Dallas Morning News* is worthy of this cognac."

Boston produced five glasses. "Where'd you get this?"

"Carol and I went to France last year. We were driving around in the south, trying to decide where to spend the night. We ended up in Cognac late on a Sunday afternoon. The town was just concluding its annual festival. We bought a case of this stuff from a local maker, and it's better than any of the high-dollar cognac sold in this country. These are the last two bottles. In Cognac, these cost about seven bucks a cork."

"My kind of price," Brooks mumbled.

Leyland began pouring. "You know, I can be a callous, vulgar cretin. I enjoy the role and sometimes play it up for effect. But that's not how I feel. When I left the Navy, I moved on. I've had a great life, and I'm glad I'm here to tell you that. I remember Rabbi Bob and all the other men who didn't get to come home and didn't get to brag about their kids or chide us for marginal behavior or even drink this damn good cognac. I remember and say . . ."

As he carefully poured the last glass and began his final words the other men stood and toasted, "To them all."

Later, Armstead refilled his glass and walked out on the deck, followed by Brooks. The light was fading fast in the west.

"Dave, I'll tell you more about the Bo De. I've only told one other person."

Armstead turned and leaned his backside to the railing. "What's that, Franko?" Their friendship at the Academy, as among other classmates, was always special, something different from civilian college life. Each service academy bred these special friendships.

"Before Bob left with Stroud, he brought me a draft after action message to send when they were in the air. Bob wrote the original message, but Stroud edited the damn thing, striking out the real detail of the mission and adding some outright lies about Wainwright. Bob over-lined the part about Wainwright but ordered me to send the message otherwise as Stroud expected. However, he also ordered me to keep the draft until I could give it to Commander Shaw and to tell Shaw what I knew. I did that."

"What did Shaw do?"

"He asked me about Wainwright, and I told him that Camel beat him to a pulp."

"What was his reaction?"

"He smiled, folded the draft, and slipped it into his pocket. He asked me if I thought Stroud had survived. I told him I had no idea but that he was alive when last seen in enemy custody."

"Did he say anything else that you remember?"

"Yeah. He said he'd take care of the message if need be, and he was meaning if Stroud ever came out of captivity. But then he wanted me to tell him more about Wainwright. I told him about the gist of what Camel said this afternoon. We all knew the story before we got back to Cat Lo. Shaw smiled the whole time."

"What became of Wainwright? You guys seemed to have pretty strong feelings about him." Armstead thought, *there's always one of his kind everywhere.*

"As far as I know he went back up to Pastel's headquarters for a while. Somebody said he then volunteered for duty north of Da Nang. It doesn't make sense, though, that he'd want to be around Marines."

Brooks sipped his Cognac. "I don't know what Shaw did after that. It couldn't have been much, or Stroud never would have made the Senate."

"We never know about that. Some real turkeys strut and gobble on the floor of the Senate. Stroud isn't the first and sure won't be the last."

Armstead tipped his glass toward Frank and then drained it.

"I owe you for this, Five Buck."

Without knowing details, Frank Brooks was the kind of man who could smell deeper meanings. He knew the business about the Bo De was more than of passing interest to Armstead.

CHAPTER 77
Breakfast Boat Ride

A clean ray of sunlight was streaming through the window on the east side of the cabin. Two loons screeched out on the lakeshore, and the smell of dark-roasted coffee filled the air. Bill Boston had put out milk, fruit, and cereal for breakfast. Armstead, out for a jog on Echo Trail, had just returned. Sam Taylor was thumbing through a book about shipwrecks on Lake Superior. Brooks and Leyland were still down. One of the Cognac bottles had gone to the recycling bag and the other into a cabinet for another special occasion, maybe not this year.

Sometime last night, with the appearance of Wild Turkey and Bombay Gin, the conversation degenerated into an almost endless recitation of whatever happened to whom. Pecorino, Boston's engineman, was a successful car dealer in Denver, now hanging on by his teeth waiting for the economy to turn. Leyland told several stories about Bowers, particularly in law school. Bowers, unwilling to put up with professorial arrogance, always made high grades.

Taylor didn't divulge the identity of a former crewman, but the group enjoyed hearing about this former Swifty grown so fat from high living that he was more comfortable traveling in a jogging suit. Something turned him around. He got on a diet and exercise routine. As his general health and weight improved, the man made other changes. Today, Sam reported, he is wealthy, healthy, and a good guy.

Brooks asked about Ringer, the man working in the detachment office the night before the Bo De operation. Taylor laughed and said, "That's another story. Ringer went to college on the GI Bill and got an accounting degree. He then went to law school somewhere and joined the FBI. His first office assignment was in Houston. He was really a good agent and worked a case that my crewman was involved with.

Finally, everyone turned in.

The framed photograph had not been hung but was lying on the big table near the fruit and cereal. The eastern sunlight bathed the picture in its ray. Armstead saw this and decided to move the photograph out of the light. He didn't know if the glass covering was sufficient protection. For the first time since the previous evening, he was able to see detail in the picture that he had missed. As the framing crossed the right edge of the grouping of men, Armstead noticed that there was a partial face showing next to the wood.

"Bill, this picture has someone in it cut off by part of the frame. Did you see that?"

"Yeah, David. The problem is the frame and not the photograph. Your copy in the tube shows who that is. It's Stroud."

Armstead crossed to one of the bookcases where the tubes had been stored the night before and opened the one with his name on it. Pulling out his copy, he unrolled the picture like he was about to read a scroll.

"You're right, that is Stroud. Why was he there?"

Taylor spoke next. "That peacock heard about our ambush and came down from the hill that morning to see what we got. He sort of muscled into the picture so he could be photographed with us really tough guys."

For a fraction of a moment, Armstead froze. He then looked up and around the room until he spotted a magnifying glass next to a box of road maps Boston's family collected over the years. Returning to the light, he peered through the glass to the edge of the photograph. He tried to adopt a poker face. Putting down the glass and feigning ignorance, he asked, "What kind of pistol is that in his holster? It's got a weird grip."

Taylor and Boston almost simultaneously answered. "That's his Lugar."

Taylor continued. "He went everywhere with that Lugar. Given his coloring and bearing, I thought he looked like a Nazi. That grip is sort of rounded like a broom handle. In fact, that's how the grip's described. That's his Lugar."

"This picture was taken a couple of weeks before I got shot. Was he carrying that when he was on the Bo De?"

"Oh yes, like Sam says, he always had it."

Whatever David thought to be his best poker face noticeably dissolved. "I'll be damned."

Recovering quickly, he looked at Taylor. Taylor was already there. "Say, David, would you like to go for a boat ride? I'll show you a little island down the lake on the west."

"Sure," looking at Boston, "Can we grab breakfast when we get back?"

* * *

Boston's father bought the boat in the early 1960s. Its ten-horsepower outboard motor was a simple engine. You put it in neutral, center the collective on start, pull the rope, then adjust the throttle downward for a bit, put it in gear, and go. This aluminum boat and motor had about forty-five years of summers flawlessly hauling kids, guests, lovers, dogs, and old folks. Its rumpled skin testified to its hard use.

Armstead sat well forward to counterbalance Taylor's weight in the back. The lake surface this early in the morning was like glass.

"This little island we're going to is hardly bigger than most folk's living rooms, but it's a nice place to visit. Bill and I took my sons out there when they were just young boys. I had found an unopened LURP we decided to fix for them," a reference to the Long Range Patrol ration developed for US Army Special Forces.

This ration was a freeze-dried, packaged, individual meal in a bag further within a waterproof canvas-like bag. Mixed with water, hot or cold, the contents reconstituted into one individual meal. A case of meals contained twenty-four packages of eight different meals.

"This one was chili and beans. I brought it home from Vietnam, and by the time we took it to this island, it had to be fifteen years old. I couldn't keep it forever."

Armstead smiled and nodded. "Was it any good?"

"Sure, and the boys loved it."

Taylor slowed as they got closer and appropriately cut the engine, gliding in between two water-soaked logs and over some gravel. Armstead stepped from the bow, pitching the makeshift anchor to the center of the island.

Taylor got out of the boat, sat on a rock and declared, "Let's talk, Bruno. I have a feeling you need to tell me something."

"Is our attorney-client privilege around here someplace?"

"You bet it is. I've been reading people all my life, and with you, I see a man who's been struggling alone with something pretty big. If I can help, this is the time and place to tell me."

For the next hour, Armstead told Taylor everything that had happened with Phan, his sly indirections and peculiar references, and finally what Phan disclosed on the Bassac River. Phan's final words of farewell in Saigon disturbed

Armstead. Taylor asked questions and penetrated Armstead's knowledge even further. David confessed his suspicion about security at the State Department. He was worried that somehow the secretary, a man he held in the highest respect, was part of the problem rather than a part of the solutions. People had been following him in California. He worried that Phan and others were manipulating him into a foolish course to wrongfully influence the November election. Based on what he knew thus far, Stroud probably did kill Hampton, and it probably happened just as Phan had described.

"Prevert, this whole matter has gotten beyond my experience. I've done a lot of tricky things in my career, but I've never screwed with American elections, and I've never done a murder investigation."

They sat for a while in silence.

"I have a bodyguard and shadow for years. I haven't even told him about all this. Do I fully trust him? Yes, and he knows I'm holding out on him."

"David, let's go back to the basics. Someone told you that Stroud murdered Hampton, and you can place Stroud at the scene. Your witness may never be available but gave you some interesting items of evidence. He gave you a pistol, some bullets, an expended shell casing, and a holster. He also gave you Bob's dog tag and his red patrol notebook. This morning you learned that Stroud's pistol, admittedly unique, was in his possession at the time of the Bo De raid if not in Stroud's control when Bob was shot. You can't get a ballistics match because you can't find the expended slug. Still all that is so tantalizingly close that you might be misled into thinking the case would stand up at trial."

Armstead nodded affirmatively as Taylor ticked off the points.

"Bob's letter home to his wife is nice, but not of much value in building a case against Stroud. Even if you had the slug and could prove it was fired from that Lugar, you would still be unable to prove that Phan or his men didn't shoot Bob themselves. To get anywhere you would need Phan to testify. His written statement alone might be admissible, but I wouldn't count on it. If Mr. Phan isn't on the stand to counter a defense lawyer's suggestion that this was all a diabolical setup, on a technical level you're dead in the water."

Armstead's dejection was apparent.

"Bruno, look at the evidence independent of Phan. Circumstantially, you have built a pretty good picture of the conditions under which Bob died but not much as to who killed him. Before you get all bent out of shape and begin thinking I'm crazy, start seeing the evidence as though it's a child's game of connect-the-dots. The picture you have drawn without Phan or his statement fails to depict Stroud as the shooter. And the law is going to say that when all the dots are on the page, as to the identity of the shooter, that evidence must exclude every other reasonable hypothesis that someone else shot Bob."

"So I'm wasting my time? What about Shaw and the edited message?"

"What Frank told you last night was interesting. You might look up Shaw if he's still alive and swab him out on all that. So he got the message, and the officer in tactical command disagreed with the draft prepared by a junior officer. That's what OTCs can do. That's what they are supposed to do if they think the message is inappropriate."

"Sam, this is a bunch of crap. I've been agonizing over this for nothing?"

"Let me paint the picture even darker. You, Sir, can be portrayed as a conniving pipsqueak like Wainwright, scheming to destroy an honest-to-God, decorated war hero who just happens to be in the political party that your bosses oppose. Heaps of shame on you, Mr. Armstead, and shame on your bosses. With the state of the record as I see it, some rum-soaked municipal court defense lawyer could look like Clarence Darrow, Percy Foreman, and Johnny Cochran all wrapped up in one."

This time Armstead began shaking his head left and right.

"I'm screwed. I'm done. Phan's gone, and I've got nothing even if Stroud did it."

"That's not entirely true, my boy." Taylor began smiling. "You do have something that might be more important than anything you've told me."

Armstead looked skeptically at Taylor. "What the hell are you talking about?"

"It's called guilt, not the guilt in the courthouse, but the guilt that's in that man's heart. I call that the wild card. Most people have a tough job living long with guilt, and one way or another, they break under the strain."

"So I just waltz up to him and tell him he's a guilty asshole, and he'll drop to his knees and confess? You're kidding?"

"You're not there yet, David. I've painted as dark a view as I can imagine, but the bright side is that you are probably right, and he is definitely wrong and knows it. It's safe to assume that, despite what your suspicions are about others, Stroud doesn't know what you know or how much you know. That all works in your favor; I don't know how it will play out. Guilty people do some pretty stupid things without much help from anyone."

Armstead lifted a large stone and heaved it into the lake. The waves from its splash rocked the stern of the boat.

"Now that I've dumped all this lawyer stuff on you, two points are very clear. First, if you have Phan testifying, you've got a case that can go to a jury; that is, the judge won't kick the prosecutor out of the courtroom. The second point I've only implied is that guilty people trying to hide even the whisper of a crime can be dangerous and will nearly always fail to make a realistic assessment of the evidence against them. Their fears of discovery prevent them from seeking a professional opinion. My bet is that no one around Stroud really knows the truth. In that case, there's always a wild card to be played."

"Thank you for giving me a clear look at the situation. I don't know where this is leading, but I'm going to keep at it. I can't stop now. I'll find Shaw and pray that he tells me something that puts Stroud away."

"Good, that's what I wanted to hear. I'm honored that you trusted me with this. Now, let's go back to the cabin."

Taylor stood and got the anchor. "Do you want to drive?"

"Sure, I might as well put it all on the line." While Armstead liked Taylor's pragmatic manner, David didn't always understand his friend's metaphors. David surmised that every card in this game had been wild.

As they drew near the dock, the same fisherman was on the other side of the point seventy yards east of the house. Taylor didn't see Armstead's gesture, but just as they tied up and got out of the boat, Barrett Johnson motored in and pulled up to the other side of the dock.

"What's going on, Boss?"

"Could you join us for breakfast?"

Taylor took this all in stride except to think, *God, I love this.* He whistled the opening notes of "Dixie."

* * *

As the three men walked into the cabin, Brooks and Leyland were cleaning up from breakfast. Boston was tightening a clamp on a new lake water filter and saw the stranger. He wasn't exactly a stranger.

Armstead took the matter up without waiting for questions.

"I'd like to introduce you to Maj. Barrett Johnson. He's my shadow and a good man."

They stood to greet him.

Boston smiled and said, "How was the fishing?"

"Hold the interrogation for a minute, Double. I need to tell Barrett about you all. These are the best men you will ever meet. They drove Swift Boats in that other war, and you can trust them. I trust them. Looking at Taylor, Armstead continued, "and I trust Barrett every day with my life."

"Let's cut to the chase, Bruno. Barrett, was the fishing any good?" Leyland asked.

Barrett was quick. "Only before you fellows woke up."

"Are you staying down at the lodge? You might as well move up here. You can keep a good eye on Bruno, and I guarantee the food's better with us," Boston said.

Johnson turned to Armstead. "When are we heading back?"

Armstead had no qualms about discussing his schedule. More to the group than directly to Johnson, he said, "Before I got here, I was planning to bail out tomorrow and canceling Alicia's flight. I'm not doing that now. What I've got to do in DC will still be there next week."

"I was hoping you'd stay. Everyone else is in. Maj. Johnson, don't sweat the space question. There's plenty of room here or over at the Peterson cabin."

"Thanks for the offer, Mr. Boston, but I need to visit with Mr. Armstead first."

"Barrett, you can hold the formality here. This group responds better when addressed as 'asshole.'" We try to avoid such terms back in the seat of government, but not here and not now, at least until the ladies arrive. Let's go out on the deck."

As Armstead closed the sliding glass door behind them, he heard Leyland emitting one of his classic hooo-aaaahs.

"David, I've got good news, and I've got bad news. Well, actually, it's only questionable news. I have an address on your Commander Shaw. He's retired and living in Annapolis. Ms. Lokey passed on a message from Secretary Brady to the effect that Mr. Phan has really disappeared. The Vietnamese government advised Brady and the Center in Hawaii that a medical doctor named Dang has been assigned the liaison function replacing Mr. Phan. I have other contacts trying to find out what happened to him."

"Did Lokey know if I was still going to be working with Dang, and do you know of any reason I need to go back to Washington?"

"I asked those questions. The secretary's only hint to her was to say that Phan's replacement might 'be of passing interest' to you. Regarding getting back to Washington before next week, she said people are already leaving the city. She said she put in a leave request herself and expected to be gone, beginning Thursday."

Armstead nodded in understanding. "That's good enough for me. Barrett, you need to take Boston's offer of hospitality. I haven't felt this relaxed in years." David realized that this feeling only came to him after he and Taylor spoke on the island. He also remembered Phan's new English word—perspective.

"Maybe it's something in the water, but I can tell this has been good for you. I'll reconfirm my arrangements for your wife and check out of the lodge."

Johnson started down the path to the dock. He stopped and turned.

"I almost forgot. I had someone do two or three drivebys on your street. The old guys are gone."

Armstead smiled and went back into the cabin.

CHAPTER 78

Senate Office Building

As Stroud's post-holiday staff meeting concluded, he asked Lester to his private office. On the way through the door, Stroud told Mrs. Baxter to track down Billy Fern for confirmation of their meeting later that morning.

"Report," Stroud spoke without cordiality.

Depression had crept into Wainwright's mood. Resigned to abuse, he recited his current understanding of events.

"Armstead is back in town. Apparently, he was in Minnesota, but I haven't been able to find out why or where. Capt. Quinby said that Armstead's goon, an Air Force major who does things sometimes for Secretary Brady, asked his help two weeks ago in finding a retired Navy Commander Shaw."

At that Stroud began a hard look at Wainwright.

"That's right, Senator, our old friend Delwood Shaw is a person of interest, probably to Armstead. I don't know why anyone else would care about Shaw."

Wainwright had his own bad memories of Shaw. He enjoyed seeing Stroud squirm. Stroud no longer complained about Wainwright's conversations with Quinby, giving up on that issue. Wainwright staged his report to see Stroud's further reactions. Lester didn't know the true dimensions of Stroud's fears; he only saw evidence of them.

"I paid the investigators in California and got their final report Saturday. They lost Armstead late the preceding week, and then Mrs. Armstead gave them the slip last Wednesday."

Stroud's predictable disgust with the assumed ineptitude of the investigators was increasingly visible. It was time to disclose their more fruitful performance.

"Their report had some interesting features. They spent considerable time at the cemetery in Fresno. In nauseating detail, they prepared a grid of graves wherever Armstead had been seen walking. They overdid it, jacking up the bill. Here's the list." Wainwright tendered the multipage document to Stroud, who accepted it with impatient silence. Stroud began thumbing the pages.

"Go to page six, toward the bottom. You'll see a familiar name."

The expression changed on Stroud's face, but there was no verbal reaction. Wainwright was more intrigued by the appearance of Hampton's name than what he saw in Stroud's face. After a moment, Stroud spoke.

"Why do you suppose Armstead would be interested in Mr. Hampton?" There was an air of puzzlement in Stroud's voice.

Wainwright was disappointed. He hoped to see Stroud go over the edge, but oddly he appeared calm. Lester could have added another fact.

"Beats me, Senator. Maybe he wanted to pay respects. The report is clear that the dirt over that grave was reasonably fresh, which sounds like an exhumation."

Stroud swiveled his chair away from Lester taking in the view from his window. "I can't imagine why, either," he said. "Got any ideas, Lester?"

Wainwright could not see Stroud's face, an aspect that often guided Lester in his subsequent behavior around people he wanted to manipulate. For once, Stroud was not raging at him, a point of relief. *Maybe we can get past this paranoia,* he thought. *If Fern's plan is going to work, we must be focused on the convention, not the past. This all got started because Stroud fears Brady, not because he might fear anyone else.*

"I could follow Armstead myself and see where he goes or hire someone like I did in California." Wainwright had run out of ideas.

"Do what you can, Lester. I need to meet with Billy in the next few minutes. You let me know if you find anything interesting." There was an odd imbalance in Stroud's voice, so odd that Lester decided he had better stick on Armstead like glue, if that were possible.

* * *

Fern lumbered into the senator's office without his usual bluster. He appeared determined and pensive. The dark business suit and accessories he wore were appropriate in all respects; he actually looked and was dressed like the serious-minded advisor Stroud always wanted. Stroud had been told to watch for this display from Fern, evidence of Fern's conviction that his plan for the candidate was maturing into solid results. Without invitation, he took a seat.

"I've had significant meetings in the last sixteen hours. The people I met with called me and wanted to discuss your interest in being on their candidate's ticket." His voice and language were void of his usual crudities.

Stroud smiled. Most often Fern's reports were recitations of ongoing efforts rather than accomplishments. Stroud was a working participant in Fern's plan. If successful, Fern gave his clients the credit and a handsome bill. Failure was always shared.

"I don't know which of these two is going to win the nomination," Billy said. "The key is uncommitted delegates. None of the other primary candidates have enough delegates to force a decision, but together they can name the winner."

If Fern had to pick the candidate he personally preferred, he would go with the guy from New England and not the woman from Arkansas. For purposes of getting his client on the ticket, he didn't really care. Significantly, both camps surveyed Stroud's availability.

"For you, Senator, the bottom line is that they are interested in you as their running mate. They say their vetting has already begun. Neither wants to be the other's VP, and Mrs. Olsen's people are adamant on that. Both are adamant in refusing to take VP spot. Neither anticipates nodding to anyone as a condition of getting enough delegates to win. There isn't energy for that at all."

Fern and Stroud smiled.

"Senator, let's talk about what can kill the deal. I've been unable to answer satisfactorily their questions about Mrs. Stroud. They perceive that she is less than a public person; that doesn't particularly bother them—or me. They asked whether she will be a liability at any time through Election Day." Billy thought, *these bastards care about no one the day after.*

Stroud frowned. He was being forced to do something about her situation. Now that his goal was within reach, this was the time to follow Fern's advice. He worried that he might have waited too long.

"Billy, tell them the truth about her drinking problem. Make it very clear that I have agonized with her over this for some time but recently decided to take the hard steps to restore her to health. I'll have her somewhere before next week. Imply that Mrs. Stroud also recognizes her problems and wants treatment. Be sure to tell them that I fully understand if they decline to further consider me. I will be honored to serve in any capacity they desire and will continue fighting for their election. Ask that they pray for Elaine's speedy recovery." Even Stroud was surprised by his seemingly spontaneous generosity of spirit.

Fern's view was less complimentary. *This is one cold SOB.*

CHAPTER 79

Washington Navy Yard and Annapolis

Armstead spent his first afternoon back in Washington in the archives section of the Naval Historical Center at the Navy Yard on the northwest shore of the Anacostia River. He searched old message traffic, looking for the after-action report that Frank Brooks transmitted on the morning of the Bo De operation. On finding it, he made several copies, trying to get the best product from the old and faded message. The text conformed to Frank's recollections.

Of more than passing interest to David was a peculiarity in the punctuation used on the substantive text of the message. The sender's punctuation, quotation marks, flanked the body of the message, Stroud's version. These marks, abnormal for military communications, Armstead concluded, were Brooks' method of transmitting that version without implying an endorsement of the assumed truth of the message. Brooks was allying with Bob Hampton without overtly saying so, a predicate that could support whatever action Shaw might take later. As expected, there was no mention of Wainwright, or the O-in-C's salvation of the 69 Boat.

That evening Armstead telephoned Commander Shaw at home. Following a brief introduction, he told Shaw he wanted to visit with him soon. Shaw was cordial and invited Armstead to his home the next morning.

The drive to the eastern shore of Chesapeake Bay was pleasant, the traffic moderate for midmorning. He found Cantwood Court, a tree-shaded, dead-end street running north from Old Mill Bottom Run. Shaw's home was a beautiful, red-brick, two-story Georgian structure with a carefully maintained and flowered front yard.

Shaw opened his front door before Armstead reached the porch. Although in his eighties, as further confirmed by his crenulated face and sparse gray hair, Delwood Shaw's weight and apparent physical fitness seemed not to have changed since his days in Vung Tau. He was dressed in a yellow golf shirt, beige slacks, and walking shoes. Armstead followed him back to the kitchen.

"My wife is out in the garden. She wants to get more flowers planted before lunch. Can I offer you anything?"

Armstead declined.

"Thank you for seeing me, Commander. It's been many years since we last met, but I needed to talk with you about the old days." Armstead had not decided how to approach the topic, except to do so with some candor.

"I remember you, Mr. Armstead. You damn near got killed somewhere around Coastal Group 35. I never expected you'd live. I'm glad I was wrong. You look all right today. And from what I know, you've come up in the world."

Shaw turned toward the refrigerator. "I'm gonna have some orange juice. Sure I can't offer you something?"

"No, Commander, thank you. You were Senator Stroud's executive officer in those days, weren't you?"

"I was also the intelligence officer." Shaw drained the small glass, washed and dried it, and checking to see that it had no smudges, returned it to the cabinet.

"I've never been much on military protocol since I retired, but the Navy sent me home as a rear admiral, and I'm proud of that if not much else."

Armstead nodded and smiled. Shaw went on.

"Believe me, I'm not offended. There's an old judge I play golf with who lives down the road. He sat on the Supreme Court of Texas many years ago before retiring here. One day we ran into a younger fellow who remembered my friend when he was the attorney general of Texas. He called him 'General' and not 'Judge.' I thought that was strange."

Armstead realized that Shaw was about to make a point.

"The man didn't apologize, but explained that calling him 'General' was a respectful reference to a time that he believed my friend had greatly served Texas. For that fellow, calling my friend 'General' was a higher honor."

"Admiral, I'll call you whatever you'd like. My subject has to do with your time with Stroud."

Armstead needed to show deference to his senior, but he also needed to keep the man on topic.

"A few days ago, I visited with some Swift Boat fellows who said when they were in trouble, you were a fine man to have up on the hill in Vung Tau. One of those men was Frank Brooks, who retired from the Navy a few years ago. Given your story about the golf-playing judge, Brooks might also call you 'Commander.' Do you remember him?"

Shaw looked at Armstead, a smile forming.

"Tell you what, Mr. Armstead, let's you and I take a walk. The orange juice gets me jittery, and I need to spend some energy."

Armstead followed Shaw to the attached garage where Shaw grabbed a baseball cap from a worktable as they stepped through a side door. Walking down the driveway, Shaw commented, "I don't need the sun burning off what little hair I have left."

As they moved toward Old Mill Bottom Run, Shaw began speaking.

"Sure, I remember Brooks. We had a long conversation when he got back to Cat Lo. I asked him to come up to the hill. Stroud was still being dragged through the jungle by the bunch that captured him."

Armstead reached in his shirt pocket and produced one of the copies of the after-action message. Handing it to Shaw as they strolled down the hill, he asked, "Did you and Brooks talk about that message?"

Shaw took the paper and moved it around in the light as they walked. "Sure did. Those are my initials in the little routing box up there." Shaw pointed to the scrawled "DS." "Why do you ask?"

"Brooks told me that the two of you talked about the handwritten draft of that message, and I was wondering if you remember such a conversation or the draft."

"Yeah, we talked about that. I remember that the draft was seriously edited and then re-edited. Seems Stroud and another officer couldn't agree on what happened or what was needed in the message. We're talking about a fellow named Hampton. He was killed by the commies."

"Did you ever do anything about what you and Brooks talked about?" Armstead saw that they were close to the end of the street and felt they were nearing the end of the discussion.

"Not really, Mr. Armstead. Let's go back up to the house. I need a trip to the head."

Shaw escorted Armstead back into the kitchen and disappeared. Through the large rear window, Armstead saw Mrs. Shaw kneeling in the garden near the back fence. Every so often she came upright, reached for another container of flowers, and moved further along the fence. A few minutes later the Admiral returned and gestured for the two of them to sit at the kitchen table. He was carrying a small folder.

"I got this out of my office in the back." Handing the folder to Armstead he said, "The draft is what Brooks gave me. Still in pretty good shape after all those years."

David smiled and accepted the folder. He read the draft. This original writing of Hampton and Stroud, victim and killer, could be used to establish the existence of a conflict between the two and hence a motive for Hampton's murder, he concluded.

Armstead was certain that Sam Taylor would consider this draft a strong and final piece of evidence against Stroud, a corroboration, at least of Phan's statement. Armstead felt humility, reading this revealed truth. He was also disappointed because he understood that without Phan's testimony, the case against Stroud was subject to all the defensive claims outlined by Taylor in Minnesota. Finally he looked up at Admiral Shaw.

"Why have you kept this all these years?"

"Mr. Armstead, when young Hampton died and Stroud got captured, I supposed that little struggle between them ought to die, too. Part of me believed that Hampton's reputation, especially after death, would come out on the bottom of that contest. You and I both know that in this kind of confrontation between a junior and a senior officer over the adequacy of the senior's leadership, whatever the result, a junior loses a career. From what I knew of Hampton, he was going to make a great officer one day. Other people around him knew that, too. It seemed better to let things be and not risk tarnishing that memory of him also."

"Believe me, Admiral, I know life isn't wrapped up in nice little packages of black-and-white decisions and absolutes. With all that was going on in the country, the craziness, I don't fault your rationale on any of this. Hypothetically, if you'd made a stink over it, assuming Stroud survived captivity, this whole mess would have been seized upon as just another reason we shouldn't have been in Vietnam."

"I kept that paper in case there might be a chance of using it. By the time of Stroud's escape, I was back in the States on the way to other duty. Then I read that he and Hampton had put up a hell of a fight. I didn't like Stroud, but all that national prominence made him, and by implication Mr. Hampton, genuine war heroes. There seemed little point in returning to old business that could only make the Navy and maybe Hampton look bad. Hampton was dead, unable to defend himself."

The older man ran both hands across the top of his head. "You know, my big regret is that I didn't do more to protect all those boys that day on the Bo De."

"Why do you say that?" Armstead knew that senior officers far behind actual fighting don't always see battle images in the same way as close up combatants.

"When I came up on watch that morning, I realized that our timetables were all fouled up. I was worried that we wouldn't be able to keep the air cover, and then I learned that the cover had been canceled by Stroud."

He drew his hand across his mouth as if clearing away some felt, but unseen debris. "I got on the horn and spoke with the OV-10 people. I told this fellow that some damned fool had canceled the air, and I wanted it back. I told him not to ask who the damned fool was, but he already knew. I told him that I'd sure appreciate it he wouldn't get them booked up for a while, just hanging out."

"Sounds reasonable, Sir. What more could you have done?"

"I could have told him to put his planes right over the operation going in. Those bastards needed big nuts to shoot our boats with Broncos right over them. Might have been a different day if I'd done that."

"If you don't mind me saying so, you shouldn't spend time dwelling on what you might have done. All these years later, it's not much use."

Armstead suppressed the temptation to volunteer his own doubts to Shaw. He wasn't sure that he wouldn't, when the day was done, also smother the truth.

"You can have that folder. I almost threw it away myself two or three times. I'm glad to be rid of it." Shaw paused. "What are you going to do with it, anyway? This is a nasty political year. You going to use this against ole Stroud?"

"Admiral, I'm following a string out to its end." Armstead felt dishonest in his evasive response. He need not have worried; Adm. Shaw understood that Armstead was making smoke.

"We wouldn't be having this conversation if Stroud had stayed in the shadows and been some ordinary guy. You do what you have to do, Mr. Armstead. Just do better than I did."

"Sir, I'll try. By the way, these boys also told me about someone named Wainwright, who was on that operation. He's that person indirectly mentioned in the first edit. I didn't know him when I was there. Was he on your staff in Vung Tau?"

Delwood Shaw's face, for the first time that morning, broke into a broad grin. "I tried to fix that son-of-a-bitch. He caused that operation to get fouled up, the manipulative little bastard. Brooks told me what happened and that one of the other officers beat the hell out of Wainwright for his cowardice. I booked his little ass up to the DMZ to serve as a naval gunfire support officer. If the commies didn't kill him, I wanted the Marines to do it. As luck had it, he conned his way out of that job and beat me back to the States. Have you met him?"

Armstead stood up from the table. "No I haven't, but from what I've heard, he's a . . ." Shaw interrupted Armstead with a hand held up.

"We called him the Miserable Little Bastard. It still must suit him."

As they walked toward the front door, Adm. Shaw placed his hand on David's shoulder. "Mr. Armstead, come back any time. We'll take another walk, and maybe you'll have some juice, too."

* * *

Back across the bridge heading west on US Highway 50, Armstead saw a silver Jeep Cherokee following him. He exited the highway, proceeded to the next on-ramp, and then moved back onto US 50. The Cherokee still followed. Armstead decided to use his cell phone.

"Barrett, someone is following me again. Are you in the office?"

"Yes, in a manner of speaking. I'm in my old truck behind the silver Cherokee that's behind you. It's got Washington State plates; I'm checking."

"Barrett, I am tired of this crap. What can we do?"

"Pull off on the next exit where there's a gas station. Stay there until you hear from me."

Armstead complied. He stopped on the service station apron.

The Cherokee drove past the station and stopped on the road shoulder about eighty feet down. Armstead saw Johnson's white Ford pickup roll by the station and pull up behind the Cherokee. Johnson got out of the truck, carrying an opened road map. He seemed to be having trouble with the wind blowing the map in his face. When Johnson arrived at the Cherokee, he began talking to the Cherokee driver. Then Armstead's cell phone rang.

"Come over here and meet someone. He'll be happy to talk with you." Armstead acknowledged the invitation and drove forward. He thought he heard some sort of howl as he ended the call.

When Armstead walked up to the Cherokee, Johnson's right arm was extended into the driver's compartment. He had a grip on the driver's neck just at its base on the man's left shoulder. The man was moaning but conscious.

"Say good morning to the man you have been following," Johnson quietly commanded.

The man moaned and said, "Good morning."

"Address him more properly, Sir." Johnson pressed the man's neck. The man screamed.

"Good morning, Mr. Armstead."

"Now if you would please, tell Mr. Armstead first who you work for and why you are following him."

"I wasn't . . ." He screamed again.

"My name is Lester Wainwright, and I'm an administrative aide to Senator Edward Stroud. The senator wants to know what you're up to." Lester was trembling. He was clearly worried that Johnson would tighten his grip.

Johnson hissed in Lester's ear, "I'm going to turn you loose, and you are going to step out of the car. I'll refrain from hurting you further as long as you answer every question Mr. Armstead asks. Do you understand me?"

Lester could barely speak but nodded his comprehension.

David liked Johnson's style. He decided to benefit from it.

"When did you start following me?"

Lester stared at the ground. "This morning when you left your apartment."

"Did you know the person I saw this morning?"

"Of course, I did. You saw Commander Shaw. I guessed you would." Wainwright reached up with one hand and began massaging his left shoulder and neck.

"What made you think I was going to see Shaw?"

"I was told you wanted to find him."

"Told by whom?" Johnson interrupted.

"By someone where you two work," looking at Armstead.

"Look, you turd, who told you?" Johnson was like a cobra, ready to strike.

"A man named Quinby. He's a Navy officer on temporary duty over there." Wainwright's eyes darted from Armstead to Johnson and then back to Armstead. Tears were forming in his eyes.

Johnson moved very close to Wainwright's face and again hissed. "Are you the dung brain who put the old farts on Mr. Armstead out in California?"

Lester nodded. He would have given up his mother to the electric chair if Johnson had asked him. He was beginning to panic; in broad daylight on a late weekday morning these men were going to kill him, and there was nothing he could do but answer every question.

"Why is Stroud interested in anything Mr. Armstead is doing?" David detected an ominous, but soft growl coming from Johnson. Armstead had never seen this aspect of Johnson.

Wainwright was about to collapse. "I don't know. You gotta understand Stroud. He's a funny guy. He gets a notion in his head, and nothing can change him. He's afraid of your boss, Mr. Brady." Tears streamed down Lester's cheeks.

Barrett looked at Armstead and stepped back from Wainwright. A dark stain now spread across Lester's trousers.

Wainwright cried. "I don't know. I don't know why Stroud's doing any of this. I do what he tells me. All of us do."

Johnson looked at Armstead. "Do you need anything else?"

Armstead motioned for Johnson to follow him to the back of the Cherokee. Johnson told Wainwright not to move an eyelid. When they got to the back of Lester's car, they spoke in muted tones.

"Jesus, Barrett, you even scared me. I'm through with him, but I want him to leave town, and I mean really leave. I don't know where he calls home, but I want him out of Stroud's service and to keep his mouth shut."

"I can get the point across, Boss. Don't worry your balding little head about this." Barrett was pleased this had gone so well.

Armstead was concerned. "Don't kill this man. He needs to live with himself a long time."

Johnson nodded his assent. "Why don't you go on, and I'll finish my little talk with Mr. Wainwright."

"One other matter we need to agree on, Barrett, is about Quinby. Let's do nothing to him yet. We know the truth; that's an asset. His time will come."

"Sir, I totally agree."

Armstead returned to his vehicle as Johnson walked back to Wainwright, handing Wainwright the Cherokee keys.

"Mr. Wainwright, I have a couple of things to tell you before we get back on the road. From this moment on, you are to have no further contact with Senator Stroud or anyone in his office other than to phone in your resignation. Do you completely understand me?"

Wainwright nodded.

"I'll let you live," he paused, "today and tomorrow and as long as you do as I tell you. You will never speak of today to anyone, and you will leave here and go back to wherever you called home before Stroud. You are to lead a quiet and inoffensive life. If I learn you are messing with anyone—Armstead, his family, or anyone—I will find you and kill you. You know I will. This is the best break you will ever get in your miserable life. You better take it. Do we have an understanding?"

"Yes we do, Mr. uh . . ." Wainwright realized he had not recognized his tormentor. And then he understood. ". . . Johnson."

"That's right. When I said you were to talk to no one that includes your scum friend Quinby. Are we clear on that?"

"Yes, we're clear. He's no friend of mine. Just another one of Stroud's flunkies, like me."

Johnson stepped back from the Cherokee as Wainwright opened the door. Lester turned to speak this last time to Maj. Johnson. "Mr. Johnson, I know this is going to sound strange to you after all that's just happened, but thank you for letting me go and for giving me an out from something I never should have been involved in. You'll never hear of me again."

Johnson watched Wainwright until he was out of sight.

* * *

Armstead's rearview mirror reflected Johnson's last conversation with Wainwright. David wondered where Johnson had perfected his capacity to menace without lasting injury. Cocktail party elites would recoil at Johnson's behavior, something they otherwise enjoyed seeing in movies and television shows. Johnson was a professional, however, and not an evil brute. In truth, Armstead remembered his own violent capacities years ago when Brady recruited him. Had Brady seen in him the restrained and mastered violence David now saw in Barrett Johnson?

Armstead reached for his phone. Sam Taylor needed an update.

"Sam, can I run recent developments by you? Do you have time?"

"You're lucky I'm in today. I took my time driving back from Minnesota, and I'm not sure how long I'll stay here, but go for it."

Armstead summarized his conversation with Admiral Shaw, the big differences between the after-action message and its draft, and the encounter with Wainwright. Taylor laughed so hard at Wainwright's predicament that he could not completely hear David's report. Repeating the information, Armstead requested his friend's legal opinion.

"Bruno, if you had Phan available as a witness, I'd get an indictment of Stroud so fast it would make your head swim. Even Lester might be a good witness against Stroud. If Stroud failed to testify at trial and was convicted anyway, there'd be enough evidence to sustain his conviction on appeal. And if the bastard did testify, he'd have one hell of a problem explaining all of this different evidence that I see as cross-corroborating. Any prosecutor could reconstruct that day on the Bo De with just the testimony of our Swift Boat people you saw at the lake. We might want to track down that air crewman who watched Pastor Bob hobble off into the jungle to find Stroud and possibly one of Hampton's crew members just to nail down what we all knew then, that Stroud froze up during the firefight. The day we lost Bob Hampton has never dimmed for any of us."

Taylor paused. "That brings us to the moment of truth—proving that Stroud actually pulled the trigger on Bob. You have him by the balls, if Phan is in this country and can testify. Stroud's other lies would also be exposed. Without Phan, Stroud could walk out of the courtroom a ruined man, but not convicted. Kind of like O. J."

Armstead remained silent. The confluence of all this information wouldn't have been possible even a few years ago. It's as though this day was ordained, he thought.

"David, are you there?

"Yeah, I'm here. Just thinking."

"Well, think on this, Bruno. You could wait until you locate Phan and make a decision then. On the other hand, you probably don't want to wait too long and let Adm. Shaw die on you. He'd be an effective witness on a lot of points. The rest of us are in good shape and ready to do what is right."

"Yeah, Sam. For a bunch of old toads, you Swifties still looked reasonably lethal." Armstead's admiration for these friends out of the past was palpable.

Taylor, ever the cautious lawyer, hedging against his gut feelings about the strength of the case, continued. "Look, I haven't really thought much on this, but there are some federal court rules about preserving the testimony of a potentially unavailable witness in an investigation; you know, like someone who is dying. I don't think you need to be in a hurry just quite yet. I'll call you Friday, and we'll talk more on the evidentiary questions and the steps you could take with the Justice Department. Don't be discouraged and remember this: legal solutions aren't always the best solutions to everything."

"I've got one more question for you. What do you think of the proposition that all this was a shameful attack on a fine American for political purposes?" David was prepared to say more, but Sam's growled reply shut him down.

"To hell with them, Bruno. Those people know no other way than to attack the messenger. They're helpless in the face of truth. Get Stroud in a court of law with the evidence that you have, and those assholes will shut up. More importantly, the public and a jury will know just how bad Stroud is."

"Thanks, Sam. I appreciate your insights." Armstead's tone lightened. "I really enjoyed seeing you and the others. Minnesota was a good thing for me, and thanks for pressing me to go there."

Armstead's comments gave Taylor time to calm down. He was getting too old to be an attack dog.

"Going up there has always been good for me; this trip was no different. I'm making long overdue changes here. I'll keep you posted. Let's talk Friday. Got to go."

Armstead knew from Boston that Sam had not been happy since his wife's passing, more like going through the motions without having a heart for it. Armstead also knew the importance of always having a heart for what you do.

CHAPTER 80

Armstead's Office and Apartment

Washington, DC

Armstead spent the rest of the afternoon in his office intermittently pondering his action while dealing with paperwork Ms. Lokey had set aside. His distraction was compounded by her cheerful interruptions to bring in more paper. Finally, defeated by the tedium, he decided to leave for the day. Some clear path might be revealed once he got home. He made one last phone call.

"Barrett, did Wainwright get your message?"

"Oh yes, boss. When he changed his pants or before doing so, he was to phone in his resignation. He's out of the picture."

As Barrett and Armstead were talking, Wainwright had completed packing his Cherokee and arranged for the Salvation Army to come by his apartment the next morning to pick up the rest of his other possessions, furniture, and linens. He deferred his resignation call until after the end of the workday. He had a few personal effects in his office to pick up in the evening, enough to fill a large briefcase, and then he would be off. On the road out of the city, he planned to call Mrs. Baxter at her home and ask her to convey his regrets to the senator. Well before midnight, Lester hoped to be on Interstate 81 South, approaching Roanoke, Virginia.

"Anything about Mr. Phan, anything at all?" Armstead asked.

"No. A puff of smoke would have left more of a trail than he did. David, I've kept my mouth shut about all the spook stuff that's gone on with you in the past few weeks. You'd tell me when you thought I needed to know something. Are you anywhere close to doing that?" Friendship spawned Barrett's question.

"I appreciate that. I'll tell you as soon as I know the answer. Thanks." David hung up and left his office.

When Armstead got to his apartment, he pulled off his suit coat, tie, and shoes, poured some Wild Turkey, and sat down in his small living room. He finished the drink and rested his head on the back of the overstuffed chair. *No decisions come easy these days*, he thought. He drifted off to sleep.

The television set and a table lamp were on a timer, a long-established minimal security precaution used when Armstead was traveling. The television volume was moderate; so was the voice of the political analyst, a media pimp found often within the beltway, paid to predict that which his employer of the season expected.

"Yes, Phillip, it's a toss-up for the top spot in New York at this point."

Phillip delivered another slow pitch to the guest whore. "Then what about the vice presidency, who'll be a running mate?"

"That's the real story emerging these days," the analyst intoned. "Understandably, neither candidate is talking except in general terms and to deny that they would play second fiddle to each other, a smart position at this time. They've got to look like there's a world of difference between them; if they agreed on the number two person before their convention in Boston, there wouldn't be much excitement, would there?"

Recognizing his cue, Phillip smiled, characteristically arching one eyebrow. "Is there someone out there they would prefer on their ticket?"

"The sources have been very tight-lipped on this whole question, Phillip, but my analysis points to one man as a likely bet, Senator Edward Stroud from Indiana. He could be selected by either candidate."

Satisfied that he had wrestled a special insight from his guest, Phillip pursued supporting information. "In the primaries and other events of the past year, you would admit that Senator Stroud hasn't been a very serious candidate. Why then do you think either of them would want him joining their battle for the White House?"

"On the contrary, he has been serious. He probably understood that he could not win the nomination, given the higher profiles of the other competitors, but he could attract attention and votes as a running mate. There are many reasons for this, Phillip. Stroud's politics are straight down the party line, and he offers that time-honored commodity of geographic diversity. Not least, however, are

Senator Stroud's personal qualifications for office. He's a decorated war hero; he's mature and, frankly, he sounds like he knows what he's talking about. In these days, that's more important to the general public than actually knowing."

They both indulgently laughed. Neither man recognized their elitist and manipulative attitude toward the masses or the gravity of publicly announcing that an empty suit had as good a chance at the White House as anyone.

"A terrific speaker, he's polished, and some might say he's handsome. Finally, in a political party that's been terribly divided this year, he's been the one person out there consistently and optimistically talking about unity and the future. I'm jaded in my old age, but Senator Stroud really wants to and believes he can help heal the political anger in America."

Phillip paused thoughtfully and, placing the fingertips of both hands together almost as in prayer, spoke with gravity, "Thank you for being with us tonight. After a short break for our sponsors, we'll be talking with . . ."

Armstead was unable to recall when he became aware of the discussion between Phillip Carr and his guest analyst. Mr. Carr was well known for his mature good looks, carefully rehearsed but shallow intellectuality, and the parade of political prostitutes he regularly invited to his show. In cruder circles, he was known as Pimp Phillip or Madam Carr.

David Armstead believed he no longer had the luxury of time or of carefully constructing a criminal case against Stroud. Legal advice notwithstanding, Armstead knew that events were once again threatening to overwhelm a long-suppressed truth. If he waited one more day to sort through competing considerations, legal arguments, and evidence, he would inevitably enter a swamp of indecision and defeat. Once again, Stroud would emerge from a darkness of his own creation to appear as a gallant, heroic American. This time, he could be only one death away from the presidency. Not now, David Armstead vowed. Not ever. It's time to play Sam's wild card.

CHAPTER 81
Stroud's House

Elaine Stroud spent the morning on the telephone with her mother, a seventy-five-year-old widow comfortably living in Terre Haute. Elaine's mother, also a gentle spirit, had been blessed with a kind and loving husband. Economic success had not spoiled the small family, but the death of Elaine's father had burdened both women. Elaine had no other close family. She called her mother daily.

Following a light lunch prepared by Doris, the housekeeper, Elaine telephoned Janet Brock, an energetic, hard-bodied mother of two elementary school children. Mrs. Brock's husband was an economist in the Department of Commerce, and Janet supplemented their income by helping women who could afford her services as a personal shopper. Janet's clients sometimes had bad taste or no taste at all for the right clothing in any situation. Others had no time for shopping, and still others considered Janet a status symbol. A very few, like Elaine, lacked confidence that their own selections would meet spousal and public approval. In shape and coloring, Janet was a younger version of Elaine. Senator Stroud admired Janet's wardrobe and thus was inclined to approve selections made for Elaine. Janet had sensed uncomfortably that the senator's interests extended below her clothing.

Elaine explained to Janet that the senator had indicated they might be traveling to Terre Haute soon and then on to the convention later in the month. Could Janet suggest items that might be appropriate? Indeed Janet had in mind four items that might be suitable for late summer in both cities. The ladies agreed that Janet would pop by midmorning on Friday after dropping her children off at Vacation Bible School. Janet mentally noted that Mrs. Stroud, frail in spirit, was enthusiastic about the coming trip.

Later that day, Elaine worried that she might be going too fast in calling Janet. She should have spoken with Edward first. She called Mrs. Baxter but was unable to speak with the senator; he was in conference. Her worry deepened, but this time she would not venture into the back of her closet. She would instead take a nap. Doris would prepare dinner and leave before Edward arrived home. Also by then, Elaine would awaken feeling better. That would be a good time for her to speak with Edward to confirm his approval of the meeting with Janet.

When Stroud arrived home, he knew that Elaine was asleep upstairs. He removed his coat, got a glass of red wine, and returned to his study. There he reviewed literature on two clinics in Indiana that might be suitable for Elaine. Wainwright had assured him that each would be discreet and sensitive to the senator's needs. Stroud made his selection. They would fly to Terre Haute late Friday afternoon for Elaine to be admitted Saturday morning, a low-profile occurrence unlikely to attract media attention. Unencumbered by Elaine, Stroud could then focus on his political future.

Turning on the television, he listened to the first part of the *Phillip Carr Show*. Stroud expected Fern to call later that evening, asking for the senator's opinion of the segment, *not bad at all.* He got a second glass of wine and, switching on his computer, began typing lists for Wainwright's and Mrs. Baxter's attention until he returned to the office late Monday. They needed to get him ready for the convention and the short press release announcing Elaine's hospitalization. It was better to put this out on the table, rather than have the press wondering about her absence. Surely the Carr program would stimulate particular interest in both Strouds.

The telephone rang a little after 8:00 p.m. "Mrs. Baxter, to what do I owe this call?" Mrs. Baxter never called him at home unless her news was important.

He listened. "Did Lester give any reason?" He listened further, his face darkening. Wainwright was tired of Washington and the stresses of work. Mrs. Baxter's recitations omitted Lester's specific comments about the senator's verbal abuses and shady use of campaign funds, the latter item unknown to her. She also did not disclose the unguarded relief she heard in Lester's voice. From long experience, she knew the hazards of delivering bad news, but making it personal with this senator was dangerous.

"Thank you, Mrs. Baxter. This will be all right. We'll deal with this in the morning. Have a good evening."

Stroud dialed Lester's cell number. The phone immediately rolled into its messaging format. "Call me, Lester. Tell me to my face what the problem is. This is a very important time for me."

Replacing the receiver, Stroud took another sip of wine and thought. A moment later, he hurled the glass against the wall. *Lester, you coward*, he raged. *I've got to get you back, though. You're my only way through back doors.*

The front door chimes gently rang. *Ah, that could be Lester. We ought to be able to work out this little problem before things get out of hand.*

The senator failed to look before he opened the front door. There stood David Armstead, dressed in a business suit without a tie. Stroud's stomach tightened, a feeling he had not experienced in years.

"May I come in, Senator? I must to talk to you briefly."

Many times in public settings, Stroud had seen Armstead but never in social or private circumstances. Of course, he remembered him from their days in Vietnam and knew that Armstead worked for a man that Stroud detested. This would be a time to clear the air.

"Come on in, Mr. Armstead. May I offer you some wine?"

Armstead declined. As he moved into the study and to the chair offered by the senator, he noticed broken glass on the floor to the right of the doorway.

Stroud closed the door behind them and said, "I was startled by your ring. Knocked my damn glass over."

Armstead saw red splash marks of wine going up and arcing across the wall and wondered how a knocked-over glass splashed its contents up as high as Armstead's chest. He believed that Stroud, as was said of a former US president, was "an unusually bad liar."

Stroud realized this wasn't a social call. As Stroud settled into his swivel chair, he casually reached for his computer mouse and closed the screen.

Armstead, Stroud remembered, was well considered and direct in his speech. In Vietnam, he had a reputation among senior officers for stating his views and then shutting up. He never argued or attempted to bolster his views, but he always made it very clear where he stood. Stroud waited.

"I met one of your people today, Lester Wainwright. He was in Vietnam during our time, but I never knew him. He told me you had an active interest in what I do or at least what I've been doing for the past several weeks. I feel an obligation to tell you directly so you need not speculate further."

What could that fool Wainwright have told Armstead? Stroud thought.

Armstead was known for a rough past before he started working for Secretary Brady. Without compassion, Stroud supposed that Armstead had become physical with Wainwright, something Stroud himself had barely resisted. The senator appreciated this man's unexpected civility, a fast-disappearing commodity in politics. Stroud's appreciation was brief.

"I'm responding to this obligation not because I give a damn about you in any capacity but because I deeply care about this country. Based on the truths I know, you will understand that you're finished in all senses of the term."

"Oh really? You're pretty confidant of that, are you?" Stroud had been threatened before. Defiance was his best shield. "Why don't you get to the point and stop wasting my time?"

"Certainly, Senator. In November 1969, following the Bo De River raid, you brutally murdered Lt. Robert Hampton, and I can and will prove it."

David did not expect Stroud's silence, but he did notice a slight twitch on the outside corner of his left eye. He went on.

"You shot him in the back near the base of his neck with your Lugar and then surrendered to the NVA." He saw a second twitch.

"Mr. Armstead, you seem to be having a fantasy. Have you considered all of the implications of this preposterous story?" There was a third and fourth twitch.

"I'm not going to argue with you or play games, Senator. Rationally, you have four choices facing you; all four bring you disaster one way or another." He moved forward slightly in his chair and continued. "First, you could try to silence me by persuasion or killing me. The first part's not an option, and even if you had the nerve to kill me, you'd be ruined anyway. There is at least one other person out there who knows everything I know, and he's no wimp."

"And the second choice?" Stroud's face became stone. *This man knew how to deliver threats.*

Armstead's voice was clinical and void of malice. "That's the one I like. You could blow your brains out." Armstead paused. "But you're too much of a coward for that. Moving on, you might want to fight me, test me on your fantasy argument. I like that also because it means prolonging your ultimate ruination, whatever the outcome. Your fourth choice is the reason I'm here."

Stroud smirked. "I can tell you've given this thought."

"Oh I have, Senator. I'm here to make you an offer. Withdraw from all political life, resign from the Senate tomorrow, and inform your people that you no longer have an interest in any public life. If you do this, I will consider our business concluded, and the country will be spared from anything beyond useless speculation. For Bob Hampton, I will have secured your public destruction, but you will retain your physical life and freedom, although I can't imagine what that would be worth. Beyond that will be God's judgment."

In the middle of Armstead's statement of the fourth option, Stroud began looking around the study, his eyes not really focusing on anything. David shortened the fuse.

"I made a similar offer to Wainwright today, and he wisely accepted. One way or another, as I said, you are finished."

Now the eye was twitching too often to count.

"Tomorrow doesn't mean all day to accept my offer. It means before noon. I'm going to the Justice Department after that. I'll listen to the noon network news if I haven't already heard something through the grapevine. Do you have any questions?"

"No, it's time for you to leave." Stroud's voice was flat, defiance vanished. He rose from his chair.

Armstead also stood. "I agree. I'll let myself out." Before Armstead reached the study door, Stroud spoke.

"I didn't mean to hurt Hampton."

"I believe you, Senator. You were driven by fear. You lacked the courage that others find day after day. It's time to pay up, to answer for that. Good night."

Out on the street Armstead felt a special freshness in the summer evening air. The meeting with Stroud hadn't taken long, and it had gone well. For the first time in weeks, David was at ease with everything, at least for now. He would call Alicia when he got to the apartment, take a shower, and go to bed early. Tomorrow would have its own issues and play out as it may. Given Stroud's final admission, David would confide in Secretary Brady only if Stroud rejected the fourth option.

Stroud continued standing but motionless, hands palms down on his desk, head bowed, and eyes closed. He had to think; there must be a way. When Wainwright told him of Hampton's grave in Fresno, Stroud glimpsed his fast-approaching doom. He had ignored the darkness coming up over him and pressed on with Fern's plan, hoping somehow that his fears were misplaced. Now there was no escape. Fern could help. Stroud reached for the telephone.

"Billy, can you get over here?"

"Sure. Did you see Carr's piece on you? Our man did a good job."

"Never mind that, Billy. We've got a problem, and you need to get over here quickly."

"Gimme twenty minutes." Fern had never heard the senator speak this way. Fear raced over the wires.

Stroud replaced the receiver, sat, and restored the computer screen. He had to think this through, to assess the options without panicking. He began typing.

* * *

Elaine Stroud subconsciously heard the door chimes and felt her dream receding. It would be grand if she could stay in Terre Haute for the whole summer instead of going to the convention. She wasn't there yet and still needed Edward's approval. She lay in quiet suspension between her dream and reality. Then she opened her eyes. Getting off the bed, she straightened her clothing and checked her makeup. Surely Edward was home by now. She went down the stairs.

She knocked gently on the door to the study. Not hearing a response, she cautiously opened the door and saw Edward seated and staring intently at his computer screen. She also saw broken glass on the floor. His eyes were red-rimmed.

"Edward, are you all right?"

He refocused, ignoring her question. "What do you want, Elaine?" he asked coldly.

"Since we're going home before the convention, I was wondering what to wear. I called Janet today, and she's bringing some things over tomorrow morning. Is that all right with you?"

Stroud looked at her with questioning amazement. *This is about clothes,* he thought.

"I didn't know what to do without talking to you. I tried to call you today, but Mrs. Baxter said you were busy."

Elaine's weakness showed with every word. *Didn't she know that?* His mind was snapping.

"You never know what to do." His anger rose.

"What? I just thought . . ."

"You bitch! You never think." Stroud's face turned red.

"Please, Edward. I'm sorry . . ."

"Please? You never pleased me or ever tried to. You're worthless. I should have dumped you years ago." By then, Stroud was standing and advancing toward her with an open hand ready to slap. She backed away as he screamed, "Get out. I'll deal with you later."

"Deal with me?" she stammered. "What do you mean?" She reached for the doorknob, and he screamed again.

"Get out." He slammed the door behind her. That sound filled the house.

Elaine ran to the far wall, turned, and sobbed. She had not cried this way in years and never saw Edward so threatening. "Oh God, please help me," she pleaded and sank to the floor.

Eventually she came up to a sitting position with her back to the wall. Tears streaked her makeup. She jerked her head as she remembered his screams and the sound of the door being slammed. "Oh God!" she pleaded.

Later, she would not recall how long she remained on the floor, but then a calm came over her. She looked around the hallway. The mahogany table had belonged to her dad's father. Edward had allowed her to place it in the hallway only after their decorator had approved that piece as complementary to the other furnishings. Elaine loved that table; its gentle simple lines and rich finish reminded her of her parents. She stood and walked to its front, caressing its surface, and then testing its drawer for smooth quietness.

Her eyes fell upon the deadly object inside. This evil thing did not belong in her table. Her mother and father never would have allowed such an obscenity in their home, much less in this table. Elaine would give the pistol to Edward. He could find some other place for it.

She opened the door to the study and entered. Edward, again looking at his computer screen, turned. His anger had subsided but was now replaced with peevishness. Fern should be there soon, and Stroud wanted no further interruptions. He was formulating a plan. He did not see the pistol held next to her right thigh. "You didn't knock."

Only a moment of incomprehension crossed his face as her right hand came up. She had an odd look on her face. The first shot hit his left shoulder and the second quickly followed, striking his twisted right side just above his waist. His eyes went wide and mouth agape. The third shot hit his right cheek, just below the eye, throwing his head to the side and against the high-back leather chair and exposing his throat for the fourth bullet. That slug passed through Stroud's larynx.

With each shot, Elaine took one more step toward Edward. She marveled as his arms flailed with each impact. He was speechless. She wondered what he would tell her about this in the morning. She smiled, and her aim declined. Of the last four .32-caliber slugs, two hit either side of Stroud's high-back swivel chair, one smashed his right wrist as it was swinging in the air, and the last slug harmlessly plowed into a wall-mounted photograph of the newly elected Congressman Stroud, shaking hands with President Carter. As the party in power changed over the years, he moved that photograph from his office to his home.

Puzzled that he was no longer flailing, Elaine placed the empty pistol on Edward's desk and returned to the hallway.

There, my table's clean. I don't want him putting ugly things in there again. A loud banging startled her. *Was Edward slamming the door again,* she thought. Then she realized there was someone at the front door. She smiled and opened it.

Fern walked past her and into the study. Returning to the hall, he placed an arm around Elaine's shoulder and said, "Let's go across to the other room."

"Okay, Billy. I've been worried about my clothes. You know we're going to Terre Haute and then the convention. Do you think I'll look all right?"

From the parlor, Billy made two telephone calls that night, the first from his cell phone and the second to 911 from the house line.

CHAPTER 82
With Police

Metro detective Carl Parker's call had come in before the late night news. At this stage in Joseph Dooley's life, routine was more pleasing than a phone call from an old friend. Both men were nearing total retirement from law enforcement, and Joseph assumed the call was significant.

"Father Dooley, I've got something you might be interested in seeing. It won't be on the regular news quite yet, but tomorrow is another matter. Here's the address."

Dooley copied. "Can you give me a hint, Carl?"

"Yeah, Joe. That's Senator Stroud's home in Georgetown, and there's been a shooting. Looks like his woman used him for target practice, but we're playing it cool for now. He's gone to the hospital. He'll probably not make it. Her lawyer was there when I arrived and won't let her talk. She seems like a sweet lady. You'd think she was receiving guests for dinner instead of a bunch of street cops and old guys like me." Carl knew how to put you at the scene.

"You think she's gone over the edge? Sounds like that's what you're indicating. Who's her lawyer?"

"Another Irishman, McGonicle, and this time, he may be in the catbird seat. I smell a shrink waltzing up in these facts. McGonicle had her hauled off to some private clinic for white folks." Joseph never believed his black friend was prejudiced, but they agreed a long time back that they were both ethnic realists and that their friendship was bigger than all the sleeve-worn sensitivities of those days.

They first met in New York City when Dooley was a first office FBI agent and Parker was a street cop attending law school. They met at a shared inside hallway during a stand-off in a bank robbery. An old bank guard had died behind the tellers' area, and a woman was being held hostage at the dead end of the hall leading to the safe deposit department. As the guard fell, he mortally wounded one of the two robbers. Between the screams of the dying robber and the shrieks of the hostage being dragged down the hall, there was enough distraction for the street cop and the puppy agent to slip into the bank and follow the remaining robber to the head of the hall. Flanking either side of the hall entry, both young men without speaking formed a bond that would last their lifetimes.

Istvan Resizk was a Hungarian national illegally in the United States via Canada. His first taste of killing and hatred at the age of fifteen was in Budapest during the Hungarian Revolt of 1956. The Russians crushed the revolt while the world stood by and took photographs. Istvan's parents were part of the grist. His last sight of them was their naked and twisted corpses lying in the street fronting their dingy apartment building. Like new-fallen snow, quick lime dust covered their decomposing bodies. Istvan always hated snow.

Seven young Russian soldiers died by Istvan's hand before he escaped into East Germany. Rootless and with a taste for violence, he eventually made it into the West. There he became an accomplished thief to support his drug habit. American-style European grocery stores were his favored target for armed robberies. Surmising that the mystique of robbing American banks might be more exciting and lucrative, and recognizing that life was getting too short in Europe, he managed his way to Canada and then into upstate New York. When the weather turned harsh, shutting down his construction job, he and a Czech refugee friend traveled south to rob banks. This was their third in Manhattan.

The Russian AK-47 he wielded was a fabulous and familiar weapon, sporting heavy slugs and lots of noise. He had stolen it in a gun shop burglary in Ohio. The owner illegally possessed the weapon, and thus its loss went unreported in the investigative inventory. Its only limitation was in close quarters further made difficult by holding the terrified and screaming woman with one arm while aiming and firing the gun with the other.

Resizk blasted the entry when he saw the two men dive for the floor on either side of his line of sight. The AK should make them rethink their choices. Stephan had stopped yelling and was probably dead. Too bad. Istvan grinned. Maybe there was a way out. As he turned slightly to grip a doorknob, the woman stopped screaming, probably exhausted by that effort and fainted, slumping away from his grasp. In that instant, Joseph and Carl opened fire, striking Istvan with every killing shot, sprawling him back against the wall. The AK clattered to the floor. Istvan Resizk's last thoughts were to wonder when the snow would fall.

Reloading as they moved toward the fallen woman and Resizk's body, Carl kicked the AK away and looked down at the Hungarian. Most of the shots were to the chest, but two struck the underside of Istvan's jaw as he was falling back. Blood pooled around his head. Joseph lifted the woman, telling her she was safe. As other officers poured into the bank, Carl and Joseph emerged into the sunlight. Only then did they speak to one another by way of formal introduction.

The adjustment to New York had been easy for Dooley, who had been raised in Philadelphia, but it was tougher for Parker, whose folks raised him in Acres Homes just north of Houston, Texas. The multi-ethnicity of New York has always been a challenge for newcomers.

In those early years in Houston, being black wasn't a tribute to civil rights or equal opportunity, but the black community was strong, relatively cohesive, and spiritual in a religious sense. Education, albeit separate and probably unequal, was a parental commitment in all of the black enclaves in and around what has been called old Houston. Carl attended Jack Yates High School, an all-black school named after a post–Civil War Baptist preacher, who along with other ex-slaves, built Antioch Baptist Missionary Church, now nestled among the tall buildings of downtown Houston.

Carl became a postal worker and attended Texas Southern University, another Yates stamp on Houston, but by then drugs and crime had begun dividing his world. His mother's death from breast cancer triggered his need to leave Texas. He was able to get on with the Postal Service in New York City and finished college. His next goal was law school, but the concept of being a police officer also took hold. By the time he got his law degree, he was married with two sons in middle school. Instead of changing careers, he decided to continue working for the police department. It had gotten into his blood.

Joseph's track was different. A Roman Catholic boy to the core, Joe had been a full-time student at Penn State, graduating with an accounting degree. He spent two years in the Army just after the Korean War and returned to Philadelphia to get his accounting certifications. His dream had always been to join the Federal Bureau of Investigation. He saw himself as a numbers sleuth, detecting and preventing financial crimes, penetrating the shifting ethics of the American business community. His self-image wore a blue suit, a hat, a plain tie, and a white shirt. Bureau agents called this ensemble, "Hoover Blues," a reference to the expected attire for its agents.

He never imagined that his first action would be a desperate gun battle on the floor of a bank with a Hungarian international robber, a fight that would propel him into the elites of the crime-busting Bureau. As years passed with new assignments to other cities, Joseph steadily climbed the ladder. He retired from the Bureau while assigned to the Justice Department's Public Integrity section, an entity charged with bringing to account corruption of governmental organizations, administrators, and politicians. This included election crime matters. These days, he was an investigator for the Senate Ethics committee. He had come a long way from violent crime scenes. Younger agents and Carl Parker also knew Joe, a soft-spoken and compassionate man who rarely showed anger, as Father Dooley.

Parker, on the other hand, was recruited from the NYPD by the Metropolitan Police Department for DC for his street-cop savvy and brilliant investigative skills. He thrived on situations that called for tact and diplomacy when the blood on the walls came from or because of the high and the mighty. He, too, had come a long way.

"Okay, Carl. I'll be there in half an hour. Let's get a glass of milk afterward," a euphemism for Irish whiskey, a taste they shared over the years.

"That's fine. Stroll up to the house. I'll be looking for you. The media is beginning to get a whiff of this, so I expect they'll be swarming soon." After a moments pause, he continued, "Tell Cassy I'm sorry to pull you away and that Beth and I will make it up to you both."

It had been a long time since violent crime had touched the political class of the national government. Maybe their kids or relatives would be involved, but crimes by and against the big boys or girls were generally nonviolent. The public expected, even hoped, for scandalous behavior from their national leaders, so that they could feel confirmed that the entire political process was corrupt. Even more exciting was the notion that the lives of politicians drifted into the dark realm of street crime and domestic violence. Tonight's call signaled the beginning of a frenzy of news media attention, endless speculation, and agonizingly inaccurate analysis.

CHAPTER 83

The Crime Scene

By the time Dooley approached the Stroud home, most of the emergency vehicles had gone, replaced by a horde of news vans, lights, and earnest young reporters looking for that one big story to mark their careers. One young woman was checking her makeup, and another reporter was brushing back his hair and adjusting his jacket, each preparing for a live feed back to their stations. Across the street, clusters of spectators were gathered to see what might be seen and to speculate on what could have happened inside the house. The scent of exhaust fumes and the feel of unhealthy tension replaced the freshness of the air that Armstead smelled earlier in the evening.

Dooley's practiced effort to appear nondescript over the years paid off. Hardly noticed, he passed through the line of yellow tape and young officers. Detective Parker had been leaning against the front of the house, chewing on a stubby but unlit cigar. He promised to stop smoking but said nothing to Beth about eating the damn things. Pitching the cigar into the nearby gutter announced to the cordon of blue uniforms that his friend was coming up and should be passed through without commotion.

Stepping into the house, Joseph said, "So we find ourselves in another hallway. What do you have that I'm supposed to see?" Following Carl into the study, both men characteristically jammed their hands into their pockets to avoid accidentally touching anything.

"Bloody chair, broken glass on the floor, messed-up photograph of Jimmy. Was she trying to kill her husband for spilling wine, or did she not like Mr.

Carter?" Dooley observed. Callous humor expressed out of the presence of civilians was a protective hedge against the tragedy of such scenes.

Parker nodded at the uniformed officer standing by the doorway, a signal for him to move out of earshot. Carl got to business.

"Joe, when I got here, the street officers had secured the immediate scene and identified the civilians present. The EMTs arrived just afterward and hauled Stroud off to GW," a reference to George Washington University Hospital. He was still alive but was in bad shape. So, the senator's wife Elaine, Jack McGonicle, and the senator's political advisor, William Fern, were in the house when I got here. Fern was the first on the scene. He apparently heard the shooting from outside and entered the house, finding the senator sitting there bleeding like a soaker hose and Mrs. Stroud smiling like a socialite. Fern called 911, and he confirmed that, but there's a time gap between the time of his call into the system, and the time of the reported shooting. Right now, all this means is that Fern first called McGonicle, who beat me here."

"So Carl, I missed the late news to see a domestic shooting scene?" He smiled wanting to see his friend's reaction.

"Joe, you can be a real asshole in your senior years. I'm glad I'm your friend. Now boy, step over that broken glass and tell me what you see that is interesting."

Dooley scanned the room ignoring the blooded clutter. "The computer is on standby."

Parker's face broke into his famous broad smile. "You got that right, Father Dooley. That screen was sleeping when the officers arrived. Nobody noticed that until after the soaker hose was rolled up and carried off to leak somewhere else. That boy I just shooed off was standing around being bored when he saw that screen blinking. He reached down and hit "enter" a couple of times and turned away. He didn't see the screen come alive, but I did. I ran him off and took a look."

"Carl, getting you to the point is harder than shooting Hungarians, but I am a patient man."

"I had Mrs. Stroud, McGonicle, and that Fern fellow all back in the kitchen. After I did a little light reading, I told the officer to stay out of the study and let no one else in there 'til I said it was okay. I then talked to McGonicle and got him to get Mrs. Stroud's permission to remove whatever I thought was material to the investigation. I insisted that I hear her agree. I could tell that Jack felt he had a slam-dunk of getting her off the hook, so it didn't matter what we took away as long as we left a good inventory. Joe, you need to understand that I consider the computer tower may contain evidence material to my investigation." He looked very carefully into Father Dooley's eyes and emphasized the word "my." He continued, "And you are welcome to sit in my office tomorrow afternoon as I see what my victim was writing in his computer just before he was shot."

Dooley moved to the keyboard, pressed enter twice, and waited. He scrolled up a bit and read. Turning to his friend, he smiled slightly and said, "I'll hang around until you're ready to get some milk."

CHAPTER 84
Brady's Office

David Armstead arrived in his office before 6:00 a.m. His morning run calmed him and provided the necessary mental focus he would need for the day's events. He attacked Ms. Lokey's paper pile and planned to get his desk clear before the storm he expected that afternoon. Stroud, he now believed, would reject the best and most discrete option.

He usually received no telephone calls until after 8:30. The time was 6:43. Secretary Brady's voice was firm.

"David, you weren't home when I called. Meet me in my office in forty-five minutes. Speak to no one until then—I mean no one. You understand?"

"Yes, Sir." The line was dead before David further responded.

Armstead saw the secretary as the two approached his office from different directions. Brady looked neither right nor left and spoke no words until they were both behind his closed door.

Brady pitched his briefcase on a chair, grabbed the television remote, turned to Armstead, and said, "Senator Stroud has been shot. Did you have anything to do with this?" He clicked the power button as he spoke; the screen and sound appeared.

". . . and news of Senator Stroud's shooting is racing through Washington and the country," the commentator said. "Few details are available, but Senator Stroud apparently was injured around 9:00 p.m. last night at his Georgetown home. Mrs. Stroud is under the care of a physician. Her attorney Jack McGonicle, a short time after the shooting made these comments . . ."

Initially Armstead's mouth fell open. Then a crooked smile was replaced by confusion.

The screen shifted from the commentator to the front steps of the Stroud home. There, in polished business attire stood Mr. McGonicle, one of the toughest criminal defense attorneys in the Mid-Atlantic States.

"We anticipate fully cooperating with the authorities in their investigation. Mrs. Stroud is understandably distraught and is in no condition to visit with anyone or me this evening. Her doctors are quite concerned. Obviously we all pray for the senator's speedy recovery."

Reporters pressed for more information, but McGonicle gave his usual initial press conference smile and standard closing, "That's it; we'll find the truth."

Brady pressed the mute button.

"Sounds like Mrs. Stroud shot the senator. David, what's your answer?"

"I sure didn't, and this is all news to me. I went over there last night and left probably before 8:15."

"Why did you go there?" Brady's anxiety declined.

"Mr. Secretary, that's going to take some time to tell you, I planned for us to talk about this after lunch."

Brady sat in his chair and waived David to another. "Let's talk now."

The outline of events had become crisper in David's mind, and so without careful nuance, he related most of the mileposts of his knowledge and actions. Brady's mind recorded everything, including the treacherous behavior of Capt. Quinby.

"Why didn't you tell me about any of this earlier?"

"There was always the possibility that I was being manipulated by Phan if not others. I wanted to protect you from that accusation."

Brady appreciated the nobility of David's words but also understood that Armstead probably considered the possibility that Brady might have been among the suspected manipulators.

"Why didn't you trust Maj. Johnson?"

"I feel bad about that, Mr. Secretary, but I wasn't ready."

"Why then, dammit, did you trust these Swift Boat fellows that you haven't seen in thirty years?"

"Time has no bearing on that kind of trust, Mr. Secretary. If you'd been in the military or knew these men as I have, you'd know what I mean."

Armstead regretted tweaking Brady for not having served; he could not have served given his visual impairments. David loved the story that a draft board, late in World War II, had sent a notice for Brady to report for a physical. Despite being half-blind, young Brady, knowing the serious drain of the war on America's manpower, appeared as ordered. One of the clerks at the board laughed and disappeared into an inner office. Soon one of the members of the board came out and spoke with Brady, then a student at Rice Institute. Spoke was not exactly descriptive. More embarrassed and flustered that they had failed to look at his original registration record, setting forth his disability, he babbled that things weren't that bad off with the war, that the government expected Brady to finish college, and that if they needed him to help finish the war, the member would call him personally and even send a car for him.

"What possessed you to confront Stroud last night? That was pretty dammed brash."

"My lawyer on this, one of the Swift Boat bunch I saw in Minnesota, reminded me how powerful guilt is, and he made a point of explaining that our guilty hearts convict us faster than the courts. He called that kind of guilt a wild card. I thought I was playing a wild card."

"It was wild, all right," he sniffed. "You could have gotten hurt yourself. I can't afford that. I haven't brought you along to have you get involved is some domestic disturbance." The paternalistic tone caught Armstead by surprise, but this was the first time Brady had admitted to higher visions for Armstead. Brady reached for his pipe, a sign that he was considering a decision.

"So far as you know, did anyone else see or speak to you at Stroud's home?"

"No, Sir. I found a parking space down the street and walked to his door and rang the bell. He answered, and we went right to his study. The house seemed quiet as a tomb. Our visit was brief, no voices were raised, and I left. I have no idea where Mrs. Stroud was."

Brady unmuted the television. "Stroud has been in the Senate for the past twelve years and was being mentioned as a vice-presidential running mate. A real war hero, a tragedy for Indiana and the nation; Gwen?"

Turning to Gwen Perez, his female co-anchor, she said, "Yes it is." Dramatically wincing with implied concern, she continued. "A representative of George Washington University Hospital says the senator's condition is grave. We'll have more on this sad story as it develops." Brady clicked the mute again as the salesman, poorly costumed as one of Snow White's seven dwarfs, Sleepy, and began his animated pitch for low-cost, luxurious, king-size mattress sets.

"David, I'm not going to tell you what to do, but we ought to sit on this until the afternoon, if not tomorrow morning. Keep your calendar open." Armstead nonetheless took Brady's advice as an order.

As Armstead left Brady's office, the secretary leaned back in his chair and thought. *Moles are everywhere in government, self-serving and despicable sons of bitches. Quinby won't enjoy even retirement when I'm finished with him. Among the many good men and women, there are always bad ones. At least I'm blessed that David is with me.*

When David returned to his office, Ms. Lokey smiled with her usual brightness and told him that Sam Taylor had just called and was holding for him.

Picking up the phone, David spoke first. "Not me, Prevert. I wasn't anywhere near the home when she shot him."

"That's good news, Bruno. I know this guy, McGonicle. He doesn't suit up without a big sack of money being paid or some other very good reason. Someone made quick arrangements for Jack to beat the cops to the scene. Mark my words, Bruno, he knows how to make fat ladies sing his song," referring to operatic conclusions.

Armstead liked Taylor's delivery. "Let me tell you a little of what happened last night, and you tell me what I should do."

David's quick report caused Taylor to jump to Brady's final questions, concerning whether anyone other than the senator knew that Armstead had left the house more than forty-five minutes before the shooting.

"Stand fast, Bruno. This case is going down the old domestic disturbance trail. McGonicle is good at that. You might have played the wild card, but you didn't cause Mrs. Stroud to pull the trigger. Just sit on this. Stroud's out of commission and may not survive. You can come forward later if that's appropriate."

"That's what the secretary told me although I'm not sure the secretary wants me coming forward at all."

"That may be right, but watch out making any statements. I'm the only safe ear. I'll call you tomorrow."

That day's the *Washington Times* and *Washington Post* in their own way had grabber headlines about Stroud, "Stroud Shot" and "Senator's Shooting Tragic." With slightly different layouts, these newspapers reported presently known information and quoted from portions of a statement made on behalf of the senator's family.

"William C. Fern, a longtime family friend, issued a brief statement this morning describing Mrs. Stroud as grief-stricken and confused over the plight of her husband. 'Mrs. Stroud has been under a great deal of stress for many years,' Fern observed. Mr. Fern concluded his statement by saying that 'he hoped everyone would be patient with the investigative process and pray for the senator and his distraught wife.'"

For the first time in their marriage, Elaine Stroud was of more interest to the public than her husband.

Billy's carefully written remarks did not include his statement to the police that Mrs. Stroud may have been a long-term victim of at least verbal abuse and that he had asked, to no avail until recently, the senator to seek treatment or counseling for her problems. Fern expressed the view that Elaine's apparent alcoholism probably masked deeper problems and that Senator Stroud had ignored his pleas. Likewise, he did not disclose that he called a former client, now a prominent criminal defense attorney in the region and asked him to help Mrs. Stroud.

Fern had taken two risky and critical steps, possibly saving Elaine. He planted seeds suggesting abuse by the husband, a view he had suspected for some time, and he lined up a superb lawyer, who would also indirectly protect Billy's personal interests. According to McGonicle, she might not even be charged, particularly if Stroud survived and maybe even if he did not. Despite his press statements praying for the senator's speedy recovery, lawyers like Jack McGonicle, defending trigger-happy wives, preferred them to be sad, abused widows by the time of trial.

When the lawyer McGonicle heard Billy's initial telephone outline of the facts and Billy's erroneous belief that Stroud was dead in the next room, McGonicle coarsely opined, "Ah, the dead man made her do it." On that basis, Fern hoped that Elaine could ultimately leave Washington and rebuild her life in Indiana.

Fern wasn't the only person wishfully anticipating Stroud's death.

The Thursday evening television news continued reporting developments of the day. One station carried a brief exclusive interview with an unnamed female staff member in Senator Stroud's office, a mature woman, off camera, who thought Elaine had been a "virtual prisoner in her own home." This same woman said that Stroud only rarely took Mrs. Stroud's telephone calls.

Mrs. Baxter, while she was a dutifully loyal employee, was also candid with the police in saying that the only time the senator expressed to her any compassion for his wife, she thought it was an act.

Finally, most of the television and radio stations carried a related story of denial from representatives from both top-tier competitors that Stroud was ever under consideration for their ticket. A spokesperson for one of the candidates was disturbed by reports of Stroud's personal behavior with his wife, which if true, was dreadful. The *Phillip Carr Show* made appropriate reference to Stroud's shooting but ignored its role in the previous night's charade.

These embarrassments would be buried before the first shovel full of soil fell on Stroud's coffin.

CHAPTER 85

George Washington University Hospital

Intensive Care Unit

Cold. Soft voices. Where am I? Am I dead? A dream? Can't move. If I'm dead, why am I dreaming? Sleep returned. Edward Stroud lay sheathed in a cocoon of white, connected to monitors and tubes of fluids.

Still cold. Billy's voice, but where is he?

"Jack, he looks dead. No, I didn't check his pulse. He's got blood all over and isn't moving. I'm sure he's dead. What should I do?" A pause. "I left the gun on the desk. No, Jack, I didn't touch anything."

Who is Jack? I'm not dead. I can hear you, Billy. Talk to me and not to Jack.

"I don't know. I got here and heard the shots and went in. Mrs. Stroud let me in. She seems okay but is acting strangely. When she opened the door, she looked weird; mascara was running down her cheeks, and she was smiling. How long before you can get here?" Another pause. "Yeah, yeah, I'll call 911 when we hang up. Just get over here quickly. I don't want to talk to the cops until you're here."

The smiling bitch shot me, and you're worried about yourself? You fat Heeb. When I get back to the office, I'm going to fire you. Stroud's pulse raced; his breathing labored. Hands touched his left hand, gentle hands. He smelled a feminine breath and calmed. Billy's voice went away.

"Call Dr. Rhodes. She should look at him." The Filipina nurse's voice was heavily accented. Stroud slipped away somewhere.

CHAPTER 86
Parker's Office

Carl concluded a telephone call; Joseph held his copy of the sheets printed from the senator's computer.

"That was my man at the hospital. He says the senator was moving around a while ago, but the doctor put him out again just to make him rest. He is stable for now, and she thinks he should remain that way through the weekend. That will give us some time to gather a few more pieces."

"What do you make of this?" Joseph waved the sheets in the air.

"I thought you'd tell me first, Joe. My case is clean, but you're the man with the interesting circumstances. It's clear the wife shot him. I'm sure we'll find her prints on the pistol whenever McGonicle allows us to take them. In these cases, there's a feminine quality to the facts: the first shots are usually dead on, so to speak, and then as they begin to enjoy it, their aim gets bad. In other words, the shooting pattern points to a woman. Also, no one else was in the house when the shooting, heard by that Fern guy, started. Proving she did it is the high point of my facts, but convicting or confining her goes south from the point Mr. Fern got in there." Carl Parker ticked off the salient information predictive of the outcome of his case.

"From all the on-scene accounts, she was probably not of sound mind at the time of the shooting. Then, between the statements of Fern and our interview of one of Stroud's main secretaries, it looks like he may have abused his wife. Stroud sho' was gonna plant her at a funny farm; he had their little pamphlets on his desk." Part of the fun of working with Carl was his occasional shift into street talk, something he abandoned on the witness stand and in interviews.

"And then you get into what he typed about her along with this other stuff. So far as we have learned up to this point, Elaine Stroud doesn't even know how to turn on a computer. It's no stretch, based on what he wrote, to believe he wanted her out of his way or dead. There was a tough old bird in Houston who was famous for getting folks found not guilty for killing other folks. One of old Percy Foreman's standard defenses was to prove that the deceased 'needed dying.' It looks like the esteemed senator may have deserved what happened to him. McGonicle will know how to play those cards."

Joseph knew when he asked Carl what he thought that his responses were likely to be clear, extensive, and correct.

"But Joe, you didn't really want to know my thoughts about the domestic aspects of this case but about all the other stuff. Stroud had other problems his wife may not have known about." He picked up one of the sheets and began to read.

"Find LW. Persuade or erase LW and LW tracks. Blame LW. Continue to erase ES."

"Lester Wainwright was the senator's administrative assistant, at least until sometime earlier in the evening when he phoned in his resignation. He's supposed to be on the road back to the State of Washington. Now how about this next section?"

"Persuade or pay DA. Test DA. Delete DA. Delete me. Resign and leave. Live."

"I've got people checking if there are any district attorneys in Indiana or around here that have something on the senator, but I think that's a blind alley. "DA" stands for a particular person, but what really got my attention was the word 'erase.'"

Dooley was listening with satisfaction. You don't often get legible crime-scene scribbling from victims, and even less so on personal computers. Correctly interpreting the meaning is, however, the main exercise, especially when the writer is dead or is otherwise unavailable. Stroud was certainly unavailable.

"Carl, 'erase' takes on a different connotation when you look at what he wrote later."

"You bet, Father. He was computer literate for sure." Flipping to the second sheet, he continued to read, "Check w/ Q. Delete log. Delete 2nd books, Remove paper copies and destroy 2118. Lay off on LW."

"These things have to do with your case, not mine. Now, you tell me what you think. I've said enough."

Joseph had been analyzing the writings all along. This kind of brainwork was common exercise for both men.

"Erase is physical, and delete is technical. LW is a person, and so are DA and Q. Second books always means second set of books, one clean and one dirty. And when you delete a set of books, you need also to remove and destroy the paper copies. My only question is, where they are? When I see them, I'll know how dirty they are. I have no idea what 2118 means yet. But when you find Wainwright, we'll learn all about that and maybe the alphabet identities. I am sure that ES refers to Mrs. Stroud. Putting her in an institution certainly is one form of erasure. Stroud has written a roadmap. We just need to interpret it accurately."

Parker nodded approvingly.

"Now let's talk about timing. Stroud's typing about Wainwright most likely began after his resignation was made known to him. That being the case, your people can pin down the time by speaking with Mrs. Baxter. These are running notes reflective of things that were happening and his thinking about them. Maybe there was contact with DA after Mrs. Baxter spoke with Stroud but before he wrote about deleting things. Mr. Fern told your boys that he got a call from Stroud about twenty minutes before he got there. Fern said that the senator was agitated and told him, 'We've got a problem.' Just speculation at this time, but I don't think Stroud's 'we' problem was about his marriage. That was nothing new and not a huge cause for agitation. Seems like Mrs. Stroud was an inconvenience and a passing one at that. No Carl, this had to do with DA. Maybe it was telephone or a personal contact, but DA had something to do with Stroud's agitation. How's that strike you?"

"Joe, there's another element. The language gets progressively more urgent. Compare the early entries about LW with this stuff about DA. The DA material is posed as alternatives, but the final entries, deletions, and destruction talk look imperative."

Both men became silent, each with their private thoughts. Carl Parker spoke first.

"What do you want to do with this? Are you going to open a case with your committee?"

"Not yet, Carl. My presence in this is to be off the record for a while. Let's see if your victim survives. In the meantime, maybe you can locate Wainwright and get him back here for an interview, which may help us identify DA. Have your techies been through everything in the senator's hard drive?"

"No, Father. I told them to look only at the last writings. What I read at the house last night was enough for me to call you. If you want to keep this as a local matter for the time being, that's your call. I need to find Wainwright anyway, and there's a Mrs. Brock, who came by the Stroud house this morning. I'll get her interviewed and let you know what she has to say. Do you want to come up here Sunday morning and take a look at my victim's hard drive?"

"I don't think so, Carl. Let's see what Wainwright has to add. The hard drive is safe; the senator isn't going anywhere except maybe to his grave, and Elaine Stroud is in competent hands."

What both men knew without saying so is that they were engaged in a dance with the laws of search and seizure. This dance began with Parker's late evening call to Dooley, a dance that required them to maintain a polite distance, ignoring their instincts in favor of an objective accumulation of information to support a search warrant, if needed, into Stroud's hard drive. This would be a search for evidence beyond the information contained in Stroud's working document at the time of the shooting. As long as this United States senator remained a victim, the orderly revelation of information they, by long experience anticipated, would inevitably lead to hard evidence converting Stroud into a criminal defendant for campaign fund abuses. Parker and Dooley were patient dancers.

CHAPTER 87

George Washington University Hospital

Intensive Care Unit

The duty nurse saw Stroud's feet moving under the covers of the bed. Adjusting his covers, she spoke to him with her soft and engaging Philippine accent, but he did not react. Dr. Rhodes had ordered that this patient be brought back to consciousness slowly and that attention be paid to any indications of infection, always a possibility even in the best of hospitals. His life-threatening initial condition was slowly improving, but as this process occurred, new threats could emerge: infection and potential blood clots. Intravenous cocktails would be adjusted to account for these threats and the increasing prominence of pain the patient would suffer. Immobility was, for now, the best circumstance to encourage healing. Nurse Crystal Ramos, age forty-two, was looking forward to the 11:00 p.m. shift change. She intended to call her aging mother back in the Philippines. It would be Sunday afternoon for her.

That voice, her smell. . . . I'm floating. I'm warm. . . . Things are stuck in my mouth, my penis, and my rectum. One side of my face feels dead. Can't swallow. Can't move my right hand. I feel strapped down. Try to open my eyes.

Stroud's brain attempted its inventory, but the work was too exhausting. *Too heavy. Easier to sleep.*

All 172 pounds of Nurse Lavonia Booker lumbered through the double doors, intent on relieving Crystal and enjoying the quiet time of this watch on a Saturday night in ICU—no visitors and no real interruptions. She would just do her job and go home before the morning rush hour.

"What you got goin,' baby? You ready to get out of here?" Lavonia called everyone baby regardless of age, gender, or station in life. Lavonia, ten years younger than Crystal, had large eyes, full lips, and hair tightly pulled back in a fluffy ponytail. Her cheerful, husky voice always had a gentle tone that made people smile. Her white uniform rustled as she moved toward her little friend, Crystal. In the subdued light of the ICU, the big momma bear Lavonia reached out and hugged the small Asian nurse. Everyone loved Lavonia. She was good for the patients and a comfort for worried visitors. When death came calling for some, as it often did in the early morning hours, Lavonia was there to stroke a forehead or hold a hand as a soul left the room.

"Lemme see the clipboard." She carefully studied the notations and physician orders for the few patients sleeping there. One by one, she went over with Crystal the special considerations of each patient and then walked to each bed, dutifully followed by Crystal.

Standing at the foot of Stroud's bed, Lavonia inquired, "Has he come around at all?"

"No, Lavonia, he hasn't. He's better than last night, and I thought he would show some signs of waking tonight, but that hasn't happened. Poor man." Crystal was compassionate with every patient. She made the assumption that whatever evil circumstance brought people to her ICU, it was God's will for her to show kindness and to shield them from further harm. Lavonia was not as generous.

"Baby, you haven't been watching the news like I have. You don't think that po-lice officer is outside just to protect him, do you? The senator's wife put all those holes in him and from what I heard on TV, he deserved every one of them and then some." Lavonia had a particular intolerance for men who were unkind to their wives. "It just breaks my heart, seeing pictures of that little white girl he's married to. She doesn't look like she's got a mean bone in her body. Gawd sure will protect a little one like her."

"Lavonia, you ought to let God do what he does, and you need to not be talking like that here." Crystal's mild scolding of her big friend had the right effect. Lavonia's smile fell as did her eyes. She was embarrassed that she had spoken carelessly in front of this patient, even if he was asleep.

"I'm sorry, baby. You're right." Crystal smiled, shouldered her small purse at the nurses' station and walked out. As Crystal touched the double doors, she heard Lavonia's final defense, "I can at least be happy this boy won't be goin' to no convention."

Stroud had awakened four minutes earlier hearing Lavonia Booker's muted voice, discussing other patients. For the first time since he was sitting in his study, he knew where he was and why he was there. He was able to open his left eye and see his surroundings.

The bitch. She believes what the media are putting out. Why are they doing this?

Stroud could not have known that Jack McGonicle had his own contacts in the press and knew how to play the media. He was orchestrating the music for the Fat Lady's song.

Billy should be fighting this. Lester, too. Oh Lester, I forgot. You've run away and left me, too. This is a media fight. We can handle this. I can deal with Armstead if he hasn't shot his mouth off. If I can just get out of here, I can . . .

Stroud moved in one substantial jerk. The restraints held him, but not enough to immobilize the surgical repairs and bandages. Pain seized his entire upper body all at once. Most of all the right side of his face felt like it had been smashed with a baseball bat. His brain wanted to scream, but no sound came forth. The pain was overwhelming him.

"There, there, baby. You gonna be here a while, so just settle down. You won't hurt no more tonight." A big, warm, soft hand touched the left side of his forehead. Stroud then heard skin against fabric "Baby, this will take just a little time."

He began to relax. The pain subsided, but he had the sensation that something large and heavy was embedded in the right side of his face. He heard his own words in his head, but nothing sounded from his throat.

Nonetheless, as clouds began to surround him, he was content. *One good eye, two good ears, and my brain still works. I need to remain here and rest. I'm safe here.*

Lavonia noted this event, and her actions on his chart and moved away to check on other patients.

CHAPTER 88
Parker's Office

"You Feds don't go to work early like we do over here at Metro. You trying to avoid the traffic?" Carl liked starting his Monday midmorning phone call with a little needling.

Ignoring the dig, Joseph took a friendlier tone, sort of. "Did you have a good weekend? Did Beth get any work out of you for a change, or did you flee to the office to get some rest?"

"She had me cutting grass and trimming hedges. I thought I'd avoid being a yardman when I left Houston and came up north. My Yankee wife ain't any different from my momma. Momma had me doing the yard every Saturday and had me in church every Sunday. Beth is just the same. Joe, I love every minute."

They chuckled and got down to business.

"The boy is still alive, and my people got ahold of Wainwright over the weekend. He's agreed to return to town. He wants to lawyer up, though, but says he'll cooperate. Right now, this is just an investigation into the shooting. You can slide into the corruption stuff during the interview. We'll see if his lawyer is on his toes."

"We can assume he will be. One of the committee lawyers brought in a copy of a television news piece from Thursday night or Friday morning quoting an unidentified female employee on Stroud's staff about how he treated his wife. This committee lawyer suspects the woman—I assume it's Mrs. Baxter—knows more than she's been asked about. I agree. These old trolls generally know more than they ever let on. Maybe you and I ought to interview her before we do Wainwright."

"I'll set this up for tomorrow morning, Joe." Parker paused. "Hey, do you want to go with me to see our victim late tomorrow afternoon? I thought we'd take a look just to verify he's there, and besides, it's kind of sad. This guy is nationally prominent; he was a possible vice-presidential candidate and a war hero. The uniformed officer at the hospital says nobody, not even from his office, has come to visit him. He has instructions to log everyone in who tries to see him. It's a blank page. Sounds like folks, even in the Senate, know more than we do."

"Good idea. We can grab a glass of milk afterward, and I'll give you some advice about finding a smaller house with an even smaller yard and no hedges."

CHAPTER 89
Interviews

The interview with Mrs. Baxter took longer than anticipated, and Wainwright's newly hired lawyer called Detective Parker's office that morning and left a message that he wanted to talk before submitting his client to an interview. In these circumstances, Parker and Dooley postponed a visit to the hospital. Stroud had developed a temperature in the meantime, and the doctors were said to be changing his antibiotics. News reports were putting the senator's life in the balance.

Lester's lawyer, a polished young man who had just entered private practice from the US Attorney's office for the Northern District of Virginia, wanted to limit the interview to matters directly pertaining to the shooting investigation. He correctly surmised that his client shouldn't be talking about sensitive matters unrelated to the specific crime facing the senator's wife. Parker told him that was agreeable, but he was having trouble determining the perimeters of that case and that Wainwright ought to be able to clarify all that. Parker understood his own double talk but wasn't convinced that Lester's lawyer had a clue as to how far down his client's pants would be pulled before it was too late. Cops understand these things; the good ones don't abuse these understandings.

Mrs. Baxter showed little hesitation in repeating the comments she made to the television reporters and the slightly more detailed statements she made later to other detectives. By the time Parker and Dooley spoke with her in Stroud's inner office, she had heard enough of the anguished news reports about the senator's condition to assume that his death was imminent, and she had no fear of reprisal. She freely commented about the senator's false compassion for his wife, noting that her sad situation was an open secret to the entire staff. Her most chilling comment was that the senator always "calculated life in terms of its benefit only to him."

With a guiltless conscience, she also revealed Lester's statements about the senator's abuse of campaign funds and her own views of Lester's personality, including an obvious weakness of character. As to the numbers "2118," she had heard references made to them by the senator and Wainwright, and assumed it was a room number of sorts, but she knew nothing beyond that. Concerning "Q" she speculated that Capt. Quinby might be the person so identified. Mrs. Baxter had never met Quinby but provided his contact information at the State Department where she knew he was on temporary assignment from the Navy. She volunteered without examples that she thought Lester and Quinby came from the same mold. She had no idea about "DA."

Her knowledge of William Fern was limited. Beyond his community reputation as political and campaign advisor, she found him to be foul-mouthed and sloppy in appearance. She sensed that he kept his distance from Lester, although in fairness, he also did not deal with any of the staff. He appeared to limit his advice only to the senator and did not get involved in campaign expenditures or financial reporting. She had overheard Fern pleading with Stroud to do something to help Elaine and thought that Elaine Stroud's welfare was important to both Fern and Lester, although for different reasons.

Finally, she advised that she had no idea how long she would remain employed in Stroud's office because she had received a direct call from the governor of Indiana. He was anxious to be apprised daily of Stroud's condition and particularly of his death. The governor was prepared to appoint a temporary replacement, pending the usual elective process to fill the vacancy. She believed the appointee would want to clean house. What she did not know was that Governor Allen had been a high school classmate of Elaine Stroud. He wanted the best interests of the people of Indiana protected, and that included Elaine.

* * *

Lester Wainwright collapsed faster than either Parker or Dooley expected. He was nervous from the beginning of the interview, conducted at his attorney's office in McLean, Virginia, and it only got worse as the interview progressed. Readily corroborating Mrs. Baxter's statements about the general staff knowledge and the senator's callous regard for his wife, Lester gave up more about Senator Stroud's selection process when it came to a place for Elaine's commitment. Beyond confidentiality, his greatest test was cheapness of the institution.

Lester, too, assumed death was imminent for Stroud and lost no time in tarnishing his legacy. This was payback time. It felt good to do so.

Lester's secret euphoria was deftly punctured when he was asked about "2118." He muttered something about that being an off-site storage facility for archived materials. As he answered, his eyes went to the floor, and he shifted in his chair, companion signals missed by his lawyer but not by these experienced investigators. When asked for the facility address, he identified a public storage warehouse near the Key Bridge just across the Potomac River. His lawyer also missed Lester's involuntary tug at his tie.

Wainwright explained his sudden resignation as the result of the strains of working in the highly charged and poisoned political environment of Washington, DC. He had seen all he needed to see and wanted to return to his home state. Yes, he was tired of the senator's demeaning attitude and harsh demands. Lester omitted any mention of the demands of David Armstead or Barrett Johnson. When shown a portion of the last words typed by Stroud concerning erasing and blaming LW, Lester stiffened. Without pausing to speak to his attorney, Lester blurted out, "Look, I was doing what Stroud told me to do. He can't blame me. How he handled campaign money was his business and not mine." Finally, Lester's lawyer perked up.

"Let's go back to something else. Do you have a key to 2118?" Parker asked.

Before Lester's attorney jumped in to prevent an answer, Lester had already said he did and began reaching for his pocket. There was a brief and very awkward silence among the four men.

"Lester, could you step out to the reception area? I want to speak with these gentlemen before we go any further. Get a cup of coffee. This will take just a few minutes." The lawyer knew he had to do some fast dealing before his client totally bombed out. The interview concluded two hours later with a trip to the warehouse.

CHAPTER 90

ICU

Stroud opened his left eye. Daylight. Was it his imagination? He could hear familiar sounds, a television, but the volume was muted but clear.

"Indiana Governor Allen has announced the appointment of Randolph Perry to fill the vacancy created by the shooting last week of United States Senator Edward Lewis Stroud. According to the Certification of Vacancy issued by Indiana's Secretary of State, Senator Stroud's injuries are so incapacitating as to prevent his continued effective service in office. Senator Perry hopes to prevail in the special election to be held later this year for the remainder of Stroud's term of office."

Allen, he thought, had been a friend. Perry, too, had been a supporter but maybe only waiting for his chance. Stroud wanted to scream, but he could not. He wanted to move but sensed that severe pain was lurking nearby.

They know something. I'm alive; I can think. Why are they moving so fast? Surely, they could give me a chance to recover.

He heard hushed voices of women. "Oh God, turn that off," and "I'm sorry. I thought he was out." Then, "He is, but you'll learn soon that people float in and out while they're here and what they hear and remember if they survive will amaze you. Listen to the news elsewhere." The rebuke was stern.

Survive? I'll survive; I must. I can't let them destroy me. The heat on my face . . . Where am I?

His mind began drifting. Pain came out of the shadows, and his head throbbed. His hands were cold. He felt fluid draining from his left eye and nostril. For one brief moment, he heard a distant male voice, saying, "You'll be all right," and then he slept.

* * *

Parker and Dooley arrived at the hospital just after general visiting hours had ended. They had worked all day on the materials found at the warehouse and further debriefed Lester Wainwright about his use of campaign funds at the direction of Stroud. Parker had essentially given up on finding any evidence that portrayed Elaine Stroud as other than a fragile and tormented spouse. He intended to speak with the District's US Attorney's office about being very open to a lenient plea if offered by McGonicle, especially if Stroud died. The senator's survival, of course, might alter all of these views. Parker, then, began assisting Dooley on the public corruption aspects of the case.

Dr. Rhodes required more intense and continuous ICU monitoring. Parker spoke briefly with the officer on duty outside the room, learning that Rhodes was becoming alarmed about an infection that was not responding to medications. In addition, Mrs. Baxter had sent a couple of staffers the day before to check on the senator's condition. A congressman from Terre Haute had also stopped by later that evening and was overheard on his cell phone speaking to a person he addressed as "Randy."

Stepping into the dimly-lit room, they saw Stroud still penetrated by an array of monitoring devices, tubes, and drains. They heard a periodic gurgling sound. Stroud's lips were pale. Both men stood silently for about three minutes.

"Kind of sad when it all comes down to this," Carl mused to Joseph. "Whatever a guy has done, good and bad, doesn't seem so important at times like this."

Dooley had developed a particular habit of speaking out of the side of his mouth when imparting confidentialities. Regardless of his surroundings, the number of people present, or the importance of the topic, Joseph always preceded such speech by looking around to see who might be in earshot. Carl had joked with Joseph that God was always listening however quietly Joe spoke.

"Yeah, but I'd love to interview him before he goes. And if he sticks around, what his wife did to him is minor, considering what we found at the warehouse."

"That's not happening tonight, my friend. There is nothing we can do here. Let's go get some milk."

Driving out of the parking garage, Dooley had a change of mind about milk. He told Parker that he wanted to turn in early. Tomorrow he planned to call David Armstead for an appointment. Parker accepted Dooley's preference that the interview be solely between Dooley and "DA," whom they had identified through Wainwright and the papers at the warehouse. Both men understood that, depending on Armstead's revelations, a memorandum of interview might not be prepared. Meanwhile, Stroud dreamed of black-robed judges speaking and dark, angry faces he did not recognize.

CHAPTER 91
Armstead's Office

Ms. Lokey announced Joseph Dooley's call on Line 3.

"Good morning, Mr. Armstead. I'm an investigator with the Senate's Ethics Committee. I wonder if you would have time to talk with me today. Maybe you could fill in some blanks about Senator Stroud."

Armstead paused, *So much for lawyer predictions.* "Let me have a call-back number. I need to see if I can clear my schedule this morning." Armstead felt stupid for such a pretentious reply. Dooley, on the other hand, had heard these often-evasive remarks for decades from prospective interviewees who needed to think, gain time, or speak with counsel. He expected these dodges in his work.

To Dooley's surprise, Armstead continued, "Give me about thirty minutes."

Hanging up the phone, Armstead considered calling Mr. Brady but opted to track down Sam Taylor. Twenty-five seconds into their call, Taylor started laughing.

"Did you say Joe Dooley? He was here in Houston as an agent when I was in the US Attorney's office years ago. We called him Father. He's the straightest shooter I know. Did he say any more about what blanks he had in mind?"

"No. I told him I'd call him back shortly. What's your advice?"

"Bruno, we can do this one of three ways. Decline, defer, or go for it. I see no important points supporting the first two valid options, but then if you go for it today, I can't be with you except by speakerphone. My gut says for me to be on the speakerphone, listening. If there is any reason to shut this down, I can do it. How's that strike you?"

"If you can be clear this morning, I'll call him and set this up. My only problem is that I don't want to do it at my office. I have a speakerphone capability on my cell phone. Can you deal with that?"

"Sure, Bruno. Just as long as you aren't meeting in a noisy titty bar. Hold on, though. I have a friend over at Hogan and Hartson. He can lend me a conference room for you two. I'll call him now and get that arranged. It's not as entertaining as a titty bar, but it will be quiet."

Armstead smiled. "I'll get back with you."

Dooley's surprise continued. Of course, he remembered Taylor, and he acknowledged his priestly nickname. He also agreed and welcomed Taylor's presence by telephone. Dooley did wonder about two items. First, Armstead appeared to have anticipated Joseph's call or at least a call from someone inquiring about Stroud. Therefore, Armstead had something to say. Second, he was amused that with all the high-powered lawyers scurrying around Washington, Armstead's lawyer was in Houston.

After the exchange of amenities primarily between Taylor and Dooley, Joseph crept into his purpose for wanting to interview David.

"I cannot divulge the nature of my inquiry, but I have come across an investigative report by private individuals revealing that you were the subject of surveillance at and near your home in California." Handing a copy of the report to Armstead, he continued. "What do you suppose was the senator's interest in your activities?"

"The nature of my activities involves many things, some of which are not ordinarily disclosed, if at all, except through judicial proceedings."

"Mr. Armstead, I am here to determine if there is a need to go through more formal proceedings. Allow me to show you another document. It's a copy of what I call computer doodling, but it is very interesting in its references to 'DA.' Are you 'DA' and have you had recent contact with Senator Stroud? Have you spoken to the senator in any way within, say, the last two weeks?"

Before responding to Dooley's questions, Armstead described the doodling to Taylor. Additionally he described the other language about LW.

"See, Bruno, this is what a wild card can lead to. You never know the consequences. Hey Joe, are you going somewhere with this?"

"Sam, that's up to you. I've got a dying US senator in the hospital, and his wife is responsible for that. There is plenty of information about the senator that if he lives, his life will be very uncomfortable. Prison clothing may not be to his liking. If what you and your client know is just interesting, then it goes nowhere with me. I may not write it up. Your call."

"David, take me off speaker and let's talk."

Dooley walked over to the credenza where the Hartson staff had placed soft drinks and coffee for this meeting. Armstead listened while Taylor spoke.

"Bruno, this is one of those situations where we go on our instincts. I recommend you give him a pared-down narrative similar to what you told Secretary Brady. Go ahead and tell him about going over to the Stroud's home and your conversation. Let him know that you have all that stuff that Mr. Phan gave you and what our Swift Boat pals will say. Then let's see what Father Dooley has to add."

"Thanks, Sam. I'm going to put you back on speaker." Armstead walked to the coffee, poured a cup, and said, "Mr. Dooley, this will take a while."

Dooley remained silent throughout David's narration. For the most part, he sat with his hands held behind his head or walked around the conference table. No notes were taken, and he asked no follow-up questions. When Armstead finished, Dooley stood and walked to the speakerphone.

"Sam, we'll let this matter stay here. It's best for the country. Stroud is publicly dead even without this business about Lieutenant Hampton. If you ever get to DC, let me know," Turning to David, he reached out to shake hands. "Mr. Armstead, thank you and Sam for your service thirty-five years ago and especially today. This isn't said often enough."

CHAPTER 92

The Hospital

How did it all come to this? So tired! I'm lost. My head is coming off. That voice, speak louder.

He strained to hear. "You'll be all right," the male voice says. And then another voice—a soft, kind voice, "Baby, you gonna be all right. Gawd gonna love you, too." He felt that familiar hand on his cheek and a sad emotion first in his stomach and then in his chest. He wanted to cry but could not even breathe. Her voice again, "That's okay. Lawd's here for all of us."

Then the male voice spoke again, a strong hand on Stroud's shoulder. Now Stroud is sitting in a forest. It is peaceful. "Come on, Commander; you'll be all right." *Why is he calling me Commander?* Assured by the man's voice, he rises and turns to follow. He can't see the man's face but sees his green fatigues, all clean and well ordered. The man is so young, he thinks, *maybe I know him.*

* * *

Allen Parkway and Memorial Drive flank Buffalo Bayou on the near west side of downtown Houston and provide two of the many fast tracks into the central business district. Some workday mornings, the traffic slows as the price drivers pay for Houston's street renovation program. Sam Taylor needed to be in the office by 8:00. He wanted to visit with Mary Jacobs before things got too busy. He normally refused to turn on the car radio during high-traffic times. He didn't need the distraction. Besides, often he used driving as a "think time" and even billed clients for his ponderings.

Today was different. The traffic on both roadways had stalled. Because of the meanders of the bayou, he was able to see a large crane up ahead that appeared to be moving across the flow of automobiles. He was going to be late. In frustration, he pushed the radio's power button and then station switched until he found KPRC, a twenty-four-hour news-and-talk radio station. The morning host finished recapping the results of some inane listener survey such as what would you do if you were the mayor of Houston. A chatty female then gave the day's weather and current traffic conditions. Then the network news began.

"Good morning. Washington, DC awoke to learn that United States Senator Edward Stroud of Indiana died this morning at 3:23 Eastern Daylight Time at George Washington University Hospital. He never regained consciousness after his shooting last week. Hospital representatives have advised that the severity of his injuries and post-operative complications made his recovery doubtful. No one has been charged in that shooting. On a lighter note, a hostage crisis in South Florida ended peacefully with the surrender of the lone gunman, who . . ." Taylor hit the off button as traffic began to move more steadily.

CHAPTER 93

Various Matters

That morning Secretary Brady was in good spirits. He invited Armstead down for coffee and rolls. Armstead declined the rolls.

"David, your business last week with the senator passed unnoticed. It will continue to do so. Stroud was a beast in secret who so dominated his wife that she lost her mind." He paused. "It is interesting that this poor woman had enough presence of mind to inflict on him several potentially killing shots." Brady smiled as he brought a roll to his lips.

David decided not to contradict Brady's conclusion that the business had gone unnoticed. *Nothing to be gained there if Mr. Dooley was good for his word.* "I'm sorry she's in this mess, Mr. Secretary, but when I look back, he probably abused people all his adult life. One day or another, it would catch up with him."

"You've done excellent work on this, David. With all your running around, the exhumation, attorney's fees, and old Moore's expenses, you must have run up quite a tab. How much are you out of pocket as far as the Stroud matter is concerned?"

Armstead chuckled. "I thought you'd never ask, Mr. Secretary. Excluding the trips you ordered me to take and the Minnesota trip, this has cost me a little less than ten thousand dollars. I've got receipts."

"Good for you. Prepare a voucher, and I'll sign it." He hesitated somewhere in additional thought. "What would happen to the costs of government if we never paid until after the work was done satisfactorily?"

"I can't answer that, but I didn't have a bottomless bank account or gold credit cards. I tried to watch the expenses."

"If there are other loose ends, tie them up, put some perspective on this, and move on." This blind patriarch was almost giddy.

Spurred by Brady's unusual and relaxed joviality and the secretary's readiness for Armstead to move on to other projects, David's mind raced like the scrolling of a computer screen full of seemingly unrelated combinations of letters and numbers, then stopped abruptly on one word: perspective.

"You knew, didn't you? You knew everything about Phan and about Stroud? Why did you use me?"

Brady's demeanor changed. He paused, taking the measure of Armstead's feelings. Brady hoped not to lose David's trust or respect.

"You struggled with the possibility that Phan was using you, to interfere with our domestic politics and trying to influence our elections to some advantage for his country." Brady brushed some dusty remnant of a roll from his pants. "I do have other sources. I heard that Phan was disappointed in the behavior of his post-war colleagues, but I had no idea where that would lead. I arranged for us to meet by accident early last year in Paris. I tried to sound him out on the truth about all this POW/MIA business, but he wasn't receptive. We had no shared background. He was an aging warrior; I was simply aging. I backed off and pushed you into more involvement. I assure you, David, I had no idea of any of this business of Stroud's connection with the death of your friend Hampton until your disclosures last Friday. I knew Phan had a secret, but I had no concept of what it was."

Brady could feel Armstead's suspicions subsiding. *Good,* he thought.

"This was maddening for me," Brady added. "You also knew something and kept it from me. You wanted time off for personal business and then behaved as though you were on a mission. I talked to Johnson, but you kept him in the dark, and then Phan disappeared. Something was going to happen and all I could do was wait."

David admired and respected the secretary beyond description. But that didn't mean that he believed Brady was above convenient feints and deceptions, especially when it came to faithfully doing his job. David smiled.

Brady smiled, too, as he reached for another roll. Armstead finished his coffee and left.

On the way back to his office, he passed Duane Quinby in the company of State Department security guards. Quinby, unsmiling, was carrying a small cardboard Dole Fruit box, containing desktop items and a few photographs. Armstead's eyes met Quinby's.

"Lost your patron, have you? See you around, Duane."

Anger flashed across Quinby's eyes as they passed, but the shoulders of the escorting guards kept him otherwise in control.

Early that afternoon, Armstead telephoned Katherine McCullough at the US Attorney's office in Fresno.

"Katherine, this is David Armstead. I hope I'm not interrupting your busy morning."

"Oh no, Bruno. I wondered when I would hear from you. I can call you Bruno, can't I? It seems so natural."

"That's fine; my wife does." He wondered how many more people were learning of this name. "I wanted to give you an update. My concerns about Bob's death have been resolved. He died trying to save another man's life. I don't have to tell you; Bob was a good and decent man to the last."

Kate's voice was soft. "Thank you. I never need to be reminded, but to hear that from you and others . . ." her words trailed off.

Kate remembered people telling her that Bob died a hero while he and another man were fighting communist soldiers, but she never read any news accounts of Bob's death and pushed any details she might have heard far back in her memory.

She resumed. "When we last spoke, I knew you were going to do something about Bob's death. This call suggests that you're satisfied with the outcome. I don't need more than that."

"I am." David suspected from her last words that she understood that Stroud's death, now spread over the national news that included the highlights of his Vietnam service, was the significant, but unstated provocation for David's call. He also sensed peace in her voice, relief that she no longer had to be concerned about the exact circumstances of Bob's death.

"Kate, are you going to be all right?"

"Absolutely, Bruno. It's all a God gift. The timing is interesting, though. Bob junior's being ordained Thursday, and he's received a call as an associate in a church outside of Sacramento. This, too, is a blessing. When I get a date, could I send you and your wife an invitation to his welcoming Sunday?"

"I can't imagine anything that would keep us away."

Later that afternoon, Sam Taylor telephoned his law partner, George Lindsay, at a marina on Galveston Bay. George was getting a head start on his weekend and his social activities.

"Hey, Sam, what do you have?"

Not being ready to waste time, Sam spoke briefly. "George, I thought you ought to have time this weekend to think about my news. I'm withdrawing from the firm, effective at the end of the month. I'll be moving to Austin, but that's not certain."

Sam heard ice rattling in a glass and a sucking sound. "What in the hell are you going to do, Sam?"

"I'll practice law, George." Then he decided to add, "Maybe."

Taylor did not want Lindsay knowing quite yet that Ms. Jacobs was considering going with him. It might be difficult enough just dividing clients.

"Sam, what am I going to do?" Lindsay was merely saying the words he was thinking, not expecting an answer.

"I don't know, George. You'll work something out. See you Monday."

CHAPTER 94
Northern California
September Morning

David and Alicia struggled during their married life to achieve stable familial cohesion. This was never easy, given Alicia's business and David's line of work, but the payoff was immense. Big-ticket items, such as healthy, happy, self-reliant daughters and sons you could trust to be ready to meet the world, were obvious blessings.

Less obvious blessings were more telling. Without giving up anything of importance, either as husband and wife or as parents, David and Alicia were selflessly dedicated to one another. Whether they were geographically separated or not, the family regularly attended church, and for David's travel schedule, the term "church universal" had a special meaning.

Going to church was an act of normalcy, although for the Armstead family, church meant more than regular attendance. David had in recent years begun to think of his Christian faith in a nondenominational sense, avoiding inordinate reliance on the personality or wisdom, if any, of the clergy of any particular church house. This allowed him to listen with critical interest to sermons without feeling a need to grumble afterward to Alicia or the preacher if the sermons lacked biblical authority or were infected with secular fads.

Another act of normalcy was a Sunday morning unhurried drive to church. This Sunday was special, however. They needed to leave San Anselmo early enough to find the church near Sacramento before the service. Alicia and David chatted as he drove the Yukon on the north side of San Pablo Bay. The traffic was light. Once they got to Vallejo, David turned northeast on Interstate 80. The steady hum of the wheels on pavement and the flickering of morning sunlight on her side of the car eased Alicia into a pleasant doze.

As David set the cruise control, the last four months passed in review. He had followed carefully the reported internal and public machinations of both party conventions. To his knowledge, not one word was publicly uttered by the media about Stroud. The Indiana delegation in New York was led by the mayor of South Bend who seemed to grope through his voting announcements. The senator's death was complete. Elaine Stroud continued under psychiatric evaluation; no formal charges had yet been made against her.

Lester, according to an earlier call from Sam, was "going to be wearing wire" for the government for a while, and if things worked out, he might get probation. Sam also said he believed Lester was so afraid of Barrett Johnson that he never mentioned the matter to Dooley. Sam was convinced that Dooley would have told him if Barrett's name had come up.

The other gatherers in Minnesota had also called him. They had connected the dots of Stroud's demise without any information from Sam. David promised more details next summer. Richard Leyland's way of closing his phone call, was his usual "hooo-aaah."

"David, where are we?" Alicia climbed up out of her sleep for just a moment.

"We're about twenty minutes from the church. I want a good look at Sam Taylor's girlfriend before we go in. I'll wake you in plenty of time."

"Yes," was all Alicia could manage before again slipping off to sleep.

When the invitation came to Armstead, he called Kate and asked if she would also invite Sam Taylor, another friend of Pastor Bob's. She was delighted to do so. Armstead then called Taylor.

"Bob's widow, Katherine is sending you an invitation to their son's welcoming Sunday at a church near Sacramento. He's going to be an associate pastor or whatever they call them in that church. Can you tear yourself away?"

"As a matter of fact I can; I haven't sold the house here in Houston and haven't quite decided where I'm going to go. So sure, I'll be there."

A few days later, Taylor called back saying that he had a friend living in Incline Village on the north side of Lake Tahoe. Taylor assumed it would be okay for her to attend the services as well but he didn't want Armstead worrying about Sam's transportation or accommodations.

"Sam, is this a serious friend?"

"She's a great girl, but we'll let things go along that way, at least for a while." Armstead accepted the polite dodge for what it was. After Stroud's death, the two men had continued to talk from time to time about each man's future. Armstead wondered if Taylor would find government service interesting but had never raised that issue directly. This weekend would be an opportunity.

As David turned off Interstate 80 and onto Interstate 5 north, he reflected on one of the best developments to come out of the Stroud mess. After his work monitoring the conventions and a restful Labor Day weekend, Armstead returned to his office in Washington, DC. Rummaging through his junk email account with Hotmail, he found a message sent several weeks earlier.

Dear Mr. Armstead:

My family is now living in Bangkok. I was worried that I might have lost your email address but found it this morning. If this is still a good address for you, please respond. We live in an apartment near an Internet Café. I go there daily. My father sends his best wishes.

Phan Vu

David was excited; he paced the office thinking about his response and before sitting down to type, he made one call to Secretary Brady.

Anh Vu:

I'm delighted to learn of your safe circumstances. If you or your family need any assistance, any at all, please go to the American Embassy located at 120/22 Wireless Road, Bangkok, and ask to speak to Mr. Huso or Mr. Clarke. These are good men. The new ambassador, Mr. Boyce, may not have settled in yet, but any of these gentlemen will be more than happy to assist you. Please convey to your father my best wishes and hope that in the very near future we may resume our stimulating conversations.

David

As Armstead drove into the parking lot of the church, Alicia came alive with anticipation. David recently told her the outlines of the events that brought them there. She admired her husband's role in this and the men and women he had worked with. She, too, liked Sam Taylor's mixture of gruff good cheer but saw in him the sadness he was living without his wife. Alicia also wanted a good look at the girlfriend. The reception following the service and lunch later that day would be good opportunities to see if this woman could change his sadness.

They met on the steps to the church and entered together. Katherine was just inside. She greeted and escorted them to the last of three rows in the front on the right side, designated for family. They sat next to Sam and the attractive girlfriend. The church was packed. Just as they found their places, the organist began a Bach prelude.

The service, like the sanctuary, was simple, beautiful, and unpretentious. There was a genuine feeling of spiritual reverence. Sam Taylor was enchanted from the beginning. His church in Houston focused on form, a substitute for substance, and on the personality of the rector. Membership was dropping like a stone. Here among these strangers, however, Taylor was comfortable.

Both men were stunned by the appearance of the younger man, who walked in with the pastor, each in vestments. David and Sam exchanged startled glances when they first saw the younger Hampton, a duplicate of his father thirty-five years ago. Tears welled in Sam's eyes, and David's throat tightened. Carried by the dynamics of the service, they eventually calmed down.

The sermon, delivered by a man in his mid-fifties, was an interesting examination of the dangers of two competing views he called the demons of moral life: pluralism, on the one hand, in which there are many right answers and really no wrong answer, and rigid religiosity on the other, he said. The chief evil of both, he concluded, is that each leaves no room for discernment, a softer, more acceptable word today than judgment; and no room for spiritual growth.

David liked this pastor's approach. Not only did he expect self-examining work from the congregation, he made it clear that he, as the pastor, was not the center of God's church. David had a test for measuring whether or not a pastor, minister, or priest by any title was self-absorbed. David counted the first-person, singular pronouns in the sermon; in other words, how many times the preacher said "I." This pastor passed.

The sermon ended with a prayer. He then told the congregation that he wished to introduce a new face to them. Robert Hampton stood.

"Our church, its membership, and its community involvement have grown. New people come in our front door every week. Now we've decided an associate pastor is needed to help with our work, adding more action to our mission statement. Bob Hampton worked as a financial manager here in California after a stint in the military. He then decided to go to seminary. Reports on him are good. Please join me in welcoming Robert Hampton as our new associate pastor, along with his family and guests."

The congregation applauded. The pastor gestured for Rev. Hampton to approach the lectern. In a clear, strong, and even voice, Robert Hampton introduced his wife and daughters as well as his mother, Kate, her second husband, Ted, and other family members by name. As he did this, his eyes paused on David and Sam. He smiled briefly and then moved on to his remarks.

"Thank you all for being here at this most important event in my life. Pastor Carlyle asked me to wait until next Sunday to give a real sermon." The congregation laughed and shifted in their pews. "I'm compelled, however," he continued, "to talk briefly about someone who could not be here today."

"I didn't know my earthly father, Robert Hampton, Sr. What I know of him is what my mother and others, through her, have told me. Mother generously shared his letters to her. Their wedding and photograph albums depicted two young people full of love for one another with expectations of a long, happy life together. His military citations from Vietnam revealed other aspects of him: his heroism and leadership. His Navy buddies called him Pastor Bob. A few months before my birth, my father died in combat."

"Recently, I've learned more about my father. He died trying to save another man's life; his friends with whom he served never forgot him or his steady manner in the face of cruel reality. They honor his memory. These men who do so go nameless today, but I call them *decent men*. Despite the evil around all of them, my father lived and served in the company of these decent men. On his behalf, today I thank them."

"If he had survived the war, this naval officer would have taken steps to be ordained. What is not speculation, however, is that because of my father's character, the love and support of my mother, stepfather, and my wonderful wife, Suzy, I found my way here and do know my heavenly Father and the great sacrifice He made for us, to give us hope and save our souls. What a special gift. Thank you for being here. I look forward to meeting all of you."

ACKNOWLEDGMENTS

Putting books into the hands of readers doesn't just happen. The writer needs coaches, cheerleaders, critics, advisors, and role models. I am blessed with all of these.

My agent, Paul Shepherd, has patiently encouraged me before *Mixed Company*, the first book in this series. Larry Carpenter, my publisher by whatever corporate manifestation, has provided solid advice and counsel in the process. I have been especially fortunate to have readers for authenticity of characters and events portrayed in the story. Art Shelton, Art Storey, Susan Pierce, and my shipmate, Weymouth Symmes, all contributed their special talents to my effort. William Rogers very generously provided relevant maps. My wife, Sylvia, has exerted a loving and unique encouragement of my goals for the Decent Men series. Likewise, readers of *Mixed Company* looked forward to this second book. What a reward. The third book in the Decent Men series is a work in progress, focusing on the later lives of the main characters in the earlier books and their offspring. I promise to deliver new characters and situations for my readers.

The gentlemen mentioned in the dedication of this book embody the steadfast leadership and inspiration that are by far the majority in the American naval and military services. Words like *courage* and *duty* fail to fully describe the spirit of service within them and most women and men in uniform. Each in their way paid their dues; Admiral Hoffmann started in World War II on a destroyer in the Pacific, continuing at Inchon, Korea, where his minesweeper was sunk. No novice to naval combat, his career path crossed those of Captain Plumly and then Lieutenant Bernique in the Mekong Delta of Vietnam. Captain Fugit, an Army helicopter pilot, daily put his life on the line. These men and those who did not survive the Vietnam War are the inspiration for this book.

www.ingramcontent.com/pod-product-compliance
Lightning Source LLC
Jackson TN
JSHW071700170426
101040JS00022B/438

* 9 7 8 1 9 4 5 5 0 7 1 6 8 *